Steve and Me

Patricia Menzel-Tinkey

PublishAmerica
Baltimore

First printing

At the specific preference of the author, PublishAmerica allowed this work to remain exactly as the author intended, verbatim, without editorial input.

ISBN: 1-4137-9271-5
PUBLISHED BY PUBLISHAMERICA, LLLP
www.publishamerica.com
Baltimore

Printed in the United States of America

Dedication

To my husband, Jerry, my firefighter and EMT-B, who has been there through the good and bad times of the last twenty-two years, and who put up with my writing at all hours of the day and night. Thanks for being at my side!

Acknowledgements

Many thanks to everyone who helped me along the road to this finished project—Jerry, for all that you do and all that you are in my heart; my parents, Howard and Kathryn, who never let me fall; Salt and Pepper, who curled in my lap as I wrote, purring their approval; my brother, John, always in my heart; the many special employees of Woodstock Residence, including Vanessa, Melanie, and Kim, who kept me motivated with their kind words, Alissa, who proof read and suggested necessary changes, and Jan, who can always make me laugh (I miss you—get better soon!), and Dee, on whose shoulder I cried several times; my best friend, Pat, always there when I need you; and a special singer whose words touched my heart and soul, and always made everything alright with his voice, his smile, his being.

*1*975—shag, feathered haircuts were all the rage, but my mother said absolutely not. John Travolta was one of Mr. Kotter's sweat hogs before any of us knew he had an incredible ability to dance. Mary Tyler Moore was still throwing her hat into the wind in Minneapolis, and President Ford survived two assassination attempts within 17 days of each other.

Beaches were deserted as Jaws scared everyone out of the water, and George Lucas went to the future as production began on *Star Wars*. Jack Nicholson flew over a cuckoo's nest; Warren Beatty shampooed women's hair and did a little bit more than hairdressing in the back room; and *Rocky Horror Picture Show* was acted out in its entirety in theatres by movie-goers who wanted a really good time.

We were wearing hot pants and bell-bottoms, halter tops and peasant blouses, and men were steppin' out in—gasp—the dreaded three-piece polyester suit, as everyone boogied the nights away.

Charlie Chaplin was knighted by Queen Elizabeth; *Wheel of Fortune* debuted and turned us all into puzzle-solvers; *Saturday Night Live* also debuted with George Carlin as the guest host, and we were introduced to improvisational comedy and the not-ready-for-prime-time-players. Males fell in love with Valerie Bertinelli one day at a time, and females couldn't decide who was the bigger hunk—Starsky or Hutch (did it really matter?—they were both gorgeous). Norman Lear and Garry Marshall each had multiple shows in the top 20 for the year, and *M*A*S*H* reminded us that, not only is war hell, but it could be funny too.

The music of the 70s was as varied as every previous generation—starting with the decline of true acid rock that had turned into fusion rock and funk. The slow, harsh death of disco ended the era as records were steam-rolled in the streets, and punk rock took over.

In 1975 there was everything in between acid and punk rock: country, blues, soul, bubble-gum, pop, hard rock, soft rock, country rock, metal rock and too many one-hit-wonders to remember.

Bruce Springsteen was becoming The Boss; Fleetwood Mac welcomed Stevie Nicks and Lindsey Buckingham to their folds and soared to the stars; The Bee Gees released *Jive Talkin'*, which changed their image and sound, catapulting them to disco dance floors everywhere; Barry Manilow would write the songs everyone would sing; and Elton John's *Captain Fantastic* would be his biggest selling album ever.

Earth, Wind and Fire; Captain and Tennille; Frankie Valli; Stevie Wonder; The Carpenters; Minnie Ripperton; John Denver; The Ohio Players; and the Ozark Mountain Daredevils were just a few of the bands and singers who took their place in the top 40 song list of the year—a wide variety of singers and musical styles, all of which defined a generation.

And, tucked securely into this timeline of my life was that year: 1975—the militant revolution of the 60s was a distant bad dream, and the me-me-me over-indulgences of the 80s were still to come. I was a teenager in this year, during which my life changed drastically and dramatically in an instant one summer night. The 70s was an exciting era, made all the more invigorating by a young man who sang his way into my life.

I was 15 when we met; strangers put together by fate; held together by love and passion and something magical, something undefined. I never stopped believing in him and everything he became; I never have; I never will. I can't stop believing in him.

And, I never realized, until now, thirty years later, just what we meant to each other. My Administrator at my nursing job told me that I was home to him, his comfort zone, his retreat from the harshness that had taken control over his life—she told me I represented his family, and where he had come from; she was right. I was the one he turned to in the chaos of popular music and idols and fame. I was the one he held on to when he needed a shoulder, a smile, a laugh, or simply someone to listen.

We made a connection on a hot summer night in San Francisco, locking eyes and hearts across a room, bonding ourselves to one another in a friendship, a love, that would last. Three decades of history together speaks to the relationship that he and I had, and continue to share—love, passion, patience, sadness, loneliness, and a true devotion to each other.

The party may be over in some ways; he walked away from it when the music seemingly could have gone on forever, but, his music plays on in our hearts and minds, and he and I go on, we endure, we love and we survive. We took a midnight train in the darkness, and went to hell and back to make it to each other as we hid in the night and tried to go on.

Strangers—friends—lovers.

Love can always find a way.

I met him in late July, 1975, during a family vacation, touring the coast of California. We were in San Francisco—me, my parents and my younger brother: my evil, always in the way, little brother—the bane of every teenage girl's existence.

My dad was driving us in a rental car; thank goodness he had, at least, let us fly across the country—I overheard my mom and dad at one point, discussing driving across the country. God, what a nightmare that would have been: me in the car with my mother for several days straight. No, thank you.

Dad actually got stopped by the police at one point, in San Diego—a first. The officer was very nice and politely explained to him that he was going the wrong way on a one-way street. We had a good giggle over that; no ticket was issued to the wrong-way out-of-towners.

We were from the Midwest—Ohio—and this was a big deal, even if it was a dreaded family vacation that no self-respecting teenager should be forced to go on. And, being 15, I was feeling very grown up that summer, confident with my new-found blonde hair, thanks to a bottle Sun-In.

We were in a large San Francisco hotel near the bay—the Golden Gate Bridge was visible from the hotel room that I was forced to share with my brother. I wanted desperately to see the street corner made famous by every news program during the late 60s and early 70s—Haight and Ashbury but would my parents even drive by? No. That type of thing would simply not be seen nor tolerated. I wondered how I could get there on my own. Always the defiant one if only in thought and desire.

Luckily for my brother and I, and much to the dismay of my mother, Dad had arranged a business dinner while we were in town. After much bitching and arguing about it in the next room, they were finally ready to go, leaving brother and I to "go out on the town," which really meant, "stay in the hotel." We could order room service or go down to one of the restaurants.

Okay. That may sound really boring, watching your little brother, but I parked him at a computer terminal the hotel had in the lobby—computers were just coming onto the scene and he was fascinated with the way it worked, drawing pictures and playing games—cards and word games. So, my brother was hooked; I could leave him there and not worry.

Now it was my turn to find something to do—swimming was out—didn't feel like it—not hungry—not into computers at that time. The lobby was interesting, watching people come and go but I couldn't do that all night—too boring. Then I heard something and had to find out where that sound that seemed to drift on the breeze, was coming from; it caught me by surprise and off-guard. I was still listening to teeny-bopper music like David Cassidy and Bobby Sherman, and just beginning to discover Elton John, and other bands, but found this jazzy, soulful, fusion sound irresistible.

A sign in the lobby announced a band playing their bar that night—it must have been them that I was hearing. A bar. I was 15—how was I going to manage this?

I made my way down the winding hallway, and found the door to the bar as the music grew in my ears, making me sway to its rhythm like no music ever had. The instrumental had a haunting sound; the vocals were lilting, emotional, passionate; like nothing I had ever heard before. There were people crowding the doorway but I didn't see anyone really barring the way so I went in, trying to hold my head high, trying to look like I knew what I was doing. I must have looked out of place in my jeans and Elton John t-shirt, but nobody paid any attention to me.

I made my way toward the small stage, taking in all of the sights and sounds that were around me. There were a lot of people in this place, smoking, drinking, making out. The lighting was flashy with strobes, and blue and red lights. I could see smoke trails in the lights, and smell its pungent odor. My mom and dad would probably think I had taken up smoking: one more thing to worry about.

I finally got close enough to the stage to take a good look at the band. They were all men—5 of them—one guitar, one bass, one keyboard, one drummer and one lead singer.

The lead singer was the focus of my attention—he wore a white silk shirt, unbuttoned and tied at the waist, occasionally flopping open to reveal a hairless chest. His pants were tight black—looked like he had been poured into them and yet he moved with the agility of a cat onstage. He had long straight brown hair that hung about six inches below his shoulders and swayed with his body to the songs.

I was hooked by their sound—something unlike anything I had heard before; it had more raw emotion than I had ever experienced. The instrumental pieces were warm and without harshness, and the vocals sent waves of warmth and peace through my soul. I know that sounds really pretentious but it was true. Maybe I felt the way I did because this was my first time in a bar, in a strange city, this close to a band. I had been to concerts back home but never this close to the actual performers.

The lead singer had a voice that could reach any height. When he opened his mouth and let the words fly, you could feel the honesty and see the sincerity in what he was singing. He could have been singing anything at that point and I would have ...oned. The sound was distinctly alto to tenor and he could hold a note forever and not be winded. His voice would become the voice of the 80s (in my opinion). I didn't know the destiny that was waiting around the corner for the band, as they played several sets that night. I don't even know if they knew that they were about to soar to greatness.

I stood off in a corner watching them, enjoying their banter between songs. There were a few times that the audience could tell they were playing a song in which the kinks still needed to be ironed out. They would laugh trying to get through some. The guitarist seemed the most serious up there, frowning when things did go wrong, and turning his back on the audience frequently. The bass player had the biggest sense of humor, always smiling widely, laughing to ease the tension that was an obvious undertone on stage.

But the lead singer, the youngest member, was the friendliest with the others as he sang and swayed and lost himself in the music. You could see him get swept away in the lyrics as he would close his eyes and sing. I found out later that he closed his eyes either when he was feeling very nervous or when he was trying to picture the lyrics in his head so he could sing them correctly. But, he was the one who seemed the most at ease being on the stage, and yet seemed the most shy when speaking to the audience.

We locked eyes once and I had to turn around to see if anyone was behind me to be sure he was looking at me. Considering I was backed up against, and leaning on, a wall, it had to be me he was looking at.

When the song finished, he asked, "So, girl in the Elton John t-shirt, how did you like it?" I blushed, feeling the heat well up in my face, and gave him a "thumbs up" sign. Dopey. I couldn't even come up with anything to say.

They were in the midst of the last set as he and I continued to lock eyes through the remaining songs—it was as though he were singing to me and only me at that moment in time. I was his prisoner: captured by his voice, held there by his eyes, and the fire within him, swept away by the words of the songs.

When they were finished, it was midnight, and I turned to leave; I figured I had better gather up my brother, who would still be playing computer games, and get him to bed before the folks get back and kill me. I had taken a few steps when I felt a hand on my shoulder, tentative at first and then heavier as I began to turn. It was him—the lead singer. My breath caught in my throat as I turned and faced him full on. I couldn't leave now. I wouldn't leave now.

He smiled gently and asked me if I would join him at a table for a few minutes. We sat down; the silence between us for the first several minutes seemed deafening. I could not imagine why he had chosen to be here with me when he could probably have anyone in the room. He finally spoke first after ordering a beer from the waitress who had made her way through the crowd to the table. I had ginger ale.

He wanted to know what I thought about the band, about him, and wanted a critique of the performance. They were getting set to go out on the road as the opening act for another more popular band and needed some feedback on how they sounded. He told me to ignore the mistakes and the obvious bobbles on stage—they would be cleaned up in rehearsals.

Of course I gushed and said they were wonderful. What else could I say—it was the truth. He was sweating and wiped his brow with a cocktail napkin several times, and kept apologizing for it. He was soft spoken with almost a shyness about him; hanging his head often as he spoke—strange for someone who had just been up on stage in front of hundreds of people. Stranger still for someone that was about to be on stage over and over, in front of thousands of people. But the shyness was refreshing.

I was 15—he was 25.

He talked and I listened. Listened to him tell me all about the —that he was new in it and was still only learning the ropes. Listened to him tell me about his family in the South and how proud they were of his accomplishment.

I couldn't say why he came up to me that night and why we spent the next several hours together. It didn't make any sense that he and I would connect in this bar. None of it made any sense. I wasn't even supposed to be in the bar but that didn't seem to matter to anyone. Except to my father, who found me there.

Dad pulled me politely away from the table, out of Steve's earshot. I was anxious as I figured I was going to get reprimanded for being irresponsible, something I rarely was.

But, Dad was calm—he asked who "that young man" is, emphasis on "man," and what was I doing in a bar? And, he reminded me, had Mom known, I'd really be in for it. I didn't need that particular reminder.

I was honest—that I came in for the music and "that young man" was actually the lead singer of the band that had played. How do you explain to your father that a man had just singled out his teenage daughter in a crowd and just wanted to talk? And, how do you further convince him to let you stay awhile longer?

Dad did let me stay, after he went back to the table and I introduced them. "Steve Potts—Dad. Dad—Steve Potts. Now, can I stay?" Something like that. Dad was gracious; Steve was quiet and reserved. Dad actually told him to "get a haircut" then added, "Isn't that just what a father should say?" Steve laughed; I was still holding my breath.

Dad told me to get back to the room safely; Steve assured him he would see to it.

The bar closed at 3 in the morning; I was shocked when I realized what time it was. As we sat at our table and talked, Steve continually pulled his long hair back with one hand and threw it over his shoulders. He seemed uncomfortable in his clothing and had untied his shirt at some point and buttoned it up nearly to the top. Too bad—I had kind of liked the view.

We walked slowly to the elevator, and even more slowly to my room on the 8th floor. We were walking close together, touching shoulders, silent in the hallway. I stood at my doorway and told him it was nice of him to walk me up there and so great to meet him; I am sure the way I said it sounded stupid—like a gushy teenager, even though I was trying to act older.

He asked what our family plans were for the next day—I had no idea even though my dad had given us all a neatly typed itinerary every day so we knew what was going on. He told me to meet him at the hotel pool at noon that day. We were staying in San Francisco one more day, so I figured I *had* to do this. I had to show up and see him. I had to be there, no matter what the family plans were. And we said good night.

I watched him walk down the hallway to the elevator, watching those tight pants walk away from me. He turned and gave a half wave to me, stepped onto the elevator and was gone.

I changed and went to bed, only to watch the time tick away as I lay there, wondering about what had just happened. Why had he picked me out of a crowd of beautiful women to speak to? With all the ladies that were there that were closer to his own age—why me? What kind of connection did we spark that night? And would we really see each other the next day?

I had friends back home that were boys that I had crushes on but no one else's presence had made me feel so alive and so inadequate all at the same time. I couldn't help but continue to fuss over whether or not he would really show up the next day at the pool, or if he had been toying with me.

There were so many questions and no answers.

That night I couldn't sleep. Go figure.

*T*he family plan for the day was to go to Alcatraz and Ghiradelli; it did not sound like fun. Family vacation—a drag. I had my own plans and nothing was going to keep me from them. My parents figured since I had been out so late, it was okay if I stayed at the hotel. They had an ulterior motive— they knew if I didn't get any sleep I was terribly grumpy; they didn't want me spoiling their fun. Thank heavens.

I am still somewhat at a loss to understand why they had not questioned me about the man I was with or why they let me stay in the hotel alone when it was pretty obvious I was excited about something. I never thought to ask them later and the subject still has never come up. I would imagine the answer would have been something sensible like I was a level-headed kid, straight-A student, knew right from wrong and would not do anything stupid. That was me—always the practical one.

Noon came and I went to the hotel pool, one piece tank suit (all the rage back then) underneath a robe, large white hotel towel in tow. And he was there, sitting in a lounger at the side of the pool near the deep end. And he was gorgeous.

He had a bathing suit on that left very little to the imagination, stretched out with mirrored sunglasses on his face, hair pulled back in a pony tail, hands folded on his stomach.

There was a towel draped on the end of the lounger and a bottle of beer on the table next to him. His feet were crossed at the ankles, something he would always do when he was relaxed, and he was softly tapping the top foot to a rhythm only he could hear, something else he would always do when he was relaxed.

When he saw me, he sat up straight and patted the lounger next to him; lifting the sunglasses up onto his head and smiled at me. There was something there that I couldn't put my finger on, something I had never felt before. It was as if a jolt of electrical current connected us and, when I was close to him, someone hit the juice.

We talked some more and he told me more about him—he was from Atlanta; his family was still there. That he had come to California—Los Angeles first, in search of a career in music and barely made it for years, nearly ready to go back home and work in the family hardware business.

He talked of very tough times he had had, how he begged, borrowed and, sometimes, stole food stamps to survive, and worked menial jobs, any job, to make ends meet. That he had lived on the streets for several months, holing up in doorways and sometimes in shelters. When he spoke of being homeless, he seemed embarrassed, hanging his head slightly, his voice becoming softer.

He spoke of life on the street and the danger that had been around him. He was in his very early 20s at the time and had considered doing many things in order to make ends meet, including selling himself, which, according to some of the people he hung out with, was the way to make good money. But, he never went that far. There was always something he found to make a few dollars.

Then he decided to leave Los Angeles—decided there was nothing for him there—he had been unable to find steady work and certainly wasn't being discovered—time to move on. So, he hitch-hiked to San Francisco. The hippie culture was still in vogue there, so he was able to find help with some of the counter culture, joining communes just to have a place to lay his head at night.

He sang on the street a lot with the others and began to let his hair grow out; to fit in, he said. He kept in close touch with his family but he never let on that he was in any kind of trouble. When he was discovered singing on the street, his hard times were left behind and he was on his way with this new band that had just lost their lead singer to a college scholarship.

Sitting poolside, listening to him, I could hear sincerity in his voice and some trepidation—he didn't know if the band would make it in any way—I wish I had had a crystal ball at that time—to tell us where he was going—we didn't know just how far he was about to rise out of poverty.

When he finished telling me his story, he wanted to know about me, and I wasn't quite sure what to tell him. I was just a high school student, in the marching band, on the school newspaper. Big deal. The most rock-bottom I had hit up to that point in my life was when the power went off and there was no TV in my bedroom. He laughed at that.

He asked about my family and said that he thought my dad was okay. I told him, yes, he was, but watch out for my mom who could be hell on wheels at times, especially when it came to her daughter. She had been divorced when I was very young; married my dad when I was four; he adopted me and things had been great, but don't mess with her daughter. My brother, John, was five years younger than me. He was their son, but there had never been any difference in their love for either of us.

And we had a dog—a dog that had grown up with me, who was now in failing health. My dog, Charlie, was a mutt but she was my friend and saw me through all my growing years, 14 years. She looked like a red fox, and there were times when my friends, on their first visit to my house, were afraid of her. But she was very gentle—not a bite in her. He seemed to like the story about my Charlie. He was an animal lover too; he had grown up with cats and a dog—that meant he had a very special soul that could love animals.

He wanted to know more about me and I admitted there wasn't much more. I was about to go into the tenth grade. I played saxophone and clarinet in the band. I had just learned how to play; a girlfriend had taught me on her back porch the summer before, and I had managed to get a spot in the high school marching band. I wanted to tell him I was excited by that; didn't, though, because that would have been silly. But he said he too had been in his high school band—he played the drums.

I told him I wanted to become a writer, that I was one of those girls who kept a diary and wrote everything down. And that I made up my own stories about television characters, in particular, *The Partridge Family*, because all I wanted to do was write. I was going to become a journalist—go to college and work for a newspaper. My cousin worked for our hometown newspaper and I think she inspired me quite a bit. I had been a writer for the junior high paper and hoped to be one in high school too.

He asked me if I would write about our meeting and I admitted I already had—that morning. He smiled again and cocked his head slightly. Said he wanted to read it and I told him there was no way. But, he's read it now—in these words.

I had never been out on a real date. I don't know why I blurted that out to him.

I felt foolish sitting poolside telling him menial things about me. I wanted to be sophisticated and older and all I could muster was the fact that I was trying to memorize songs for the marching band, looking forward to the first football game in September.

But he sat and listened to me, appearing interested. He said it was refreshing to meet someone "real," unlike the people he had met in California. I reminded him of home. I was guessing that was a good thing.

We finally decided to go into the pool—that meant I had to

take off my robe. I was suddenly very self-conscious. Not a prom queen, I was slightly overweight and knew I was not pretty by any stretch of the imagination. Meant I had to take off my glasses too—I hoped I wouldn't trip over anything.

I hesitated to take off the robe, but he helped me from behind and slid it over my shoulders. There I stood, in a suit that was a definite 70s paisley print of purples and blues. He tossed his sunglasses onto the lounger and pulled my silver-rimmed John Lennon-type glasses off my face and laid them on top of the robe. He didn't even seem to mind how I looked; he just grabbed my hand, pulling me into the pool after him.

We swam around for a short time, above and below the water. We finally came to rest at the edge in the water where it was about 4-feet deep. There were no words spoken between us as he stood very near to me in the water. I looked at his face and saw deep caring in brown eyes that spoke volumes. I felt his arms go around my waist under the water and my body suddenly felt as if my legs would collapse—thank goodness we were in the water that lent some support.

Then he kissed me. Softly at first, lips closed, gently on my mouth. Three or four times he kissed me and my breath came in sighs. He pulled back and smiled at me, as if to ask if what he was doing was okay. How could it not be okay? Then his mouth was back on mine, this time an open mouth. His tongue probed and I opened my mouth in acceptance. I could taste the beer he had been drinking, and felt the unevenness of his bottom teeth.

We were locked in the kiss for what seemed like forever, and, as far as I was concerned, it could have gone on forever. My hands touched the skin of his back, feeling the muscles ripple as I held my palms against him. His hands were holding my jaw on each side. We must have been quite a sight there in the pool. And neither of us cared. Especially me. This was the first man I had kissed and held that close. I didn't know what I was doing and yet I knew I didn't want it to end. Ever.

We were silent as we stared at each other, skin glistening

from the water and the hot sun overhead. His face was serious and his eyes were a darker brown than they had been. He suddenly smiled at me and the dimples appeared at his outer cheeks, his eyes crinkled nearly shut. His smile captivated me and held me in its wonder.

I smiled back, wondering if my smile had the same effect on him that his had on me. He took my hands under the water and held them firm, then placed them on his shoulders and wrapped his around my waist. We stayed in that position for minutes, looking deeply into each other's eyes, not sure of what was happening.

It is hard to describe the feelings you have when falling in love, and, even at the tender age of 15, I was sure I truly was falling in love. There are few words that will attest to the emotion and the physical attraction that occurs. I had never been kissed by anyone; the feelings were all new to me. I felt as though I was full of electricity, that every sense I had was coming alive. I felt acutely aware of everything that was going on around us, yet I was focused only on him. Where he touched my skin it burned with a heat I had never experienced. When his hand brushed the skin of my arms, I tingled and my breath was rapid for a time.

I am sure, as he was 10 years older, this was not a first for him. I never have asked about prior experience and never will. He has told me some stories, but I never asked. At that point, in that pool, it didn't matter.

He suggested we go to his room and I hesitated for the span of a few heartbeats; he quickly stated he wanted to get out of the sun. He did have very fair skin that was already sun- speckled with redness so we got out of the pool, retrieved our belongings, and headed inside, my insides all a-jumble with a flock of butterflies.

Once we were in his room, I sat in the chair near the bed and he lay down on the bed after turning on a radio; the tunes of the day were playing—Elton John, the Bee Gees, and others. There was a chill from the air conditioner, even though it was 90 degrees outside. I wondered what the heck I was doing, but didn't want to think about it too much.

Steve was quiet for awhile, hands behind his head, ankles crossed, right foot tapping to the music, staring at the ceiling. Nothing on but the bathing suit, which, now that it was wet, was even more revealing. I had draped the robe across my lap and leaned back in the chair, looking around his room.

He had a few pictures in frames on the dresser—looked like one picture of his parents, another of what I presumed was his brother. There was sheet music strewn about—some printed, some that he was obviously writing himself.

A duffel bag was thrown in the corner with some clothing spilling out. One dresser drawer was open and I could see more clothing there. A pair of tennis shoes—high tops—was sitting looked as though they had been kicked across the room, laces undone and twisted. Tucked into the frame of the mirror was a copy of the poster I had seen in the hotel lobby announcing the performance of the band. Tonight was their last night in town. Mine too.

He shattered the silence by telling me to come be with him on the bed—to be comfortable. Uh huh. He had turned over on his side to face me, to make room for me at his side. He propped his head up on one arm and the sway to his hip in that position caused stirrings in me that I was not familiar with. He looked very sexy. The last person I had seen looking that good in that type of position was the Burt Reynolds centerfold in Playgirl. And that was paper—this was the real thing.

Here I was with this half-naked man, looking at him on his bed and the thoughts were racing. Could I really be doing this? Was I really with this man? His chest was void of any hair but below his navel was a line of dark hair that went into his suit to places I had yet to know. He had let his hair out of the pony-tail holder and it was hanging in wet strands about his shoulders

21

and chest. His feet were still crossed at the ankles, continuing to tap to the music.

I went to him. Shaking inside. Heart fluttering. Breathing shallow and rapid. How I ended up in the bed next to him, facing him, in his arms, I don't even remember. He pulled me to him and held me as close as we were going to be without me going through him. He put his arm underneath my head and I leaned on it.

The light was on over the bed and I took a good look at his face—the mole on his chin and the small pimples that were on his nose. He was still a young man with acne. His face had deep lines near the corners of his mouth and crows feet at the outer edges of his eyes. He was about to embark on a concert tour and whirlwind beginning to a career that was to last many years.

He moved his face to mine and we kissed again, probing and drinking in each other. There was nothing between us but two layers of spandex and I felt him hard against my lower abdomen. A sensation I had never felt before. His hands caressed my skin and made me feel as though I had a fever as I flushed seemingly from my toes to my head and back again. We remained in each other's arms for the rest of the afternoon. Talking, kissing, getting to know each other.

He never made any moves more than running his hands over my bottom, and occasionally brushing against a breast. Our kisses were long and passionate and loving. I ran my hands through his lustrous hair and enjoyed the feeling of it as it ran through my fingers. His fingertips brushed lightly on my skin and sent me into a head rush like no other. I explored his back with my hands and allowed them to brush against the backside of his bathing suit as well.

Five in the afternoon came a lot sooner than I had hoped and we pulled away from each other. He was due at the hotel bar in three hours, and Dad probably had a posse out searching for me, since I had been away for so long. I called my parents room and discovered they were not particularly worried. They wanted me

22

back for dinner, but I convinced them to let me be with Steve for the night—for dinner and his show. Reluctantly, they agreed—we would be in Carmel tomorrow and away from this man. They had no idea and neither did I.

Steve and I parted for a few moments as we both got dressed—I left him in his room with his promise to come to mine in 30 minutes. I dashed to the 8th floor from the 6th and quickly changed after showering. We were going out to dinner, leaving the confines of the hotel and taking a chance on the outside world. A real date. What to wear? I settled on a peasant blouse and a pair of dressier jeans. When he knocked on the door, it was all I could do to walk to it and open it.

He took my breath away. There he stood—tall and handsome in dark blue jeans that fit tightly in all the right places, and a white cotton shirt, tucked in with the top two buttons open. A simple gold chain hung around his neck, small, understated. His hair was dry and hung free at his shoulders and chest, parted straight in the middle, curling slightly at the ends. A 70s shag cut—the kind I had always wanted but was never allowed to have. And his signature tennis shoes; always the tennis shoes.

He had a small car that had seen better days, but he held the passenger door open for me, then climbed into the drivers' seat. I had no idea where he was taking me so when he asked where I would like to go, I was taken aback.

I told him there was only one thing I really wanted to see in San Francisco—Haight Ashbury, so off we went. We even had dinner in that vicinity at a cute little diner. The hippie culture was there, and they were all pretty nice to us, and anyone who passed by. Some even remembered Steve from his time with them, as we walked the street. He was very polite to them, introducing me as we passed, singing with some of them, dancing with some of the girls who had flowers and ribbons in their long hair.

I was suddenly jealous and those feelings took me by surprise. The air was thick with the strong scent of incense, food and what was probably marijuana (what did I know?). People were everywhere, all ages—from infants in their mother's arms, to the elderly. Music was everywhere too. Peace and love. I felt so at home, holding the hand of that man, walking and talking, in that place, with those people. I was, however, a long way from home.

We went back to the hotel room to spend the remaining time before the show—we had about an hour before he had to be on stage. We filled the hour by kissing some more on the bed. The passion was evident and I knew he wanted more, I just wasn't sure how to let him know that it would be okay.

But, we had to go—time for his show.

He had a table reserved in the front of the bar, at the stage, and we sat there for a few minutes until his band mates were all on stage. He stood and turned to join them, hesitated, faced me and gave me a kiss: a quick, wish-me-luck kiss.

Their show that night seemed smoother, with less obvious mistakes. They were all still learning each other's moves and nuances, it still needed some tweaking, but, to me, it couldn't have looked or sounded better. He was perfection on stage.

Steve sang with a force of energy and soul—singing to me, and people noticed. Even the band members noticed—everyone but the drummer. I sat mesmerized by the drum performance: like a machine gun he pounded out those rhythms. I spent the whole night, resting my head on my arms, elbows on the table, a breech of proper etiquette.

They performed three sets with half-hour breaks in between. Steve disappeared with his band mates after each set for a few minutes, then came to join me at the table. People randomly stopped at the table now and again to pat him on the shoulder or shake his hand, tell him he sounded great. While acknowledging their presence and comments, I got my first glimpse into his dislike of fandom and fame.

I didn't know it until much later, but my dad was in the audience, in the back of the bar. He had come to check out this band and see what I was up to. The most he saw was Steve's arm across my shoulder, quick kisses as he went back on stage, and him singing every note, every word of love to me. He must not have been too disturbed because I never heard about it for years. Typical father of a teenage girl.

Time was quickly up for us as the show ended much too soon. Instead of remaining in the bar, we took a walk out by the pool, and he took my hand in his as we walked slowly, ever so slowly, around the water's edge. He finally took me to my room.

He answered my silent questions with surprising replies. He told me he wanted to keep in touch, that, when they were in Ohio, he would come to see me, and that I was to come see them play. He wanted more than a summer fling; that we were destined always to be friends, good friends, maybe more at some point. He promised to call and write; we exchanged phone numbers and addresses there in the hall with paper and pen I had in my purse. Then we kissed passionately at my door.

I wanted him to stay; I wanted to go with him. I never wanted to let him go, yet I knew we had to part. Tears in both our eyes gave proof to our feelings for each other, which had grown so much in just two days. We said goodbye, and suddenly, very softly, as he hugged me, he whispered into my ear, "I love you." I let out a sigh and pressed into him and said the same back. Our lives had changed in the span of a day, and, as I was to learn, would never be the same.

We kissed again, long and heartfelt, then again I watched as he walked to the elevator. He blew me a kiss as the doors closed around him and I cried as I walked into the room I shared with my brother. My vacation was over; I was not the same person who first walked into that hotel room a few days ago.

I left San Francisco behind the next day and managed to tolerate the rest of the family vacation. I can't say how it wrenched my heart to see Steve standing in the lobby the morning that we left, watching me from across the great hall. I wanted to drop everything and run to him, hold him, beg him to take me with him. How childish would that have been? Instead we both smiled at each other, raising our hands in silent good-bye waves as I kept walking away from him. My parents were unaware of it all; my brother noticed but, amazingly, said nothing. I cried in the backseat of the rental car as we pulled away from the hotel.

There was so much left to see in California, yet I wanted nothing more to do with it. I was moody, sitting in the backseat of a rental car, pressed into the corner of the seat where it meets the door, as tightly as I could manage. I wanted to be left alone to wallow in my grief.

What did my parents want to do? Talk. Talk about what had happened the last two nights. Talk about "that man."

My mom was first with the intrusion into my depression.

Who was he? Steve. How old? 25. Twenty-five! Isn't that a little too old for you? No. I think it is; what could he possibly want with you? (That sounded a little nasty and mean-spirited.)

We're friends. Why you? Why not? Your father actually said he was nice but that his hair is too long; is he nice? Yes, Mom, he is, and his hair is fine.

Then my dad—He did seem somewhat enamored of you—how do you feel? (I have to talk about this with them?!) I like him. What did you do all day? (Made out.) Swam, went to dinner, he sang in the bar. How'd you get in the bar again? Walked in. Did you drink? Ginger ale.

He never let on that he had been there that second night.

Do you love him? I shot John a look for that question he had felt the need to ask, but said nothing in response.

My parents did not seem to disapprove of my new friend, but I don't think they believed that I would ever see him again either. They figured this was a summer vacation infatuation on my part and that he was toying with the heart of a teenager.

My heart—I left it in San Francisco that day; couldn't help but run that song over and over in my head for the rest of the trip. *I Left My Heart in San Francisco*—I had heard that song so many times in the past and thought it was hokey, didn't make any sense. Now it seemed to be the theme of my summer. I knew I would never hear from that man again but my heart ached to see him again.

When we arrived home from the vacation, I immediately called my best friend, Patty, and told her to come get me. She and I were a year apart in school—she was older—but we had become the best of friends, spending most of our free hours together and with the others who ran with the two of us, or, rather, who could put up with us.

She drove over in her Datsun and off we went to the nearby park, our place to commiserate and tell secrets. I was so full of excitement and anticipation to tell her what had happened that I could barely contain myself until we got to the swing set. She knew something was up because I was acting like a giddy schoolgirl, something I rarely did. Usually I was the one who kept her head about her when all others were losing theirs; this time I was the one all a-flutter and bursting at the seams.

Patty finally heard the news—I had met a wonderful man in California, one like no other. Older and smarter and more talented than anyone I knew. I told her of the band, how they were going to begin touring with another band as the opening act and were working on an album, trying to get off the ground and make something of themselves.

Then I told her how we had kissed in the pool and eventually in his room. How his touch made me sigh inside and out; how his hair brushing against my face sent chills to my toes. She almost didn't believe me until I pulled something out of my pocket that I had brought home—(it was a picture of he and I—one of the few we would ever take together, because I hate to have my picture taken—something about preserving an overweight person on film just didn't seem right to me). It had been taken at the hotel bar the night that we sat and got to know each other, after he had finished singing.

He had his arm around me in the picture and a bright smile on his face, looking into the camera with pleasure and happiness that I could still see in his eyes. I was looking like the teenager I was, but, nonetheless, there he was—with me. There was no denying it.

Patty squealed with delight in that way only she can do and asked if anything else had happened. Regretfully, I said no but that he had promised to write and get me to some of the shows. Then I told her I didn't really believe that would ever happen, but a girl can dream, can't she?

We sat on those swings for hours until the evening began to set in. I told her my feelings about Steve: that I was probably in the midst of a very big crush that would be difficult to get over. I had wanted him to take me right there on the bed but with my age being what it is and his age being what it was, nothing good could come of that.

My summer vacation had actually turned into one that was worth talking about and I could only tell a very select few who would not only believe me but who would keep my secrets. Patty drove me home, then called me later that night.

Typical teenage girls—we were on the phone for nearly an hour, something that never failed to irritate my mother. I didn't have a phone in my room and had to resort to sitting in the kitchen, at the small desk there, speaking in low, hushed tones so as to not reveal anything to parents who were sitting on the other side of the closed door in the family room.

My secret had been put into words and told to a friend. I waited the rest of that month of July to hear from Steve while I went out with my friends and began rehearsals in marching band. I didn't hear from him and really wasn't all that surprised, but the disappointment was pretty evident to those who knew what was going on.

I lost my appetite, and spent many hours in my room alone—not really sulking, but owning up to the realization that my summer fling had been exactly that—a summer fling. I knew, in the back of my mind, my teenage, rational mind, that I would never see him again; but my heart, my teenage, irrational heart, kept my hopes up, kept me believing that he would contact me.

Then, one day in August, my friends and I—Patty, Mark and Eric—were riding in the Datsun—our go-mobile—when I heard the radio announcer say the name of the band: they were announcing a new release that was "taking the country by storm." My heart flipped as I reached from the back seat to turn the music up. There was the intro and then the vocal—that was Steve—I would know that soulful voice anywhere!

I hushed everyone in the car and made them listen.

Perfection
By Steve Potts

She was a child when my eyes met hers, locked in a magical gaze
She touched my heart, captivated my soul and stole my love
She was older than her years, timeless in her charm, impossible to resist
She enchanted my life with her endless fire, her laugh—forever in her love

My lady came to me as a girl and invaded my psyche
When she laughed, she sparkled, when she spoke she gleamed
Everything I am is because of her
Forever in my life she will remain

To her I am perfection, the reason and meaning of her life
To me she is everything, the glint in my eye, the keeper of my driving force
When we came together it was a power like no other, a passion, an intensity
And she knew and I knew, as we met with open arms and hearts, we were one

My dreams came true one July day
My life changed and turned around
Secure in her life, in her love
She is the one

There were tears in my eyes by the end of the song that was about me—I was pretty sure about that. Patty was too—she had recognized in it what I had told her about. The band was on their way now; there would be no holding them back. They were destined to be stars—big stars—and that meant the true end to our relationship. I was sure of it.

Six weeks after I had arrived home from vacation, two weeks after that day in August when I heard him on the radio, I received my first letter, postmarked Denver. He wrote me—he actually wrote to me! His letter was four pages long, written in pencil, on music paper; probably all he had with him. He included a picture of the band—a promotional shot—an article that had been written about them from San Francisco, and one of the passes from the Denver show. He sent me momentos! He sent me stuff! I dashed to my bedroom, slamming the door behind me to read his letter, tears in my eyes.

He told of the band's tour, and the fun they were having. Of the screaming crowds, the girls who flashed them while they were on stage. His writing was stilted, almost as though he was uncomfortable writing in regular sentences, as opposed to the song-writing he was doing. He misspelled a few things (only a person in journalism would have noticed), and his words were smudged in places as if that was where he had rested his hand in thought, then continued to write, drawing his hand across the pencil marks. His writing was a little difficult to read, but once I got used to it, I had no problems.

He asked how I was, how the family was, how school was. He wanted to know how band was going, if we had won our first football game yet. I cherished every word, every question. He ended his letter with, "Love you, Steve."

I couldn't write to him; there was no way to keep up with a band on the road in a bus that he described as a "junk heap on six wheels." He told me of the road trips in the old school bus that they had had to paint (shades of a *Partridge Family* episode), and of the seats with springs that hit the guys in all the wrong places. He continued to write me—several times per week I received a letter, which I held close to my heart and shared with no one.

He told me of being tired after every show and wanting nothing more than to go to sleep; of having to endure the sounds on the bus of the other band members taking advantage of groupies. Sex was all around him in places he would never have imagined—he was still an old-fashioned boy from the south, still not sure how to take all the new-found fringe benefits of being in a band on the road.

There were drugs they had been exposed to and he told me that he had tried them: experimented. He told me of cocaine, a new drug making its way onto the scene; that it had to be snorted—it burned his nose, making him sound like he was "speaking and singing through an elephant's trunk." It changed his voice—he couldn't afford that.

And, of course, marijuana was everywhere—he said he felt as if he had to use it in order to be a part of the rock and roll world. But he didn't like the way it made him feel—so out of control and out of himself. Plus, it too made his voice sound different as the smoke irritated his throat.

Then there was the heroin he tried—injecting it into a vein in his arm with some of the other band members after one of their shows. He didn't much care for pain, so he said, and couldn't stand the thought of piercing his skin often enough to continue doing that drug on a regular basis.

So he left them behind. Beer was his drug of choice; even too much of that made him sleepy very quickly.

He also spoke of his family—a lot. He was very family-oriented, which would help lead to his downfall eventually. He loved his mother very much and missed her desperately. His dad was not in the greatest of health, though he never said why. His brother was still in high school, three years ahead of me; he told me all about his problems, kind of advising me not to get into some of the jams his brother had gotten himself into. Steve wanted me to do well in school and to go to college—something he had never done.

He was growing up on the road, becoming more and more popular with fans. The band put out their first album, *Come Meet Us*, which he sent to me, autographed, of course. Another one of the songs he had written for me—it spoke of life changes and stages, and of being faithful, trusting. I played that record on my little portable record player and drove my family nuts.

The band began to get more and more airplay on the radio and they were touring constantly, soon out on their own as headliners, with very little time to stop and enjoy the success. They had interviews and photo sessions; public appearances and autograph signings at record stores. Fans followed them wherever they went and, to Steve, it was annoying and distracting. For the other guys in the band, and the road crew, it was exciting and intoxicating.

I didn't see Steve for months. We talked on the phone when he called from the road, which he started to do in November of 1975—he called the first time to wish me a happy birthday. Then the calls continued every couple of weeks. We would spend hours talking—he would tell me the trial by fire they were under, then he always wanted to know what I was doing even though my life was so much more boring by comparison. I was a high school student—what could I say?

I told him about band and working for the school paper, writing articles about other students and their accomplishments, and about things going on at school.

I told him about my friends, what we did on the weekends—mostly hung out at each other's houses and watched TV or played music—his especially—or played cards. One of my friends had an Atari game system so we went there a lot to play video games. Big deal. My life as the straight-laced teenager was nothing to tell to a rock star, but he wanted to know everything.

March, 1976—the band finally came to Ohio—to play Cleveland, and I had to go. Steve sent four tickets by messenger—it made me feel so important. My parents were a little nervous about the whole concert thing, but figured I was going with friends and wouldn't get into any trouble.

They had been surprised that he had contacted me and had kept doing so; they never truly expected him to be in my life after we left California. I kept his letters in my desk, in the middle drawer, not under lock and key, but I never thought my parents would read them. Never underestimate the curiosity of parents. I did know my mom went through my stuff from time to time—any mother who says she isn't snooping is probably fibbing. There were times when I would come home from school and not know what she had been into because clearly everything had been touched and rearranged ever so slightly.

And then there was a time in ninth grade—my mom removed a pair of jeans from my closet and burned them because I wouldn't throw them away. Turns out she burned twenty dollars that had been in the pocket. She paid me back.

So, there was no doubt that she had read his letters. It really wasn't a big deal—there was nothing in them at that point. His writing and misspellings probably bothered her more than anything. Otherwise, he asked about school—told me to study; told me about the band; signed his letter "Love you, Steve." It may have been a good thing that she had read them—she could see what I meant to him; that I actually did mean something to him.

The passes he sent were like gold in my hand, but my parents wanted to talk before my friends arrived to take me to Cleveland. Both of them voiced some concern about my age—16—and his—27. He was a man—on the road—alone—about to see their only daughter, whom he hadn't seen in eight months. The questions, the statements they made were only indicative of their own over-protective nature, but also proved one thing—they loved me.

We never brought up sex but they alluded to it by reminding me that I was too young, and I agreed. They did ask me if I loved him, if I thought he loved me. I said yes—to both—we had said it to each other in San Francisco. That kind of set them back in their chairs.

They let me go to Cleveland, knowing that a relationship with a grown man had been set into motion. They knew I would go to him regardless of their permission—it would have been the first time I defied them.

My dad understood it more than my mom, but Dad had met

the man—briefly—he had laid eyes on him. There wasn't much awareness about pedophiles back then and no one really questioned if that was a part of this relationship—no one in my family really knew Steve; heck, neither did I. I didn't even consider that he might have been someone who liked little girls, even though, at 16, I didn't consider myself a little girl. I considered myself all grown-up and ready for this relationship to go forward. Is a 16 year-old a child to a 27 year-old? I didn't know, and didn't think about it for very long, although I am sure my parents had many discussions about it.

My dad would tell me years later that he could see the love Steve had for me in his eyes; the love I had for him. He had had to work on my mom to soften her up and make her see what he could see. He never considered that Steve was anything more than honest with him and my dad was never one to be trifled with—he could see the truth, smell a lie and would call anyone on it. He trusted me and, eventually trusted Steve. That trust would soon be tested.

Patty picked me up, noticed some tension between my parents and me, but didn't mention it. She drove us—me, her, Mark and Eric—in her blue Datsun to the coliseum. We were swept away by the amount of people who were already there, waiting to get in.

The backstage passes let us bypass the gate lines to go downstairs to the band lounge. I had a blue pass, my friends had green—we realized the difference when they were ushered into a large room, which was bustling with all kinds of people—fans, road crew, band members—I saw Richard, the drummer, and Ned, the guitarist. I recognized them from San Francisco, even though they had changed a little. Ned's hair was bushier, and Richard had grown a moustache. They looked good, though.

Patty squealed with excitement as she went into the room, causing Ned to look toward us, Eric and Mark to roll their eyes and probably make them wish she wasn't with them. I don't know if Ned recognized me or not—I would guess not.

I started to go into the room after my friends, but the door was closed in my face, and I was directed to another room down the hall, let in with no words.

There he was—dressed in tight jeans, torn at the knees and fraying at the bottoms, and a yellow t-shirt with something written on it, I can't remember what. His head was hanging low; he was stretching his neck, sitting in a folding chair. The tennis shoes he had on were blue—new ones—last ones I had seen him in were red. There was a dressing table to his right with a mirror and lights all around it. So cool—this was the dressing room of a star. Hair spray and other assorted hygiene items were on top. There was also some sheet music there, and a picture. I focused on the picture through the tears, which were swelling in my eyes and saw that it was he and I in San Francisco! It was pretty dog-eared and wrinkled, but it was us.

He was holding a brush in one hand, as if he had just stopped brushing his hair a few seconds earlier, a beer in the other, and was tapping the brush on his leg as he continued to rotate his neck around in stretches.

His hair—I finally noticed—had grown since we had been together. It was probably eight inches past his shoulders now. I fell in love with that hair from the moment I first laid eyes on him. And his sideburns had grown—they were down along his jaw line to about two inches from his chin.

I stood silently, and watched him for a few minutes, not sure what to say. We hadn't seen each other in months—eight months to be exact. I had last seen him in July; now it was March. The touring was in full swing. I was surprised to be there and yet I had been expecting it.

I was unsure how he would react when he saw me. Would he be happy? Could that really possible? Happy? Really? Now? Here? How would I feel when I looked into his eyes again? Am I in love? Really? With him? After all this time? Love? I suddenly felt as though I was drowning, like someone was holding my head under water. Then I realized I wasn't breathing.

I drew an audible breath that he must have heard—he realized someone was in the room and looked up. Was it happiness I saw in his face? He smiled his wide, tooth-filled grin at me and came to me, dropping the brush onto the floor. We met in the center of the room and he held me close, nearly crushing me in his arms.

He started to say something but I didn't give him time to finish—this time it was my turn to kiss him: full on the mouth. The taste of him had not changed—mostly beer—and he took full advantage of my open mouth as our happiness turned into lust right there in the dressing room. I was so excited to be with him and didn't ever want to let him go again.

We didn't have a whole lot of time before he was to go onstage with the band but we made good use of the minutes we had and hugged each other deeply, holding on for dear life. There were few words spoken between us at that point. Our faces said it all. He stepped back and took me in—I was back to being a natural brunette, which he said he liked better, and he was looking a little more tired than he had in San Francisco.

There was soon a knock on the door; one of the other band members stuck his head in the door—the bass player with the long dirty-blonde hair, and huge moustache and goatee. It was time to rock-and-roll. Time to let go. His name was Joss; he gave me the once over with his eyes, and looked at Steve with raised eyebrows. Don't know what that was all about; I didn't much care.

Steve led me out and gathered up my friends and I introduced them to each other. Patty was as giddy toward Steve as I had been when I was telling her about him. He took us to one of the roadies and pointed where he had reserved seats in the front row. Best seats in the house. He kissed me on the cheek behind the stage, and readied himself for the start of the show. We took our seats and got strange stares from people around us—kind of like, how did we rate? Who the heck were we to be up that close?

The performance was amazing: this was not the same band I had seen in San Francisco. Same band members but a whole new direction—more melodic rock as opposed to the jazz and soul sounds they had been playing last summer.

Their sound was unique and energized. They played a lot of ballads and a lot of soft to moderate rock. All their own music. Steve had the energy of a boy on stage, running back and forth, dancing around. He held the microphone in his right hand and gestured with his left—his fingers were stiff and he almost looked like it was difficult to move them at times, but move them he did—he would point and curl them into a fist to show his emotions. The veins on his arms and hands stuck out—don't know why I noticed that.

The lights were hot; they would end up, in later years, playing under even more lights and heat and pressure. Steve sang to the audience, not just for them; he even pulled a girl from the audience—a not so pretty girl—and brought her onstage to sing a song to her. I found out later he did that at every show. When they sang the song he had written for me, he found my eyes in the front row and never let go.

My friends were impressed that I knew this man, that I had gotten them this close to a real live rock band. Patty was in heaven as she watched the connection between him and I. Mark and Eric were equally impressed but they never would let on. What a way to spend a Friday night!

When the show was over, there were a lot of girls suddenly backstage that had been gathered up by the roadies, who make their way through the crowds in search of the "appropriate" girls to bring back. With my blue pass, I was escorted past them, but, again, my friends had to go in the other room. That was okay with them—they would be with the other band members—and would have great stories to tell when we got to back to school on Monday.

I went straight to Steve.

He was upset about how the show had gone. He lamented to

me the fact that there had been too many mistakes made, and that the mix was all wrong. I told him no one in the audience noticed, that they had sounded wonderful. But he knew that there was a problem. Being the perfectionist that he was, this would *not* happen again. It took him some time to cool off, pacing the floor, running his fingers through his hair.

He finally stopped and jotted a few things down on a piece of paper on the dressing table, then turned to face me. I had taken my place on one of the folding chairs, waiting to see what he would do next. I could hear the noise from next door and realized there was quite a party going on over there. I asked him about it and he said it was an every night occurrence; that he stayed away from it.

He smiled then, and asked me to go home with him that weekend. The band was off for three days and he wanted to go home—to Atlanta; and he wanted me to go with him. He said he didn't want it to be over tonight. Not tonight. He wanted this night to go on—forever.

I called home on the pay phone that was out in the hallway—collect. No cell phones back then. I asked my dad, practically breathless, if I could visit with Steve longer than this night—could I go home with him to Atlanta? My homework was finished. It was a weekend. Nothing I would miss. No tests Monday. Nothing to worry about. We were just friends who wanted to catch up. Could I go to Atlanta? Please?

My father hemmed and hawed on the phone, no outright absolute no—yet. I was surprised. He wanted to talk to Steve—he was going to embarrass me, I could just feel it, but I reluctantly handed the phone to Steve who was standing next to me, as anxious, I think, as I was.

"Yes, we are just going to my parents' house. No, I don't have anything in mind for her, sir. (*Oh, God.*) Yes, both my parents will be there. Yes, I know how old she is, but, sir, I do love her. (*He said that to my father*?!) Would you like my parent's phone number—here it is. I will have her back to you Monday night—

is that okay if she misses one day of school?" (*This was beginning to sound promising.*) He handed the phone back to me.

Well, Dad?

More hemming and hawing—he was discussing it with my mother; she was not sounding good about any of it. She kept talking about the age difference, that he was probably only using me and did Dad realize we were probably sexually active and was that okay with him? My dad, exasperated, nearly ready to say no, suddenly said okay, almost as if it were out of spite; I could hear my mother losing it in the background. My dad assured her I still had a cool head, that Steve and I were friends; we were going to his parents' house, after all, not some hotel; they would call his parents and talk to them.

A rock star, and a friend. He finally said that he and Mom were going to have to meet this man soon if I was going to—how did he put it?—"run around with him." Meet him? Formally? Meet my mom?! How could I get through something like that? Oh, God in heaven—I had to avoid that.

How many fathers would allow their 16-year-old daughters go off with a rock star? There probably aren't too many, but I think my dad figured I was going regardless—this way, at least, he felt like he had some control over the situation. Dad had met Steve once—he had seen the same sincerity and honesty that I had fell for.

I hung up the phone, leaving my dad to deal with my mother. Poor man. Steve was such a gentleman on the phone with Dad— was this really a rock star I was dealing with?

*T*his would be my first of many trips home to a small house on the outskirts of Atlanta. His parents' home was humble—neat and yet, disorganized. Does that make sense? There was so much of Steve all over the place. His parents looked like my parents—just as normal. His dad wore reading glasses all the time, peering at people over the frames; and when he was home, he had a pipe between his teeth, sometimes lit, but, more often than not, it wasn't. His mom always had on a full apron and a dress—I don't think I ever saw her in a pair of pants. She reminded me a lot of Edith Bunker from *All in the-Family* in her appearance and mannerisms. She was heavy-set and buxom, and fussed over Steve all the time.

She was the typical proud mama of a famous son—she had every article ever written about him and the band stuffed into one scrapbook after another, and she took great joy in showing me those articles, the pictures, the letters. She was the keeper of the archive. Steve seemed embarrassed by it all but looked over his mother's shoulder, more than once, to see himself in print.

James, Steve's younger brother, separated by nine years to Steve, lived at home. They, apparently, had been the rowdy boys of the neighborhood when they were younger: I was treated to stories of their hell-raising, including the tale of Steve dangling James by his ankles from the roof. As a grown-up, James was more serious, preferred James to Jim, and idolized his older brother.

Steve was a ham when he was at home. Much more relaxed and able to kick back, be himself: a man with a good sense of humor—funny, witty and smiling. That was the Steve I loved most: the homebody who liked nothing more than to sit in his family's living room, listening to music, lost in the melody with his loved ones around him.

He and I always ended up on the couch in the family room. That couch—I'll never forget it—it was the one piece of furniture that seemed so out of place in a house of new pieces Steve had purchased for his family. He spent the money he was making on his parents and his brother. And spent it to get back to Atlanta as often as he could—it was his place to unwind, regroup. And he spent his money on phone calls to me. His mother would not part with that couch, though, and I was glad for that. The couch was older and had been recovered several times. This incarnation was a gold- and brown-toned material with big flowers. The cushions were over-stuffed, into which you sank when sitting on it, and generally needed help getting out of.

That was our place. He and I on the couch, his arm around me, my head on his shoulder, quietly listening to music and answering his mother's questions about the band and his life. Was he getting enough to eat because he looked awfully skinny? Was he getting enough sleep because he looked awfully tired?

She didn't quite understand what our relationship was, but, of course, neither did I. Steve had told them about me in a letter, but didn't say much more than I was a new friend. He introduced me to his parents as "the girl I told you about from San Francisco."

We were friends and yet we were so much more. I didn't know where I truly stood in his life but I did know that I wanted to be in his life, in any way possible. Here I was in his family home, with his parents and his brother, and I felt comfortable—as if I belonged there.

Did I want to be a groupie the rest of my life? At that point, if it meant being with this man, then, yes, I did. The problem was—I didn't like the limelight anymore than he did. And, with my age being what it was, still in high school and trying to get into college, it was almost equally as hard on me as it was on him. He was an adult, in a band touring the country and eventually, the world, hounded by thousands of fans. He needed a woman who could be with him, on the road, and love him in the way he deserved. So, what was he doing with me, I wondered.

On this first time he took me home, I had an idea that I was someone special. His mother had taken me aside and talked to me a bit, asking me many questions, mostly about who I was and where I was from. She told me that I was the first girl that he had brought home since he dated in high school. That made my heart jump in my chest, my breath catch. She looked deep into my eyes and told me not to hurt him—I assured her I couldn't.

He and I spent the night together in his parents' house that March, sleeping in the family room on the couch. We were curled up in each other's arms and had fallen asleep where we lay.

We slept on the couch even though he had a bedroom upstairs in which he could have slept—I would have been content to sleep on the floor so long as I was in the same house with him. He took me up to his bedroom—first one at the top of the stairs. It was a typical teenage boy's room that a mother had preserved.

As we climbed the stairs, I suddenly realized I was going to see his bedroom—the place where he had grown up. Maybe I would touch his dresser that had held his clothes; maybe I would touch a lamp that he had read by; maybe, just maybe, I would touch his bed—the bed he had spent so many nights in for 20 years—the bed that had held his secrets and dreams.

He opened the door and stepped back to let me go in first.

There was a twin bed in a simple wooden frame, with a quilt, bearing the names of NFL teams, something similar to what my brother had on his own bed. The wallpaper was also sports-related—a beige/grey with drawings of hockey, basketball and football, not that he had ever been all that interested in those sports.

He had a bulletin board with two high school letters tacked up, awards from being on the swim team for 2 years, he told me. He said they went to the state finals when he was a senior and, to prepare and improve their times in the water, the whole team, six guys, had shaved their heads. I couldn't imagine him without his gorgeous long hair. He wouldn't show me the pictures, ever.

Below the bulletin board was his desk—two drawers with a chair. A pencil holder was on top, along with several sheets of music paper. There were two pairs of drumsticks perched on top of the paper and a well-used drum practice pad. He picked up one pair of the sticks and held them, curling his fingers around each one. He lightly pounded out a rhythm on the pad for a few seconds; he still had it even though he hadn't played the drums, formally, in years.

A simple dresser was in one corner, a bookshelf kitty-corner to it. I looked at the books—Hardy Boys, drum books, music books, swimming books, SAT books (which he never did take). There were a few stuffed animals from his early childhood on the top shelf. I didn't look in his closet, but probably would have had he not been there: I am one of those nosey people who will open medicine cabinets in other's bathrooms.

This was the room in which he had grown up—the room of his youth, where he had dreamt of being who he had become; the room to which he had been sent when he was naughty (which, he said, was often); and the room to which he escaped then and now. This is where he came these days to leave the star behind.

We could have slept there but neither of us felt comfortable enough with that yet—he even offered to sleep on a cot but it was my choice, my nervousness, to say no. I don't know exactly what I was thinking but we slept downstairs.

Our first night in his parents' house was short—we arrived hours after midnight and had talked with his family for awhile. They finally went upstairs at around 4 AM. He threw his legs behind me on the couch and lay down, pulling my face down to his.

He told me he was so glad I had come—where we could be away from the fame and just be us. He kissed me all over my face, finally coming to my mouth. He was so relaxed; it was so natural to be with him—it felt like we had never left San Francisco.

I lay down next to him, pushing his back farther into the couch, facing him. His eyes were drooping slightly from lack of sleep—he had been in concert for two hours just a little while ago. With his arms around me, he drifted peacefully off.

I watched him as he slept—his eyelids fluttered at times and I could tell his eyes were moving underneath. I wondered what his dreams were. He was breathing slowly from his nose and snored very slightly every so often. He smelled of concert sweat and excitement, still in the same t-shirt he had worn on stage. I kissed his forehead and tasted the salt of the sweat that had been there.

I was mildly uncomfortable being in his parent's house. Every time I thought about it, my stomach ached and my heart got a shot of adrenaline, a little jolt just to let me know my nerves were firing. Why was I so anxious? I really didn't know. I had spent many nights, at many friends' houses over the years—boys and girls. Mostly slumber parties or just falling asleep. Never thought much about it before.

But this was his house. This man, who had taken me to his family, and let me in. This house smelled of last night's dinner—

spaghetti (his mom had offered leftovers but we had declined), and of the cherry pipe tobacco his dad smoked.

It was quiet, except for the bubbling of an aquarium to the side of the couch, and I heard the cat—a grey kitty named Nip—crunching his dry food in the adjacent kitchen. And Steve's occasional snores through flared nostrils.

I finally fell asleep, no longer able to keep my eyes open.

The second and third nights that we spent at his parents' house were also shared on the couch, but Saturday night was different. He had spent the entire day in the house; he didn't want to go anywhere, and that was fine by me. He spent some time with his brother who desperately wanted to be a rock star too, and he spent time down in the basement with his father who was always down there tinkering with some project.

I helped his mom in the kitchen and we got to know each other some more. She and I cooked for the men, and I answered her questions that danced all around her son's and my relationship. She saw that I had the same clothes on as last night—didn't bring anything as I had not been expecting to take a trip, so she hustled me into the car to go shopping—with Steve's money.

When we returned, we had dinner, played some cards with the family and turned in early as the night before had been such a late one.

He and I were going to spend another night on the couch so I had bought a nightgown, which was "sensible." Not flannel, but high neck and to the floor, with long sleeves. His mother had picked it out. When he appeared in the doorway of the family room after he had changed, and saw me in it, sitting on the couch, he laughed. He was in short—very short—running shorts and nothing else—obviously—very obviously.

He came to me on the couch, stood in front of me, giving me a great view of the shorts. I looked up into his face to see that he was still very amused by my choice of night attire. He told me I looked like a spinster; I told him I had plenty of gowns at home like this because this is what is worn to slumber parties. Slumber parties?! Had I actually just said that to a rock star?! I wanted to sink into the couch and disappear. Plus, I had been shopping with his mother—what was I supposed to buy—something revealing?!

But he laughed again, a small giggle, and sat down next to me. I could smell his aftershave—he had trimmed back his sideburns, on his mother's request. His scent was spicy and sweet, and set my heart aglow. He touched the fabric of the nightgown and giggled again—he sounded so young, so relaxed.

Hell, he looked young and relaxed in those shorts—there was still no hair on his chest—just that line of darkness below his belly button that disappeared under the shorts. And he had dark hair on his legs.

He drew me into his arms and held me; he had showered, his skin smelled of soap and of him—he had his own scent that was all him.

I felt very vulnerable that night, even more so than I had in San Francisco. There was something about the way the material felt between us and the way it heightened every sensation, every movement. I loved holding this man, feeling his body pressed to mine, experiencing him with all my senses.

I could have made love to him right there, allowed him to take my virginity with abandon, and never look back. But, he was brought up to be polite and decent and not take advantage of anyone. At least that is what he told me that night.

He sat back from me and brought one of his legs up under him on the couch, facing me. He told me that our meeting had changed him in San Francisco and that he had hoped it had changed me too. He had slept with other women—two to be exact—one in high school and one in Los Angeles. He thought he was in love both times but said that he didn't feel with them what he felt with me. I had hoped we wouldn't have this conversation but he started it; I was going to allow him to finish.

He didn't understand why he connected with me in San Francisco—what had pulled his heart toward me. He hadn't realized how young I was when he first laid eyes on me, then, once he found out, it no longer made any difference. He called it magical. I couldn't have agreed more.

He asked me about my past love life and I think I laughed at that. What past love life? I was 16—remember? I told him I had never been on a real date. I had friends and we all went out together as a group thing, even went to Homecoming Dance as a group. But there had never been anything more than a goodnight kiss with one of the boys of the group—Mark. And it was not much more than a peck on the cheek.

My group—he wanted to know about the kids in my group of friends. He had met three of them—Patty, Mark and Eric. We were 4 of 10 who did everything together—all in the band. I was one of four of us who were a year behind the others—we were dreading the end of the upcoming school year—it would signal the loss of good friends.

We were rowdy in school, most of us straight-A students, so our behavior was a little unusual. A lot of my current friends say they probably would not have liked me back then when they hear the last B I received in school was 6th grade. But I wasn't a goody-goody bookworm; none of us were.

We were the practical jokers: the ones who put saran wrap over the toilet bowls in the teachers lounges, and the ones who set off smoke bombs in the hallway; all in good fun. We had teachers in the palms of our hands because we did have the grades and would even hang out at some of their homes. We didn't smoke, didn't drink, certainly didn't do drugs—we were simply having fun being teenagers, being together, making the grades. You can have fun learning.

Steve pumped me for more information about my life—particularly about what we did on the weekends. This was all so strange that someone like him wanted to hear about my little life. It was a little disconcerting. What was he expecting me to say? That we had wild orgy parties? Hardly. We spent time in each other's houses, at teachers' houses, or, even sometimes at the high school as some of us, including me, had the key to the band room door.

There were a few nights when we would venture out to toilet paper someone's house, before it became illegal. Usually it was someone we liked, we were just letting them know that. I told Steve of the stern looks we would get from cashiers as we checked out with as many rolls of toilet paper that we could hold. I made a grumpy face and a tsk-tsk and he smiled. Here we were, at the beginning of a conversation about sex and he wants to know this stuff!

I guess I poked holes in the blanket of tension that had settled around us, so I continued.

The most famous toilet-papering incident was last Fall; it even made the local newspaper. There was a senior girl who had a crush on Eric, but Eric wanted nothing to do with her, but she pursued him mercilessly. He and his family went out to eat one Saturday night so we toilet- papered her house, then his, and connected them the block and a half with strands of paper in the street.

I told Steve I still do silly things because I am still a kid. Did he understand that—that I was still a kid? I think he did.

Then he asked—about sex. Here we go. I was so naïve and didn't want him to know that, but there was no avoiding it now. I didn't want to tell him that, less than a year ago, when I had seen him on stage for the first time, singing about making love to a woman, I really didn't know that meant sex. My mother had handed me the book *Everything You Always Wanted to Know About Sex But Were Afraid To Ask* when we got home from vacation because she was so uptight about answering any questions I may have had. And I had a lot of questions, but truly was too embarrassed to ask anyone.

I blurted all this out to him finally and he laughed at me again—he laughed hard and then shushed himself so as to not awaken his family. I humphed and told him it was true—that I was a silly Midwestern girl without experience, without a whole lot of knowledge. How could he possibly want to be with me? A virgin; a very naïve virgin.

But he was so sincere; again told me how our meeting me had changed him. That he hasn't been with anyone since, despite nightly opportunities, having to look at girls flashing all of their body parts. He said every time he sees that he thinks of me. That every time he feels excited, it is because of me. That every time he wants sex, he thinks of me. That he is willing to wait.

Wait? Wait for what? I wanted him. Right there. Right then. I didn't really fully understand what sex was; I thought is was an expression of love that two people feel for each other and do to show it.

He wanted me to be able to make the decision once we knew each other more, once I was an adult—18. Two years away. It seemed like a lifetime. I felt like I had been slapped in the face but then I realized it would be harder on him—he was out on the road, alone; yet he wanted to wait for me to catch up.

As much as I wanted him then, as much as I loved him prior to that moment, I wanted him and loved him even more. But I was still a girl—a teenager. He held me against him; he was so relaxed and gentle and loving. I knew at that moment, in a little less than two years, I would feel all of him, be a part of him even more and have him be a part of me.

Two years…would he wait? That was my only question.

That Sunday we both stayed inside the house, watching TV— some old movie on that afternoon, and we were together on the couch again, his brother on one side, me on the other. The town was buzzing with the news that he was in town (his dad had let the cat of the bag on Friday at his hardware store that his boy was coming home), and a small crowd had gathered just to see if they could catch a glimpse of him. He was a star now; it was big news that he was in town. Even the town newspaper sent a photographer to try to catch a picture—this was the first time I was exposed to this part of his life. I was beginning to understand his disdain for it all.

Some of his high school friends came over—two from the swim team, and his best friend. They spent time reminiscing—Steve wanted to talk about the old days, but his friends all wanted to know about the spot light. He introduced me to everyone as his girlfriend and I received more than my share of surprised glances during the day.

Steve was not a big talker; he listened as tales were told of what people were doing with themselves, but the conversation always turned back to him and the band. It was very frustrating for him; there were times when I physically felt that frustration, as he would tighten his grip on my shoulder.

Fortunately for him, no one stayed all that long. He didn't say much after everyone had left. Quiet—deep in thought. He would later tell me that he had been wishing he could trade places with any one of the friends who had come by, and "just be normal again."

The end of the weekend came too soon; he had to be off for Detroit and I to Ohio. Monday morning he put me on a plane to Cleveland. He took me to the Atlanta airport in his father's car, wearing a goofy floppy hat, similar to a fedora with a more relaxed brim, pulled low on his forehead to cover his face, so as to not be recognized. That hat would become a wardrobe staple in his quest to be anonymous.

Leaving him this time, I cried on his shoulder as he held me tightly against him at the gate. The teenager and the rock star—both growing up and trying to find our places in the world, not knowing what truly was in front of us. This had been an important weekend: we made it clear to each other that we were in love, that we were going to try to make it work. In my heart, I knew that he was on his way and I was nothing; I would be left behind at some point. But, for now, we knew what we had and wanted it to last. This was becoming more serious than I had thought it would, and I did not want to go.

He finally let me know that I could come with him over the summer leg of their tour if I wanted — if my parents would allow it. I could tell them I was going to work for the band as a roadie; maybe they would be okay with that. It was worth a shot. To be on the road with him for three months — my heart was thumping wildly as I told him I would make it work — it was going to happen no matter what.

My tears stained his blue shirt as I held him one last time. He kissed me hard and I took one last touch of his hair. He smudged my glasses with his nose and kissed my face, bumping my forehead with the brim of the hat. We said good-bye and I left him.

When Dad picked me up, he could see that something had changed but Dad was too prim and proper to ask. We were silent on the drive home until I gathered up all my nerve and asked him if I could work for the band over the summer as road crew. Dad was silent; I thought for sure he was about to say no. But he looked at me from the drivers' seat and could see in my eyes that I was determined; I would go whether or not he gave me permission, just like Atlanta.

The end of my sophomore year could not have come sooner. I had been granted the okay to join the band; it was spread all over school what I would be doing with my summer vacation. This vacation would be a whole lot better than being with the family. This was to be my summer. My summer of love and discovery and Steve.

*S*teve picked me up in Ohio the day after I finished my sophomore year—June 3, 1976, a Thursday. I had made it through 10th grade with straight A's, Dean's List and National Honor Society. I think, had I not been doing that well, I never would have been able to go with him. But I was a "good girl," according to my parents and would be "safe" with Steve, whom they had insisted come to dinner the night of our departure, so they could talk to him and get to know him. I don't know what I was thinking but Steve actually told me on the phone that he was looking forward to it.

This was the time I had been dreading since we met. I knew it would have to happen if I continued to see him so I figured we would get it over with now and save time later. My parents had sat me down for the lecture, prior to his arrival—they had taught me values and they hoped I would not let them fly by the wayside. They understood that I was enamored by this man; probably in love; they wanted to meet him and see if they could tell how he felt about me. God help me, I hoped they weren't going to actually sit him down and ask what "his intentions are."

They had heard all his records over and over up to this point in his career—I blasted them from my stereo, which could be heard all over the house, and some of the songs talked of passion and making love. They were just songs—he had a wonderful writing talent and when the mood was right, he could put anything to music and make it sound sexy. My mom was worried that all those love songs were about me; I had to assure her daily that they were not—that his writing partner in the band also had a life, as did the other guys, and the songs dealt with all of them and their lives. Sometimes a name in a song was just a name that fit with the rhythm, or it was someone else's girlfriend or wife.

So, he was coming; there was nothing I could do to stop it. Deep breath. It was only one evening—hopefully, it would go quickly.

It is not an easy thing in a small Midwestern town to have a rock star over for dinner, especially when he arrives in a limousine—a big, black, stretch limousine. Not something seen too often in our neck of the woods. I had told my closest friends he was coming but my brother, the big mouth, might as well have told the whole town. People kept their distance, hanging out on the street in front of our house, kind of like some had done when we were in Atlanta, but it was worse—there were more people here; more shouting and trying to get his attention. He was gracious and waved as he got out of the back of the limo. It was more and more evident what he meant when he complained about being recognized. He was seen in countless teen magazines and music magazines. The fame was trying to consume him as he was trying to keep his feet on the ground. He had gone from a virtual unknown to a rock sensation in a matter of minutes. He was now every female's fantasy. It was beginning to stress him.

I was standing on the front porch waiting for him, my brother, John, hanging by my side. He seemed to be just as excited as I was but for a far different reason—he wanted to meet a rock star; I wanted to see the love of my life. When he pulled into our driveway, and climbed out of the limo, my heart leapt—I hadn't seen him in nearly three months; he was as handsome as ever. He had cut his hair a bit—it was still below his shoulders but only by a few inches, and was layered more. And he had a moustache! A moustache! A dark brown moustache, above his mouth. That was a new look. It wouldn't last too long—thank goodness—anything that hid any part of his face was not a good thing.

He was dressed in a suit—a dark black suit with a white shirt and a black tie. And tennis shoes—black ones this time, to match the suit. He carried two bouquets of flowers—one assorted which he gave to my mother, and a dozen roses, which he gave to me along with a quick kiss on the mouth. He shook my dad's hand and said it was nice to see him again. My mom was overwhelmed because of the flowers, not sure what to say. My brother was star-struck, standing there with his mouth open. Steve shook his hand too; John just stood there—nice to see him quiet for a change.

We went into the house where our new Golden Retriever puppy greeted him with tail wagging, jumping onto his legs. He knelt down and hugged the dog that slobbered all over him. Then I had to show him around the house, at his insistence. I think he really wanted to see the bedroom where I spent most of my time these days.

We went upstairs, my brother close at our heels. John showed Steve his room and it was funny—while I was standing in the doorway, watching Steve be very gracious, I realized how much John's room resembled Steve's old room—teenage boys—are they all alike?

Then there was my room—next to John's. John tried to follow us into the room but Steve looked at him and asked if he would give us a minute. Amazingly, he did.

My room—a canopy bed with frilly white lace and a matching bedspread, two dressers, shelves on the wall, a desk; my dad had glued cork to one wall so I could pinup all my stuff. Steve went right to the bulletin board—there were pictures hanging there of him and the band, along with everything he had sent me over the past months. My airline tickets were there, and the backstage passes, napkins from our dinners together.

Sprinkled in between all of my memories of him were my own keepsakes—pictures of my friends, my band uniform feathers from the cap, a piece of the bass drum that was broken during one of the halftime shows last fall. There were articles from the school paper I had written; he stood there and read them all.

My National Honor Society certificate was there as well as my own high school letter—from band. He looked it all over. Then he moved on to my books.

He had had the Hardy Boys—I had Nancy Drew. And tons of other assorted books—I loved to read. My stuffed animal collection took up most of two shelves and he remarked that he didn't realize I liked them so much—if he had, he would have given me his when we were home—and that he still will.

Then he turned back to me—I was sitting in the desk chair, watching him from behind, liking the view very much. He had gained a little bit of weight since I last saw him—he was probably eating better now but still burning most of it off on stage. He looked so good in a suit—all I had ever seen him in were jeans and semi-dress shirts. He looked tired too—very tired—and a little worried with two small wrinkles between his eyebrows.

He told me I looked great—I didn't buy it—I too had gained a little more weight—now about 30 pounds overweight. My hair was growing. I had had my ears pierced—my parents had finally said yes. Whoopie. He walked behind me, kissed me on the top of my head and brought his face around to mine and kissed my cheeks then took me into his mouth, holding my face. I stood up and turned to him; we held each other tightly. We were silent, breathing in unison. He whispered that he had missed me and that he loved me and that there was so much he had to tell me.

I was the one he told his secrets to—sometimes he would let them out on the phone but he preferred to let them out in person. Later—we would have plenty of time to talk.

He pulled out of the tight embrace and told me we had best go back to the family—he was so considerate. He looked at my bed where my suitcase was—ready to go. He told me now he was really excited—this was really going to happen.

Dinner was very nice—my brother was refined in his behavior—thank goodness; he didn't embarrass me too much. My parents managed to do so, though, by pulling out the family albums and making him sit through the pictures after dinner. He looked so funny on the living room couch between my mom and my brother, going through the album. But he didn't look as uncomfortable as I thought he would be. He seemed perfectly content where he was and with what he was doing. This is what he loved—family.

He seemed especially pleased when my dad proudly showed him my report card. I thought I was going to fall through the floor with embarrassment, until Steve looked at me and smiled. He told me he knew I was smart; that I could do whatever I want with my life.

My parents never did do the "We have to talk" thing with him—they did ask where the tour was going; he handed them a typed itinerary which outlined all the cities, arenas and the hotels we could be reached at. Thankfully he didn't mention that we were sharing a room, which even I didn't know.

My parents also told him to keep me safe, not to let me work too hard—uh huh—they thought I was a roadie—a roadie picked up by the star.

The night, thankfully, did go by quickly; we had a 1 AM flight to Atlanta to catch—going to his parents' house for a few days; then onto the tour, starting in New York City. I said good-bye to my folks as the limo driver loaded my suitcase into the trunk. It was dark outside, after 11 PM, yet there were still about 100 people milling about. Amazing.

Steve was gracious, signed some autographs and shook hands. That was when he truly looked uncomfortable.

This was going to be an interesting summer.

We arrived in Atlanta around three-thirty in the morning—delay out of Cleveland due to severe weather over Tennessee. We were always arriving in Georgia during the wee hours of the morning. That was Steve—he figured there would be fewer people at the airport to recognize him. Someone always did manage to pick him out of the crowd on the plane, though. Flight attendants generally knew who he was but they were polite and professional about it; keeping the gushing to a minimum.

Our conversation on the plane was all him, which was nice for a change. He was becoming increasingly unhappy with fame and fans; people pushing him to do things he had no interest in; reviewers who took cheap shots at his music. All he wanted to do was sing, but, with singing came responsibility; with responsibility came hassles.

But, on the other hand, he was managing to have some fun—when he was on stage. The stage was becoming his refuge—even though that was where he could be seen by thousands of people. There was no hint on stage that he had had a major blow up with Ned just prior to being introduced, or that a fan had managed to get back stage and "attack" him moments before. He could be himself, singing without a care in the world.

Very much a private person, not willing to share his personal space, Steve had begun to travel from show to show separately from the others. While the band had purchased two new tour buses—one for the band, one for the road crew—much nicer than the school bus they had started with—Steve wanted to be on his own, generally renting cars and driving on ahead—he would soon graduate to limousines. This way he was free to stay in the hotel that he wanted to, away from the fans and hangers-on; and he could go home to Atlanta when he wanted to, catching up with the band at the next venue.

This, apparently, had caused a great deal of friction between him and other band members who would have preferred he ride with them. But he couldn't—he was left out of things by his own choice; left to fend for himself, be himself, in his own world. He reminded me of me in some ways, as I often secluded myself away in my room, away from family and friends, preferring to be left alone. Steve's mother had told me he had been a loner all his life and had not trusted many people.

It was an issue of trust—he trusted very few people and confided in even fewer. But, this matter of traveling separately would come up more and more in the future becoming a source of some very bad blood running through the band.

Our flight into Atlanta was slightly over an hour; he talked and drank beer the whole time, holding my hand tightly. A little too tightly, I thought—he's hanging on for some reason. He squeezed my hand several times, particularly when he was obviously agitated by what he was telling me. His grip was strong.

I listened to his fears and his regrets. He seemed as if he had grown years since we last saw each other in March. He had adult problems—finances, touring, privacy. I wanted to make them all go away but knew that was impossible. His life was changing; everything was changing. The band was evolving and changing too. I didn't want to see that change but, as with all things, change is inevitable.

James picked us up outside the airport after we grabbed the bags. Steve had on his floppy hat and sunglasses to walk through the terminal—how I hated that hat and yet, I knew he had to wear it. It was his protection. He ended up wearing it on the cover of a solo album just because he knew I would hate it. Ornery.

Steve fell asleep on the drive home—too many beers on the plane—too much anxiety spent at my parent's house—too little sleep, period. His parents met us at the door—they always stayed up for their boy to come home, no matter what the hour. They quickly disappeared to their rooms, as did James.

Steve, still feeling the effects of the beer, grabbed me and held me to him as tightly as he ever had. Something was definitely going on but I didn't know what it could be. He kept repeating to me that he loved me; it seemed that he was nearly in a panic.

It was a mix of emotions I was seeing and feeling from him: intoxication, love, happiness, relaxation, nervousness. All were coming from him as the adrenaline pumped into my system; I didn't know what was going on and was fearful that he was going to break up with me—a typical teenager reaction.

But, when he parted from me, he looked a little more at ease, smiling, seemingly genuinely glad that I was there. He took my bags and his and we went upstairs to his bedroom to change and get ready to go to our couch. It was 4:30 AM—this was going to be a short night. It was obvious that he had spent some time in the room. Just as it had been in San Francisco, his room was messy now—clothing strewn around here and there, tennis shoes kicked haphazardly into the corner.

There was a lot of sheet music piled on the desk with several different colored pencils on top—red, green, blue and lead. He always had sheet music with him these days, never knowing where a song inspiration might come from.

He had added a few things to the bulletin board above the desk since I had been there. Black and white publicity photos were pinned up, as was a picture of me in my band uniform he had wanted me to send him—and my Charlie was there—he had a picture of my dog that I had loved so much and was so heart-broken about when we had to have her put to sleep shortly after returning from California—on his bulletin board. He had my life tacked up in the sanctuary of his room. Me. This man never did cease to amaze me.

When I looked back at him, he was in the process of undressing—pants off, suit coat off, both discarded onto the bed. Tennis shoes a few feet away, laces still tied. He was struggling with his tie, looking comical in his helplessness. I watched his frustration grow, but eventually he managed to loosen it enough to get it over his head, tossing it past me onto the desk. The shirt came off next. He was wearing plain old Fruit of the Loom underwear. Cute. Very cute.

God love him—this rock star was standing in front of me in socks and underwear, hair tousled from the difficult tie removal—and I loved him so much at that moment that it hurt—it had become a physical ache. He had to have been able to read it all over my face. Hell, anyone who saw the two of us together had to be able to see it.

Seeing him standing there, in the seconds that he was actually still, brought a flood of emotions to my core—desire, lust, passion. But, at the same time, I felt sorrow, pain, loss of any control. Can't explain it fully.

He turned and dove into a dresser drawer, threw on a t-shirt, then sat on the bed to remove his socks. I decided, what the hell, opened my suitcase, removed a nightshirt and then came the dilemma—do I change here in this room or leave for the bathroom? He had changed here but it was different—he was a little high, and this was his room.

With nightshirt in hand, I looked at him on the bed, clothing all around him; he was smiling in that sad way he had about him. Not a word passed between us, not a sound, not a breath. I started to leave the room but he stood up and came to me and, in my ear, told me to stay.

Okay—take a deep breath—remember you have to breathe. I kicked off my shoes and rubbed the bottoms of my feet against the carpet until my socks came off; the lazy woman's way to remove socks. The jeans came next; I threw them over his desk chair, over a pair of his. The shirt was next—this was not an easy thing for me—I was very apprehensive. This would be a first for me. Okay, a second—my group of friends had all gone skinny-dipping late last fall. But, a first with this man who was standing so close, watching me with fire in his eyes.

The overhead light was on and I glanced at it with a grimace: too much light; way too much light at this point. He understood somehow and turned it off, returning quickly to my side. The room fell into semi-darkness—the sun was just barely beginning to come up with a warm orange glow outside that cast a pale, very dim light on both of us.

Without a word, he leaned against the desk, facing me, crossing his arms in front of him. I didn't need to see his face to know he was smiling. I pulled the blouse I was wearing over my head and laid it on top of my jeans. The bra came off next and took its place over the desk chair. I turned to him, as I had seen women do in the movies, and could see him a little better as my eyes adjusted. Biting my lower lip, I stood in front of him, wondering what I was doing wrong as he took me in, his eyes moving up and down my body, making me feel exposed but in a good way.

He took me into his arms and held me close without a word, then kissed me, the kiss becoming increasingly frantic as he moved his mouth against mine, his tongue fierce inside of me, our teeth scraping together.

I wanted him to touch me, to put his hands on me and show me what it was to make love to someone. I wanted him in everyway possible, to feel more than the excitement in his groin pushing against me.

But, it was not to be—not tonight. He was still cordial, play by the rules Steve, uncomfortable with my age; and I was still me, full of longing but also just a girl, not quite all grown up yet. He pulled away from me and, with a breathy annoyance, he said, "I can't—not yet." We both swallowed—hard, and I knew he was right. Damn, I knew he was right. He turned away from me and told me he would meet me on the couch.

I put my nightshirt on while he went into the bathroom down the hall, then I went down to the family room. It seemed like he took an unusually long time in the bathroom. I didn't ask, but he appeared more relaxed when he came to me on the couch.

We slept on the couch for a few hours, tucked up against each other, his back to me; like two spoons in a drawer, we were a perfect fit. I heard his parents in the kitchen and heard the screen door close as his dad went off to work in the store. James came thumping down the hall; he peeked into the family room; I raised my head and waved at him; he was in pajama bottoms.

I jumped slightly when I felt something touch me lightly on the shoulder, but smiled when I saw Nip laying on the back of the couch, pawing at me. Steve never stirred—he was out and I was stuck with my back against the couch.

I lay still for a time, surprised when James and his mother came in and sat down. I was also surprised that someone, probably his mother, had covered us at some point with a light blanket. Then I realized she had seen us there in shirts and underwear, and the awkwardness of the situation reared its ugly head.

She smiled at me from her chair across from the couch but I could sense the undertones of a mother's concern, curiosity. I propped my head up onto my arm and looked at her over her oldest son's head. We stared at each other uncomfortably; her eyes seemed to bore right through me as if she wanted to pick my brain to see what her son and I were doing together.

James had turned on the stereo and was listening to Steve's album through the headphones, oblivious to the silent exchange between mother and girlfriend.

She spoke finally, with a mother's firm, protective instinct, but softly, so as to not wake Steve up. She told me that, first, she did not disapprove of him and I, however the age thing did concern her. Maybe not as much as it would someone else as she and her husband had married when she was 17. But she desperately wanted to know if we were sleeping together, because, even when we were simply looking at each other, we appeared to be making love.

"The looks that pass between you two are nothing less than love."

I asked her if she would be disappointed if we had slept together, and she told me no. But I assured we hadn't—not yet. Due to my age, he wanted to wait. It was his idea, and he was sticking to it. We were waiting until I turned 18. His mom visibly relaxed her face and smiled. She told me he had written to her about me and she was not to be concerned about my age. She was scared, she admitted, that protective parents might accuse him of statutory rape. I told her they never would; that she needn't worry.

Her words warmed me and I told her I very much loved her oldest boy, that it didn't matter to me if he was a rock star or a construction worker or anything—I would stay at his side as long as he wanted me there.

That did it. Steve moved his legs and giggled. He had heard our whole conversation. Men! He rolled over onto his back, rising up to give me a quick kiss on the mouth, then blew a kiss to his mother.

We stayed with his family four days until joining the summer tour. He shaved his moustache the day after we arrived. Apparently the fans had made it clear to the record company that they didn't like it. Neither did I—anything that hid his face met with disapproval from me. He spoke many times with a couple of the band members on the phone, working out some kinks, banging out long-distance melodies on the piano. I think the only person he didn't speak to was Ned. Not a surprise.

I saw Steve's temper flare a few times when one member suggested he change a line in a song. If there was one thing Steve wanted, it was continuity; no songs were going to be changed now; they were to be played the same way every time. He quickly got over his anger, but it was a different side of him.

We walked around the block our last night there, hand in hand; finally arms around each other's waists. He pointed out his old school to me, and a tree he had hit when he was learning how to drive. Being there with him made him a person like me—

a regular person, even though he would never be a regular person again. Fame had taken that privilege away from him.

We came to rest on the steps of his parents' home and sat there watching the sun set. He asked me if I would stay with him if he quit the band. This was the first he had ever admitted that there was something nagging at him inside to get out of the band.

I had seen his temper spark a few more times, subtle hints of his irritation—little things that were beginning to nag at him like a pebble in your shoe that begins to feel like a boulder. He barked at band mates on the phone more and more, unhappy that things were being changed without his approval or consultation. He ran home to Atlanta when feeling overwhelmed, perhaps to re-energize in the security of family. He ducked his fans to protect what little of himself he had left.

And, most of all, he drank, sometimes to excess, as he had done on the flight here. He didn't seem to drink anything but beer and coffee. Never having been exposed to alcohol, I didn't know what to think so I thought nothing. He could go all day with one beer, nursing it for hours, and, on other days, he would have six to seven in a very short time; it depended on how often he talked with band mates.

He kept most of his demons well hidden inside of him, but, in the secure arms of his family and the hometown, he was ready to let them out

He told me of the backstage things that went on. Girls were always there; they were hard to ignore. They frequently came at him and the other band members with their tops off, willing to drop every other piece of clothing just to be near them. Some were much younger than me; some much older.

He looked off into the sunset and continued to tell me of the fans who wanted a piece of him at any expense. That they dig through the garbage left behind for any little scrap. They hang out wherever the concerts are and hound the buses and the cars, wanting to touch him, grab his clothes, make him notice them.

His voice grew quieter as he described other fan activity—hiding in the bus when they could, or in the hotel hallway. Sex became synonymous with rock-and-roll and he didn't always look the other way. He hadn't slept with any of them but it was tempting. He said he wanted to wait for me for now, that he could resist, so long as I was willing to trust him, and so long as I loved him.

We were in the very beginning of any kind of relationship and I trusted him—it was everyone else I didn't trust. I was glad at that moment that I was touring with him through the summer—that would keep some of them away at least.

Then he talked about the drugs. He had written to me about the drug activity but now, for some reason, he seemed to want to tell me what had gone on and what he had done.

The drugs were everywhere behind the scenes. Whether it was hard-core heroin or simple pot, there was no end to it. From the roadies to the groupies to the band members, use ran freely and he had not resisted. He showed me the marks on his arm at the inner elbow where he had injected heroin several times, not just the one time he had written me about. The skin was visibly bruised and red, an angry look, infected. His vein bulged in several places where he had abused it with a needle—I had noticed before but wasn't sure what to say.

I held his arm in my hand and I know he could see it in my face—my life was crashing down into those track marks on my boyfriend's arm. This issue suddenly encompassed my whole being as if I was experiencing my last day of sanity.

He hung his head and admitted to being so high the first several times, that he had forgotten time and had lost himself in the confusion of a wide-open space. He didn't know what he had done on several nights, didn't know if he had been alone in the fog. He was scared that he had done terrible things to betray him and I. Listening to him, I was frightened too; I didn't understand the pull of addiction—this was all too new.

My head felt like darkness had come over me, covering me in

a wash of confusing messages and emotions. My love for this man was suddenly overshadowed by fear, anger and dismay. Tears threatened but I willed them away.

Why my emotions crashed in on me at his revelation, I don't know. I didn't understand it all, I guess. And I really focused in on his statement about not knowing if he had been alone in his disorientation. That hit me like a knife to the stomach, pushing ever deeper with every word he spoke.

Heroin. Just the mention of the word evoked a fear in me like no other. Why heroin? Heroin. Heroin?! The tears finally came.

We sat in silence on his front porch, his back to me, head hung in his hands, face covered. He sniffled a few times, each one sounding more and more liquid — his tears were flowing too. I didn't know what to do, what to say, how to make it all better. Could I make this all better? He was obviously feeling a good deal of shame, probably wondering why on earth he had told me.

I touched his back after a long period of stillness, touching him between the shoulder blades. He didn't move. As the wordlessness grew, a calm swept around us and drew us in, the skin beneath my hand becoming warm and sweaty in the evening heat. It was at once difficult to breathe, difficult to think.

He finally lifted his head and faced me, my hand still on his back. His face was flushed — his cheeks and nose crimson. His eyelids were puffy, dark circles had appeared under his eyes and his long eyelashes were glistening with tears. His brown eyes seemed lighter, distant, veiled by his hair.

My hand left his back and trailed down the arm I had held earlier — the scarred vein, the skin over-pierced, over-used by needles. My fingers ran lightly over the scars and he let me do it, but grimaced in places as my touch settled on skin that was clearly not healthy. He tried to pull away once but I wouldn't let him, holding the arm in my hands.

I asked him — had to know — how many times? He admitted to nightly use, increasing for two weeks, at least. He felt he had become very quickly addicted (as heroin will do) and had to fight his way out of it, and was continuing to fight. He said two shows in Houston were a mess as he was in a drug-induced hallucination and delirium.

He was still not feeling like himself, battling daily to not give in and inject again. He was fighting the feeling that he had betrayed everyone: his family and himself and me. His greatest fear was that he would lose me.

He truly did not know what he had done; when he did have pieces of memory come to the forefront, they were shrouded in haze. He couldn't even trust that what he was remembering were true recollections or hallucinations. What fraction of memory he did recall was radically small.

His head was hanging again, as if he couldn't bear to look at me, his face twisted into sadness I cannot describe, and that I do not want to remember.

Did I still love him? You bet. No doubt. Did I still trust him? That took some thought. Again, more silence between us—like a raging river separating us onto our own shores to face off and face each other's fears.

Trust—I wanted to believe him when he said he wanted to wait for me, that our bond was strong and would not be broken. But now, could I be so sure of that? What experiences had he had while high? And did it make it a different situation due to the fact that he was under the influence of a powerful drug, which causes a loss of control?

I just didn't know. And not knowing would nag at me for a long time.

So, did I trust him? Did I?

At that moment, in the sunset over Atlanta, on his porch, I had to admit to myself that I did trust him, simply because I loved him. I had to swallow my tears, swallow any hesitation I may have been feeling and be there for him.

I leaned my head onto his shoulder after brushing the hair off it, and whispered, "I love you," into his ear. There wasn't anything else that would have been more appropriate. Still we sat, hushed in our little world that had suddenly become so complex so unexpectedly.

Steve was unsure of everything then. He broke our silence by asking me if we were still together? Of course we were. What if, on the road this summer, I hear stories of something he may have done? Would I stay with him? Could I still be his? Would I still love him? His words came in a barrage of frightened rapid-fire questions.

Would I still love him if he was no longer in the band? Could I love an out-of-work singer? Someone who didn't know how to do anything else?

The intensity with which he bombarded me about our future and our choices almost scared me. His face showed the signs of passion and fear I had first seen when he was on stage in San Francisco. His tone was desperate, his demeanor reckless.

It suddenly hit me—this was a man who wanted to run away! I hoped—I prayed—it wasn't me he was running from; in my heart, I knew it wasn't. It was the person he had become, the star, the band, the life. Running wasn't a part of his repertoire and I wasn't about to let him start now. He was a fighter—he had been homeless and made it out of that life to where he was now, and was about to rise even further.

I just had to get him through this bump in the road. I had to hold his hand and his heart, calm his mind and get him to the other side. I didn't know it then, but this would not be the last time he leaned on me.

*W*e survived the agony of our last night in Atlanta, June 1976. Steve's parents could see something had changed; so could his brother. Steve was unusually quiet when we went inside, and unusually clingy to me, following me wherever I went, including, to my dismay, the bathroom. Uncomfortable? Sure, but he wasn't going to let me out of his sight at that point.

Mrs. Potts (she had tried all week to get me to call her Marta but I just couldn't) shot me a look across the family room that questioned what was happening, and I shot her one back that said I really didn't know. But I did.

The next morning we said our good-byes to his family, flying off to join-up with the rest of the band. They too had scattered a week ago, meeting up in Philadelphia for the start of the tour.

The Summer of 1976, the 200th birthday of our nation, I traveled around the country in a limousine following the tour buses of a rock band, in the arms of a rock star. We celebrated the Bicentennial in Chicago—the concert had been in Soldier Field, home of the Chicago Bears, off Lake Michigan. The city had an awesome fireworks show planned and, when it started, the band stopped playing for everyone to enjoy the lights in the sky. I was in the front row of the show and Steve motioned for me to come backstage.

He had taken nearly a whole month to recover from our talk in Atlanta, but still clung to me as if, when he let me go, I would disappear. I never did. I never could.

He held me on the other side of the stage, the side that backed up to a wall of empty seats, as we watched the brilliant lights. Some of the roadies were there; Richard came back with his girl of the moment. The explosions went on for nearly an hour, Steve holding me the whole time, in front of him, arms around my waist.

His pants were tight black, laced up in the back—a 70s thing. Don't think he would be caught dead in them today, but they sure looked good back then. His shirt was silk—red and buttoned at the bottom. He smelled of sweat and his own scent that I longed for when we were apart.

They finished their performance when the fireworks were over, then we moved on to another town. The entourage had grown to three buses, four semi tractor-trailers, two limos and hundreds of groupies.

Steve always went by private car now to all of the shows. It cost a lot but he was paying for it with his own paycheck; it was his choice—his insistence. However, the more vocal band members had other ideas; Ned and Phil were at the head of that line—they made no bones about the fact that they felt they should all travel together—the five of them; that a band that travels together, plays better together, and stays together.

Many nights the three of them had words—loud words— about the travel arrangements. And, many nights, the three of them angrily separated and were "never going" to speak to the other again. Steve and the two others had extremely narrow ideas of how this, their first full-blown tour, should go. Neither of them wanted to budge.

The other band members stayed back from the anger and the personal issues. Joss was the fun one—he just wanted to entertain with his music. Richard only wanted the girls despite a beautiful wife and two children at home. Phil got over the hard feelings and went about writing songs and having fun on the road. None of them were best friends—they all led separate lives—but they had to get along, for the time being, for the good of the band.

Steve remained sturdy in his desire to travel alone. I have to admit, it was fun arriving at stadiums and concert halls, climbing out of a limo, arm in arm with him, passing the line up of fans beginning to gather early. Mostly screaming girls, willing to show any body part just to catch his eye. There was my self-esteem issue rearing its ugly head. He was mine—at that time he was all mine.

Late July, Steve surprised me back stage, an hour before show time, with a dozen red roses delivered to me in his dressing room. It was July 20—one year after we met. He remembered.

One year. He had changed so much over the year due to the circumstances of fame. He was still haunted by his heroin use, not wanting me out of his sight; it was almost as if, as long as he could see me, as long as he knew I was there, he would be safe.

What was going to happen when I returned to my real life?

God knows this really wasn't real life.

I hadn't thought about it, but, at that midway point of the summer, I realized there is very little glamour on the road. Sleeping in cars or buses to get to the next show. Dodging fans and, even worse, the fanatics, at every stop; unable to get out of the car or bus, for fear of being recognized and mobbed. Eating whatever can be kept on a bus, grabbed in a gas station, or bought at a fast food restaurant along the way, provided there was someone willing to get off the bus to gather up a huge order of food and drinks.

Road managers—they had two at that time—arranged for hotels, not always booking the band into what could be considered decent. They couldn't yet afford to stay at a Hilton every night, but generally they could have afforded better than a Bob's Motel or a Paradise Inn at the side of the road. Another reason Steve preferred to stay separately from the others. Of course, even then, we ended up in some run-down, off-the-beaten-path places sometimes.

The loneliness took its toll on everyone at times—the roadies, the managers, the band. While there was always someone around—a kid who had run away from home to join the rock and roll circus life; the manager reserving a block of rooms in the next town, fighting with a hotel manager for a better price; a family member of the band traveling along for a few cities, it could still be a very desolate lifestyle.

Someone was always on a bus, in one of the semis, hanging out on the stage. You could always find someone to be with when it seemed no one else was around. But the solitude could still be overwhelming. Waiting in line for a phone in the hall at a concert venue, only to hear no answer on the other end once your turn comes. Hoping against hope there will be a familiar, friendly face in the crowd. Waiting for the mail to catch up, but never hearing your name called.

It wasn't an easy life. Day after day—same faces—same idiosyncrasies—same nagging irritations. We counted on the comedians to make us all laugh, keep up smiling; those who could be spontaneously funny to break the tension, or simply make us feel better about being there. They were invaluable assets on a tour that became more and more grueling in the heat of a long summer. Not that I wasn't having a ball—I was. I could have been home, either helping out with summer school or just hanging out with my friends. No, this was much better—this was like nothing else I had ever done. It was special. I was watching new stars in the making.

I was privy to backstage goings-on—the fights, the madness, the jealousy, the love. I saw the drugs Steve had told me about—but, per his demands (and they *were* demands, not just a request), use was more secretive. I was glad for that, but it was still readily available. If he wanted to back slide into that hellish insanity, it would not be hard.

Late July, he finally began to relax, be more like the free spirit he had been a year ago, even a few weeks ago. He was able to let me go hang out with the road crew while he rehearsed, as long as he knew exactly where I would be. I enjoyed the roadies— some of them were close to my age—we had some things in common: the love of the band and of this tour. They worked the hardest of anyone on the tour, setting up and tearing it all down every night, very much like a carnival crew, traveling from town to town.

And I was very appreciative of what they did—they kept my Steve safe, assuring proper set-up of stages and electrical equipment, assuring the tape was placed on the platform correctly so he knew how far he had to the edge.

The rest of my summer continued as a flurry of shows, the band playing audiences of 500 to 20,000, depending upon where they were.

Then it was over; time for me to go home to Ohio. The band had two more weeks on the road before heading for California to record a new album, their second, *The Life of a Song*.

My last night with Steve was spent in a small hotel in Bismarck, North Dakota. They had played a small arts center— about 3500 people there. Not bad for those parts. It was a very intimate crowd—a nice change.

We went to our modest hotel and collapsed on the bed. He was becoming increasingly tired as the tour had worn on, looking forward to just singing in a recording studio for awhile.

We had become closer over the summer; his dependency turned back into love. As we watched the minutes tick past on our final night, he warned me about the upcoming year—that recording would keep them busy until at least December. Then they would be in preparation for a new tour, a bigger tour if the album did well. His voice sounded tremulous as he told me that, most likely, we would not see each other for a time.

He assured me that he would be "okay." That he "can resist any temptation now." So long as I love him, and write him and answer his phone calls. I was his lifeline, his safety net; a lot of responsibility for a 16 year-old.

I did love him and wanted him to lean on me. I hoped our love would last forever but suddenly, in that dingy room, that seemed extremely unrealistic.

The sweat was still hanging on him from the night's performance, so he left the bed to go shower, dropping his clothing on the floor as he walked away from me. I watched him from behind step into the shower, and close the curtain around him. Nice behind, very nice. First time I had seen him without clothes, even if it was for a matter of a few seconds. And it had to be in this hotel. Sigh.

He showered for nearly 15 minutes; I watched from the bed as the steam rose over the shower curtain. I could see the slight outline of his body behind the curtain, was excited by the sight of him.

18 couldn't come soon enough.

I went home the next day—he put me on another airplane—in another airport. Again with the floppy hat—it was so tiresome but becoming more and more necessary. I didn't want him to get out of the car and take me to the gate but he insisted—he wouldn't hear of simply dropping me off.

We practically hung on each other the whole walk to the gate. It was time to say good-bye again, something we would do many times in our relationship. We would probably say good-bye many more times than hello, if that makes any sense.

My whole family was waiting for me in Cleveland—surprise! So were Patty and Eric—they had come along for the ride in the Buick—big car; good thing. I had to tell them everything—well, almost everything. Patty would get the whole story later—the behind the music story.

School started back up in two days and it seemed like I was the most popular girl there for a few days—everyone had known I was on tour with the band—everyone had to hear all about it. I was finally given the entire front page of the school newspaper's first edition that year so that I could write about it. My first big story and I couldn't tell it all. My headline read: *Rockin' On the Road With Stars—A Groupie Comes Home.* That was me. I was suddenly special.

Steve wrote every week and called about as often. He tore a picture of himself out of *16 Magazine* and sent it to me, signed, to put into my locker at school. On it he wrote that he loved me, his usual "XOXO" and a smiley face; and he added something new—a statement he would use a lot over the next year: "C'mon 18!"

The tour ended in Los Angeles, where they stayed for the recording of their next album. He didn't even go home, which was a surprise—I figured he would try to get home at least once before settling in but no. Phil, the keyboardist, and his wife, graciously opened their home to Steve for the duration of the recording of the album. Phil was the quiet one of the group—if anyone could keep an eye on Steve, it was Phil.

I read his letters with a keen eye—looking for any sign that he might have backslid—I dug out his old letters and could see from the writing, the way he phrased things that something had been different—I just never chose to see it before. Now that I knew what to look for, I did so, but never saw any tell-tale signs of a problem. Not that I thought I would but I had done a lot of reading since being home; heroin was not something that was easily kicked; it could be returned to in an instant.

I drudged through band practice, and my studies (not that I ever had any homework), and my extra-curricular activities—I decided the best thing for me was to keep busy. If I sat around and thought about him too much I suddenly became a brooding, moody teenager who never wanted to leave her room. I was irritable and cried at everything (commercials on TV, the dog when she scratched at my door, couples at school). I was a basket case; there was nothing I could do but wait to hear from him, so I had to keep busy.

I became a trainer for the football team—a student trainer who helped with the injuries. I was on the sidelines with the team during the game, and on the field with the band during halftime. And I became a timer with our swim team. The swim team, because Steve had been on his school's swim team. I wrote for the paper and eventually became the editor of the news section—the boring section but it was mine nonetheless. I kept busy with my friends and had fun. We crashed the Homecoming Dance in the late fall and had a ball in our jeans and t-shirts among the jocks and the cheerleaders in their formal wear. And still I waited every day for the 3:05 PM bell to ring so I could dash home to see if I had a letter waiting. And then dash right back to school to football practice.

My 17th birthday rolled around in November; it had been three weeks since I had heard from Steve. I was devastated by the drought—I wondered what he was doing, where he was. I had his number at Phil's house; there were many times when I dialed the first few numbers but quickly hung up. I didn't want to seem like a hanger-on, like a silly teenager who just wanted to hear his voice. I didn't want him to think—think what—that I loved him, couldn't go on like this? No—I had to wait—see if he would call me.

My parents threw me a surprise birthday party that year, inviting a lot of people from school—they must have invited everyone in the yearbook. We had a big house, but it was bursting at the seams with teenagers. Unfortunately, I was in a funk—not having heard from Steve was making my heart literally ache; I didn't really want to face anyone.

10 PM came and the phone rang. I figured it was the neighbors calling to tell us to keep it down even though we weren't being all that loud. My mom answered it—I didn't know it at the time but she knew the call was coming. She silently handed me the receiver; when I said hello, the band was singing me Happy Birthday. Sounds really hokey but it was the best present I ever got. They all sang to me! How cool.

It was 8 PM in California; they were just wrapping up for the night. Steve had had this planned for awhile; that was why he hadn't written. It was all supposed to be a big surprise. We talked for an hour while my guests hung out.

I had to finally take the rest of the call on the phone upstairs, not really wanting everyone to hear me gushing. His voice sounded so good but there was an undertone of fatigue, his normal tenor tone very muted and low. I asked him about it but he changed the subject, glancing it off as hard work in the studio.

He sounded good overall—sober, thank heavens, happy with the way things were going for them. He told me I was the song he was singing, that I was the one who made his life worth it, and made it more fun. That I opened up a door for him and made him walk through it into something he never thought he would find. His words sounded like a song. Turns out they were.

He figured about three more weeks, then he would be going home to Atlanta and then, when was my Christmas break? My heart leapt into my throat, I swallowed hard—why? Why Christmas break? Come to Atlanta, he said—come home to me—I miss you—come back. His words were ringing in my ears as the blood rushed, making me swoon.

I would be there—the last day of school was December 15— come then? He would arrange it all—airline tickets, James will pick you up. And guess what? I already talked to your parents.

He made me cry—he thought of everything. He and my parents had been having an ongoing dialogue about the two of us; his feelings, their feelings and concerns. Nice that I was made a party to it, but I felt extremely lucky to have found Steve, and for the lengths he was going to. He truly wanted me there for Christmas—he was going to make it possible for us to be together whenever we could. This was becoming very complicated. I had no idea how much more complicated my life would become with him in it.

We said yet another good-bye and, like a true teenager, I didn't want to hang up the phone because hanging it up meant we were truly apart.

When I rejoined the party, my parents met me at the bottom of the stairs—he had sent roses to me with a—a ring?! My mother was holding the bouquet—her heart had been melted somehow—I was going to have to find out what he did.

The ring was white gold with a topaz in it—a large, beautiful golden stone—the stone of my birth. That man was truly a romantic, even if he didn't think so. The card on the flowers had four words—"Miss You Come Back." Four words I would read and hear often.

He had touched my soul; I had touched his life. We were destined for something, but as a 17-year-old, I couldn't look ahead and see what. My mother and I had a talk after all my friends had left. Patty stayed the longest—had to ogle the ring and smell the flowers one more time, hug me, tell me how jealous she was.

But now I had to deal with Mom. She sat me down and told me that I appeared to be truly in love and that Steve sounded committed (at least she didn't say that he sounded like he needed to be committed); he had told her he was in love with me—she hoped it was love. She gave me "the talk" then—the sex talk, and this time she didn't just hand me a book and send me to my room. She told me Steve had told her it was his decision to wait until I was 18; she was very impressed with this, particularly in light of his chosen profession.

We talked for awhile; it was the first time my mother and I really connected; I felt like I had grown up a lot that night. We spoke to each other like adults, like we were friends, not the adversaries we had been so many times in the past. She told me the party was set up between her and Steve. She knew he wasn't going to write for a few weeks; I got a little honked off at that—she knew I was agonizing over his lack of communication yet she let me stew in it for so long and kept quiet. Hmphf.

That Monday I was back at school, in my own limelight—everyone had to know about and see the ring, which I wore on my left hand 3rd finger. They just had to know where I was really going over break—I told them Atlanta; no one believed I would actually go to his parents' house. But, that was becoming our place.

The next six weeks were the slowest of my life. A new grade period started in there somewhere; report cards came out—straight A's, naturally. I didn't have to study much—it was as if everything came very naturally to me—once I heard something, I remembered it, at least long enough to be tested on it. If you asked me anything about ancient history or chemistry or calculus today, good luck getting an answer. A candidate for *Jeopardy!* I am not.

Steve sent me a tape of the rough cut of *The Life of a Song* the first week of December—they were wrapping up in the studio—a few musicians would be over-dubbing some of the tracks but this was pretty much the sound they were going for. I listened to it all night long. Their sound had grown, matured into a mellow, soft melodic rock with guitar riffs that were stunning and a drum backup that held you in its pounding then sent you away with the cymbals. And that voice—there was no match. He sounded better than ever—able to hit every note with ease and carry your heart on the breeze.

They had obviously worked very hard—Steve and Joss wrote a lot of the songs; Ned would add his own thing with his guitar; typical rock band of the time. They took inspiration from everywhere—there was a lot of love in the songs but there were also a lot of other things going on if you listened hard enough.

One song was about the home town of Joss—he missed it terribly and when it played the picture of his town came clearly to his mind; one song spoke of looking in to the future and trying to see what it has in mind for them; one was about being alone; one spoke of sailing, Phil's favorite past time. A few of the songs were very slow and took on a sadness all their own.

Christmas break finally arrived—it was time to put me on an airplane to the man of my dreams. My family drove me to Cleveland—I was seeing a lot of the insides of airports. He called the night before, just to say he was waiting for me to come to him, that he couldn't wait to see me. We were like two teenagers on the phone, speaking in low tones and giggling—he made a good teenager. I wish I had known him then, but I would have been a pre-teen. Ugh. There was that difference in ages again.

He sent my family presents for Christmas—my dad a tie with golf all over it, his favorite game; a new robe for Christmas morning for my mom; new computer games for John's new-fangled toy; and even a box of dog bones for Misty the Golden Retriever. My mom helped me pick out presents for his family but they weren't near as nice as these. He was so thoughtful. There was so much more to him than a rock star—he was a person who hadn't yet let it all get to him.

When I got off the plane in Atlanta—he had sent me a first class ticket so I was one of the first ones off (would have been even if I had been sitting in the back of the plane—my excitement could have carried me over everyone ahead of me). I looked for James at the gate but saw Steve—that damned floppy hat and sunglasses on a man, leaning up against a pole, jeans and a t-shirt, the band's logo emblazoned on it—daring— and his tennis shoes. I have an old pair of those tennis shoes to this day, buried somewhere in a closet.

His hair was pulled back into a pony tail, his arms crossed over his chest, hip cocked out to one side. He had gained more weight—probably a whole size by now—I think I had too by that time—but he was still looking fine. He saw me and raised his sunglasses briefly so that I would see him—how could I not see him?!

I was in Atlanta for the holidays—two whole weeks parole granted from the family. There were tears streaming down both our faces when we grabbed each other in the terminal. My legs felt as if they couldn't hold me up. The love was still there; the passion equally as evident.

We were going home.

Christmas in Atlanta is different than Ohio, where there is snow, and cold winds that blow, chilling to the bone; ice skating and sled-riding and hot chocolate and fireplaces. Atlanta is warmer—sun and short sleeves and soda. The airport was decorated with Christmas ornaments and a Santa in shorts. My winter coat was suddenly out of place and way too warm.

We gathered up my luggage and, amazingly, made it out to the waiting car without anyone recognizing him. I am not sure if he was pleased by that or a little disappointed—the radio stations were playing more and more of their music; it was an amazing feeling to hear his voice everywhere.

James picked us up—he had become our "official" chauffeur. He was in his first year of college—accounting school. It was either that or nursing—he said he had really wanted to be a nurse but "men didn't do that." Steve had told him to go for it, be whoever and whatever he wanted, but James got pushed into the numbers direction. I thought about being a nurse too but everyone was pushing me to journalism—small world.

Steve and I sat in the back seat and were all over each other before we left the airport property. I was a little embarrassed— James kept looking in the rearview mirror and smiling. Being apart had not been easy on the two of us—him more than I. It was a little easier for me as far as the sexual aspect—I had nothing to compare and long for, but I was learning.

It was dark by the time we arrived at his home; his parents greeted me at the door with open arms, taking me in as if I was their own. This was a remarkably humble, remarkably normal family that happened to have a son who was about to become world famous. We had dinner—they held it for my arrival—and then we all settled into the family room—to the couch—our couch; some things never change.

In this light, I finally had the opportunity to get a look at Steve's arm—the scar tissue from his heroin use—the track marks. The infection had long since healed—he had had to get antibiotic therapy in the middle of last summer's tour at my insistence. But the skin was darkened, still bruised slightly, appearing sore and inelastic. I rubbed my fingertips across it and he pulled out of my reach slightly but soon allowed me to continue. This was so uncomfortable for him—he had yet to tell his parents. James found out at some point, but never said anything to the folks.

We were practically sitting on top of each other on the couch while he related tales of the recording sessions, and the fights and arguments and nagging that went on. It was hard to tell if it all irritated him or amused him. He loved to sing and he loved to write his songs. If it meant he had to put up with someone else's "crap" for now, so be it. He would do it, just to keep doing what he loved. For now.

He had been home for two weeks prior to my arrival, and his parents had heard his stories but they sat and listened anyway, glad to have both their sons home for the holidays. They had decorated the house with an assortment of Christmas—there was a large tree in the living room that could be seen through the front window. A live tree that gave the whole house an odor of pine—my favorite scent, next to Steve. There was an odd assortment of homemade and store-bought ornaments but they told me the homemade ones were done in school by the boys. So cool.

Other decorations were here and there but nothing extravagant. There were a few presents under the tree but the main presents had already been given—he bought his mom and dad a new car, and one for James to travel back and forth from his school in the city. While other rock stars were spending their money on drugs, women and luxury, this man was buying things for his family, those he loved, and saving it for later. Later would come soon enough.

His parents went up to bed, leaving James and us alone in the family room. James was so much like his brother in many ways and yet, so different. He looked like an accountant—always well dressed, shiny shoes, sensibly short hair. Wire rimmed glasses, like mine, but mine were the aviator-style which Steve hated because they were a "man's frame," which he always said with a scowl. James and Steve had the same facial features, particularly the long nose, chiseled at the end, inherited from their mother. And they were both pretty much the same height, around 5'9", something inherited from their father.

Taking a hint was not something James did well. He had been with his brother for the last two weeks but, hoping some of the star quality would rub off, he wanted to spend as much time with him as he could. So, it was Steve who had to take the initiative and tell James to go to bed. It was time. It was after 10. Get it? Go! Reluctantly, he did.

Finally alone, Steve pulled me close and held my face with his hands. There were no words we could have spoken to each other at that moment that could have said what was in our hearts, what was passing between us, what was growing inside. We could put voice to our feelings with our kisses, but even that wasn't enough.

This was no longer a man clinging to me because of shame from a past mistake, or a man who was singing for his supper in a bar in front of a teenager in the throes of a crush. This was a man whose wings were spreading, a little wider every time I saw him, widening with a sense of purpose and star quality. A man who was clearly on his way to becoming more confident and comfortable in that control, and yet he was still so uneasy and uncomfortable in the limelight.

Steve's eyes swallowed mine and tears formed first in mine, then his. My tears were those of complete and total happiness, a joy of being in his arms again. More joy than I had ever experienced. Were tears brimming in his eyes for the same reason? I didn't know.

Without speaking, he kissed me, passionately from the beginning, his tongue soft against mine, slowly building to a probe exploring my mouth with more urgency. No beer taste tonight. It was all him—a slightly salty, slightly pungent taste.

My hands went to his pony tail and sent 20 inches of brown hair loose, releasing the scent of shampoo and him into the air around us. His nose ground against my glasses, smudging the lenses with the oil and sweat that had made his nose shiny. As I ran my hands through his hair, he touched mine, which was short again; he fingered the earrings I had on—hoops of brown and orange, my school colors—we had had a pep rally for the basketball team the night before the break; I never changed the earrings.

Our kiss went on for minutes, our breathing increasingly rapid, the heat in the room rising, enveloping us. There was no one but the two of us—or so we thought. His mom was suddenly in the kitchen—I hadn't heard her come downstairs.

She was in the refrigerator—forgot to take her insulin—something she frequently did, being a newly-diagnosed diabetic, already showing signs of kidney disease. We pulled apart and he went to her; I wouldn't have had it any other way.

A few minutes later, after straining to listen to them whispering in the other room, he came back, smiling, but with an undertone of concern. His mom poked her head in the door and knocked on the wooden frame, causing Steve to turn to her. She smiled and simply said, "Get on up there, youngsters."

Then she was gone, whincing, rubbing her upper arm where Steve had given her the injection.

We wound up in his bedroom upstairs; he had discussed it with his folks prior to my arrival: he didn't want to spend two weeks on the couch, but he didn't want to be without me in the night, but he didn't want to disrespect his parents. After much discussion, they were okay with me in his room. They knew of the plan to wait for me to get to 18. They understood, about as much as my parents. I truly don't think either set of parents believed us when we said there had been no sex. But, at some point, they all had to trust us and give us the benefit of the doubt and know they had raised good kids.

That past summer on the road, we had not shared a bed through the night; one of us always ended up on a chair, a couch, the second bed in the room. We had slept on plenty of couches together but no beds. Yet. This was going to be our first night together in a bed—his bed.

His clothing and paraphernalia were all over the room—yep, this looked like a room that he had lived in for two weeks. The man was talented, gorgeous, a star, and still a slob. His desk was piled high with sheet music—two piles of it. There was a 12-string guitar in the corner between the dresser and the wall—I didn't even know he played. There was a lot I didn't know about him. Two pairs of tennis shoes littered the floor, along with a t-shirt and a pair of jeans. My letters to him were in a neat pile on the dresser.

I noticed the book shelf next—the stuffed animals that had been on the top shelf on my last visit—a bear missing one eye and a nose; a cow with an old rusty bell on a leather collar around its neck; a lion with a tangled mane and crooked whiskers; and a very worn, tattered light blue bunny with no eyes and one ear practically torn off—were all on a shelf at eye-level. Each one had a Christmas bow and a tag—4 different tags: "Take me home," "Free to a good home," "Merry Christmas," "I love you dearly."

My emotions were suddenly out of control with love and surprise; no Christmas gift could have been better. He was giving me a piece of his childhood: a piece of who he had been; a piece of the little boy that still lived in his heart. Standing behind me, he encircled my waist with his arms and I leaned into him, overwhelmed by his gift, overwhelmed by him, period.

That night, our first on his bed, we were careful and patient with each other. He stripped off his jeans, I changed into a nightshirt and we lay down in each other's arms. The bed had not been made since he came home, so the sheets were already in disarray. This was a twin-sized bed, not much larger than the couches we had been on.

He held me to him, face to face, legs wrapped around each other; his toes curling around mine made me tingle. His arms around me made me feel safe. He kissed me all over my face, using his tongue at times, leaving a slightly wet trail where he had been. My glasses were already off and on the desk, sitting on top of sheet music—a stack of soon-to-be-hit songs.

Then it happened—for the first time ever—he sang to me. Very softly, very loving, he sang to me—a song from the new album—a song about my eyes and my decisions and my love. I was lost in *his* voice, in *his* eyes, in *his* love. This was the first time that I finally truly believed he was in love with me.

Beyond the Glory
By Steve Potts

Beyond the glory, there was a stillness
Beyond the fame, there was a passion
Beyond the celebrity, there was a silence
Before all of this, there was you

Too many nights, there was a stillness
Not enough times, there was a passion
In the darkness, there was a silence
You were there—I had you then

From the passion to the silence, you always had my love
Did you know it—could you feel it—did it mean   something

Past all the glory, away from all the fame, beyond the celebrity
Did we know what we had, could we feel it through it all
Two hearts that came through it all, beating as one,
Magical in their space, we had it all

Beyond the glory, you stood at my side
Beyond the fame, you were my lead, my shining star
Beyond the celebrity, you saw me as me—only me—every time

In this world of make-believe and tales never-ending
It was you, only you, who knew who I was
You—only you—who made it all worth doing
You—only you—who could take me beyond the glory

When he finished the song, he kissed me lightly on each cheek and laid his head on our pillow. There was nothing I could say, nothing I could do to convey to this man the love I had for him. This was a rock star, loved by thousands of girls, who would give anything to be in the position I was in, yet he was with me. Me: a teen from Ohio. When he could have been with anyone. He was with me.

I loved him and he loved me. It was on his face, in his song, in his touch and in his patience. I told him I loved him; he held me until we both fell asleep.

*G*oing to back to my ordinary life after being with a star can be quite a let down. Christmas in Atlanta had been a dream come true as Steve's and my love grew together and brought us to a passionate understanding of each other. He gave me the new 1977 tour jacket for a present; a diamond bracelet; and his continued love.

I spent a lot of time in my bedroom, the door locked, ignoring my family and friends, brooding in my own misery after I got home. I wanted to be with him, forget school and my family and my friends; run to him, cross the country with him, love him, marry him.

The rambling thoughts and dreams of an obsessed teenager.

Steve and the band were again spending more time on the road, promoting their second album: *The Life of a Song*; he was not happy either. His letters were rambling tales of anger with his band mates, disappointment over so-so reviews of the album, discouragement over the set-up of the tour schedule for the summer, and not seeing me. His phone calls were often overburdened with worry and stress. He admitted to fear of failure, fear of rejection.

The band and its management hastily decided to go back to the recording studio in California for a third album in March—

Distance—it would give extra oomph to the tour. What it meant for Steve was increased work, writing and arranging up to 12 songs. He was not happy but felt he had no other choice. He also formed his own production company at that time to protect his earnings, his name, his integrity.

The album's first single, *Beyond the Glory*, was released in May, 1977 as my junior year was ending. My world was crashing around me as many friends, my best friend included, were graduating and leaving me. I had begged my parents to allow me to graduate early—I had all the necessary credits—but my mom didn't think it was a good idea. I knew why—she figured I would have run off with Steve—she was probably right.

School ended in June, and I met Steve in Jacksonville, Florida for my leg of the summer tour. Our reunion was as if we had never been apart. The passion and the love were still there. We spent every free moment together, whether it was in his dressing room, in a corner behind the stage, in a limo; we were together. His kiss, his touch, set my heart on fire as we grew closer everyday.

But he also used me as a sounding board—he leaned on me when things weren't going well. There were frequent spats between him and the other band members, particularly Ned, who had become more vocal than on the last tour. Both men were extremely professional, extremely gifted, extremely volatile when together. Ned wanted more guitar and other instrumental solos written into the music to highlight his talent and that of the other band members; Steve felt his voice, his instrument, was the solo; they would have to live with it. It was a no-win situation, further tearing this band apart.

Steve wanted me on his side, which I was, and used me to listen to him—calm him. He frequently had small panic attacks prior to the beginning of a concert. This band had hit it big very quickly, perhaps too quickly, with little time for its members to become accustomed to the screaming adoration of thousands of fans.

I didn't really understand how it would feel to be on the stage, night after night, staring out at the thousands of people all screaming your name, crying their everlasting adoration, pushing each other forward into the stage. So he let me have a taste of the mania.

To look out at the massive span of people from the stage *is* an awe-inspiring sight. Standing on the platform at the far end of a football stadium, staring at rows of seats, first on the field itself, then the arena seats, seeing them all full of fans screaming and yelling and chanting is truly overwhelming.

Steve had told me about this, that there is a buzz; a buzz like nothing else. That is what excites him — to be with the crowds while he is on stage; he could be himself, everyone would be his for the night. The girls are in love with him, the boys want to be him.

I had never been out on the stage before — front row, yes; back stage, behind the scenes, but never standing here, where he would be in a few minutes, singing for all he is worth, entertaining this capacity crowd of 105,000. The numbers are staggering, even more so now that I was looking out over all of them.

Standing on stage, aside the road crews who were busy making the final touches, I could understand, to some degree, what Steve meant. There is something in the air and it was building as time drew nearer to the concert. He convinced me to get out there; to take a look. I am glad he did but I didn't ever want to do it again; my nerves were now more on edge for him than they had ever been. It was mid-evening, just the red stage lights were on, casting a bloody sheen on everything; I could clearly see people in the first several rows before they became a blur farther back.

The roadies like this part of the show — five minutes to the band — the seats are full with only a few last-minute people straggling in. The stadium, bursting at capacity, and the road crew gets to show off, ham it up a little. One screws on and off a cymbal nut and bolt, careful not to overdue the act and screw up Richard's kit. One young man is rearranging Ned's guitars — only slightly because Ned will hang him if he screws something up. Another is checking microphone height. And still another, the most important one, in my opinion, is laying the final pieces of tape on the platform — tape that will let my man know where the edge of the stage is in the darkness. He is also taping down the line-up of songs to show Steve the order; it's easy to become confused and begin singing a song out of order while the band is playing something entirely different, even though, as a practical joke, that happened more than once.

This is part of the road crew job — to assure final preparations are set. Out of the 35-person road crew, four get to come out on stage prior to show start — they play cards, draw straws, roll dice to see who will be the lucky four. Another will win the opportunity to be the one who assists Steve with his microphone cord — if he gets entangled during the show, there will be a roadie there, hiding in the shadows, to quickly untangle him, as unobtrusively as possible.

Why is this such a privilege? Because, to an audience member, these guys are cool — they are special — they are doing things the audience wishes they could do — they are *with the band.*

The audience hushes some while the roadies do their thing. Their appearance means the band is not far behind. Tonight the band is late — as always — about 20 minutes. Rock and roll is never on time. Me? I am always early; rock is always late.

I was standing back from the edge of the stage — no way I was going up front to get a better look — afraid of heights and on a platform about 12-feet off the ground, not my favorite place to be. I stayed back in front of the drum platform where Richard had his kit all set up — six cymbals and nine drums of assorted sizes and sounds. Suddenly the screen behind me was illuminated with the band's logo and the crowd came alive, to its feet, screaming louder, stomping in the stands.

To see over 100,000 people standing, clapping, cheering, and watching your every move was making me a little nauseous. I didn't like standing there but, I was riveted in place. I couldn't even stand up in front of 30 people in my class and give a speech. *This* was surreal. I marveled at how the band could do it night after night to this kind of crowd.

As the band's eerie intro music began to sound through the massive speakers, growing in intensity and volume, the crowd became more animated. Mostly girls, mostly my age or a little older; they were "jiggly teenagers," obviously wearing nothing underneath their t-shirts emblazoned with the name of the band, or worse, Steve's face.

That was a little weird—seeing breasts bouncing beneath his likeness.

It was all so incredible—there is no other suitable word. I understood how he felt—magical. He had described how his heart would pound nearly out of his chest and he would have small panic attacks. How he dreaded walking onto the stages night after night in a new town every few days. How the screams drowned out everything he sang and said on stage, and haunted him into his sleep.

Maybe that is why he downed several beers before hitting the stage: to calm his doubts, to calm his mind, and allow him to feel the adoration, not the apprehension. It would have taken a lot more than beer to get me to do what he did. Maybe that was the motive for the heroin.

Now, with the intro growing, sweeping through the stadium, pounding out a rhythm from their past, the band was approaching the stage. But I was still frozen, basically unable to move. The stage went dark for a few seconds and then was draped in blue light. This was it and I still couldn't move. I was going to get stuck on the stage. When the lights would throw everything into daylight, I would be there, not only embarrassing myself, but Steve too. This was not a great place to be.

Suddenly there was a boom from behind me: Richard had climbed into the seat behind his drums, and hit the pedal for the bass drum—his way of saying "hi"—he knew I was there. He began playing a cymbal with the sticks—his intro. I was out of time—there was no way he could help me. I looked up and caught his eye. He smiled, continuing to play the cymbal, nodding his head to the side as if trying to convince me to "exit—stage left." I couldn't. Panic was definitely settling in and taking hold. My feet felt like lead—why wouldn't they move and get me away from here?!

The stage was suddenly dark again—the only light was from the back lit screen and a small light under Richard—great—now people could see me better, a perfect silhouette in front of the light.

The crowd was increasingly loud—cheering, whistling, screaming. A frenzy of noise that was amplified on the stage.

Then, Steve was next to me, holding my hand, leading me off to the left side of the stage, into the protection of a roadie. He smiled at me as if to say, "Didn't I tell you so?" squeezed my hand, kissed me quickly on the mouth, and dashed back onto the stage. He rescued me—thank heavens—just in time—he actually had to start singing before grabbing the microphone.

My legs were heavy, I felt more than embarrassed but, Curtis, a senior roadie, told me he'd been caught out there too—they all had at one time or another. Hazard of the job. This band happened to be very understanding, but he had heard stories of other bands that were not so nice about it all. Roadies had lost their jobs for making critical errors like the one I had just made.

In the middle of the concert, Steve came off stage, as he always did, for two instrumental pieces; I was still shaking and he held me, swaying to the music. He was drenched in sweat, summer heat—energized from the show. Curtis was still with me when Steve came off the stage; Steve patted him on the back. He was very friendly with the road crew—they were the only people around that didn't want a piece of him.

When Steve prepared to go back on stage, he looked over his shoulder at Curtis and said, "Take care of her." He kissed me and bounded back onto the stage to thunderous applause and wild screaming. There was no doubt that he was the star of this band, of this entire era.

It was mid-July, the halfway point of my time with him. The tour had been incredible to this point, his band more popular with every stop. The decision had finally been made a month ago to hire security for them due to several disconcerting incidents. The worst involved Richard and one of his many encounters with a groupie in Dubuque—she insisted he was a new daddy—she presented him with—of all things—a baby doll. Then she presented him with a gun in his face; just a little break with reality there. Scared the hell out of Richard. Rightfully so. But I think he was more afraid that the whole episode would hit the papers and his wife would get wind of it. She did, but he double-talked his way out of it. Smooth.

There were other occurrences of fans getting back stage only to hound and attack band members; break-ins at the hotels: burglary of clothing, any souvenir that could be carried out; vandalism of the bus, which I never quite understood. It was unbelievable that these people, who purportedly loved this band, would do such things. There must truly be a fine line between love and hate and fanaticism.

And, from what I had been told, this band's fans were much better behaved that the fans of heavy rock and metal bands. I had never been to a metal concert until that summer. Steve's band was playing Boulder the night after Black Sabbath finished their two-night run. He and I arrived in Boulder in time to catch their show. What an interesting night that would turn out to be.

I had heard tales of these concerts—didn't much believe them, but the people in my high school who came to school on Mondays with their new t-shirts from a weekend concert, wore those shirts like they were a badge of honor—they had survived. They were the "stoners" at school—I didn't like that name but even they called themselves that. They were the smokers out on the loading dock, who walked around school in a daze, as if they had a cloud of smoke around their heads. I didn't have much contact with them, although one was the brother of Sarah, one of the girls in my group. She often tried to deny that they were related.

Anyway, there had been tales floating around school of pure debauchery, to put it mildly, at these concerts. Some concert-goers threw meat at the bands, live chickens (?!); sex ran rampid in the seats, with drug and alcohol use prominent.

Steve and I were going to see the spectacle. He had been to several metal concerts over the years; hard rock, soft rock, pop rock—he loved music; loved to watch different performers. If asked whom he admired, he had no one answer. He liked most everyone: John Denver to Barry Manilow to Jimi Hendrix to the Boston Pops; quite a span of different styles.

So, we were off; it became the first time that I was ever so glad that he played in a soft to medium rock band.

There were drugs and alcohol everywhere; no one had been kidding about that. Steve wore his hat down over his brows and eyes so that no one would recognize him but I didn't think it was really necessary; this was not a crowd he played to. This crowd was truly different—75% girls—teenage girls in various stages of undress; most without bras—obvious even with the shirts still on. Short shorts and ripped t-shirts were the haute couture this night.

Alcohol flowed freely; bottles, thermoses, pop cans emptied of their sugar-filled soda, to be replaced with the pungency of scotch or vodka, Southern Comfort or Jack Daniels, passed through the crowd.

The sweet, yet acid, scent of pot hung heavy in the air, mingled with the cigarette smoke, swirling in the lights from the stage. The teenage girls thought the cigarettes made them look older, more sophisticated. And when they replaced the cigarettes with the pot, they figured it was even cooler.

We saw harder drugs that night too. Occasional cocaine was snorted from the backs of hands (cocaine was still fairly new on the scene at that time); here and there people were injecting what I assumed to be heroin into arm veins that were well scarred. Steve seemed to watch the heroin use more intently that anything else going on around us.

This was a totally different scene that what I was used to. Many, many of the girls received passes from road crews who circulated among the crowd. Didn't see any teenage boys get handed a pass, though. If they were there with one of the lucky ladies, I imagine they went out and waited patiently by the car until the after-the-show party was over, which could be hours.

Steve told me before we went to the concert about "the list" that some bands have. Sometimes hand written, sometimes typed, sometimes drawn up on a computer as computers gained popularity. The bands had a list of girls in each city—phone numbers, physical attributes (particularly hair color and bra size—always a bra size, be it an actual number or some vulgarity in its place). And the last, most important piece of information on every list—what the girl would do sexually.

This was not unique to metal bands but it was the most prominent in that group for awhile. Steve laughed it off, almost in an admiration of the sexual prowess of the band members who partied every night with different girls, sometimes multiple girls each night. This was the era when AIDS was still a distant continent away.

So, we went to the show, took in the sights, smells and sex of a metal concert. I saw more teenage breasts that night than I ever needed to see. It was actually more fun watching the audience than it was the band. These girls knew every word to every song (most of which I couldn't understand), every dance, every word to scream at the band to get noticed.

Sex, drugs and rock-and-roll; groupies of every age, mostly teens and early 20's. I was a groupie too but didn't do these things—didn't flash the band, didn't have to do drugs, didn't have to drink in order to feel good about being there. I wasn't on some list that stated what I could do well in bed.

Steve and I left the show early. The pot fog and the sheer madness of the crowd were overpowering, too much for me. I think he was happy to go but he never actually said. He was quiet as we walked to the rental car and drove off toward the hotel. He still had on his hat so I couldn't see his face, couldn't read his emotions. His silence was maddening but my ears were still ringing with the noise from the concert. Felt like my ears were full of cotton—everything, every sound was muffled.

There was a question I wanted an answer to but was afraid to ask—I wasn't totally sure if I would like the answer. It was about the list…did his band have a list? Did I want to know? Yes/no. How wishy-washy can you get?!

We continued to drive in silence through downtown Boulder. It had been a warm day but the evening was much cooler but we had the car windows down, the rushing air further muffling any sound.

I finally reached across the front seat, grabbed the hat from his head and threw it into the back seat—it was making me crazy. Then I asked the question nagging at me that I knew would tear me up inside until I had an answer. Did his band have "the list"?

Silence—no answer. His facial expression remained neutral—was he thinking up a good answer? One that would appease me, make me easier to live with?

We came to a stop at a red light; he sighed heavily and ran his hand through his long hair. Here it comes—he turned toward me and looked at me, furrowing his brows in that way he had when he was trying to be serious.

Yes—the band had a list borrowed from another more raucous band. Yes, two of the band members had taken advantage of that list and called some girls to come to concerts for the after-show festivities.

My heart sank to my toes; I sat shocked in the passenger seat.

I hadn't heard much that he said after, "yes, the band has a list." Funny how quickly the mind can block things out that you really don't want to hear. I pressed back against the seat and felt as if my world had come crashing down on me. The tears that welled up in my eyes threatened to roll down my cheeks as I fought desperately not to blink.

The thoughts about this list came crashing through my brain like rapid-fire. What all did it actually have on it? How many girls were on it? And, most importantly, how many girls had Steve taken advantage of by calling them, inviting them to him?

The traffic light had turned green and we were moving. Thankfully the hotel was only a few more blocks away. Don't know what I expected to do once we got there—my jealousy, my envy had kicked in. I dreaded the thought of him being with anyone else but I also realized I couldn't expect him to remain chaste for me. He was a man—a grown man—a gorgeous man with needs and desires.

We pulled into the parking lot—the rest of the band was across the street at another hotel. I could see the tour bus parked to the side of their hotel. Steve and I remained in silence, walking across the lobby, then down the hall to the room.

Once inside, he broke the silence. He told me he wasn't the one using any part of the list—he didn't go in for that sort of "stuff." He sat down on the couch and I chose a chair; there was only one light on in the room, which cast eerie shadows on the walls.

He said nothing more, just sat there and looked at me though the dimness of the room. He propped his feet up on the coffee table, hesitated, kicked off his tennis shoes and placed his feet back on to the table, crossed them at the ankle, tapping his right foot slightly. He gathered his hair in his right hand and threw it down his back, leaning forward a little to do so.

This was the conversation I had dreaded since the summer of 75: the sex talk. He and I had decided to wait until I was 18. This was partly bowing to the wishes of my parents—they let me go with this man because they trusted my judgment, my intuition. They trusted that I would wait.

The question was on the tip of my tongue: did he fool around with the girls? There are some things you just have to know but can't know. This was one of those things.

The room was quiet with only the occasional on and off running of the fan of the air conditioner. The night had turned cool, the room felt just right. Steve was either lost in thought or avoiding my stare, his head still resting back on his hands, foot tapping. His eyes were closed now, his face relaxed. I watched his chest rise and fall with rhythmic breaths.

This was our first night in Boulder, the first night we ever really had a disagreement, and that isn't even what I would call this. He was tired and he had some insecure high school girl nagging him. I went over to the couch, sat next to him, facing him. He put his arm around me; I laid down, my head on his legs, looking up at him. His hand rubbed my shoulder, down my arm, and back; still the silence.

He asked simply, "We okay?"

"You bet." He relaxed. We fell asleep on the couch even though it was still relatively early, by our standards—11 PM. Must have needed the sleep.

This was the first time in several weeks that we didn't sleep in the same bed. Last year, while on the summer tour, we had maintained a distance for most nights. Even at the beginning of this tour we didn't slept together in a bed—on a couch, in the limo—but not the bed, even though we had slept in the same bed in Atlanta at Christmas. Maybe that was subconsciously considered safe due to the proximity of his family.

That all changed in Dallas.

*I*t was a steamy summer night in the heat and humidity of Texas. We had to sit through a horrendous thunderstorm that delayed the first night's concert by an hour while the county went under a thunderstorm warning, and, soon after, a tornado warning. Then we had to put up with the stifling, humidity-dripping heat. I was not, and still am not, a fan of hot weather.

The concerts in Dallas turned out to be some of the best up to that point. The crowd was energized and the band greedily fed off of that energy. The stadium had set up a huge platform for them and Steve spent the two hours running from end to end, singing his heart out, pouring his emotion into every word, making eye contact with fans at every corner of the audience.

These were the concerts he loved the best—the ones during which he could connect with fans from the stage. And the ones when he could be most mobile on the stage; he was not one to stay still if he didn't have to—he loved to move and shake things up a bit. Where he got his incredible energy from I didn't know.

To watch this man run across the stage and sing to the girls in the first several rows was a site I will never forget. His face was a sea of emotion, whether he was singing a ballad or hamming it up. To think that this is a shy man, who would always prefer to be a recluse, was not in mind while watching him perform.

The night of the first concert in Dallas, he was high with the music and the cheers. It was as if, when he came off the stage, he had done some kind of drug. Maybe he had. That was the effect it all had on him sometimes. He was almost in a manic state—highly excitable, not able to stay still, talking incessantly.

He actually joined the other band members in the large dressing room/lounge, dragging me in there by the hand. They were as shocked to see him there as I felt being there. He left me standing off to one side by a long table to flit around the room like a bee in search of the perfect flower. He went from girl to girl, and there were plenty in there to flit to; he shook hands, laughed loudly, had his picture taken over and over.

For awhile I felt very lonely, like I was off in a corner: solitary confinement. It was a horrible feeling: me in the corner and him with seemingly every girl in the place. My heart was aching as he spent more and more time away from me, and more with them.

Richard finally came up to me, one arm around a girl's shoulder (who looked ½ his age) (I'm sure his wife would have liked to have seen her), the other hand holding a beer. He looked drunk or very much on the way; smiling at me as if to say, "Are you okay?" I nodded, the tears welling up. He and the girl sat on the table behind me and began to make out; just what I needed to see. What I wouldn't have given at that point for a camera and the address to his wife and children. No, I really wasn't that nasty. Not really. I don't think.

After what seemed like hours but was probably only thirty minutes or so, Steve made his way back to me. I felt hot (it was too warm in that room with all those people there), fat (most overweight girl in the room) and left on a doorstep (like I truly did not belong there). He was still on his manic high, working on his second beer. He was sweating—his forehead glistening, his hair in wet strands about his face. There was a crowd of girls following him at a distance of several feet. Their expressions were pure anticipation and sex; they would sleep with him at the drop of a hat if only he would ask them. I wondered how he felt.

Breathless and hoarse from the concert, he told me to "Come on," and lead me out of the room to his private dressing room. The gaggle of girls gave me strange looks and wore very disappointed faces as we left. I swear I heard one of them say, "Why her—she's fat?" Things like that were said behind my back a lot, just loud enough for me to hear. I was only about 25 pounds overweight at that time but, unfortunately, that was enough. There are a lot of prejudices in the world—none of which make any sense.

If Steve heard the comment over the noise of the party, he didn't let on. He was on such a high that I doubted he heard anything. He pulled me into his dressing room and slammed the door shut behind us, leaning up against it. He said one word, "Incredible!" and swept me into his arms, kissing me hard on the mouth.

I was stunned, to say the least, but relieved as well. I loved this man, there was no doubt in my mind about that, and it broke my heart to be left in a sea of pretty girls who were also in love with him and would do anything to prove it. Anything.

I melted into his arms and leaned up against him, pressing him further against the door. His kiss was long as his tongue curled around mine. He tasted of beer and the piece of pizza I had seen him eat about 15 minutes earlier. His chin was rough with beard stubble and scratched against mine. I felt his arms close around me tighter as the kiss went on. He sighed heavily against my mouth; it went through me like a bolt of lightning.

His breathing became heavier and faster and something changed between us. Suddenly we weren't just two people locked in a kiss, but so much more. Our relationship seemed to be rising to another level, to a deeper level. Unlike the many other times we had kissed, this one was full of excitement, full of a raging fire, full of each other and full of something sensual. He was pumped with adrenaline and it was bringing us to a whole new understanding of each other.

In that moment, I wanted him. I wanted to experience the sensation of our skin touching, of him exploring parts of me no one else had. I wanted him to make love to me and promise we would be together always. I could feel his longing for me as well as his hips gyrated slightly and he moved his thighs against mine—he was hard beneath his jeans and I was damp beneath mine.

There was no denying it at this point: we both wanted to be together; it was fast becoming quite obvious to us.

It seemed like we held our position up against the door for minutes, our lips grinding against each other's, hands groping each other's backs. The room seemed to be getting hotter as time passed. I felt a flush travel from my groin outward—it seemed as though my skin was burning wherever he touched me. I broke into goose flesh several times causing me to shudder against him. We both audibly sighed many times as we breathed in unison.

When we finally came out of the kiss, he put his head back against the door, arms still around me at the waist, and looked at me. His eyes were glistening with tears that, at any moment, would be released and run down his flushed cheeks. His gorgeous face framed by his brown hair. Sweat sparkled on his brow and his brown eyes suddenly darkened to a chocolate, a smoldering chocolate brown.

He touched my soul at that moment. I can't describe what it is that I felt when it happened; I just know that he did. I felt light-headed and my knees were gelatin, wobbly, about to collapse. It felt like my heart would leap out of my chest, beating so erratically.

He must have felt it too because his face changed. It changed from a smile to a glow. He swallowed hard and closed his mouth that had been slightly open.

We stared at each other, taking each other in. The noise from the party down the hall was gone. The smell of this place—underneath the stadium, near the locker rooms—was gone. The light—harsh overhead fluorescent—seemed to dim and was nearly gone. It was just he and I in that place—in that moment—in the whole world. Everything else was gone and didn't matter. It was just he and I.

We had told each other that we loved each other—since the second day we were together—but tonight there were no words. No words to speak that would be the right thing to say. No words that could sum up what had passed between us.

He became even more a part of me that night in the Dallas Cowboys stadium. A part of me I knew I would never be without—that, in some way, we would always be linked—always be together—even if it was because we were standing under the same sky, we would always be together; no matter what.

He pulled my face to his again and we were locked in another kiss—equally as passionate and loving.

He again was grinding his pelvis to some rhythm deep in his own mind, and it felt natural for me to do the same thing. He pulled me even closer to him, pressing my body against his. His hair hung over my face and lightly caressed my cheeks. He slightly spread his legs apart, placing one foot up onto the door, opening his legs wider. I placed one of my legs in between his, leaning into his body more. Just there—as close as two people can be without actually having sex.

His hands went underneath the back of my white button down shirt—it was one of my dad's shirts and hung loosely over my faded jeans. He caressed the skin of my back, occasionally sliding his hands underneath the bra strap, and daring to come forward ever so slightly.

My favorite part of him was his hair; my fingers toyed with it, twirling it around my fingers. I touched his face with his mouth on mine and felt the roughness of the stubble and the gentle downward slope of his perfect nose. I touched his closed eyelids and ran a finger lightly over his unusually long eyelashes.

I ran my fingers along the sharp line of his jaw and felt his muscles move as his tongue searched my mouth. My hand went around the back of his head and held him against my mouth as we lost ourselves in this sea of each other. I could feel his breath against my face as it washed hot over my cheek.

Still lost in the kiss, he brought his hands around between us and began to work on the buttons of my shirt, slowly unbuttoning them one by one. I didn't protest; couldn't have even if I had wanted to—he was taking my breath away. Once the shirt was totally undone, the kiss ended and he began to nuzzle my neck, sending shivers through every nerve ending in my body. I was his at that point, to do with whatever he wanted. If it was going to happen, let it be now—I was ready. I wanted him. I loved him. It was okay.

He worked his kisses from my neck to the rise of my breasts over the top of my bra. He was gentle and loving as he kissed every inch of my skin, pulling me closer to him with every move. We were crossing a line that we had invisibly drawn from the beginning; we were moving into territory that I no longer had to simply dream about.

Then, seemingly as quickly as this had all begun, he stopped. He looked up at me and simply said, "Let's go back to the hotel." Talk about stopping short. I had heard jokes about coitus interruptus—I guess this is what they all were referring to.

I nodded, still lost in his spell, beginning to button the shirt, decided to hell with it, and tied it in a knot around my waist, pulling the two edges closed in the front. We quickly left the dressing room and made our way to his waiting limo. We practically sat on top of each other in the limo, exploring each other's faces with our kisses all the way to the hotel.

The walk to the room seemed endless. We walked in step, arms around each other's waists, still kissing as we made our way down the long corridor. He still had on his clothing from the concert and that damned floppy hat. He was recognized in the lobby by several fans who had on band t-shirts; they had obviously either been to that night's concert or were going to the next night's affair. Thankfully, they were an older group of people and respected our privacy, didn't come close. But they pointed and giggled and shouted hello. Steve acknowledged their presence, waved, then was lost in me again.

Once we were in the room, we nearly fell onto the bed, wrapped in each other, clinging to each other. He was laughing—I don't know what about—but it was so nice to hear that laugh. It meant he was relaxed and at ease with things—I didn't hear that laugh often enough these days. No one did.

He stripped off his t-shirt and threw it to the floor, then kicked off his tennis shoes, flipping them so far that they hit the opposite wall with a thud. He untied my shirt and let it fall from my shoulders. "I want to feel your skin against mine," he said, staring into my eyes, looking into my being.

I answered with, "I want to feel your hands on me, Steve."

He reached behind me and, with some minor difficulty (which actually made me feel kind of good), managed to unsnap my bra. He left his hands on the fabric, bringing them around to the front, brushing against my breasts as he pulled the bra down my arms and off. My eyes were closed and he told me to open them.

There we were, naked from the waists up, alone in a hotel room, with the glow of a small wall lamp that illuminated our passion. He grabbed me and pulled me to him once again. As our skin touched, the sparks flew—literally. I swear I felt as if someone had set me on fire as he pulled me to him and we fell onto the bed. I wanted to cry—I wanted to shout—I wanted to love him.

We stayed silent, simply in each other's arms for a time, listening to each other breathing, enjoying the feeling of each other. He was extremely sensitive in that he wanted to take the time I needed, as this would be my first time. My first time for what—were we actually going to make love this night or, as my friends would have put it, "fool around?" I didn't care—whatever he wanted to do I was willing. I would be 18 in three months; three lousy little months. Did it really matter?

He pulled his head up away from mine, again melting me with his stare. Our legs were entwined together; he kept running his stocking feet against my calves. I touched his face with my left hand and held him by the chin. He leaned his face into my hand, which he kissed as his mouth met my hand.

He took my left hand in his right and kissed my fingertips, softly but hard enough for me to feel his teeth. When he got to my thumb, he kissed it, then laid my hand onto his chest, and laid his hand flat onto mine, just where the skin began to swell into my left breast. His hand hesitated as he tilted his head and said, "I can feel your heartbeat." That was a song from the *Partridge Family*—why did I think of that? I was still such a teenager.

Where his hand lay, the skin became hot, blossoming into a fever flush. Still looking up into my eyes, he drew closer to me and we kissed again, this time with a little more urgency, a little more abandon. As we kissed, he slowly, ever so slowly, caressed the soft curve of my breast, at first drawing across me, following the curve, and finally coming to rest with his palm over the nipple.

I drew in a quick, sharp breath, both with pleasure and surprise. He continued to slowly draw his palm over my skin that was rapidly contracting and hardening against his touch. The pure ecstasy of this moment caused stirrings in me I had never felt. As I sighed into him I could feel him smile in our kiss.

Our mouths separated and he licked his bottom lip. I think I bit him a moment earlier when he first began exploring me because I had tasted blood. He smiled, his eyebrows in that position that made him appear sad and thrilled at the same time. He looked at me and simply said, "Okay?"

I nodded—I couldn't even speak. My breath was gone.

His hand remained on my breast, continuing its slow rotation of the palm, his fingers gently reaching outward, touching my skin. He lowered his head and rested his mouth against his hand. He was breathing through his mouth; his warm breath on my breast through his fingers was almost more than I could stand.

Lips that had been against his hand were suddenly on me as he drew his hand around to the underside of my breast, lifting it to his mouth. He kissed the skin in short bursts, drawing ever nearer to the tender nipple. When his lips met it, the feeling was just like the movies—fireworks, lightning, stars, love. I lowered my face onto to the top of his head and drew in his scent as he tasted me.

His hair smelled of an unusual blend of shampoo, sweat and cigarettes. I squirmed around slightly as his mouth both tickled me and took me to a level of excitement I can't describe. His tongue in my mouth had been a heady feeling; his tongue on my breast was unbelievable.

Steve's hips were again gyrating against me, his leg over mine with the other leg next to me. I could feel him straining hard against his jeans as his excitement grew. I ran my hands down his back, using my fingernails—not realizing I had managed to scratch him in the process. He never let on.

My hands came to the top of his jeans; I slid under them and the band of his underwear, feeling the slight rise of his cheeks. Steve drew back from me and, for a moment, I thought I had done something wrong but his next move buried that thought for good. He unbuckled his belt, unbuttoned his Levis, and unzipped them, allowing more room for my hands.

He hesitated for several seconds as though he was wrestling with what to do next; suddenly he rolled off the side of the bed and stood up. His body was in shadow by the dim light in the room. He was so thin—his collarbone and ribs clearly visible. I rolled onto my back and considered getting up myself—to do what, I wasn't sure, but I didn't have to worry about it.

Steve pulled the bedspread back and I rolled over it when he removed it from the bed. As he took the spread a few feet to the chair, I crawled under the light blanket and sheet, still in my jeans, and laid my head down on the pillow, face up.

Steve came back to the edge of the bed. I had pulled the sheet up almost to my chin in an attempt to cover myself from his gaze, a little embarrassed; but he reached over me and pulled it down; I didn't press the issue. I looked at him standing over the bed and realized he looked almost comical with his pants just starting to fall down over his hips, open at the fly. I giggled and he wrinkled his nose at me. In one swift movement he dropped his pants and climbed under the sheet with me.

He laughed again a little—nervousness, sexual tension? He turned toward me and laid his head on my shoulder, one arm draped across my chest, hand over a breast. He told me he loved me, didn't want to be without me, that he wished I could be on tour for the rest of the year and not leave him. His voice was tender and soft, hoarse and breathy. My emotions were soaring as he nuzzled up against my neck, throwing one leg over mine.

I told him I loved him back, and, if I could, I would never leave him; I so wanted to be with him wherever he went; I wanted to follow him to the end of the world and back again if I could. I loved him so much—my rock star whose star was just beginning to shine with a brilliance he had yet to realize. I was still a teenager with school ahead of me, and parents who didn't really understand the attraction. I was a teenager; he was a man. This relationship was an odd one by most people's standards and yet, at that hotel, nothing seemed more natural, more true.

His hand slid down my belly to my jeans, which he unsnapped and unzipped, then rubbed the skin of my stomach where the band of the jeans had just been. My mind raced with a thousand questions and thoughts, all of which remained silent.

Steve sat up and helped me get the jeans off, then laid back down, both of us in our underwear and socks—what a sight that must have been. He rolled on top of me and held himself above me with his arms. His hair hung down around his face and drifted across my chest, causing the same explosion of pleasure that his hands had. His pelvis was tight against mine. He felt large and stiff against me; I could see his manhood straining to escape the thin cotton.

He looked deep into my eyes; his face was so gorgeous, so sincere. I could see his love for me in his face now, like something I hadn't seen before. He was so relaxed, yet so serious.

He lowered himself to me, taking my mouth onto his, kissing me hard, hands coming up to hold my face, forcing his weight onto me. He took my breath away—literally—as I wrapped my arms around his back and downward. I could feel his desire emotionally and physically, and wanted him to be a part of me.

He came back from the kiss and suddenly told me he couldn't go "all the way. Not tonight. Everything but."

The disappointment must have been evident in my face and he smiled at me; told me it was the age thing, he wanted our first time to be special—to be somewhere special—he already had it all planned.

Hmmm…everything but…what did that mean? He asked if that was okay and I started to say no but quickly changed it to yes as it came out of my mouth. He kissed my neck and again worked his way down, taking one of my breasts into his hand and again lifted it to his warm mouth. It brought me such pleasure that I actually arched my back a little, causing my chest to thrust into his hand.

He let out a large moan, dropping one of his hands to touch me through the underwear which was now wet with desire. His fingertips danced across the fabric, lightly touching me, and himself, at the same instant. The sensation of his fingers between my legs and his mouth on my breast was overpowering. I could hear myself breathing louder, almost panting, as he moved his pelvis up and down mine, his fingers lightly stroking me.

He suddenly arched his back, pushing himself onto me, his

hips moving faster in his passion. His breath was coming faster too, in short bursts. His head raised and he moved his face up to mine, crashing his mouth down onto mine, moaning as he did so. He moaned several more times, pushing his fingers a little harder against my underwear, and occasionally touching himself. When he touched me again, I exploded into waves of feelings that were new to me and amazing.

At that instant, as I let out a small gasp, he moaned very loudly in my mouth, stopped his thrusting as his body became suddenly stiff. His pelvis quivered on top of mine and I felt movement that I wasn't familiar with. He collapsed on top of me, his mouth falling away from mine, his breathing slowing some. There was a wet sensation between us and I realized what had just happened. I may have still been a virgin, but had done the reading—he had climaxed. No penetration—not yet. He had said everything but. The pleasure was there—the love was there.

From that night on, we spent our time in the same bed, at times doing what had happened that night; at times simply loving each other without anything sexual. The sexual tension grew between us over the summer and, as time grew near for me to take my leave of him, go back to school, we knew the time was fast approaching when we would make love—slow, warm, passionate love, and be truly together and one.

C'mon 18!

*S*ummer ended and again we were forced to say good-bye. We spent our last night in Houston at a crazed concert that seemed to go too fast, followed by a last night in bed. He put me on a plane early the next morning. This was becoming increasingly more difficult; he knew it; I knew it. But there was nothing either of us could do about it; I had to go to school; he had to be with the band.

I hung on to him at the gate until last call was announced for the flight, wanting to savor every last touch, smell and look of him before I left. I never looked back after we finally let go of each other—if I had taken one last look that would have been it—I wouldn't have gone; I would have run back and made him take me with him, to hell with everything and everyone else.

The day after I got home, I had band practice, then football practice. Band practice was okay right up to the point when I realized the next new song we were going to be rehearsing was one of Steve's songs. I shouldn't have been surprised—our band director always arranged a few of the popular songs for us to march to—I just never imagined it would be one of Steve's. It was a bit heart-wrenching. My band director said he did it to honor us both—he always was an old softie. Couldn't wait to tell Steve about it.

Football practice were two-a-days—two practices per day—I was kept busy tending to injuries, trying to prevent new ones. Working with the guys on the team was fun—most of them had high hopes of going off to college on a football scholarship, then being drafted into the NFL. High hopes with such little chance. I was surprised 10 years later to see a familiar name playing for the Cleveland Browns—I used to tape his ankles!! Pretty exciting.

School finally started in September—this was my senior year—the "best time of your life." Right. I was, basically, miserable in my loneliness. I had my friends and we hung out as much as the previous year. Plus I had made a few new friends, girlfriends, and we had a blast together. One girl was the statistician for the football team; we became very close—she replaced Patty, who had gone off and left me for college.

My parents were glad that I had made a new friend; they had been convinced that I would shut the world away after leaving Steve this last time. I had shed a lot of tears the first few days home; didn't want to be bothered with anyone or anything, but forced myself to get up and get moving. Steve was calling me from the road nearly everyday; my heart ached for him—truly a physical discomfort at this point, making it difficult to inhale at times while we spoke. So, Sandy's and my antics were a good diversion.

I knew November would come soon—my 18th birthday—the time we had both been waiting for. We hadn't really discussed it lately but I had hoped he and I would be together for my birthday, or, at least, close to the date. He had said he had it all planned. I took charge of things in early October and was put on the pill—a very big deal back then. Had to endure all of the doctor's prying questions—Why do you want to do this? Are you planning on having pre-marital sex? Do you know about sexually-transmitted diseases? Who is this man you want to be with? He asked that question because he was friends with my mom and dad. Then I got the standard lecture—I should wait until I am married; good girls don't; you can wait—you waited this long, what is the big deal?

I did feel a bit strange about going on the pill but it was, hopefully, a necessity. Time would tell.

I was still artificially popular at school because I had toured again with a rock band. People I didn't know came up to me, asking me questions, touching me as if it would rub off; whatever "it" was. Sophomores especially, wanted to see the senior who knew Steve Potts; then, when they did see me, there was almost disbelief in their eyes, a "why her" attitude. That same "why her" attitude the concert-goers had had.

Homecoming came in October—the weekend before Halloween, my favorite holiday. I was actually on the ballot for queen—couldn't understand it but figured it was more of that artificial popularity, or someone's idea of a joke. Steve would be on tour but offered to come for the dance. They would be in Pittsburgh—concert ends at 10:30—no encores—he could be there by helicopter in an hour or so. Helicopter?! I told him no—the whole thing would just be too much, and, besides, it wasn't that important to me. Sandy and I were going to go to the dance after the game, and that was fine by me.

The week leading up to the Homecoming game and dance was a whirlwind of marching band and football practices. Steve called and called, needing reassurance that, no, I did not want him to come; no, I would not be disappointed if he didn't; yes, Sandy and I were going together, dateless; yes, I wanted to see him but it was too much to go through for a silly high school dance. He understood, I thought.

Friday night came—the Homecoming Queen (my neighbor and good friend, Shelly, who had taught me to play clarinet on her back porch) was crowned—she reigned over the game and the ensuing dance. The stadium stands were full of present and past students, families and friends; the football team was pumped, ready to take-on our cross-town rivals; the marching band set and ready with a new halftime show.

Sandy and I hung out on the sidelines; she kept track of the plays, scores, all stats; I dealt with injuries. The halftime show went off without a hitch—we even played Steve's song that night. Okay, so I cried a little during it. Who wouldn't? I missed him so much.

I looked up into the stands as we were marching off the field, and noticed that my parents had left already. Strange that they would leave so quickly but I shrugged it off, thinking Mom was probably cold or she had had enough of watching her daughter run around on the field with the boys.

The game went into overtime, further delaying the dance festivities; we managed to eek out a win with a 36-yard field goal—not bad for a high school kicker.

After a short bus ride to the school, all my medical equipment stashed in the coaches' office, I tried hard not to look at the football players while making my way back through the busy locker room, and headed home. My house was just over a small hill from the school so I rarely drove.

I wasn't in any hurry. Sandy and I would meet at the dance, which would go on until 2 AM or so; it was only 11:30 PM now. So, I dawdled, strolling lazily through a field toward my house, head in the clouds, thinking of the game and my friends and the team and my Steve. It had been a fun evening—football and band were my best times when I wasn't with the man in my life.

Steve—just thinking his name made me dizzy. I pulled my letter jacket close around me—the air had taken on a slight chill. My band uniform was dirty—the knees muddy from kneeling next to football players on the field; the uniform jacket was wadded up in my medical gear back at school which meant another trip to the dry cleaners on Monday after school. My hat was in my hand; I was carrying it with one finger, twirling it around; dropped it a few times, causing some feathers to fall out of the plume. The white spats over my shoes bore a lovely combination of mud and a football player's blood from a nose-bleed all over them. They would need to be washed.

As I approached my house, I noticed the police car in the driveway. Police? State police: not city; not county; state. The windows of the downstairs were brightly glowing with all the lights on inside. My pace quickened until I burst through the front door.

Two state patrol officers practically ran into me as they were leaving—tall and imposing, they each tipped their hats to me and stepped past. I saw my brother sitting in a living room chair (I kind of wondered what he had done); then I noticed he was on the edge of the chair, that same open-mouthed, wide-eyed stare he gets when he looks at Steve.

Steve?

Oh my God!

He came into view from the interior of the living room, dressed in a dark suit (thank goodness—no polyester), tie, tennis shoes. His hair was very slightly grown out from when I had last seen him; it feathered around his face, falling past his shoulders. He took my breath away—literally—I wasn't sure I could continue standing and wavered a little, my father behind me, steadying me.

I would find out later that he *had* helicoptered from the concert and had received a state police escort from a nearby airport to my house, which my father, who knew everyone, had arranged; lights and sirens all the way to my house. Wish I had seen that. Parents—they will never stop surprising me.

We rushed into each other's arms, meeting in the doorway to the living room. I made sure I kept my knees away from his suit so as to not muddy it, but pinned the rest of me against him. He held me tightly, breathing into my ear, causing a shiver to run through me. My parents were watching us, but I didn't care. I kissed him—he kissed me—full on the mouth—not a namby-pamby hi-how-ya-doin' kiss—this was the real deal. His lips felt so warm, his taste so good, his scent so sexy—I could still smell the concert sweat. I could have melted into the ground. But, I had to take a deep breath and compose myself.

He turned me around until I was facing my mom who was holding a dress—a long, light blue, straight to the floor dress. I was showered and coming back down the stairs in 20 minutes—pretty good for a girl. Uncomfortable without my jeans, feet stuffed into semi-high heels, hair swept up and held in place with a thousand bobby pins, and make-up.

Make-up—I never wore it before but Mom had insisted tonight.

My dad and Steve were in the foyer where the stairs came down. I hadn't thought about it but I left him alone with my dad—oh, God, what must they have been talking about? What had they all been talking about before I got home that night?! Too late to worry about it now. Sigh.

The picture-taking was next—it was great for me—I wanted a memory of this moment, but I am sure it was awful for him to endure even though he said otherwise. Dad allowed him to drive the Buick to the dance, all the way up the hill to the school. My parents just kept surprising me.

What a stir we caused when we walked into that gym. Me, on the arm of a rock star—a rock god. There was a gradual hush that settled over the gym and dance attendees; people stared at him, suddenly acutely aware of who he was. Whispers were practically shouted between people. I don't really know what shocked people more—the fact that he was there, that he was there with me, or that I really had been telling the truth all along. I felt sorry for the trio of "wanna-be" rockers who had been hired as the band—their hearts had to be in their throats as they realized they would be playing for *him*.

People kept their distance, for about five seconds. We weren't mobbed but all of my classmates were suddenly my best friends as they gathered around us just to get a look, a touch, a glance. He signed some autographs, allowed pictures to be taken with him, and even ended up singing two songs with the petrified band. We danced together—slow songs only—and I felt like the belle of the ball. Cinderella with her Prince Charming—it was past midnight and I hadn't turned into a pumpkin, not that night.

His presence overshadowed the whole Homecoming victory, the queen, the dance. Shelly looked a little teed off until he went up to her, introduced himself, congratulated her and kissed her hand. She was pudding. He truly knew how to handle difficult situations.

When the night was over, he drove home, came inside. I hadn't even thought about where he was staying—hadn't occurred to me that he would go anywhere else. The dance had run until 3 AM. He was staying the night with us, the next night too, before he would have to join back up with his band. He was mine for a day and a half.

My world was so different from his—I wasn't sure how my parents would react to seeing us on the couch in the morning. He told me they had showed him the guest room when he got there—he had dressed there. There were two beds there—couldn't we each take one and be together?

In a daring split-second decision, we ended up in the guest room together after I had changed into a nightgown and washed the make-up off my face. He had stripped down to his underwear and was already on a bed with the sheets pulled down when I walked in. The room looked like him—concert clothing on the floor in a pile, tennis shoes kicked over by the bag, suit tossed onto the other bed.

Because the room shared a wall with my parents' room, and because the walls were pretty much made of toilet paper and spit, we were going to have to be quiet—not that we were ever loud, but I wanted so much to squeal as he pulled me onto the bed with him.

He kissed me all over my face with a need and a hunger he had never displayed before. His lips were wet and when they finally pressed against mine, our love was evident. We held our mouths against each other's and savored the moments we had been able to steal from his increasingly busy schedule. It was unbelievable that he was actually there.

When we finally came up for air, his head hung above mine, his hair tousled from my hands running through it. We hadn't really spoken since I saw him in the living room. Now was the time—quietly.

Why are you here? Missed you. How? Worked it all out with your dad—he is pretty cool. *MY* dad? Yup—pretty cool. What about the band? We're off tomorrow. How are things? Tense but I'll survive; how's school? School's school—you just met everyone I know there; they're so excited; you are so fabulous; I have missed you so. Missed you too—wish you were on tour with me; not the same without you there.

I searched his face for any sign of—of what? A sign that he was toying with me? A sign that displayed what he was thinking? His face was relaxed—those eyebrows slightly raised, drooping on the outside, sad and perplexed all at the same time. There were slight dark circles under his eyes—lack of sleep, and I wasn't helping things by keeping him up at all hours with a silly high school dance. He was here, in Ohio, all mine, for now.

Neither of us was going to get much sleep. Not tonight. My emotions were stirred into a frenzy; he was a burst of sexual tension. There was an intensity in the air around us making it difficult to breathe, at least for me. We were so close to 18 at this point—it was nearly within my reach, and yet, it was miles away.

He pushed my nightgown up around my hips, caressing my leg, thigh and hip as he did so. I nuzzled his neck as he presented it to me by raising his chin a little. His hand went underneath the nightgown and found a breast, which he tickled and stroked to hardened excitement. I wanted to moan with sheer pleasure at his touch but didn't dare. Absolute quiet—we had to have absolute quiet.

The hand that I had on his chest was suddenly taken into his grasp; he slid it down the length of his body until it was over his full arousal through his briefs. He wrapped my hand around him and moved it slowly over the length of his hardness, showing me what he liked, what felt good. His hand left mine to do as he had shown me; he wrapped that hand around my shoulders and drew me close, bringing his lips to mine, giving me short, staccato kisses.

It didn't take long—he was soon breathing very hard, his hand back over mine, helping me to hasten his excitement. I muffled the sounds of his pleasure with my mouth as he climaxed into his briefs. He lay very still for a few moments, apparently needing time to recover.

He finally whispered, "I love you." I whispered it back with a kiss.

Wasn't much for you, was it? Yeah—it was. How could it be? I was with you. You sure? I love you—I'll do anything; I want you to be happy. Only time I'm happy is with you—really happy. Really? Yup—really—I need you—I love you.

His voice was a breathy whisper in my arms, his last words ringing in my ears. He needs me—a kid from Ohio, a nobody. We fell asleep in the twin bed, totally by mistake, but it happened; wrapped around each other, lost in a love that continued to grow between us.

Four hours later, the quiet of our room was shattered. I hadn't left the door totally latched, and in raced Misty, who jumped onto the bed and made herself at home at our feet. My brother was on her heels as he bounded into the room on the pretense of catching the dog. He gave us a quick glance then sat on the other bed, pushing aside Steve's suit. John then scrutinized us further, taken aback by us both in the bed, but he quickly recovered. Steve stirred behind me as I rolled over to look at John. He was 12 now—still very star-struck; didn't see anything wrong with coming in; after all, the dog had burst in.

Steve threw a leg over mine and began to kiss the back of my neck before I told him we had company. The way he jumped, I think he thought my parents were in the room. But then he saw

John on the other bed and laughed, a little with relief, a little with the memory of his brother, James, who had walked in on him at home while he was with the first girl he ever had sex with. I did not want to talk about that.

John finally spoke. "What are you guys doing today?"

"Nothing."

"Did you have fun last night?"

"Of course."

"Does Mom know you're in here?"

"No—don't say anything."

"Can my friends come over today?"

"No way."

Steve laughed and announced, "Your mom knows. I could hear her as she and your dad went downstairs earlier. Believe me, they know."

I groaned.

We spent Saturday in the house, watching TV—old, black and white, strange little horror movies—and avoided the suspicious glances from my parents. We went out for a drive before dinner, just to get away for a few precious moments, ending up at the park where Patty and I used to go. The surrounding trees were beautiful in their fall colors, the setting sun streaming through the leaves. No crowds, no groupies, no parents, no screams, no shouts. We had found a small piece of solitude away from the world for a moment in time.

Alone, away from everything, we were just us; there was no star and no high school student. We were simply Steve and Jean—two people who had met, felt an immediate attraction and need, and were struggling to maintain it.

As the sun slowly set on the horizon, and the area around us darkened, his arm around my shoulders tightened, and he shifted in the seat.

"I don't want to leave you tomorrow; I don't know if I can."

What was he saying? That uncertainty, insecurity that I had seen in Atlanta was back.

"You have to go—there are people depending on you; you have your destiny—it's music and it's not here. You have to go."

I didn't want him to go but I didn't want to be the one accused of holding on too tightly. I had to push him back to the band, back to his music, back to the limelight, back to his future. He was predestined to be a star, a bigger star than he already was; I knew that in my heart. His star could not, would not, rise here in Ohio. He had to leave.

He tried to argue with me but finally had to agree. He was just so tired, so sick of the price of fame—the high price of fame. He said he didn't like feeling as if he had sold his soul to the devil; he didn't know where the future would take him, would take us.

I had to push him away, not in a physical sense, but push him back to his music. It was not an easy thing to do, not just because he was resisting, but because I didn't want him to go. My heart desperately wanted him to stay and, if he would, we could get married, buy a house, have a family, be a family. I wanted him at my side to have and to hold. But, he had to go.

And he finally agreed. Reluctantly.

And the next day, I let him go. My family drove him to the Cleveland airport to catch the flight back to his tour, away from my body but not from my heart and soul. He hadn't brought his disguise hat so my dad lent him one of his goofy golfing hats—I didn't know which hat was worse. When his flight was called, he shook my dad's and John's hand, half hugged my mom and took me off to the side.

He touched my face and I could feel the love leave his fingertips and travel to my heart, making it quiver in my chest. My tears couldn't help but flow. He hugged me tightly, telling me over and over he loved me with both his words and his touch. Neither of us wanted to let go—it was me that pulled out first. He bent his head to mine and kissed me many times. I didn't care who was watching.

Final call. Time to let go. Again.

C'mon 18!

124

Can't come soon enough!

Steve was an amazingly thoughtful and caring person, something I had known for a few years now, but I had no idea just how much until my 18th birthday approached. We both knew what it meant—this was going to be our first time together, finally together, able to share ourselves with the other completely.

He was out on tour—this band seemed to be on the road a lot more than others, but that just showed how popular they were, and it also showed just how much I missed him. It was only going to grow in the next decade. When the schedule for this tour was set up he asked for only one break in it—the week of my birthday. He didn't care about anything else; they were going to stop for me.

No one argued with him—no one dared argue this point. The other band members were okay with it anyway—they needed a well-deserved break at that point too. The band manager was a little upset—he would have been able to get them several "great gigs" if only Steve would relax a little on the dates, but, no, it wasn't going to happen.

He came to my house the day of my birthday, in the limousine. My brother, home from school on this special Friday, was anxious to have him sign the album he had in his hands. A newspaper photographer, a budding paparazzi, was in the street, keeping a polite distance, but ready to snap a picture of a star. Some of my friends cut class and came too. This man had such a pull on people.

He was all in black—pants, t-shirt, long leather duster-type coat, black tennis shoes. Thank heavens he wasn't wearing the hat! Again he had flowers for my mother, who graciously accepted. She and I had had another "talk" the night before. Yes, I was on birth control—no, I wasn't stupid. Yes, I will finish high school. No, we are not running off to get married. Yes, I am taking this very seriously—have for a few years now.

My dad had stayed home from work to see us off too—Dad never stayed home from work.

Steve came into the house and sat in the living room for a time. He wasn't rushed—arrived in plenty of time for socializing. My brother jumped onto the couch next to him and stuck the album in his face, barely able to say anything to the man—John was still pretty star-struck. Steve signed the album cover and handed it back—I thought my brother was going to pass out—I leaned past Steve and told John to breathe. He did.

Misty laid her head in his lap and he stroked it slowly. Lucky dog. His hair was shorter—about two inches below his shoulders and very layered now. There were a few grey hairs here and there—he was only 28—and I could smell hair spray. He really was becoming a rock star! He also looked like he hadn't shaved that morning—later he would admit that he had run out of time; it was either shave or do his hair—the hair won.

My parents asked the usual questions—how was life on the road? Hectic. Was he getting any sleep? No. Was he having a good time? Sort of. How were his folks? Okay. What we were going to do this weekend? (*Oh, God.*) Go to Atlanta for the weekend and then on to Orlando for five days.

That was news to me—I had school next week…I looked at Steve who was smiling a mischievous smile, then at my parents. Again, they knew things I didn't. My dad simply said I was 18 now and an adult; I had to be left to live my life but I only had until next Sunday but I had better be home, ready for school next Monday. Steve assured them I would be back—Sunday night. Ten whole days with the man. My parents were amazing.

We left soon after the questioning ended. Out came the sunglasses and the hat for the trip through Cleveland's airport. We were very well-behaved in both the limo and the airplane. I was going to his house to do what we had been waiting to do for two years. My heart would not stop jump-starting itself, pumping erratically at times, causing me to jump every now and then.

We arrived at his parents' house at a decent hour for a change—5 PM. We had to take a limo from the airport as James was in college classes until late, and then he was staying on campus with a friend. I expected to see his parents on the porch, or, at least, inside the front door but, when he opened it, there was an amazing quiet. Only Nip greeted us and then quickly walked away in search of a toy mouse.

Without a word, he held me in the foyer and we swayed in each other's arms to music only he could hear. He seemed timid, almost shy—I thought that was my role—as we glided around the floor, lost in each other. The light had faded; this was so romantic and so perfect.

He finally told me his parents were enjoying a night in downtown Atlanta—dinner and a nice hotel: we had the house to ourselves. That allayed some of my fear about being with him the first time under the nose of his mom. He toyed with my hair as we had made our way into the living room, standing in front of the main window. My hair was longer now, about to my shoulders, and curly—my mother said if I was going to let it grow, I would have to perm it so it looked halfway decent. Mothers! Some adult I was. I wanted to do a shag thing with my hair like he had. It would have to wait.

I laid my head against his chest, breathing him in, smelling that sweet essence I missed so much. It was all over his t-shirt. I wrapped my arms around him under his coat and held him close. He asked me if I wanted my birthday present yet and I thought, heck yes I want it—I want it to be you—tonight—now. But I answered with a noncommittal response that was mumbled against his chest.

He pulled back from me, took his coat off, tossing it aside, aiming for the piano bench but missed. I pulled my own coat off and held it as I sat down on the couch. He turned on a light in the living room and picked up a box off of the book-shelves. A small box; a velvet box. Dizziness was threatening as I wondered what on earth he had done. My heart was so loud I could hear it in my own ears. I was glad I was sitting down because I may have fallen down had I been standing—that would have made for a nice memory.

He came over to me on the couch and stood over me for a moment, before he bent down to his knees, leaning an arm on my leg. Oh my God—this can't be. It just can't be. I can't—he can't.

He looked into my eyes, which, I am sure, made me look like a deer in headlights at that point. I was lost in a whirlwind of emotions and confusion, and had bitten my bottom lip so hard it was now bleeding. He saw that and leaned forward, kissing away the blood.

He moved a little on the floor, came between my knees and leaned forward into me, opening the box. There was a perfect ¾ carat diamond ring in a white gold setting—nothing fancy—a Tiffany box and ring. The diamond shone with rainbows of color as the light hit it.

"I have known you over two years now—two years and four months and my life has not been the same since, in many ways. We came from separate worlds and collided into our own. You have been my rock, the promise of a future, the one I can depend on to pull me through anything. I want this to be my promise to you—that, someday, we will be together forever. It may not be now; it may not be soon. There is so much I want you to do first and I will not expose you to the life I lead now. But I want you to know that this is my promise for our future. Someday. I love you so much. Happy birthday."

Nothing could have been said that would have meant more. He took my left hand in his and slipped the ring on my 3rd finger, where it rested just above the birthstone ring he had given me last year.

My head was literally spinning with what had just happened. I didn't know what to say—the words were stuck in my mouth—and I think, had I been able to say something, it would have come out wrong, so silence was good. There were tears in my eyes that flowed freely. It's a girl thing. He was still on the floor, looking up at me, leaning on my legs.

"Let's go upstairs." That was all I needed to hear.

He held out his hand to me as he rose from the floor. I took it and stood in front of him. He was so handsome all in black. His hand was warm; mine was damp. He kissed the finger with the ring he had just placed there, allowing his lips to remain there for a few seconds.

We made our way slowly, dreamily up the stairs, Nip practically tripping us as the cat raced ahead. The sun had gone down, it was dark upstairs, so he turned on the desk light in his room. I saw his things neatly—neatly?—here and there. Even the few pieces of sheet music were straightened. I also noticed three syringes on the desk but didn't think anything about them, as his mom was diabetic.

There was a vase of roses on his dresser—they were emitting an intoxicating scent into the room that mingled with that of him and the house itself. His suitcase was in front of the dresser, which is when I realized we had left mine downstairs. He said I didn't need it.

This *was* going to happen.

He took me into his arms again; I buried my face in the hair on his shoulder. I was comfortable in his arms—I never wanted to leave. I was an adult now but I didn't feel any differently than I had the last time here. The love was still there, the friendship, the yearning.

I don't know how long we stayed that position. We were both so still and yet, I felt myself trembling slightly. If he could feel it, he didn't say. He sighed several times, making my knees shaky. I knew what we were about to do and all I could question was why he had chosen me. Me: a plain, high school girl from Ohio. This man—this talented, gifted celebrity—picked me to be his—at least for now.

I fingered the diamond on my finger behind his back and

suddenly felt a rush of adoration for him like none other. I tightened my arms around him; he did the same, briefly.

I looked up into his brown eyes and—did I see tears? He was so emotional, a trait I found endearing. When we were together, he wasn't a star, but a man who liked simple things, shunned the publicity and cared more for family above everything else. He was just Steve. I never really thought of him as anything else.

With a tenderness I had not yet experienced, he stroked my face with his hand, gently gliding his fingertips over my eyes, my nose, my mouth, finally arriving at my chin, which he raised.

He smiled at me and a tear fell from his eye, trailing down his right cheek. In an instant of spontaneity, I brushed it away with my finger, which I then tasted, savoring the taste of salt, the taste of him, and we smiled at each other.

There was something different about this night—about this place—about this time. This was a man to whom I had revealed so much, things no one else knew, not even Patty. And I knew his secrets and fears as well. The room seemed closer, as if the temperature was slowly, but steadily, rising. It was as if we were standing in a circle of energy that was threatening to rise and consume us, and we were pushing it back with the slow pace we were on. We had been patient for so long, I wanted these moments to last.

I didn't care if it took all night; I don't think he did either. He wasn't rushing into anything, which is what I half expected. I thought he would have me in bed by now; his composure was amazing.

We finally brought our mouths together and kissed. I kept my eyes open for a few seconds to watch his eyes flutter closed and feel his lips part mine. He tasted familiar, like home. As our kiss went on, it became more urgent, more fiery, both of us becoming more aroused—I could feel it in both of us.

He pulled back from the kiss, still with his hands locked at the small of my back, my arms around his shoulders. His eyes spoke volumes as he stared into mine—they glistened with unshed tears and love. This man loved me—in this moment, he loved me. And I loved him, more than life itself.

We moved to the bed where I sat down on the edge. The bedspread and sheets were turned down. I could smell a flowery bouquet rising from them, realizing the sheets were clean. On prior visits to this bed, the sheets had always held his aroma. We didn't speak any words after I sat on the bed; didn't need to. Words just wouldn't have made any difference. Not then.

He knelt in front of me again, and my legs came apart like a butterfly taking flight. He held me around the waist and laid his head against me, facing sideways. I could feel his breath, warm and even on one of my breasts. I held his head tightly against me, fingering his wonderful hair, which was slightly stiff with hair spray. He looked up at me and straightened his back to look into my eyes more directly. There was a question in those eyes and the answer was a gentle nod of my head. There had been a whole conversation pass between us without any words spoken. It wouldn't be the last time.

His hands, trembling ever so mildly, reached to my blouse, and began unbuttoning it. His movements were tentative as he was forcing himself to take things slow and easy.

When he allowed the blouse to fall from my shoulders, he rolled back on his knees, beginning to remove his own shirt, but I leaned forward and finished, and let it fall to the floor.

I reached out to his face, cupped it in my hands and brought it to my mouth. Our kiss was passionate with increased longing, the adrenaline flowing freely. There was a difference in the kiss that had not been there before this moment. It was urgency with a love that would no longer be denied—could no longer be denied. We were committed—there would be no stopping this time. We would be consummating a love we had shared for two years.

As we kissed, his breathing was coming at a quickened pace and I could feel perspiration on his back. My breath seemed stuck in my throat as his hands found my bra and unhooked it, still experiencing the bit of difficulty he had from the first time he unhooked it. I smiled — no, I grinned against his mouth and he laughed softly as he pulled the bra off between us. Nice tension breaker.

His hands found my breasts and lovingly caressed them; brazenly I arched my back and thrust them firmly into his hold. My skin reacted to his touch by becoming hard and sensitive. I moaned into his mouth as he drew in a long breath and let it out in a sigh against me.

He kissed my face several times then stood up in front of me, causing my heart to hurt with longing. The small desk lamp illuminated him; I could smell his sweat. I inhaled deeply — his scent was one I never wanted to forget.

I was excited, petrified, aroused all at the same time, watching him remove his socks and toss them behind him. Slowly he undid his belt and then his jeans, stepping out of them with no difficulty, kicking them aside. His arousal was evident as I could see him firmness strain against the cotton. He hesitated for a few heartbeats that seemed to pound on for seconds in slow motion, then he bent over and removed his underwear.

Naked for the first time, he was overwhelming. The tension rose in me, and my body reacted with a flood of sexual fluids. I rose to hold him but, the moment at which I stood, he knelt. From his knees, he unbuttoned my pants and pulled them and my own underwear down, assisting me to step out of them.

He touched my leg, kissing it lightly, then worked his way up from my ankle to my hip, to my belly, to my breast, slowly standing as he did so, to my neck, to my mouth. My breathing was hard, full of sighs and other noises escaping that I had not allowed to escape in the past.

As he held me to him, the skin of our bodies finally touching each other in full, I felt him probing my mouth with his pleasurable tongue, probing against the junction of my legs with his firmness. I spread my legs and let him in between, the sensation causing my silky fluids to spread over him as he moved his hips ever so gently. He moaned into my mouth, I melted into his arms.

I don't know how, but we made it to the bed, a tangle of kisses and legs and arms. He touched my breasts as we kissed, moving his hand down my stomach, coming into contact with the growing moisture between my legs. His stroking was light, almost tame, as he explored me.

He took my hand and moved it down the length of his body and, with his hand, he wrapped it around him as he gently drifted his hips back and forth against me. It was a touch that left me both impatient and ready to please him however I could.

My head was spinning as I enjoyed the many new sensations that were both internal and external. The feel of him in my hand with his own hand caressing me was euphoric. A fervor rose in me as his fingers connected with my nerve endings that felt as though they were on fire. I arched my back as he drew his body over mine, positioning himself between my legs. We broke out of our kiss as he looked down the length of our bodies; he took himself in hand and entered me. He was slow and easy as he slid into me, and, just as slowly, backed away. He knew what he was doing—how far to push so as to not hurt me, how much to pull away so as to not break away. He kept his fingers on me between our pelvic forces. His mouth was alternately kissing me on the throat, down to my breasts, and back to my mouth.

A wave of warmth, starting in my pelvis, rose to my head in a rush of heightened sensations, and I felt a flare of exhilaration like nothing had ever felt before. I could feel his excitement increasing as I worked him between my legs. A sound rose from my throat, coming out like a murmur against the top of his head. He was moaning against the skin of my breast, feeling like a small vibration.

I again involuntarily arched my back as my excitement peaked, and climaxed against his fingers, causing my body to clamp harder around him. His own body began to stiffen on top of me; he brought his mouth down hard on mine. It felt like he was trying to take me all in. His orgasm inside of me was a flood of emotion and fluids as he plunged into me one last time. Our kiss was consuming each of us. A spark moved between us that could not be denied.

The heat in the room had risen around us to an almost uncomfortable level. We were both wet with perspiration. The taste of his mouth had taken on a metallic tang. His skin felt wet beneath fingers on his back and I could sense the tension in his muscles. He felt rigid and confident within me. The air was alive with the scent of our lovemaking, an aroma of sweat and other body fluids mixed with the roses from the dresser.

He relaxed on top of me and slowly lowered the full length of his body down against mine. We lay very still for several minutes, both of us trying to catch our breath. I was almost headachy from the energy that had just run through me. He lifted his head and I finally opened my eyes. He shifted and I felt him pull out. Yet another delightful experience—I actually shuddered with pleasure.

Steve smiled at me. His face was totally relaxed, totally at peace; a sparkle in his eyes. No words—we were still enjoying each other in silence. The rock star and his groupie. I still called myself that, yet I knew I was much more to him—I was his— what? Girlfriend? Future fiancé? I didn't know. Didn't care.

So, this was what it is to give yourself completely to someone. It was an amazing thing to do and feel. I was so completely and utterly in love with this man. All that he was, all that I was—we were each other's now. We had become lost in a world of each other in that night and I never wanted to be found. I would have stayed with him, given up everything, including me, to be with him forever. I wanted to stand up and shout that I loved him, before it was too late.

In one swift movement, he rolled off of me, pulling me over onto my side to face him. He brushed the curls away from my face and lazily traced my face with his index finger. He kissed me again—the strong taste of him welled up in my mouth; I sucked him in, tasting him, savoring him.

I threw my leg up and over both of his, and could feel him becoming aroused again. I pressed myself into him as I made it clear that I wanted him to take me again. This time it was my hand alone that brought him to his full rigidity, and directed him into me.

We rolled over again, with me on top this time. He pushed me by my shoulders into a kneeling position over him, dropping his hands to my breasts, which he fondled with increased vigor. He was thrusting into me from beneath me as I quickly caught onto his rhythm.

Again, our desire rose and burst into a culmination of love and lust. His lovemaking was all that I had imagined it would be, and more. When I lay next to him for the second time, I felt so at home, reassured by his strong arms wrapped around me, full of him physically and emotionally.

I kissed his face, tasting the bite of his sweat, feeling the rough areas of a day's beard growth scratch against my lips. He was watching me kiss him, rubbing his hands lazily up and down my back, occasionally low enough to caress the skin of my bottom.

We lay in his bed for a long time, face-to-face, skin-to-skin, gazing into each other's eyes, touching each other, not speaking. My hands felt his chest, the smoothness of the skin, the firmness of the muscles; down his abdomen, tracing the line of dark hair into the coarser hair below, running my fingers lightly through it resulting in a quiver running through his body. Again, I could feel him growing beneath my fingers.

He began to kiss me, working his way down my body, scooting himself downward in the bed. He went past my breasts, kissing both, awakening my own passion again. He kept working his way down, kissing my stomach, trailing his tongue around my belly button, and then continuing again. His fingers found that tender place between my legs and worked their magic. His face was directly above his fingers; I sucked in a deep breath when he kissed me there, replacing his fingers with his tongue and mouth.

This was a strange, but extremely exciting, somewhat embarrassing, situation. It felt good; strange, but good. I felt myself tense—he must have sensed it too because he came back up to my face and kissed me, finally speaking, telling me that he loved me. I told him the same. His voice was almost breathless; it was hard for me to find my own voice.

The taste of his kiss had changed—salt, bitter—the taste of the two of us. He and I were making love for a third time, holding each other tightly, almost as if we were afraid to let go.

When it was over, he rolled off me; we both lay face up in the bed, staring at the ceiling. He drew up the sheet from the foot of the bed, covering us. Steve turned toward me, onto his side, and threw one leg over me. My thighs were sticky from the lovemaking, and he felt wet up against me. The sheet beneath us was damp with sweat and other fluids spilled through the night. I looked at the clock—2 AM; we had been in bed over six hours. Sure didn't feel that long.

We cuddled, nuzzling up against each other, kissing, occasionally touching. He told me he loved me again, the he was happy we had waited, that he felt privileged to have been my first. I loved him more at that moment—it seemed my love for him continued to grow through the night.

Do you want something to drink? No. Eat? No. Shower? No (I didn't want to wash away his scent). Did you enjoy it? Oh, my, yes—couldn't you tell; how about you? God, yes—should I have used something—you know—protection? No—went on the pill a month ago, but, what would you do if I did get pregnant? Marry you—in a heartbeat.

He wasn't kidding—his face would have given him away.

We settled into each other's arms, content in our newfound love. He fell asleep as I watched. It had been a glorious night, one that will remain in my memory forever. As he slept, his eyelashes lying gently on his cheeks, his face relaxed, the stress lines all gone, he was very peaceful, without much movement or sound. He didn't snore at all that night but, a few times, I did hear and see him grinding his teeth. What was he thinking about to cause that? Occasionally he tapped his right foot, going over music in his head, I imagined.

I brushed the hair away from his face; it was still dewy at the hairline from sweat. He slept with his mouth closed, nostrils flared. Small pouty lips; slight overbite. Strong chin. Long, straight nose.

It took a long time for me to fall asleep. Too much excitement, too much adrenaline, too much Steve. I was enjoying the sight of him next to me.

At the age of 18 I entered the world of women—not just in years. I woke up when Steve got up and went down the hall to the bathroom. 8 AM. Sun was up, brightly shining on everything in the room, including Steve when he came back to bed. My first look at him in full light. He was definitely a good-looking man—all over.

The house was deafeningly quiet as he climbed back into bed, and held me. He said his parents would be home around noon; James, for dinner. We had four hours to ourselves and took full advantage of it, including a shower together shortly before his parents burst through the front door. We were just barely on the couch, he in shorts and a t-shirt me in one of Dad's shirts and jeans.

We spent the weekend under the watchful eye of his mother, the curious eye of his father, and the stargazing eye of James. His family was wonderful, becoming my second family, but, once they were home, it was difficult for me to make love with Steve, knowing they were only a wall away.

Monday morning we flew to Orlando to spend four days at Walt Disney World, my first time there. He wore his sunglasses and his hat—was recognized several times, signed a few autographs. He could be extremely gracious to his fans as long as they respected his privacy, his right to be a regular person. We walked miles through the park; it felt like we were a normal couple, in love, enjoying being with each other.

Friday we were back to Atlanta—Sunday came too soon and we were saying good-bye. I went back to Ohio—he went back to being a star musician. He had touched me more than physically and there would be no turning back now.

*B*ack home, my parents must have noticed the diamond, but didn't mention it; they also must have been aware that Steve and I had made love—that had been the plan for the last several years. They never asked. Sandy did—had to know all the details. Other friends noticed the ring at school; some asked; some whispered, starting rumors; some assumed. If someone did have the courtesy to ask, they were told it was a "promise ring"—a ¾ carat promise ring. Right.

The winter of my senior year was a difficult one.

Welcome to 1978! The year in which *WKRP in Cincinnati* went on the air with Venus Flytrap and Dr. Johnny Fever, who would one day run from the phone cops; Debbie did Dallas; fantasies were sold on a remote tropical island; and the *Love Boat* continued to give work to actors past their prime. Queen rocked us with their *We Will Rock You* anthem, which would become a war-cry at sports events everywhere; and the *Saturday Night Fever*

Soundtrack continued to spin its disco beat, keeping us all dancing the nights away. *Animal House* made me look forward to going to college and attending a toga party—did they really have those?

The band was going to tour Japan, a very last-minute, hurried arrangement. He would be gone for months—I was heart-broken but had to understand.

The same week Steve left for Japan, we had the worst snow-storm central Ohio had ever seen and I was miserable. This was not the age of computers, with their instantaneous communication capability to send messages to the other side of the world. I was dependent upon phone lines and the USPS, neither of which were reliable during severe weather—31 inches of snow on the ground pretty much overnight.

No school for nearly a month—first, due to the snow which didn't totally get cleared from the city streets for 2 ½ weeks, then due to the extreme cold that settled in, dropping temperatures below zero—too cold to go to school. Actually the radio said it was "economically unfeasible" to attempt to heat the schools when it was that cold. We were declared a disaster area—didn't mean much to me at the time.

No school—no phone—no TV except what we could pick up with rabbits' ears antennas. Stuck at home with the family—every teenager's worst nightmare, worse, even, than a family vacation. We ate (my mom was always a food-hoarder so we had plenty), played cards, games, and listened to music. I hung out in my room a lot, staring at Steve's pictures and being depressed and gloomy, content in my misery and tears—typical teenage girl stuff. I moped around in my pajamas for days and refused to get dressed. What for? Where was I going? I managed to make my parents miserable—mission accomplished.

Almost two weeks into the weather-imposed seclusion, the doorbell rang, causing us all to jump. Turns out a friend of mine, equally as bored and disturbed with his family, walked through the cold and the snow the eight blocks to my house. Eric and I had met in 8th grade when I joined the band; he was the tuba player; tall, handsome, basketball player. We were science lab partners through 11th grade; he helped me with geometry in 10th grade but neither one of us was very good at it (fortunately we had a teacher who was also the football coach, more interested in watching football films from past seasons than in teaching); I wrote his English papers. We were the best of friends. He'd call me late at night; my mom would hand me the phone and announce, "It's that boy with the deep, sexy voice."

So, he shows up looking like a snowman who fell down more times than could be counted. What was he thinking?! But, I was glad to see him—would have probably been glad to see anyone, but I'm glad it was Eric. My whole family was glad to see him—gave us a different face to stare at—we were certainly tired of each other. Eric and I retreated to my room where we spent the rest of the day bitching, laughing, talking. There was never anything romantic between us—we used to talk to each other about our loves, our friends, our dreams. I always talked of Steve—he had a different girl every week.

Eric ended up staying the next few days with us—his parents knew he had been coming here; they were good friends with my parents so they weren't worried. No phone—no way to reach them. He looked pretty ridiculous in a pair of my dad's pajamas, Eric being a foot taller than Dad.

The phones came back a few days later. We realized it when it rang. I picked up the phone in my room, expecting it to be an equally-bored Sandy, but it was a near panic-stricken Steve from Japan.

Are you okay? Sure—why? Couldn't call for two weeks. Phones out—lines down. We saw it here on the news—Ohio looks buried—you sure you're all okay? Yes—fine, stuck here with family and a friend who hiked over. Sandy? No—someone else. Who? Eric? Who? (The tone of his voice was rising nearly an octave.) A friend from school—you met him in Cleveland at the concert and again at the dance; remember? Oh—Eric. Uh huh.

Suddenly he sounded skeptical, all the way from across the world. He grew quiet, not saying anything. I gave him 10 seconds to recover and then I spoke.

What is wrong? What are you two doing? Nothing—listening to music—*your* music; he's a friend.

Eric tapped me on the shoulder and made a questioning motion—did I want him to leave the room? I vigorously shook my head.

"Steve, I love you, I love that you're worried, that you're hurt that Eric is here. I miss you so much."

He softened. His voice was hoarse with little of the normal tenor tone left from all the singing he had been doing. There was still a bite in his words, though, but it might simply have been from fatigue. We talked for nearly an hour. The band was recording music for a movie being shot there, and then would tour the island nation. He was still concerned about Eric; I was concerned about the Asian women and their almond-shaped eyes that all men seem infatuated with.

But, he was still reclusive, even in a foreign world, climbing ever deeper into his own world as the band's fame overtook their lives. He assured me he was monogamous—that there was no one else for him. I believed him, I think. Somewhere in the back of my mind there was always a nagging voice that questioned anything and everything.

I cried when we hung up. Eric held me as I bawled on his shoulder, as I had many times in the past.

The roads in our neighborhood were finally cleared, the cold subsided, and school was back in session in a few weeks. The mail came in a huge batch a few days after the plows hit us—15 letters from Steve—15! I savored every single word. The man had horrible handwriting and had difficulty putting words together in complete sentences, unless he was putting it all to music. But, I loved his letters, every word, every symbol, every heart he would scribble onto the page. I have them all to this day. Such a pack rat.

He was beginning to feel as if he really wasn't a part of the band but knew it was partially his fault—traveling separately, leaving tours, staying in separate hotels. In his heart he knew he was a primary reason for their success, but, in his mind, in all of his troubled uncertainty, he didn't feel he belonged to any of it.

So, he compensated — over compensated. He was beginning to exert more control as far as song-writing and arranging were concerned. He had become stern in his quest for recording and performance perfection, insisting that takes be repeated over and over until he found that perfection.

The other band members, at first complaining about his reclusiveness, which seemed to them to say he didn't care, were now complaining that he was taking their control away and perhaps cared too much. Was it ego? Probably: on all their shoulders. Did I understand it? Hardly.

They were in Tokyo, so I was able to write him back, and I think I probably over did it. Wrote to him everyday after getting home from school. He wanted to know everything I was doing so I let him know. It became something like a girl's diary. He still has my letters too, after all these years. What does that say about this man?

As my senior year was coming to an end, he could sense the sadness with which I wrote about leaving school, the fear about going off to college and the anticipation of his homecoming.

Prom was nothing to me — there would be no surprise visit from him as he was in concert the whole week leading up to the dance — and I would not stand to have him fly from Japan just for that. We talked about the dance on the phone a bit. I didn't want to go — could not have cared less. He tried to convince me to go with a friend but I wouldn't budge. Stubborn — I got it from my mother.

He sent me flowers that arrived the night of the prom — orchids and roses. My God, they were so beautiful. A package came with them — the tapes of the album they had recorded. I spent the night in my room, mooning over his picture and dying to the sound of his voice. This was better than some dance.

Senior Day was Wednesday the week following Prom. By tradition, seniors skipped school that day and went to Cedar Point, an amusement park on Lake Erie. Unfortunately for us, the new school superintendent proclaimed any senior that skipped school that day would not graduate. Talk about taking the fun out of being a senior.

So, we stayed in school—and raised a little hell: threw our books out the windows at a pre-arranged time; commandeered the overhead speaker and played rock music; dumped Kool-Aid into the pool while the swim team was practicing, turning some of them a nice shade of orange (Steve particularly liked that one). And for the piece de resistance—eleven of us streaked around the building—yes, me included.

Graduation was the following week: a sad, tearful occasion. I won a journalism award and one for both the writing I had done for the newspaper and the photography for the yearbook; a band award and my varsity letters for swim team (as a timer) and football (as the trainer). I wore my white, one size does not fit all, graduation gown and flat hat with my gold top 10% of the class cord around my neck. Underneath, we girls were supposed to have on white dresses—not me- white shirt with blue jeans rolled up to the knees. I was afraid I would trip going up to the podium to get my diploma so I wore new white tennis shoes, much to my mother's dismay.

Steve again sent me flowers—roses this time—all red—long-stemmed. And a diamond necklace: one perfect diamond on a heart that floated on the chain. The man knew how to keep a woman happy.

He came home two weeks later, June 16, 1978. I met him in Cleveland; we were going to spend two nights at my parents' house, then two in Atlanta and then we were off on a summer tour—my last summer tour—this one for their fourth album, *Abandon*.

I waited at the gate for his plane from Los Angeles—he had landed there from Japan four hours ago and dashed to another gate to catch this flight. It had been six months since I saw him. My hair was short again, still brunette; I had new glasses—pink plastic frames—"girls' frames"—he should like that; jeans, white shirt—Dad's shirt actually. Poor Dad—I was always taking his shirts.

As I waited, standing at the plate glass window, watching jets come and go, time ticked away slowly, painfully slowly. Finally, a large 747 was slowly directed into the gate area. I watched the precision with which a man with two orange cones in his hands directed that huge piece of machinery into a tiny space. It brought a thrill to my heart to think my Steve was on that plane. I could see the pilots through their windows and silently thanked them for bringing him to me safely. My heart took flight as the doors were opened after the walkway was pushed forward, waiting for people to begin making their way off the plane. I couldn't stand still, fidgeting; my stomach was twisted; the strength suddenly threatened to escape from my legs.

A lady in a wheelchair was first, propelled by a stewardess (they were still called that back then). A few other assorted people came next, all searching the crowd for a familiar face. My familiar face came next down the walkway, head hanging low, but I would know that stupid hat anywhere—someday we were going to have to have a ritual burn for it! His walk had a little less bounce in it, a little more shuffle to his feet and he may have been favoring his left leg a little.

When he crossed the threshold between the walkway and the airport, he lifted his head and scanned the crowd through mirrored sunglasses. He was biting his bottom lip, his jaw looked tense, grooves around his mouth deep. Had I been able to see his eyes at that point, I would have seen very blood-shot, half-opened brown eyes with very heavy lids, darkness underneath. His hair was down and straight, several inches below his shoulders now. He had on a black leather jacket (strange for June), jeans that had seen better days, a t-shirt with Japanese writing on it, and bright red tennis shoes, one of which was untied, laces dancing as he walked.

As his sunglasses-hidden eyes found mine, he smiled, a closed-mouth smile, raising his eyebrows, and made his way to me through the crowd. I backed up against the glass I had been standing in front of as he approached. He dropped the three duffel bags he was carrying at my feet, swept the sunglasses off his face and kissed me, holding me firmly by the shoulders. As we kissed, his hands came up to my face and he leaned farther into me, pushing his hat up and off his head onto the floor. We didn't care until someone squealed and screeched his name.

We pulled apart; his face had drained of all color as he scrambled to grab his hat and bags off the floor and put his glasses back on. With my hand in his, we ran—made a mad dash through the terminal—feeling like we had been thrust into a scene from the Beatles' movie *Help!* This is what he faced everyday and what he feared most: being chased by screaming girls. I was getting a small taste of what this poor man went through everyday of his life; it was not pretty. We finally found refuge in the private lounge of his airline.

Both out of breath, we collapsed into each other's arms; he held me with an unusual amount of force, arms tight around my waist, making it that much harder to catch my breath. We remained in the lounge for 30 minutes, sitting in a dark, quiet booth in the back. Few words passed between us—I was content to simply gaze into his eyes, those gorgeous, but sleep-deprived, eyes I hadn't seen in months.

We finally made it safely to baggage claim, then to the car. Everywhere he went now people knew who he was—more so himself than the rest of the band—he was their front man—the one with the voice that launched a million crushes. Everyone wanted him. I had him.

He drove my dad's car home from Cleveland with me cuddled up against him. I wanted him to tell me all about Japan—I wanted to know everything he had done every minute he was gone—how the movie turned out, how the tour went. His answers were noncommittal, sometimes grunts. He was lost in his own world at that time—concentrating on something far away. He knew I was there as he absent-mindedly stroked my shoulder; but he wasn't really there. I never did find out where he went that day.

My parents were very nice to him, as if they had finally figured out that this relationship was going forward. Mom even hugged him; shocked me; shocked him more. John was finally more himself around Steve, mouth closed, no more wide-eyed staring; okay, maybe just a little. We all had dinner together, and Steve visibly relaxed, more eager to talk. I imagine he had a fierce case of jet-lag going on, but he was cordial, a gentleman. We sat next to each other at the table and he kept touching my leg beneath the tablecloth.

Steve and I hadn't spoken of sleeping arrangements to each other, but my parents and I had—many times leading up to this day. No big surprise—they did not approve of pre-marital sex, did not want it going on in their house—but, as I was now an adult, and, as Steve and I had been in a relationship for some time, they would, as they put it, look the other way. They knew we would go stay in a hotel anyway, so this was preferable in their minds, to that. "Just please sleep in your room and not right next to us in the guest room." Sure, put me next to my little brother who was sure to be up all night with his ear up against the wall.

After dinner, the fatigue was showing—he was nodding off during desert in front of the TV, so we said uncomfortable good nights and went up to my room. John had brought up all of Steve's bags, happy to do something for the star. Steve looked at them on the floor, sighed heavily and sat down on the desk chair.

I brought presents. You did? For everyone—have to unpack and find them; can it wait 'til tomorrow?

He was so tired, so adorable.

He was all the present I needed.

He smiled, weakly, eyes heavy and red. He started to take off his shoes but gave up—I kneeled down and did it for him. Did he get this kind of treatment in Japan from a Geisha? Why do I always think things like that?!

He stood up and removed the rest of his clothing, down to his

Fruit of the Looms and crawled into my bed—my virginal bed—holding his arms out to me to come to him. I did, eventually.

It was an odd thing seeing him in my bed under the frilly canopy of my childhood, his head on my pillow, his long hair flared out around his face on the pillowcase. I turned the radio on softly—not sure why; I wondered if they would play one of his songs. The sun was setting but it was still fairly light out so I closed the curtains to block out the light for him.

He was watching me make a fuss and finally told me to come to him before he fell asleep. As I started to sit on the bed, he told me to "lose the jeans," so I changed into a nightshirt and joined him. The man was so tired and drained—I didn't want to drain him further. I looked at him and he seemed so skinny—skinnier than the last time I saw him. His ribs were visible and I could see his hip bones jutting out. He said it was from the long hours, too much coffee, not enough sleep, too many shows. What was going to happen this summer? I had looked at the itinerary—they were playing sometimes two shows a day.

He told me not to worry—he didn't like Japanese food ("Some of it *moves* on the plate!") so he didn't eat much over there. He had eaten a lot tonight; I guess that was a good thing. I just didn't want him getting sick.

We kissed each other; he practically fell asleep in the middle of it. I let him sleep as I watched. For hours. Into the night, the wee hours of the morning, the glow from the dial of the radio shadowing us in an eerie orange light. He never stirred, never snored, never ground his teeth. Just slept. Probably the best sleep he had had in months. He seemed so at peace, so calm, so normal.

He was Steve Potts—the voice of my heart, rock star, destined for greater things—and yet, here he was in my canopy bed, sound asleep, lost in a world all his own for now, sleeping with a girl from Ohio he met nearly three years ago.

Three years—had it really been that long already? I never would have believed, if someone had told me then, that I would still be with this man—this star. I didn't believe back then that I would ever hear from him again. He pulled a bar band up from the lounge scene and into super-stardom, gold records and hits the country was singing. His voice did that—there was no mistaking it—when he sang, you knew who it was.

Unfortunately for everyone involved with the band, they had one week to get over the jet-lag, relearn the way home and get to know families and friends before beginning another tour in the Summer, 1978. It was hard and the road was going to be even harder—110 shows in 140 days. But they would endure it all—for the fans.

I was an adult on tour now. Nothing else was different. Except for the tension level between band and management, band and Steve, band and each other. The mere act of being together for so many months, day in and day out, performing, recording, doing it all over again without a real break, was beginning to wear very thin on everyone, particularly Richard, Ned and Phil whose children were growing up not knowing what their fathers looked like.

Steve was continuing to strive for perfection, which had become hard for Ned—he was a skilled guitarist who liked nothing better than his guitar rifts and solos. By the very nature of rifts and solos, they were not always note for note the same every time. That did not go over well with Steve whose pursuit of faultless music became an overwhelming obsession at times.

He always fussed after a concert about problems he had noticed, whether it was lighting glitch—their increasing use of computer-controlled lights was costing more money, more time for set up and take down, more headaches for an already tired crew; a sound mix problem; a musical screw-up; pyrotechnics that went off a fraction of a second too soon or too late—he noticed everything. No one else did. Not the fans, not the engineers (most of the time), not the other band members. It took a lot to get him calmed down on most nights.

Listening to old recordings of radio interviews and

interviews staged by their record label for promotions, his shyness and self-doubt are clear. The other band members were all eager to answer any and all questions put to them; Steve was always silent, answering only when a question was directed straight at him. And even then, his answers were disjointed, as if he hadn't been paying attention.

Their popularity continued to soar to new heights as they toured, but so did the obstacles. The more Steve leaned on me, the more out of touch he became. I began to see my presence there as detrimental, and considered leaving the tour. The other band members must have been feeling the same way as they began to avoid us—or were we avoiding them?

Toward the end of the summer, the tour coming to an end, my time with him draining away, I found out just how much I didn't know—just how naïve I still was—just how much I should have paid attention.

Salt Lake City, August, 1978—sold out—which concert hadn't been? Steve and I arrived a day ahead of everyone else—we were going to simply relax and enjoy one of our last days together. The last couple of weeks had been very hard—not only on us but everyone around us. Richard had started wrapping his wrists during performances, and icing them between shows. Ned occasionally had bloody fingertips despite heavily calloused fingers. Phil was in the midst of a painful divorce—his wife decided she had had enough of him being away so much. And Joss—he was the only sane band member with no obvious difficulty; he just loved music and loved this band.

Steve was looking forward to the upcoming break—a whole month. His tension level had peaked a few weeks earlier and was now back to a more even level. I figured it was the end in sight that caused his obvious relief. I was wrong. So very wrong.

There was something so different about him—there was no longer a tension wrinkle between his eyebrows; he had taken on an almost devil-may-care attitude; he wasn't eating much and what he did eat was next to nothing. His insecurity was gone, replaced with a hypomanic state.

I soon discovered why. He was using the heroin again—or had he ever stopped? That explained a lot—a whole lot. The sudden surges of euphoria, followed by the unusually-extended periods of sleep. I had noticed the change about a month prior to Salt Lake, and I realized that, thinking back, he was probably only using a couple of times a week—there were people who could control it—I had done research after the last episode.

I discovered his syringes, insulin syringes, probably "borrowed" from his mother, as I searched for a bandage, purely by accident. I had cut my finger looking through our travel case for a pair of earrings and caught my finger on a disposable razor. Clutz. Searching the bag for anything of a first aid nature, I found the syringes, some still with a light brown liquid in them.

Forget the cut finger—I didn't know what to do. I wasn't as shocked and disappointed this time, but I was somewhat dumbfounded, thinking, well, duh—you should have known! My first inclination was to get rid of them and not say a word, but what would that accomplish? Nothing. Then I wanted to scream, rant and rave, and generally make an ass of myself. Again, this would accomplish nothing.

My mind raced as I took this all in for a second time. It hurt that he hadn't told me, hadn't been honest with me. It hurt that he was using a drug to get him through whatever he was going through. He needed a drug; he didn't need me.

I left the bathroom, my head in a fog, carrying the syringes with one hand, bleeding with the other. He was laying on the bed in ripped jeans, shirtless, hands behind his head, right foot tapping in the silence. When he saw my bloody hand he jumped up, his face full of concern and worry; when he saw the syringes, it stopped him cold; he turned pale and stared at me, through me, heaving a deep sigh.

Three little words: "I never stopped."

What more was there to say?

I sat down hard at the foot of the bed, my legs no longer able to hold me. He got up, retrieved a towel from the bathroom, brought it back and wrapped my bloody finger in it. He held it tightly for a few wordless minutes, not able to look me in the face. When he checked it, it was still oozing but not dripping as it had been. He lifted the finger to his lips, kissing it gently, smearing my blood across his mouth.

My eyes finally met his as he looked up—I wasn't sure who it was I was seeing in those eyes. He had tears forming, releasing them to make the long, slow journey down his cheeks and jaw line; his jaw was tensed and his overbite more pronounced. I glanced down—he knew what I was looking for—he held out both arms, elbows down, for me to see the veins. They were scarred—both arms; inflammation in some areas. Nothing looked recent. Actually, his arms were not as bad as I expected.

How much? Hardly any—twice a week—max. Why? The rush—the feel—the escape—the departure—I dunno'; it helps me get through, helps me cope with me. Helps you cope with what? The guys, the aftermath of the shows, with me. Me? God, no—never you; helps me cope without you here, the loneliness and the emptiness.

He tried to explain what had been building between the band and him: that they couldn't agree on anything, that he felt so isolated, why he felt he needed this monster of a drug. Could he live without it? Probably. Did he want to? Not right now. Really only so few times? Yes, I swear.

Then he hit me with a bombshell: did I want to try it? My immediate response was to shout a resounding *NO*. I had heard stories, read things about instant addiction, severe withdrawal, death. I was not a drug-user—of course, I hadn't thought he was either. He didn't think he was addicted as he was using so infrequently and in a relatively small amount that only lasted, maybe half an hour. The frequency and amount had not increased—so he had not developed a tolerance. He had very mild withdrawal symptoms at times—nausea, muscle pain—nothing serious. Serious? What did he want?

So, did I want to try it? This man had introduced me to a lot of things—rock, love, sex. Did I want to step up to drugs? What if my parents found out? This is what they were afraid of with me being on the road, or, at least part of what they were afraid of. Now I see why.

I didn't know if Steve wanted me to try the stuff out of guilt or if he thought I would understand more if I did. I just didn't know what his motivation was in asking me to try this.

There were things I did want to know, though: what about what you told me—about being in a fog and not knowing what you had done? Took too much, too often; I truly did stop for some months—went through horrific withdrawal—was sick all the time—then I started again, in low dose and not often. Did you ever do it before a performance? No. Have you done it before we—did it? No. You've got to stop—you've got to get healthy—you will kill yourself; I can't lose you this way.

There, I said it. I couldn't go on with this hanging over us. That sounded so high school. This was the adult world with adult problems. He was a rock star with mounting fame and mounting problems in his life he felt he couldn't handle. I wanted to understand it; I wanted to get it; I decided to do it.

I was never so afraid of anything—not of making a speech in class, not of going to Homecoming on the arm of a God, not of making love to him. Is this what love had brought me to? Was I doing this because of my feelings, or because I would do anything to please him? Was this the right thing I was going to do? There was no sane answer to that question.

The more I thought about it, the less I wanted to think about it.

He came back from the bathroom, one syringe in hand that looked to be about one-quarter full. He injected a small amount into a vein in his arm that he had distended with a tourniquet.

He sucked in a deep breath, held it, let it out. I presented the inside of my arm to him; he placed the same tourniquet on me, and, with the same syringe, found a vein and injected the rest into me. We had exchanged sexual fluids, now we exchanged blood—to some degree. He still had blood on his mouth from my finger.

I suddenly had a feeling of heat spreading across my chest and, just as suddenly, had my breath taken away, causing me to exhale with great force. The room didn't spin, I didn't take flight or turn purple. My arms felt heavy; my mouth went dry. Then the ecstasy set in—slowly at first, growing into an unexpected feeling of jubilation.

I looked at Steve—he was still gorgeous—he didn't have two heads, he hadn't sprouted horns, he didn't have anything else growing out of him that hadn't been there a minute ago. My head didn't start spinning around—I didn't spew green soup.

He looked good—better every second, if that was possible. My legs began to feel heavy; my neck hurt—no, "hurt" is the wrong word; it felt as though the muscles in my neck could no longer support my head. I don't remember a lot of details after that. I know we made love—several times. I remember feeling good—so good I never wanted it to end—was that him or the drug? Both.

The high didn't last all that long. I had thought it would but it didn't. We fell asleep briefly. I felt what I figured was hungover when I awoke. Steve was lying next to me, watching me. I don't know what he expected—that I would hate him? Hate myself? Be angry? Leave him? Love him?

I was disappointed in myself—that I had taken the drug, but I had to admit, the high was an incredible feeling. The sexual sensations were intensified and I wasn't at all embarrassed being with him, having him see me naked, as I had been every time in the past.

The tour for the two of us together lasted two more weeks until I had to go home, only to then leave home in two days to go off to college. Steve's and my relationship had been a little strained in Salt Lake but we got through it and carried on without problems between us. I tried the heroin four more times in those two weeks; still have the scarred arm vein to prove it. I felt guilty for doing it, obsessed with him, which is probably why I did it, and scared for him; for us. I had begun to wonder if my love for him was nothing more than obsession, like so many of those crazed fans at his concerts.

Last concert for me was Anchorage, Alaska—beautiful piece of our country! Just amazing. Flying in over the glaciers and the mountains was breath taking. The concert was sad and tearful— even he was crying during the second encore, which he sang directly at me—I was on stage left—the poor audience was watching the side of his body as he sang that beautiful ballad to me.

When Steve was on stage, he was totally himself. There was no ego, no anger, definite certainty and security. And that night he sang with extraordinary tone, incredulous emotion. He sang as a true member of the band, not someone who felt like an outsider. It was amazing to watch, a thrill to behold. *This* was the band I had seen in San Francisco—confident but not overly so, in love with their music and in awe of what they were able to accomplish together.

What was this night's difference? This was a much smaller venue than the stadiums and coliseums they had been performing in recently. No computerized lights, no pyrotechnics. Just the band, simple lights of blue, red and white, and their Alaskan fans. A nice, informal atmosphere. Relaxed, without all the trappings of a big-name band. Fans that didn't scream all the way through the show but who sang along, couples that were making out, lighters raised in approval and gratitude. This was what Steve wanted but would rarely ever see again.

After the show we went back to our hotel—last night together. Yet another last night. He was on a high without drugs tonight—his drug had been the performance; the show had invigorated him. I had seen it before, but not in a long time. Tonight there was no bitching about things that may have gone wrong.

He swept me into his arms as we entered the room, dancing me to the bed. His tennis shoes were kicked off then he removed his t-shirt over his head, tossing it toward the dresser where it missed and fell to the floor. His belt and pants were next—I loved looking at that man in his underwear—tonight was no different.

He was already becoming erect as he unbuttoned my shirt and slid it slowly, erotically down my arms, his fingertips dancing along my skin. I turned for him, presented my back to him; he unhooked my bra and as I turned back to face him, he removed it in much the same way he had my shirt.

We kissed, pressing out chests against each other's, grinding our hips together. His hair was wet from the show; his mouth dry from singing. He took the moisture from my mouth with his tongue and suddenly he tasted of me. He smelled of sweat and arousal and passion; it filled the room.

Steve knelt at my feet, reached toward me and unzipped my jeans, pulling them and my underwear to the floor at the same time. I stepped out of them, standing naked in front of him. I could see his excitement as I looked down and was sure he could see the moisture building between my legs from where he was kneeling.

He leaned into me, kissing my rounded belly, wrapping his arms around me, pressing his hands into the small of my back. He kissed his way down to the silky hair at the V of my legs. His hands came back around to my front where he used his long, expert fingers to spread me apart, gently, as if he were opening a delicate blossom, petal by petal. He kissed me everywhere, exploring me with his tongue; when he found that very sensitive spot on a woman's body, I gasped. I hadn't wanted to, but I did. Maybe it was more like a yelp. It was both. As I realized I had done so, I felt the color drain from my face, then, just as quickly, come rushing back, stinging my cheeks as they flushed with heat.

I touched the top of Steve's head and simply said, "I gotta' sit."

He giggled—the big goof giggled! I backed up a few steps to the bed, sat on the edge, sweating and trembling all over. Steve stood up, removed his briefs, presenting himself to me in all his male glory, came to me on the bed, knelt at my knees again and continued to ravage me with his mouth. I couldn't help but lie back, unable to sit up any longer. He hadn't ever done this before—briefly the first time we were together but nothing like this. Tonight was unexpected, fabulous, flustering. He brought me to an incredible climax that shattered my composure and any doubts I had about anything between us.

He kissed his way up my body, glazing me with my own fluids, until he reached my lips with his, reaching a different set of lips with his hardness, as he climbed onto me, sliding himself into me slowly; it all worked on me like an aphrodisiac. He expertly thrust into me, holding his mouth on mine, working his tongue in the same rhythm. When he came, it was with a force greater than he ever had before.

We collapsed in a sea of sweat, fluids, love. Who needs drugs when it can be that good, that sweet?

*C*ollege was everything I had heard it would be, and more, and less. I had my own small apartment instead of living in a dorm. The reasons were simple—Steve would be coming in November to perform, and would be staying over; I didn't want that visit complicated by a roommate and a floor of dorm mates with big mouths. In an apartment I could be an anonymous tenant. Looking back, I wish I had been in the dorm in some ways—for the friendships, the late-night bull sessions.

I tried out—successfully—for the marching band—not an easy feat in college. We had early morning practices everyday and every evening—two-a-days—just like the football team. The payoff was worth it: marching to crowds of tens of thousands, which was a little overwhelming at first (*you just have to learn to not look up into the stands,* he told me). I was going to a Big 10 school—a big deal. Football was nearly a religion during the fall. Our halftime shows were legendary. This was not high school—this was college—nothing small about this.

I also worked at *The College Post* (their motto: "we never sleep"), the university newspaper when they needed something no one else would write. For some reason, I always seemed to end up with the music stories. Funny how that worked out.

And, of course, I had classes—apparently that was the main

reason for going to college—I actually thought it was all the extra-curricular activities. Classes were okay—the only ones I really remember were photography and archaeology. And they were huge—not like the 25 students in high school; there were hundreds in some of the lecture halls. I was reduced to a number and a face on an ID card, which you better have with you wherever you go or you can't go there.

College was also a sad time, a learning experience in more than just academics. I had freshman syndrome—no longer a big shot in a small high school, I was a nobody in college—a face in the crowd, a zero. Professors didn't know me from any other student, and I didn't really know them either.

But I had Steve—he had become my refuge—my love to lean on. He called regularly—thank goodness. We would be on the phone for hours, him listening to me bitch and moan about being nobody, me listening to him bitch and moan about being somebody. There were a lot of times when we said nothing to each other, simply listened to each other breathing.

And his letters continued to come. Always funny in the way he would write 2-5 word sentences with no real beginning or end. His letters were full of frustrations, isolation, sadness. They were also full of love—no reading between the lines—he still loved me—even if I *was* a nobody.

The band was back in the studio to work on their fourth US release, *Abandon*; their last release had been the album they recorded in Japan: *Distance*, appropriately named. Steve took great pride in telling me about every song and what it meant, excited to have it come out in the Summer. Sometimes it would be easy to tell—a break-up, love—but, other times, there were other things not so obvious going on in those songs. They were working on a song about one of them going through a divorce (could have been one of two of the band members); one was about children and their spirit, their joy (did he want children? I didn't know); one was simply about enjoying the outdoors. Mostly love songs—the ballads of the era.

Their songs were getting continual radio play. You couldn't turn on a top 40 radio station in 1978 without hearing one of their songs. Their concerts had been recorded in some cities and were playing on Saturday night TV. Not the same as being there but great to see him nonetheless.

All along I wondered how he was doing—really doing; if he was healthy, sleeping, eating. How his emotions were—was he continuing his self-imposed seclusion or had he decided to break out of his shell a little? Was he thinking of me?

Was he still doing his drug?

I couldn't ask—I could ask all the other questions, just not that one.

Flyers announcing the band's concert on campus in November went up in mid-October, causing a flurry of attention: people lined up two days in advance to buy tickets. I felt rather smug knowing I didn't have to go through all of that. I wore my tour shirts like *my* badge of honor to class, much like the "stoners" had done in high school, and again gained some artificial popularity as people learned I had been "with the band."

Late October I actually went out on a Friday night with a new friend, Randi, a freshman too, suffering the same syndrome as I was. For some reason we had hit it off immediately; we both loved to write, both loved the band and music in general.

I had told Randi briefly about Steve and I when we got to talking about boyfriends—she had been to apartment and had seen the "shrine" I had. I confessed—he was my first and only boyfriend. Yes, the lead singer of *that* band—he and I were a couple.

Then I got the suspicious look over her glasses—the same look I used to get from high school friends—the "Yeah, right" look.

I could have shown her his letters, sent to me from all over the United States and Japan, or shown her the few photos I had of he and I together, or shown her any of hundreds of signatures, notes, locks of hair that I had, but rejected going to such lengths. If she didn't believe me, that was okay. Very few people did.

We were headed to a downtown bar to listen to a local band play that had become somewhat legendary in their long-standing gig. Gee, another band in another bar.

Down the Rabbit Hole was tucked into a small building at the bottom of the large hill in the middle of town. It was an appropriate name: the place was dimly lit, a yellow glare from unshaded lightbulbs, smoke cascading in exhaled waves through the beams of light. Laughter rose and fell in surges, ebbs and flows of noise, as conversations were carried on among the many patrons. There were people everywhere, three and four deep at the bar, pushed up against each other. It was nearly claustrophobic.

A TV set was on over the bar—*Dallas* was on; that Larry Hagman still looked pretty good. A jukebox was belching out songs when quarters were plugged into it—disco, soul, pop. Someone even paid to listen to one of Steve's band's songs, which caused a pang in my heart. The noise level was booming as conversations competed with the electronic noise boxes.

There were booths and tables; stools at the bar. Everything looked full but Randi noticed an empty table up by the small platform stage. It was all eerily familiar as I looked at the band's equipment. Memories of San Francisco and Steve and his band came crashing into my head.

After having a beer—not my favorite drink—three men and one woman appeared on stage. Nice to see a female up there—and playing drums! The three men in front—one 6-string guitar, one acoustic, one banjo—started warming up. We still couldn't see their faces as they were in shadow. The TV and jukebox were turned off at 10 PM, and conversations began to take on a more hushed tone. The stage lights came on, illuminating the band—Country Blue.

Randi and I had heard good things about them—no one had been kidding. They were a mixture of country, bluegrass and popular tunes with the ability to lighten the mood of the whole place. They played until 2 AM with several breaks here and there during which they talked with those of in the audience— all except the acoustic guitar-payer, Chris. He stayed close to the stage, drinking a bottle of beer. Another reclusive performer?

He was taller than Steve—5'11" or so—skinny, moustache and long blonde hair—that unusual shade of blonde that has brunette filtered into it but still can be considered blonde. He reminded me a lot of Steve. I watched him the whole night. He sang lead on a few songs—he had the voice of an angel with a head cold. Not the resonant sweet sound of my Steve.

Randi and I went to their performance the next night and ended up at the same table—we would soon become permanent fixtures there on the weekends.

The second night, the banjo player took a shine to Randi and talked to her at every break. I finally took the hint and left them alone, going to the edge of the stage and sitting there, close to Chris, waiting for Dean and Randi to finish whatever they were starting.

Chris and I struck up a conversation—I don't remember who started it—but we ended up talking during the next break too. I managed to convince him to agree to an interview for *The College Post*. We exchanged phone numbers, agreeing to meet the next day at my place, then we went our separate ways.

The interview went well: my first big interview for the paper. Pretty cool. I learned about all there was to know about this man who had graduated from the college 25 years ago and remained in town, first as a firefighter/paramedic—he had graduated with a degree in fire sciences—then discovered music and helped form Country Blue.

Chris was not a big talker—his answers were short and curt; I usually had to verbally prompt him to give me more. His voice was like gravel, low in comparison to Steve's.

We became friends that day in my apartment. We talked about me after the interview—he said that was only fair since I now knew everything about him. He wanted to know all about Steve — he commented that my whole demeanor changed when I spoke of him — he could feel my love for the man. That was one of the nicest things anyone ever said to me.

Chris and I spent all of that Sunday together talking, laughing about anything. We listened to his music — he brought me a tape of an album they had recorded and were about to sell in very limited release — limited to the college. They were very good — I enjoyed the music very much and enjoyed Chris.

My Steve's band came to town on a Wednesday night before my birthday. Steve arrived the day before — not inconspicuously either. The big, white stretch limousine pulled up in front of my apartment building early in the afternoon; I was walking down the sidewalk with Randi, book bag slung heavily over my left shoulder, saxophone case in my left hand. I hadn't expected him this early, but there he was, climbing out of the rear door without waiting for the driver. He had obviously seen me as he looked up the street right at Randi and me.

My heart was in my throat, threatening to stop my breath completely. Twenty-feet separated us but I could feel his heat already. Randi, completely in shock, stopped in her tracks, taking on that same star-struck expression my brother used to. My bag and sax case hit the ground with loud thuds as I released them and ran to him. A total teenage thing to do. I was still so much younger than him.

His arms opened wide and invited me in, wrapping me in his warmth, his peace, his love. No hat — no sunglasses — out on a busy college street. He found my mouth and kissed me as we — or, rather, he — stopped traffic on the sidewalk.

Randi quickly regrouped from the initial shock of seeing him, gathered up my stuff, and shooed us both into the building before a riot ensued. People knew realized who he was and were going to get at him. Thank goodness I lived in a security building.

We went up one flight, hanging on each other, and, as I unlocked the door, I told him to "be prepared." Randi laughed.

He stepped into a room filled with him and his band—posters, tapestries, tour jackets, photos, programs—were everywhere. I had saved everything at that time in my life and everything I had saved was up on my walls, it seemed. He told me it looked like a museum.

I introduced Randi to him—he shook her hand, flashed one of his most handsome smiles—she was his. She stayed for a few minutes, not saying a word, then made a gracious departure. She mouthed "Oh my God" at me from the doorway and walked out.

We were alone at last. He looked good—no, he looked great—not near as skinny as he had been. He said he had tried to be healthy by becoming a vegetarian but it didn't last very long—about 10 minutes. Just long enough for some magazine to print it so that the rumor was that he won't eat meat. He has been branded a vegetarian since 1978 despite making statements to the contrary since.

He denied any recent drug use—I didn't ask—he volunteered. I was glad to hear it but not totally convinced. He repeated that he was trying to do the health thing—walking a lot, trying not to drink as much. Time would tell.

He noticed the tape Chris had left for me, sitting on my cluttered desk—how he saw it among all of my junk, I don't know. He wanted to know all about this man and this band. I showed him the article from *The College Post*, about Chris and Country Blue; he was suitably impressed, and suitably jealous. He listened to the first side of the tape with me, smiled, said they were "okay."

Thankfully the limo driver, after waiting over an hour for instructions, brought Steve's bags up to us, interrupting the obnoxious conversation that was extremely strained.

We continued to talk about school, the newspaper, the marching band (I showed him a video of a halftime show that had been on TV); he wanted to see my school work (he sounded like my father) so I showed him some of the papers I had written for English, and a research paper on ancient Egypt for archaeology. He seemed interested and impressed. I just didn't know.

He told me about his band—tempers flaring constantly, at times escalating to near physical violence. He and Ned were constantly at each other's throats over songs—no matter what arrangement Steve wrote, Ned had a problem with it—too sappy, too much crooning, not enough guitar time, too many vocals.

As Steve spoke of it all, his face took on an almost light-hearted look, as though he were almost amused by the whole thing. He didn't actually say so, but that was the way it appeared.

He sprung a surprise on me then: he bought a house in California. When he had found time for that, I don't know. He dug a stack of papers and pictures out of his bag and spent the next hour excitedly telling me all about it. So, he had a permanent address in Los Angeles now; the Laurel Canyon area. Hmmm…isn't that where my first teen idol crush, David Cassidy, had lived at one time? Steve said he didn't over do it— it was not a big mansion, but a nice-sized home—5 bedrooms, 3 bathrooms, swimming pool, huge kitchen, formal dining room. It had everything—"except you," he said.

Why Los Angeles? Recording studio; record label national headquarters, always wanted to live there. It had been Los Angeles that he went to first so many years ago to find work in the music business. He felt as though he had "hit the big time" now. I was surprised he didn't buy a house in Atlanta; he admitted he had considered it but his mom convinced him to go be in the city in which he spent so much time these days.

Made sense, I guess.

The band all said warm-hearted hellos to me the next night, all except Ned who glared at Steve, nodded curtly at me and went on by. It didn't bother Steve at all — he was too excited over his house, being here, the soon-to-be-released album. He had finally taken the position that he was right — everyone else was wrong — to heck with it all.

Their show was fabulous, as always — they played our football stadium — full lights, computers, pyrotechnics. It was a madhouse once again; this was no intimate performance.

But you would never know there was any behind-the-scenes turmoil; when they were on stage, it was nothing less than professional courtesy. I could see the jaws clenched, Steve's overbite intensify with stress, Ned's forehead wrinkle, Richard's grip tighten to a white-knuckled hold on the drumsticks, but no one else noticed.

Steve was involving the audience more and more, pointing at them to sing choruses, holding the microphone out to them, catching someone in his eyes, widening them, dizzying hers. He was everyone's friend while he was on stage, including his band mates.

Four encores — the last for me — and they were done. He'd spend one more night then be off to a few more shows — colleges mostly — then to California to set up his house. Could I come for Christmas? He wanted us to spend it together — in his new house — as a couple — all to ourselves. Could I come? Nothing would stop me.

*T*he tour finally ended. I received one last letter from the road that sounded exhilarated as he was preparing to spend some time in his new house. He still wanted us to be alone, together, for the holidays; my parents were disappointed as were his.

I flew to Los Angeles from Cleveland, delayed on take-off so the ground crew could de-ice the wings a second time. Steve was waiting patiently—okay, not so patiently—at the other end. No kisses when I arrived; didn't want a repeat of our last romantic encounter in an airport.

He looked tremendous in his shorts and t-shirt. Again, he had put on a little more weight, visible in his face and his abdomen, but it looked good. His hair just kept growing, and he let it, he said, because I liked it long. He had it pulled back into a pony tail—it had to be fifteen inches below his shoulders now, but the bangs were dried into wings above his forehead. He removed his sunglasses and hat as we climbed into the limo—no fatigue, no dark circles. His eyes sparkled with a life and vitality I hadn't seen in awhile. When he smiled, it was full of fire and love.

We took advantage of the long ride to his house by finally kissing with the heat and excitement of long ago. He felt and looked like a whole new person. His demeanor was easy, unrushed, unfettered by worry and stress. The band had been apart just over a month now—he was in his own groove, his own track. No one had been badgering him; no one had been belittling his writing, his singing; no one was hounding him.

As we neared his house, driving through residential streets, he covered my eyes with his hands like an anxious little boy, chuckling all the while. I felt the limo turn sharply—into a driveway?—pause—for a gate?—then drive on, swinging widely around—curved driveway? And stop. Steve told me to keep my eyes shut as he helped me out of the car. When he swept his hands away from my eyes, his house swept my breath away.

He had good taste in houses—as he did in most things— except hats. While my bags were unloaded from the limo, Steve took me by the hand, leading me around the grounds. Then I got the grand indoor tour. This was his sanctuary—his place to escape whenever he needed. He had a housekeeper—he was a slob; a cook—he didn't like going out; a landscaper—no time for that. He had had one of the bedrooms converted to a small studio with recording equipment. And he refused to let me see the master bedroom yet. Hmmm...

We had a very nice dinner—but neither of us ate very much. He kept running his bare foot up and down my jeans-covered leg under the table. When we were finished, as I gazed at him through the candlelight, he smiled, tipped his head toward the staircase. Slowly, hand in hand, we climbed the stairs together, pausing at the door.

"This house is so empty without you, so lonely with only a pillow to keep me company. I'm so glad you're here."

The door swung open to a huge bedroom, aglow with what looked to be 100 candles—a pre-arrangement with his housekeeper. Thinking back, I did realize that they had been exchanging strange glances all evening.

There was a dresser with a mirror, a large armoire, closet doors. No clothes on the floor, no tennis shoes kicked into a corner; I kind of missed that. The dresser had pictures in frames of all different sizes: his parents, James, my brother (!), my Charlie, and some of me—one of me in that band uniform, a couple from concerts, one from Disney, and that sad, wrinkled picture of him and I in San Francisco. My how we have changed! I had blonde hair then and looked hopelessly innocent; he had shorter, very shagged hair and a stunned, but happy, look on his face. We both looked so young, so naïve.

In the corner of the room was a small Christmas tree, white lights on it, no ornaments, wrapped presents underneath. I already had him—that was all I wanted.

He held me from behind, wrapping me in his devotion. I held his arms, leaning my head back against him. We were quiet and tranquil in the moment, his spirit soaring all around us.

We spent two weeks playing house; so that was what it felt like to live with someone. It was a pretty good feeling, a nice experience. We could just be us—no pretense, no hiding, no fuss. We never left his house until New Year's Eve. I didn't care if we ever went out—I knew that real life was waiting just outside his door. Real life was not necessarily a good thing.

The 1979 tour schedule was finally given to me—reluctantly. It included a five-month tour of Europe.

Europe?!

My heart dropped; felt like it fell right to the floor, to be stomped on. He hadn't wanted to tell me, putting it off as long as he could. I didn't want to let him go—that is when I realized I was hanging on too tightly again. But, he admitted to having qualms about going, particularly for so long. He, and even some of the other band members, felt that they should spend more time in the States promoting number four: *Abandon*. But, management and record label executives disagreed and overrode the band. They were committed; they were not happy.

They'd be back, most likely, the first of May, spend a few precious weeks off, getting to know their families again, then the US tour would begin. Not enough time to de-stress, but there was no way to change it all now unless they flat-out cancelled shows; that meant lawsuits, money lost, fans lost. None of them wanted that, so, passports were dug out of drawers, visas obtained, belongings packed away into suitcases, band equipment ready to go on a cargo plane.

Steve and I went out New Year's Eve—first to dinner, then to a New Year's party at the keyboardist, Phil's, house. The restaurant was amazing—the fanciest place I had ever been in. The staff was all in tuxedos and they catered to every need—almost too much. This was my first taste of the life of a star. It was a little overwhelming.

There were other celebrities at the restaurant; I was introduced to several—mostly music people. I wasn't nervous; I didn't feel out of place on his arm for a change. He worded the introductions carefully: if one key word was printed in the papers—like girlfriend, fiancé, lover—it might hurt him. He told me he didn't care what they printed but I did.

I wanted to remain anonymous to the press—a shadow in the background that is easily dismissed. I had no interest in being in the business, didn't want any fame. I had been distressed by how often I showed up in music videos, behind the scenes shots and concert footage, however briefly it may have been. I didn't want to be the cause of any embarrassment to him, didn't want him to have to explain his teenage hanger-on.

He wanted to call me his fiancé on New Year's Eve; wanted to "make it official to the world." No way; I couldn't allow him to do that. Saying I was his girlfriend, his fiance, his lover would immediately send a ripple of shock waves through his fans. Right now he was "available," as far as they were concerned, which meant maybe, just maybe, he might fall for one of them. His seeming availability gave hope to every girl in the audience. I wouldn't take that away.

So, I was simply introduced as "Jean Heck, a good friend." That was fine with me. People could read into that whatever they wanted.

I went back to college the second week of January, secure in his love; happy; fairly certain his heroin use was curtailed or, at least, *very* well hidden. We didn't talk about it at all but I snooped; didn't find anything.

Our farewell was a heart-breaker—he was sending me back to class, to writing, to Chris and Country Blue (which disturbed him greatly); I was sending him to Europe—to beautiful women, to customs of sex and love that were very different than ours. I did not want them to go, but I didn't tell him that—I hadn't quite learned to tell him the truth.

My tears seemed to last forever as I flew across the country, the distance growing ever greater. He could no loner risk being at the gate with me so we had had to say our good-byes in another private airline lounge. At least we had a little solitude there.

Once I got back to my apartment, I cried more, knowing I would not see him for five months. It seemed so long—too long. But, I had survived him touring Japan; I could survive this too. Couldn't I?

No.

It was my turn to surprise him.

In a daring move, I flew into New York City the day of his arrival there, three hours behind him, and took a taxi to his hotel near the airport. I never considered that he might not be there, or that there might be someone there with him; I did consider calling ahead but blew it off.

Standing outside his hotel room door, listening to the silence within, I wondered if I was doing the right thing—suddenly I was *full* of wonder: thoughts of him with someone else. Should I have skipped two days of classes to do this? Should I bolt now while I still had the chance?

Lost in thought, doubt, hesitation, I didn't hear the next door down open then close; suddenly Richard was behind me and grabbed my shoulders—about sent me through the ceiling.

Richard!

"Hey, girl, nice to see you. He's in there—knock."

I screwed my face around a little, biting my bottom lip and continued to hesitate.

"He's there—he's alone. Knock for God's sake!"

When I hesitated again, Richard reached over my shoulder and pounded heavily on the door. In that very instant, I became shy, embarrassed, wanted to run and hide; no idea why. I quickly ducked behind Richard before the door opened; a school girl to the end.

As Steve opened the door, a stack of sheet music in one hand, Richard told him, "I found something I think belongs to you," and stepped aside before I could stop him. The look of total disbelief on Steve's face was worth the whole trip. He laughed, shook his head, laughed some more, and took me into his arms.

We went into his room and closed ourselves away from the world, one last time; tried to make-believe he would always be there, that he wasn't leaving. All I wanted to do was hold him, never let go—keep him from getting on that airplane. I wanted that night to go on forever.

There wasn't a lot of conversation between us that night, at least, not with words. We lay in bed all night, locked together in a mad embrace. For those few hours I could pretend he'd always be there.

Morning—time to say one last good-bye. I wasn't handling it very well; actually, neither was he. It had been such a mistake to come here and yet, it had been so right. The time was drawing near; his bags were picked up by the bellman, who reminded him, "Ten minutes to the car, sir."

I held him for all I was worth, willing him to be safe, to come home, to come back to me. I had made the decision to stay in his hotel room for another hour before I would have to leave for my flight after he left; I didn't want to make a scene in front of his band mates; besides, he'd be making a mad dash across the lobby and into the waiting car. No time for good-byes then.

He took off the leather bracelet I wore my on left wrist and strapped it around his; the painted flowers on it looked a tad strange on him, but he wanted a piece of me with him. He, in turn, gave me his watch in place of the bracelet—he never wore another watch again.

As I watched him put on his black leather jacket, signaling the beginning of the good-bye, my heart ached. This was it. He took my left hand, fiddled with his diamond there, and kissed it.

"That's my promise to come back."

We kissed one last time, me sobbing all the way through it. Time to leave. I stood in the doorway of his room where he kissed me again. We exchanged I love you's, and he backed down the hall, his hand held out to me. If I hadn't leaned against the doorframe, I would have collapsed. He waited for the elevator, still staring back at me. The doors opened and he stepped in—more memories of San Francisco flooded my brain. He held the doors open a few moments longer, waved by simply raising his open hand, and then let the doors close.

He was gone. This life of being in love with a star that was always coming or going—felt like it was mostly going—was very hard. I was beginning to understand why rock marriages break up so frequently: time—too much time apart—not enough time together.

Still moping around a week after I left him behind, classes started to get interesting—I was forced to get back into life, such as it was. School was okay—nothing spectacular—nothing fun; just trying to get the prerequisites out of the way before I could start the actual journalism classes.

Randi and I spent our weekends together watching Country Blue perform. Chris and I became good friends, despite the age difference; it didn't matter to him; didn't matter to me. He replaced Eric in my life, becoming a confidant, a shoulder when I needed one to lean on, an escape from the loneliness I felt inside. He did not replace Steve; he never tried.

He lived with his brother outside of town; never spoke of any other family. The band was his only obvious means of income— I didn't know if he was independently wealthy or if the band actually made that much money playing a college bar. I'm guessing he had money—at least enough to live on.

Chris and I went out a lot—to eat, to listen to other bands, to just talk. I think my apartment, so full of Steve and his band, make Chris feel a little intimidated. He didn't talk a lot about himself, unless I pried. I was getting better at prying—a requirement to be a good journalist. We rarely went to his house, and, when we did, it was briefly.

I got to know his band mates well, hanging out at rehearsals; the four of them had been playing together for nearly ten years; there was no animosity or anger seen in them. They all seemed to get along very well, respect each other, enjoy what they were doing—entertaining drunken, rowdy college students.

Steve's letters started coming about two weeks after he and I parted in New York. He sent me flyers in an assortment of languages over the next weeks and, eventually months. When the names of the band members were listed, his was second to last, sometimes last; the publicity photos had him behind someone, usually it was Richard's shoulder. It upset me as I started noticing this again; upset him too, making him feel even less a member of the band. But, he said, it was a managerial thing.

The tour seemed to be going well; he wasn't doing a lot of complaining. The shows were not in arenas or stadiums—more like large theaters—like Alaska. More intimate, more personal. He took some solace in that.

He called late one night from Sweden—great, so I could lay in bed and imagine him with some buxom blonde bombshell. It was March already—mid-terms were next week, then Spring Break. He had been gone nine weeks—felt like nine years. I knew it was him on the phone when it rang—no one else called me that late. I immediately got the third degree when I answered.

It was the first time that he sounded angry, directing that

anger at me. I was confused—was he actually accusing me of something with Chris?

Are you kidding me? How can you possibly think I would do that to you? After everything we have been through, everything we are to each other, all the waiting, after loving you completely? How can you think that?

He didn't get it—it took a long time to calm him down, longer to calm me down, to convince him; I don't think I ever really did.

He called with increased frequency after that night, despite the 7– and 8-hour time difference. And I answered. He generally called in the morning for his time zone, nighttime for me. I started staying home, not even going to Rabbit Hole with Randi any longer. Chris was understanding when I explained to him why I wasn't there—that I had become a self-imposed prisoner in my own apartment. Randi and Dean brought Chris over several times a week, to play cards, have pizza, listen to music, watch TV, whatever. Chris had finally gotten over the anxiety he felt among all of my Steve stuff, enough so that he could spend time there.

Dean and Randi had become a couple after their first meeting at Rabbit Hole. She was 19; he was 39. Age is relative. They seemed so perfect together, at least for that moment in time. We were college students—what did we know? Why does anyone become attracted to anyone else? Can it all be explained away as a chemical reaction? Physical seduction? Is there really such a thing as love at first sight?

Steve and I had heard it all regarding our age difference, our obvious other differences. We had, many times, wondered aloud to each other why we had fallen in love that night in San Francisco; what had we seen in each other that had triggered our feelings? Did it matter that we had ten years difference in our ages, or that he was a rock star and I was a student, or that he was gorgeous and I was chubby? Nothing really mattered to us; we couldn't explain the attraction, the speed at which we fell in love, the hold we had on each other.

Randi and Dean were on the receiving end of comments much like Steve and I used to endure, only the ridicule aimed at them was much worse as their age difference was twenty years. There had been many times that Randi had come to my apartment in tears because someone had actually had the gall to say something unkind to her or Dean. People can be very cruel—whether their motive is jealousy, self-righteousness, hate, guilt, whatever—people will always have an opinion, some will have several; most are misguided.

Randi nearly broke up with Dean several times that Spring because of all the talk. It was especially difficult at Rabbit Hole when Country Blue played, as Dean would join her at the table. People whispered he was just using her as a "piece of ass" (I had heard that said about me), that he should "act his age" (Steve had heard that said about him). She and I had a heart-to-heart talk one night, discussing love, pain and everything in between.

How did I handle it—the talk, the crap? I had no answer to that. I fought with my parents about the age thing, the "danger" of dating someone older, especially since I was a teenager at the time. They wanted to keep me safe, and safe meant being with a boy my own age. Where they got the notion that boys my age were any safer than anyone else I'll never know. But I knew the danger they spoke of wasn't necessarily an age thing. Randi was getting the same from her parents as their concern grew over her relationship with Dean. My only advice to her was to listen to her heart; to introduce Dean to her parents; pray; ignore everything else.

The most important thing that had helped my parents with Steve was that my dad had met him that first night—Dad had laid eyes on him, had looked into those eyes and saw something he couldn't deny. I had thought, at the time, it was the worst possible thing to have happened. I was wrong.

As for everyone else—to hell with them.

As for yourself, you listen—you listen with all you have and follow it.

Randi asked me what my heart had told me about Steve.

It was magic, like everyone says: pure magic. When I laid eyes on him, something awoke in me that hadn't been there before. As we met and talked, my tongue felt swollen, like I'd never be able to speak; I couldn't breathe, or maybe I was just holding my breath. When we parted, I wanted to call his room just to hear his voice again, to see what he was doing, to see if he was having as much trouble sleeping as I was. Even after all these years, I still wanted to call him just to hear him—that breathy voice with the slight southern drawl.

My heart told me that something special was happening that first night, that we had a destiny over and above his music. My heart told me to do whatever I could to hold on, no matter what. I was anxious, jittery; paranoid and confident; couldn't eat and couldn't sleep. My heart told me to be strong, be myself and had allowed me to fall within minutes of seeing him.

So, she asked, how is it now? Almost four years later? Now that he's a star, an icon?

The magic is still there, still as strong as it was then, maybe even stronger. I long for his voice, wondering if he is thinking what I am thinking. I yearn for the sight of him because he completes me—he is the part of me that I do not possess. His touch is fire, his kiss rapturous, his scent inebriating. I want to be with him every minute of everyday. My heart aches for him every second that he is gone. You can never lose sight of what counts—love.

Randi sighed—she understood completely. She loved Dean, I could see it in her eyes, and could see that he loved her right back. Chris had even mentioned that he thought Dean was "hooked on her."

The phone rang suddenly, bringing Randi and I back to reality. It was Steve, from France—6 AM there. He still hadn't completely adjusted to the time change, something he would always have trouble with. He had a strong internal clock that was difficult to reset.

My heart quivered as I heard his voice: his tired, low, sexy voice in my ear; it still worked on me like a drug.

I settled into the couch next to Randi, phone in one hand, my other hand in hers. He told me, as he always did, about the tour (*It's going great but it's very tiring*); the fans (*They are much less obsessive than in the US*); the band (*Richard and Joss say hey*). It was small-talk, much like his letters had been recently. Something was wrong but I couldn't put my finger on it. It still couldn't be my friendship with Chris and I, could it?

He asked about school, my news writing, my family; skirted around the Country Blue issue. Randi laughed at something I said, I don't know what, and Steve immediately started questioning me, bombarding me with ridiculous accusations that were unspoken, but there nonetheless.

Who's that? Randi—my friend. Uh-huh—why is she there so late? We were having a girl talk. 'Bout me? Partially. Who else is there? No one. You sure? I think I'd know.

His voice had taken on an odd tone. I could tell he didn't believe me; he thought Chris was there. A tad exasperated, I handed the phone to Randi who talked to him for a few minutes then handed it back. His voice sounded a little more relaxed, a little less high-strung. He actually apologized, saying he had been so tired lately, with too many crazy thoughts flying through his head. I assured him once more he had nothing to worry about but he still didn't seem convinced.

The rest of our conversation was stilted: broken thoughts with uncomfortable silences. He didn't believe anything I had told him and was struggling to contain himself; I could hear the edge in his voice. There was no way I could convince him from thousands of miles away that I was desperate for him to come home; that there was only him.

*J*une 16, 1979; the entertainment segment on the news covered the return of Steve and the band from Europe as they made their way through JFK airport in New York City. They were greeted by hundreds of fans that somehow knew they were coming back in the wee hours of the morning.

Steve and I missed the show. He was already in my arms by the time it aired that evening. He flew from JFK into Columbus and came to me—tired, jet-lagged, disheveled. When he opened my apartment door and burst through it, I nearly didn't recognize the man, but, still, the sight of him made my chest tighten. His hair was pulled back into a pony tail, floppy hat on at an odd angle. He was thin—deadly thin—almost gaunt—hours and months of being on stage had taken their toll on him. His jeans were baggy, hanging loose on his hips.

When his eyes found me in my place on the couch, his face brightened; his cheeks flushed, giving color to the pasty appearance his face had. He threw the hat onto the couch and leaned over, kissing my forehead. The limo driver placed his three bags on the floor, wished us a "good day," and left, closing the door behind him.

We were alone—after six months of being apart, six months of uncomfortable phone calls, six months of loneliness. He sat down next to me, nearly exhausted. We faced each other, aware of the slight tension that had grown between us while he was gone.

His face was so tired in its appearance, eyelids heavy, half-closed; so scruffy with what appeared to be a few days growth of beard; and he had allowed his sideburns to grow out while he had been gone. His hands touched my face; they were cold against my skin. No words passed between us—he brought my face to his—his kiss was gentle, loving, tender; something I had desperately missed. My hands came up to the back of his head as I held him against me. His tongue met mine; the taste of him was as always—just him—his very own flavor. The feel of his breath on my face was warm, sensual. His scent was part cologne or soap (I couldn't tell which), and airliner. After spending a total of nearly nine hours in an airplane he had picked up a peculiar fragrance that could only be airliner. I was drowning in the smell of him no matter what it was.

His kiss was like coming home for me, as well as for him. He wasn't coming at me fiercely, like a man who wanted nothing more than sex, but, rather, as a man who had missed me, who was still in love with me after six months apart.

I held him to me, as our kiss ended, arms wrapped around each other and heart to heart. He felt so good, so perfect in my embrace. We backed away, looking at each other; his eyes cut through mine and burrowed into my soul. I felt like fainting every time he looked at me that way. My hands reached behind his head again as he turned to allow me to free his very long hair from the pony tail holder he had it wrapped in. I fanned his hair through my fingers, pulling it forward to spill around his shoulders in a waterfall of brown crowning glory.

As I touched and played with his hair, his eyes flashed amusement; he knew how much that hair meant to me—he often joked that his hair meant more to me than he did. The touch of his hair was like setting my senses on a high, sending fire coursing through me. I shuddered with pure pleasure.

Tears were abruptly welling up in my eyes, spilling over the rims to take a swift journey down my cheeks. He reached out, touching my face, dampening his fingers with my tears. Tears were, just as suddenly, streaming down his cheeks; I touched them and wrapped that hand around his that was wet with my tears.

I was so glad he was home—there were no words to describe what joy I felt. I ached with the knowledge that our time together would always be brief, as his career would keep him on the fast track to increased fame and celebrity. But he was with me at that time. With me and only me.

We took some time to talk—he described the final European concerts as some of the best they had ever performed. He didn't like Europe, overall, though—"Too far away," "Too serious." He did like the fans, as he had stated in his letters: they were calmer than their American counterparts, more respectful in some ways. But he still loved the American fans, the ones who were true fans and not fanatics.

The sexual tension between us was growing and he finally kissed me with the fervor and adoration of our love. I could feel his breath rise and fall heavily in his chest as he exhaled against my cheeks as he relearned the nooks and crannies of my mouth. His long hair draped across my face like a veil as we lay back on the couch, reconnecting with each other. His fatigue had turned into desire, lust and love. There would be no denying him for very much longer.

But, instead of coming right after me and initiating sex, he simply laid next to me, holding me tightly to him, kissing me from my mouth, all over my face, and back to my mouth again. It was so much pleasure that it was nearly painful. I loved that man; that star. He had come home to me. I never wanted to let him go that far away ever again.

Then, without warning, he lifted his head away from mine and started to sing to me. There on the couch I had a rock star singing to me, a song he had written with Joss while in Paris.

I Miss You
By Steve Potts, Joss Weaver

I miss you
My heart can't tell you how much I miss you
I need you
My mind can't believe how much I need you
When we're apart my heart aches for you
When we're together my body aches for you
It's love—it must be love

Don't you know that I'm all that I am with you?
You awaken my senses, my mind, and my heart
Can't you see that I'm in love with you?
My heart speaks your name with every beat
You quiet my soul; soothe my spirit
You're all I need—you are all that I am

The nights are long
When you're not here, when I can't touch you
The road is tough
Traveling without you is harder than I had   imagined
Your smile comes to mind, brightens my thoughts
Your love awakens in my heart, soothes my mind
It's love—it must be love

Don't you know that I'm all that I am with you?
You awaken my senses, my mind, and my heart
Can't you see that I'm in love with you?
My heart speaks your name with every beat
My life is complete with you at my side
Your love is my love; I give myself to you
Your love awakens my heart, soothes my mind
It's love—it must be love

Nothing had changed between us—whatever anger or frustration or suspicion he had had or I had had was gone with that song. We were so much into each other at that moment in time, I wanted to freeze it and never let go.

He eventually told me to go to my bedroom; that he wanted to take a shower, wash away "the travel crud." He went one direction; I went the other. I heard the water running and waited a few moments, then, joined him, much to his surprise. I couldn't wait any longer for him to come to me. I had to hide my shock at seeing his skeletal body—the bones were visible in most places—it was frightening to think he had lost that much weight. I worried that the heroin had begun again and snuck glances at his arms, which didn't seem to show any traces of abuse.

The water fell on us both, like the light trickling touch of a fingertip. He took me to him into his arms and held me under the water; the feel of it as it rained down on us was seductive and I felt him becoming aroused. He sighed deeply, running his hands over my bottom and hips.

We kissed beneath the water spray—I loved him so much at that moment, I would have done anything, would have said anything. My heart was aching for him, as was my body. His tongue and mouth were colliding with mine. Our energy burned around us, in the air, in the water.

We both jumped as we heard a crash of thunder coming from outside—the prediction of thunderstorms had been a possibility all day—I was guessing they had arrived. A few more clattered through my small bathroom and suddenly we were dashed into darkness as the electricity went out. There was a little light from a small window over the sink but with a thunderstorm about to hit, the sun had gone out too.

In the darkness, in the shower, with the thunder clapping around us, our passion seemed magnified. Our embrace grew in intensity, our hands roaming and touching and mentally remapping each other's bodies. I took him into my grasp and he reached his full size in my hand, evoking involuntary moaning. In an instant, I was on my knees in the shower, kissing a part of him I never had. Impulsive? You bet—but, with the thunderstorm raging, my hormones and his raging, the longing and yearning for him, this seemed right. I worked my tongue up and down the soft underside of him as he ran his fingers through my wet hair. It only took minutes before he lifted me up off of the floor, lifting one of my legs up slightly, entering me with a softness and erotic slowness.

We made love in the shower, in the relative darkness of a storm, feeling the shower's water pour over us as the sky poured forth buckets of water outside. The thunder and lightning fueled our passion and made what we were doing just that much more enjoyable and pleasurable.

Afterward we retreated to my bed and lay together, holding each other, still touching and getting to know each other all over again. The storm had died but our feelings had not. He told me many times that day and into the night that he loved me. He brought me presents and gave them to me later, as we listened to the tapes of the live concert recordings. Their concerts did sound fabulous; and, I noticed, he sang the song he had sung to me. It was part of their repertoire now. As were many others he had written for me.

We ordered pizza late that night, and waited hungrily for it to be delivered. It was nice to see that he was actually hungry—he had been the one to bring up something to eat. He put a towel around his waist to answer the door when it was delivered. We weren't even thinking about him being recognized—he had become a normal person in my apartment that day and we simply forgot who he was.

The delivery boy, who looked to be no older than 16, read the total off to Steve, handed him the pizza, then looked up at him. The total look of surprise and stun were funny. His jaw actually visibly dropped and his eyes kind of glazed over. Steve laughed out loud, smiling at the kid, and said, "Yep, it's me."

The poor kid didn't know whether to take the money, run, or what. So he stood there senseless, in a near stupor. Steve patted him on the shoulder and shook him slightly, bringing him somewhat back around. The kid didn't say anything but gave Steve a crooked smile, took the money from him, and turned to leave.

Steve just shook his head and shut the door. I love people's reaction to him, especially after we have been alone and he has been allowed to just be himself. He forgets who he is at times and does dumb things like answer the door and scare poor delivery people out of their wits. At least that kid will have a good story to tell when he gets back to the pizza parlor: "Guess who I saw?? Steve Potts and he was in some girl's apartment and all he had on was a towel and he gave me this money and I didn't know what to say to him but it had to be him because this girl had all these pictures of him all over."

The disjointed ramblings of an excited teen.

It was nice to see Steve laughing and having a good time that night. He didn't relax that much any more—not able to let his guard down all that much. Like I said, we had become regular people that day—or, at least, he had, I always was. He was no longer a celebrity known throughout the world—he was my boyfriend, my love, my sanity.

In the next several days, we did actually venture out into Columbus—drove around and I showed where I went to school—big deal. We went out to eat several times and he did get recognized each time. He didn't seem to mind it much, though—he signed autographs and spoke kindly to his fans. Most were extremely humble with him. I took him to the photography lab and showed him my photos that were hanging around the lab and classroom—some of him, some of Country Blue, which he said nothing about, some of trains coming right at the camera, which he didn't like.

We took a drive north to my parent's house and had dinner with them one night. They were very talkative with him, asking all about Europe and the concerts. My brother was so much more relaxed with the man, finally. It was nice—kind of like a normal family. A nice, normal family get-together. Wish it could have been like that always.

He was due back in California eight days after arriving in Columbus—the band was going to get together for a week or two to go over the concert recordings in the hopes of releasing some as an album. Steve was not looking forward to going into the studio for any reason—recording sessions turned into back room brawls—this was the stuff he hated—it pushed him more into reclusiveness. But it had to be done.

I took him to the airport and walked him to the gate—floppy hat and all. Some teenagers that were gathered at a different gate may have recognized him: they pointed and talked excitedly amongst themselves, but it appeared that they finally decided it wasn't really *him*.

We said yet another tearful good-bye. Always those damn good-byes. He had gotten an offer to work on a movie soundtrack so would not be coming back during the rest of the summer, as previously planned. But, when summer school was finished for me, I would be going to him for three weeks.

I sent him away on another big mechanical bird, watching it slowly pull away from the gate and taxi to the runway. He was my love, my life.

How could I live without him?

*S*ummer school was actually fun—I was enjoying my two classes—advanced photography and a graduate-level archaeology course/independent study. All that meant was that I was to write a research paper on a topic approved by the instructor—mine was the Roman catacombs. Sounds worthy of a good yawn, but it was interesting, plus it kept my mind off Steve who was at home in California, working on songs for a new album. They were ready to release the live European album, *Retreat*; and a new one slated for Spring, 1980 release, *Day Dreaming*.

I liked the photography classes I had been taking. My favorite thing to do was work in black and white film—I saw the pictures more honestly than in color. I snapped pictures everywhere I went with an old 35mm camera Dad had given me; it had become my best friend, slung over one shoulder by a guitar strap Ned had discarded on tour a few years back.

I took pictures of Chris, which he hated—he was almost as camera-shy as I was; he said the camera emphasized the lines in his face. Styx played a town nearby that summer, so Chris took me, Randi and Dean over to it—I spent the night snapping pictures of the band and crowd. A budding photojournalist? No, I liked writing better, but not by much.

I also liked dangerous pursuits: trains—the kind that rambled slowly through the southern edge of the campus. I would stand on the tracks, in their paths, dangerously close at times. But I was always able to get great shots, including a few of panic-stricken engineers; and a few more of engineers flipping me their middle finger as they passed by.

I had taken many pictures of Steve when we were together after he returned from Europe, both in color and black and white. With me he was relaxed, himself. The film was able to capture his inner star, his inner light. But it also captured the boy that lurked underneath the moneymaking, rock star façade. My favorites are of him sleeping, the only time he truly allows himself to fully relax. He hated those pictures—he could see all his own flaws—they were evident only to him. The man was such a perfectionist. I was glad he didn't look that closely at me.

I also loved the pictures of him when he was writing music, pounding out rhythms on his legs, strumming the guitar, playing the piano, pencil in hand, behind his ear or between his teeth. And pictures of him kicked back, watching TV or reading—yes, we did those things together. There were so many pictures of him on stage; my shots are the rarities—the real man behind the glow of the star.

Summer on campus was like being at an empty crossroads. There weren't a lot of students who chose to hang around—mostly science majors still perfecting experiments, or others who had nothing else to do, didn't feel like spending three months with the folks after being free spirits on campus. I could have gone home, helped out with the high school marching band (something a lot of the alums did), hung out with friends, tried to find a summer job—no, thank you very much. I could have gone to California and done absolutely nothing with Steve. That was very tempting, but he had an album to work on and neither one us got much done when we were together. But, mid-August I would turn in my photography assignments, gather up all of my catacombs research and head straight to him for three weeks. Three weeks to play house with him.

But I made a near-fatal error in judgment that summer. I had been to all the new freshmen orientations in September, during which safety is drilled into all females: don't walk alone; avoid darkness; carry a weapon—a heavy purse, keys in your hand, etc. I listened—not carefully—but I listened. I was overweight, not pretty, wore Daddy's oversized shirts and jeans all the time. I wore glasses, for God's sake! Who would attack me?

My mind was definitely elsewhere on a Saturday night in late July, 1979; 19 years old, thinking about the next two weeks and getting to Steve. Camera in hand, I headed for the train tracks, my haunt in the evening when the shadows stretch long into the horizon. No moon coming up—it would get very dark. The silence had become ear splitting in the small rail yard until a train finally approached, thundering slowly down its track. I took my series of shots and was quickly satisfied, for a change.

Sighing heavily, about to take a short walk home, I slung my camera over my shoulder, lightly touching the strap that had once been around Ned's back, securing his guitar to him, stirring memories of concerts and music and Steve. The strap still smelled of Ned, the band, and the rock scene. I realized I still had Steve's watch on, lifting my wrist to my nose, inhaling deeply as I spread the links apart, exposing a build-up of skin oils and dirt that still smelled of him—his soap—his aftershave—his sweat. I ached with longing, breathing in his essence in that rail yard. Soon—soon enough we would be together again.

Head lost in a mist of thoughts of Steve, I headed toward my apartment. Wasn't walking with purpose, wasn't really paying any attention to anything, or where I was heading. I knew I'd get home eventually; I just wasn't in any hurry. Steve was all around me—in me—he was all I could think of—all I wanted. Now I knew I was obsessed. But I didn't care. The rules didn't apply to us anymore.

I took five more steps before I heard a rock kicked up behind me. Suddenly aware of every little sound, every little movement, I was afraid to move but afraid to remain still. I held my camera strap tightly, beginning to quicken my pace, winding through boxcars and railroad tracks.

I never heard the closeness of whoever hit me from behind, a blow that sent me into a wash of black fog until I lost all light, all thought, all consciousness.

I don't know how much later it was when I started to awaken. My first thought was that I must have fallen out of bed because I was laying on something really hard—must be the floor. And the back of my head was pounding. I reached around to touch the area of pain; my hand came back bloodied. Small pangs of panic were working their way through me.

I suddenly realized, as consciousness seeped back in, that I was facing a unique set of facts:

Bloody head—did I get hit over the head?

My mouth felt bruised and I could taste blood

Every muscle ached

My jeans were gone—Gone?! So was my underwear!?

My dad's shirt had been ripped open (he is going to kill me)

My bra lifted up but not removed

Camera and strap lying next to me (thank goodness)

Watch still on my wrist (thank God)

As I moved, more curious facts came to light:

There were bite marks on my breasts

Bruises—deep purple ones—were developing on my wrists

There was fluid between my legs

Sharp, tearing pain between my legs

I had to get home.

Two blocks away.

I had to get home.

Slowly, deliberately, I got up, searing pain tearing through me. Didn't see my jeans anywhere in the darkness. Great. I pulled the tattered remnants of my shirt around me and, in the shadows of the night, thankful that Dad's shirt hung halfway to my knees; I made it home to the safety and comfort of my apartment.

I was dazed — unsure why I was bleeding — a continual trickle down my legs. I wrapped myself in a comforter and sat, and sat, and sat. I blinked and the sun was high in the sky; I hadn't moved. I was still bleeding, could feel it trickling. My head was pounding. I was a bit light-headed.

I had several options:

Call the police — immediately rejected. This was still the day and age when rape victims were considered to be mostly at fault for whatever reason. And I guess that is what I was now — a rape victim.

Call Mom and Dad — just as quickly rejected. To listen to the lectures, the "I told you so's." I didn't need that right then.

Call Steve. I wanted him. I needed him. My ideals had all been shattered. I needed him to come and make things all better. But he was all the way in California.

Call Randi — nope — she was home in West Virginia for the summer.

Call Chris.

I called Chris. Didn't say what had happened but I asked if he could come as soon as possible. He could hear something different in my voice. All I could do, through my sobbing, was tell him to come. He didn't hang up the phone, just threw it onto his kitchen table with a loud thud in my ear, and took off out the door. He was coming through my door in less then 10 minutes; I hadn't locked it; still the naïve, trusting soul.

I saw Chris' face go through a wide range of emotions in that first ten seconds — surprise, shock, anger, despair. He came to where I had piled myself, wrapped in a comforter on the couch, kneeled at my feet, touching my legs. I involuntarily cringed at his touch but quickly relaxed. He looked into my eyes, my tear-encrusted, bloodshot eyes with his eyes full of compassion.

What happened? I was taking train pictures; got hit over the head; remember nothing.

He leaned toward me and touched the back of my head, drawing his hand away, dried blood on it.

His paramedic training kicked into high gear.

"Were you raped?"

I hesitated—was I? I didn't know for sure. Don't be stupid—don't go into denial.

"I think so. Chris—I—I'm bleeding."

He paled. The rest of the conversation is a blur.

Can you walk? Yes. C'mon—van's downstairs; we have to get you to the hospital; do you need anything? Purse.

Chris stood, grabbed my large leather bag that was slung over my desk chair—insurance card, ID, breath mints, phone numbers, pictures—my life was in that purse. Even in my shock, I knew I had to have it with me.

The hospital was a surreal experience. Chris drove me to the emergency entrance; I was immediately taken into a private room where I was poked, prodded, photographed (that was kind of ironic), questioned. Chris was finally lead away briefly by the police, at their stern insistence, to be questioned; he returned 10 minutes later. He looked angry—said they made it seem like he had done this to me since his clothing was smeared with blood.

Much of what they did to me that day was a blur. I received medication through an IV that made me even more light-headed, not able to think clearly. I was told I was going to have to have surgery for severe vaginal lacerations. I signed what I think was a consent for something, but couldn't say for sure that is what it was.

Chris held my hand, standing by the gurney I laid on through the entire ordeal. He was a quiet sentinel, watching over me. I remember him kissing my forehead before I was wheeled to surgery.

Hours later I saw Chris again—still holding onto my hand—in the same clothing, still streaked with blood. My parents were in a pair of chairs on the other side of my bed. Chris had called them while I was in surgery. The police had come back with a few more questions for Chris and I. I cried through them, leaned into him for strength. My mom kept crying off and on; my dad didn't know what to do or say, so he just hovered.

The silence that was hanging thick in that sterile room was suddenly shattered as the door burst open. There stood Steve—straight from the airport, suitcase in hand with clothing literally hanging out of the bag as though he had thrown things into it haphazardly then clamped it shut. No sunglasses—no hat. From the commotion I heard drifting in from the nurses' station, it was obvious he had been recognized.

His hair was a wreck, pushed up in the back where he had leaned into the airline seat headrest. His eyes looked like my mother's: red and swollen. There were obvious tracks of tears on his cheeks. T-shirt, jeans and one untied tennis shoe completed the look. Then he took me in.

My hair was still a tangled mess with leaves and other debris, partially shaved where sutures had been placed; dried blood caked in strands. Face swollen and bruised—apparently I had been hit in the face or had fallen face forward; I didn't know which. Oxygen tubing up my nose. Two IV lines—one in each arm. Glassy-eyed from pain medication. And Chris. Chris! Sitting there, my hand in his. Oh, God!

Chris cleared his throat, quickly dropped my hand, and went to Steve to shake his hand. They exchanged a few tense words.

Hi—I'm Chris—I'm the one who called you. Thanks, man; how is she? Hurt, but she'll be okay.

They were actually civil to each other. I expected Chris to be, not Steve. My mom turned in her chair to say hello to him; Steve bent over and kissed her on the cheek, stepped aside and shook my dad's hand. Then he turned his attention to me.

He came to me in the bed and sat on the side, tears flowing as he looked at me. I didn't want him looking that closely but couldn't fight it.

Chris had quietly left the room, my mom and dad close behind—"to give us a few moments." I didn't know what to say to him; I didn't want him to look at me, to touch me. What was wrong with me? This was the man I loved, who had just flown five hours across the country to get to me, the man who meant everything to me, and I didn't want him there. I was still in shock, disbelief.

He must have sensed what I was feeling; I may have physically backed away from him, or grimaced, I don't know. He stood up from the bed without saying a word, went to the window, his back to me. His shoulders were hunched and trembling; I could hear him crying—nearly sobbing. I didn't know what to do, what to say. My heart was breaking; so was his.

The room was quiet until one of the IV pumps started alarming. A nurse quickly came in with a new bag of some sort of fluid and began to hang it as Steve quickly snapped around to face me. The nurse, a girl probably in her mid-20s, finished her duty, asked if I needed anything, said, "Hello, Mr. Potts," then left.

I looked at Steve—his face was wet with tears, fluid running from his nose, which he wiped away with the back of his arm. He was biting his lower lip, hard enough to draw blood, a nervous habit, his overbite very pronounced in this stressful state. His face was contorted into sadness like I had never seen. He leaned against the windowsill, about ten-feet from my bed, staring at me, arms hanging helplessly at his side.

He wiped his nose again, this time with the bottom of his t-shirt, and then spoke.

"Jean—*how are you?*"

"I'm alive." It was the only answer I had.

"My God! My God!" He hit the windowsill with his hands to emphasize his words.

He didn't know what else to say either.

Another nurse came in with an IV injection—she looked at Steve and suddenly became fumbled-fingered, aware of he who was. All the nurses in the place knew by now. I would find out later that the nurses working my floor had drawn numbers each shift to see in which order they would come into my room while he was there.

This nurse told me the medicine was for pain (too bad it was for only physical pain—I needed something more for the mental pain)—the doctor had ordered it around the clock for now. She injected it very slowly into the line going into a vein, but I still felt the hot flush spread through my body as she did so. She nodded at Steve as she left and we could hear her giggling as she closed the door. Why do people get so silly around celebrities?

Steve slammed the windowsill again and swore—something he rarely did.

"God damn it, Jean! What were you doing? What were you thinking?"

I hung my head; his words stinging me like a slap in the face. Didn't he think I was already beating myself up? Didn't he think I was ashamed enough, feeling entirely ignorant and humiliated? I was in the midst of a crisis, probably a life-changing experience, and my boyfriend was swearing at me.

I looked at him with glazed eyes, said nothing. I was numb. I needed a time-out. But, in the back of my mind I was screaming that I needed him most of all.

He was crying again, head hung low, hanging onto the windowsill, shoulders quaking.

"Steve?"

He ignored me, or didn't hear me, or both. He began walking back and forth in front of the window, like an agitated lion pacing in a tiny cage.

"Steven?"

He looked up, face full of tears and runny nose. Jaw clenched, muscles tense, dark eyes smoldering. The fear and anger in his face were raw emotion.

"Give me time." My words were slurred from the medication.

He finally spoke: "Can I touch you? Hold you? I don't want to hurt you. You look so broken."

His words melted my heart. I nodded.

He pushed off the windowsill and came to me, sitting near my feet on the bed. He leaned over, placing his face on my chest and cried. I wrapped my arms over his back, ever mindful of the IV lines. There we laid—both of us in tears, crying for each other, crying for ourselves. I smoothed his hair, untangling it with my fingers. The drugs were causing my priorities to be a little skewed.

I don't know how long we laid still, his face on me, his tears soaking my gown. Another nurse came in—how many were out there? Just to see if I needed anything, if the pain medication had been effective. She was a little bolder than the others: she asked, very quietly if he (pointing at Steve) was him from that band? I nodded. Steve looked up at her fleetingly then laid his head back down on me. The nurse mouthed the word "Wow" and left the room.

My parents came back shortly thereafter, opening the door slowly, quietly coming in and resuming their placed in the chairs. Chris was not with them. Steve didn't move, still obviously crying, unaware, I think, that my parents were there. When he did realize it, he sat up, wiped his face with my sheet and faced them, apologizing; for what, we didn't know.

The stillness in my room was repressive. There was uneasiness in that room that passed between the four of us. I can't explain what it was. My parents broke the silence by announcing they were going to their hotel—it was 5 AM—they were tired—emotionally and physically—but they would stay if I wanted them too, but it looked like I was in good hands. No—I assured them—they could go. They both kissed me on the forehead; Mom did the same to Steve; Dad shook his hand. Then they were gone.

He and I were alone in our anguish again. He wasn't leaving me and I wasn't about to ask him to do so. He stared at me through eyes that were sad and angry all at the same time. He looked like he had aged ten years since entering my room. His hair framed his red, swollen face, hanging six inches below his shoulders, curling slightly inward at the ends. His overbite was still over-emphasized as he clenched and unclenched his jaw.

Steve touched my cheek where a bruise was blossoming into an array of blues and violets. The pain medication was making sleepy, my eyelids feeling ever heavier as minutes ticked by. He told me to sleep—leaned forward slowly and kissed me lightly on the lips as I drifted away from him and into darkness.

The next several days were the beginning of healing—a very long process I was to discover. I had a psychologist checking in with me every couple of hours, surgeons checking their work, nurses fussing over every little thing, police with more questions, parents scared and confused, Chris poking his head in once a day, and a boyfriend experiencing the same cascade of emotions as I was—anger, denial, anxiety, grief, extreme sadness.

A week later I was released into his arms and those of my parents. I wanted to stay in my apartment, stay on campus and continue classes in the fall, four weeks away. I had received incompletes in the two summer classes, able to complete them at my leisure. My parents agreed to allow me to stay, reluctantly. They were assured that I was safe in my apartment, and then they left me and went home. In two days I was heading to California with Steve to stay at his house for the month.

The night before we flew away, he wanted to talk "about a few things." We had both seen my psychologist that day, separately and together—she had arranged for us to see one in Los Angeles. We obviously both needed the counseling right now. I had major sexual concerns, having had major trauma vaginally, with surgical repair; pain was probably going to be a big issue when I was ready to become sexually active again (which I couldn't imagine just then), and STDs were in the back of our minds—I had been put on major antibiotics and tested—all of which came back negative.

Sex, which had been a pleasurable experience between Steve and I, may now, the psychologist told us, be a terrifying experience as the rape used sex as a weapon of humiliation and control. We were both devastated.

So, that night, we talked. He admitted to me that he was exceptionally angry with me for several reasons: for being alone at night in the rail yard (understandable); for the rape itself and the person who had done this to me, who was still out there somewhere (more than understandable); and, particularly angered because I had called Chris and not him. That was what bothered and angered him the most—I hadn't called him. I tried to explain why but he cut me off, his rising temper evident.

California was a mistake. My emotions were in an upheaval and Steve remained angry with me, with himself, with the situation. We were unable to have any sort of intimacy due to my depression and fear and pain. Most nights I ended up on a couch watching TV all night, or in one of the guest beds.

Flashbacks became an issue at night as my dreams were continually invaded by the rape, resulting in little sleep; the nightmares, as if I was reliving the entire experience, frequently waking me up screaming, being rocked in Steve's arms.

Our relationship seemed different, strained, almost pushed to a breaking point. By the end of the four weeks, we were hardly speaking to each other and neither of us really knew why. He was angry, jealous; I was guilty, embarrassed. We said good-bye in his driveway—he didn't go with me to the airport.

Something had changed—we both had changed. He told me he loved me and I loved him too. But something had changed.

School started—my second year at college. I finally had some journalism classes. I threw myself into them and into finishing my summer classes, simply to avoid life. I dropped out of the marching band, and accepted very few assignments at the college newspaper. I closed my self off from everyone except Chris. He came by every evening just to check in on me. Most times we sat quietly, him watching me do my homework. Must have been a real thrill for him.

Steve wrote; first every week for about a month, then his letters dropped to occasional, to infrequent. He called every so often, about once a month, if that. He sent me flowers on my birthday in November — the card simply said Happy Birthday — no other sentiment; nothing else.

I went home for Christmas break. Never heard from Steve until the holidays were over. No card. No call. No nothing. I was devastated and retreated to my bedroom, refusing to come out, refusing to allow my family to see my anguish.

He showed up on our doorstep, unannounced, the first week of January, 1980. It was the beginning of the end. He told me he couldn't resolve what had happened to me in his mind, that he didn't understand my relationship with Chris and had serious doubts that we were "just friends." He said he wanted to take a break from us — that he needed help; I needed help. I asked what he meant and he just looked at me with a blank expression, hung his head but quickly lifted it and met my eyes.

"I don't know — I just don't feel good about this — er, about us. I know it's not your fault. It's not the sex — I can handle that. It's something else and I don't know what it is. But I am so — so — devastated. I know it's ten times worse for you; I can't imagine what you're going through. I've tried to understand; I just can't."

And he left, his words still stinging in my brain.

He couldn't resolve *my* rape in his mind?! I didn't understand that, but, then again, I could, I guess. We had both been in counseling since it happened, sometimes together, most times apart. No one had given us any guarantees that our relationship could survive this.

My world crashed. I went into a depression that sent me into a tailspin, back into my bedroom. Going back to school was out of the question—doing anything was out of the question. I ate— a lot—and did little else. I wanted to gain enough weight so that no man would ever look at me again—whether it was to date me or hurt me.

I wouldn't see Chris until February, finally beginning to climb out of the funk I was in. He and my dad had gone to school and cleaned out my apartment; put everything from it in the basement. I officially withdrew from school, and, basically, from life. Chris came up once or twice a week and we continued to sit in silence, as we had on campus. Sometimes I was dressed, sometimes still in nightgown and robe. He didn't seem to care what I was wearing or what I looked like. He didn't care that I was obviously gaining weight. He just wanted to be with me, whoever I was.

He never said an ill word toward Steve, even though Steve had said plenty against him over the time we were still together. However, Chris did have a few things to say after we saw Steve on the entertainment portion of the news one evening. He and I had been watching TV in my bedroom; I was on the bed, he was sitting in my desk chair that he had pulled up next to the bed. Steve was announcing the release of his first solo album, slated to come out next month: June, 1980: *Talkin' to Myself*.

He had gained weight—more than I expected to ever see on him—his face was actually chubby, his cheeks rounded. He had a belly over his jeans—there was actually some meat on his bones!

His eyes were lifeless, though. There was no light, no spark. When he spoke, his voice was flat, hoarse. He was sitting crooked in a chair, almost as if he were favoring his left side for some reason. His face held little, if any, emotion—he didn't smile—his eyebrows were creased in between—the lines at the corners of his eyes more pronounced. His jaw clench bordered on severe.

The album cover flashed onto the screen next to him as he answered the interviewers questions. He was standing on a nondescript street on the cover, leaning against a light pole at night. Streaks of light blew by him—time-lapse photography of cars zipping past on the street in Los Angeles. And what did he have on his head? That damn floppy hat! Pulled nearly all the way down over his eyes. Leather jacket over a t-shirt; torn and tattered jeans; old, worn tennis shoes. I liked it—I shouldn't have, but I did. Couldn't help it.

Then the interview:

"Why a solo album?"

"I wanted to do something totally different from the band—I think I was successful."

The questions, generic ones about the album, continued for a minute or so. Steve shifted in the chair several times as if he were very uncomfortable—physically? Mentally? Probably both. Then it happened—the personal questions—right out of the blue. I would have thought that a star as big as him could have said beforehand, no personal questions, but apparently not.

"It's rumored that you recently broke up with someone very close, that you have been with for several years. No one really knew you were seeing anyone. Is any of this true?"

Oh, God, how did anyone find out? Who blabbed?

Thankfully, Steve looked even more uncomfortable than he had previously—at least thinking about us made him feel that way. He lowered his head briefly then raised it, cleared his throat slightly, swallowed hard, and answered:

"I had an issue of honesty with her—pure and simple. I was faithful, on the road and at home, but she had someone else and I couldn't stand for that. Life goes on."

I was stunned as Chris quickly turned off the TV. It was too late, though. I had heard it all and wouldn't have believed it if I hadn't just heard it all with my own ears. And I did hear it all right—I have heard it several times since as I have the interview on videotape to this day. Steve actually believed that I had slept with Chris while we were together! This was yet another dagger thrown at my heart. *That* was why he left me—it had little, if anything, to do with the rape.

Chris quietly called Steve a "bastard" under his breath and turned toward me in time to see me burst into tears. He came to me, sat next to me on the bed and held me, at first loosely, almost as if he was afraid he'd hurt me, then, as the minutes passed and I gradually become increasingly hysterical, his hug tightened.

I must have cried myself to sleep because I woke up hours later, in my bed, Chris back in the desk chair, reading by the light of the desk lamp. It was 1 AM—I was guessing my family was all in bed and Chris was spending the night. My depression intensified and we talked—I talked of suicide—I truly did not want to live any longer. I loved a man who thought I had betrayed him in the worst way. I felt I was no longer worthy of anyone's love due to the rape—I couldn't expect anyone to be so patient with me as to wait out my abilities; I was a failure.

Chris listened—he allowed me the time and the patience and the understanding I needed right then. He worked me through the suicidal feelings like a pro—I made it through the night and sent him on an errand of closure the next day.

I spent part of the morning still having a good cry over the whole interview thing. But, I managed to do one good thing—I packed the engagement ring in a cardboard box, sealed it and sent Chris with it to UPS to ship it back to Steve—no note—just the box with the ring. It was still in its original velvet box that had been sitting on my dresser since January, a painful reminder of what could have been.

While Chris was gone, in a bold move, I took down all of Steve and the band's photos, passes, tour books, posters. I had a lot more down in the basement from my apartment; I was actually surprised at how much stuff I had actually accumulated—my mother had always called me a pack rat—I see why now. I considered throwing much of it, if not all of it away, but threw that idea away instead. I did figure I would never look at any of it again, that it would be too painful to look at, but could not bring myself to get rid of it all—not yet, anyway. My brother fetched me a box and we packed it all away; took it to the basement to join the rest of my keepsakes.

Steve and I had made it almost five years; close, but not quite. I truly thought we would last a lifetime—how childish was that?! Childish and naïve. But I did think our love was strong enough to withstand anything; that it would last through time and space.

I still loved the man, but apparently, the feeling was no longer mutual. How do you give up on love that easily, that cavalierly? How do you just walk away without looking back? I couldn't— I had to admit I still loved him—I couldn't shut him out of my heart that quickly.

I wondered if he ever really loved me at that point, my doubts growing. Was I nothing more than a groupie that hung on too tightly? Was I nothing more than a "piece of ass" that he could have whenever the mood struck him? Was I a trophy—a virgin he could de-flower?

As I sat in my room, waiting for Chris to return, my doubts about Steve's honesty grew. The more I thought about it all, the worse it all became, until rational thought finally took back over.

The rape had affected him, too. I had to admit that. Whether or not he chose to acknowledge it on TV or to himself in private. It wasn't all Chris—Chris was just an easy target, an easy excuse—it was better than saying, "Sorry, kid, that you went through a horrible experience, a terrible trauma, but I can't handle it—I'm outta' here." He couldn't handle my pain, his pain; the stress; the anger that both of us had for different reasons.

My psychologist told me that about half of all rape survivors lose their partners within a year of the attack. Steve's and my relationship had been reduced to a statistic.

Time marched on—Chris came up nearly every day to see me, but most days I continued to feel as though I was walking in darkness—a darkness made blacker by the nightmares, the flashbacks; from the side effects of powerful medications; and from the loss of so much of me. Chris became a therapist, a sounding board, and a shoulder.

I ended up going back to a psychiatrist in August for medication management—my diagnosis of acute depression quickly became a diagnosis of bipolar disorder, called manic depression back then. I was placed on new medications, which, fortunately, assisted in mood elevation—"better living through chemistry."

August was ending and I was finally beginning to feel human again, like I needed to get back into my life, as if I was strong enough to face the world beyond my bedroom. I enrolled in two fall classes at the local branch of the university—advanced news writing and photojournalism. Back to working toward my journalism degree—didn't want to give up on all my dreams. That dream had been a part of me prior to Steve and it continued after him. I had to continue on too.

*S*eptember, 1980. We were all talking about who shot JR in *Dallas*; CNN was on the air with the first all-news network and people were questioning if we really needed all that information all the time in our face; Post-It notes were introduced to the world so thoughts, reminders and doodles could be stuck to anything and everywhere. TV sent us cruising on the *Love Boat*, solving crime with *Magnum, PI*, and fed us in a diner owned by Mel who had a waitress named *Alice*. Record albums on the turntable included Van Halen's *Women and Children First*, Daryl Hall and John Oates' *Voices*, Prince's *Dirty Minds* and Journey's *Departure*, all which of had people head-banging, slow dancing, and, well, departing.

School started the third week of September. I was pensive about driving to the campus, walking to class; there was a strong element of fear in my mind that endured. But, I didn't have to face being alone—Chris came—every day. Five days a week he drove me to school and waited for me in the cafeteria to drove me home. His green van was my new limo. I never asked how he could afford to drive the hour each way from his house to mine, and back, just to take me to school. Chris was the type that, if he thought I should know, he would say. I was very appreciative, though, and I let him know.

Unfortunately, September ended on a disturbing note. The last weekend, Chris came up on the Sunday, late because Country Blue had played the night before, but this time, he looked a little shook. Something was wrong—it was very obvious even though he was doing his best to hide it. He was unusually reserved, not meeting my eyes. He asked if I was feeling strong enough to hear some potentially bad news.

What could be worse than what I was going through?

He handed me the Sunday newspaper and pointed to an article—a picture of Steve with a short caption underneath—Steve and a blonde—a tall, *thin* blonde. The caption said her name was Rose; she was the new love in his life, traveling with him on the road.

The medication I had been given was better than I thought. I survived.

And my life went on.

With Chris.

My parents were more distressed with our growing closeness than they had been with Steve and me. Chris was 24 years older than I—I was turning 21 in 1980—he was 45. Again, an older man; a man with long hair; a man in a band.

Chris was a friend who had given up basically everything, to be with me. He finally moved up to my hometown into a small apartment in October. My parents had offered the guest room to him many times but he was extremely uncomfortable with that. There were a lot of times he spent the night in a hotel. I never did understand that. Even Steve had felt comfortable in our guest room more than once.

November arrived and, with it, my 21st birthday—yippee—now I could legally drink; big deal. I couldn't have cared less. Chris took me out to eat, and then back to his apartment. The furnishings remained very simple in his place—a few pieces of necessary furniture, some clothing, not much else. His house had been pretty much the same way.

We sat on his couch and talked for a while. It was becoming

increasingly easy for me to be out of my bedroom, out of my house. The world didn't seem all that different—the sun still rose and set every day; time marched on. But, I was still trying to heal and I wasn't with Steve. I was different; my immediate world was different; my life was different. In an instant it had all changed. But, the only person it really mattered to was me.

Chris was my world now.

Looking at him sitting with me on the couch, he seemed different all of a sudden. He was my knight from Camelot, who had saved me from myself, not astride a white horse, but, rather, sitting behind the wheel of a green Ford Econoline van. He was Chris—the friend who was patient with me, who listened to me. Who allowed me silence when I needed it.

As we sat on his couch, he kissed me, first on the cheek, holding my face with his hands, then gently kissed me on the mouth several times, softly, without any attempts to turn the moment into a scene of passion and abandon. His moustache against my upper lip and nose was bristly and tickled a bit. He seemed embarrassed as he pulled away from me—I almost thought he was going to apologize, but he didn't. He smiled his nervous, crooked grin at me, keeping his eyes locked on mine. Then he spoke, in his low voice with the raspy quality.

Was that okay? Sure. Yeah? Yes. Jean, my motive has been more than simple friendship.

I kind of figured that by this point; I wasn't quite that dense and out of the loop. He was so serious, something he rarely was—he was usually very casual; this was very out of character for him.

He leaned into me again, giving me a hug this time. I laid my head on his shoulder, finding it comfortable, almost familiar as my cheek brushed against his long blonde hair. He smelled of after-shave and shampoo. It was nice having someone's arms around me after so long; arms that weren't there to comfort me, but were there to hold me, to convey pleasure, and, perhaps, to convey love.

Chris and I became a couple that night; a couple that shared everything except each other. I was still suffering greatly from fear; guilt and pain; unable to even consider any type of sexual activity. And he was okay with that—where did I keep finding such understanding men who were willing to wait for someone like me!?

Chris finally moved full-time to my hometown in January, 1981, quitting Country Blue completely, and found a small house to buy.

He had been a firefighter/paramedic many years ago, so he took that profession back up and joined the department. It made me a little nervous, thinking about him fighting fires, but he assured me all would be alright: Only a firefighter has the skill and expertise to go into a burning building and rescue someone without getting hurt; only a firefighter has many hours of training necessary to maintain those skills, practicing in towers darkened with smoke and brick walls without windows, locating and dragging a "victim" to safety; only a firefighter knows the hell that will be faced inside the fire and is able to stand up to it and knock it down.

So, life went on, Chris and I went on. I managed to endure news about Steve and the band. A new album was coming out in June, 1981, their seventh, their greatest hits, and a Summer Tour would soon begin. Summer Tour—that used to be my place, now it was hers. He used to be my love, now he was hers. I still read the news about them, cried every so often, but went on, never allowing Chris to see those tears. I heard they would be playing Cleveland and was desperate to go—but I wasn't so sure that was a good idea. Chris and I discussed it at length and decided it was time to get some closure in that arena too.

The concert was heart wrenching. Chris had probably been right—it was a mistake but I had had to find out. The band's new songs had a totally new feel to them from the past music they had produced. Their new music spilled more into a rock mode with less drippy love ballads, less sentiment. Not necessarily a good thing, in my opinion. But they sang the old songs too—those were the ones the fans wanted to hear—and when they sang those songs I knew had been about me at one time, I cried silently as my heart ached for his love, my body ached for his touch. What was I thinking?

Steve looked thin—rail thin—up on stage. He had lost a lot of weight since the TV interview. Didn't seem to have the same energy, the same spark, he once had but those observations were probably nothing more than jealousy rearing its ugly head—he couldn't possibly have the spark he had had when he was with me—yeah, right.

There was still obvious tension between Steve and Ned but I don't think anyone else noticed. Randi and Dean, who had come with us, certainly didn't see what I was seeing. I only noticed it all because I had been privy to it for so long, and had had to endure it standing next to Steve. The others looked and sounded great—there was no doubt that this was still a very powerful, popular band.

The four of us were enjoying the show immensely when someone lightly tapped me on the shoulder—it was Curtis, the senior roadie who had kept me safe when I got caught out on stage one time. He had recognized me, despite the extra weight I was carrying, as he wandered through the crowd in search of girls to hand passes to and invite back stage. Nothing ever changes. Passes were still given to those who "fit the requirements."

He asked if we wanted to come back, either at the end of the show or now: it was nearly over anyway. Chris and I both hesitated but Randi and Dean jumped at the chance. Resigned to remain with them, we agreed, aware of what a bad idea this probably was, over and above even being at that concert.

Curtis led us through the crowd to the area at the left of the huge stage. I had been here before—I wanted to stay there—stage left. I had a great view of the band and wanted to see the rest of the show. I came all this way, after all this time—I wanted to stay. Chris agreed—Curtis placed a pass around my neck with a quick hug, and led my companions away.

It was hard watching the band from the stage—obviously harder than being in the audience. Seeing the guys so up close after so long caused little pangs of regret to flow through me as I watched them finish their last song. Suddenly all the lights were off except for a few back stage to direct the guys, and there they came, always exiting stage left.

Richard knew me right away—he hugged me, anointing me in his sweat as he did so. Nice hug—a great big bear hug. No words were spoken between us—his smile was all I needed.

Steve was the last one off the stage—he had kept his head down, running to the side of the stage following the other four, and quickly turned to face the stage in preparation to go back out. If they were keeping with tradition, they would wait up to two minutes, and then go back out for the encores.

Would he notice me in that short time? Did I even want him to?

He didn't, and I wasn't sure if I was annoyed or relieved, but Richard, in his infinite wisdom (ha!), tapped Steve on the back with his drumstick and pushed me forward as Steve turned. By the time he had completed his turn, time was up—the band was returning to the stage to thunderous applause as the lights were coming back up, but Steve hesitated.

He looked at me—puzzled, confused, almost as if he didn't trust what his eyes were seeing. There was no time for him to react further or to speak—the intro to the first encore was beginning. He backed onto the stage, still looking at me, as he nearly backed into Joss. I had managed to shake him up—pretty significantly from the looks of things. He didn't even sing the first few verses, microphone raised to his mouth, nothing came out—did he forget the words? It was very strange. He kept looking at me from the stage, further complicating things as he stumbled through two more encores.

Between the songs, as the audience clapped and stomped

their appreciation, Steve just stood still and stared at me, a wrinkle between his eyebrows, no other emotion. I returned his stares with sadness, and, I am sure, some involuntary longing.

The last encore was a slow, melancholy song—a new one I had not heard previously. It spoke to me in so many ways, so many emotions. It was definitely about us:

One More Look
By Steve Potts

One more look at her and I could cope
A chance to see it in her eyes if we're really through
Friends say she goes on, she's on her way

One more look at her, if no one objects
A chance to see in her eyes if the magic is really gone
Has she truly moved on, truly let go

We separated too long ago
Too many angry words ago
Now apart across the miles
Long lonely spaces between us
I can still see her face, her smile
Still feel her love, her glow
What have we done? What could have been so bad?

I wish her luck and love, separate from me
She deserves that and more
Luck, love and someone else
Someone to love, someone to hold on to
Someone like me

The encore over, the lights all went dark, the band left the stage under cover of blackness, the only lights those from hundreds of cigarette lighters being raised in the audience. I half expected Steve to leave by the right side of the stage to avoid me completely but he didn't; he came right up to me, grabbed my arm, and pulled me down an empty, darkened hallway, yelling back at a roadie not to allow anyone to come down after us.

I hadn't seen him since January, 1980—twenty months ago— I didn't know what to expect.

His grasp on my arm was strong—almost too strong—as he practically dragged me down that deserted hallway. About halfway down, the lights came on, washing us both in jarring whiteness with even harsher shadows. I was slightly behind him, slightly beside him, my arm firmly in his grasp, and, though it hurt a bit, his touch still sent my heart into that flutter-mode.

We stopped at the end of the hall, where it met a doorway marked Exit. I thought he might open it and do what—go out— throw me out? But, he turned and faced me finally.

He was so thin—as he had been on his return from Europe, and during that TV interview. The bones in his cheeks were distinctly visible, wet t-shirt sticking to his unbelievably thin torso. There were lightly darkened circles under his eyes, which seemed distant and cold somehow. His beautiful hair hung in sweat-dampened strands, dark to light brown with red highlights—had he done something to the color? The grey was all gone so he must have.

And he was pale: the color of his skin was pasty, almost a sick hue. He was 30 now; he looked much older.

He leaned up against the wall, looking at me, eyeing me up and down, arms folded across his chest, reminding me of how much I had changed. I suddenly felt extremely self-conscious, wanting to run back to Chris and hide away. But, I stood firm, almost defiantly, daring him to say anything derogatory. He didn't.

"Why are you here?"

That took me aback; why was he asking that, and in such a curt manner?

"Is there some reason I shouldn't be here?"

He bristled at that remark as if he may have had a reason but decided not to speak it.

"No," he said after a long pause, "no reason. I am just surprised is all."

His voice had a gentler edge to it and he seemed to be relaxing, dropping his arms to his sides.

"I still like the music, Steve. Nothing will change that."

I wanted to say I still liked him too, still loved him, but didn't want to go that far. But then the barrage of questions and answers came:

Are you here with him? Yep—you're here with her aren't you? Oh, you know? The whole world knows. She's here—probably out in the car.

That used to be my spot to wait for him after a show. The tears threatened to well up in my eyes but I was determined not to cry in front of him—not tonight. I wouldn't give him the satisfaction.

So, how are you?

We had the typical small-talk conversation; I told him about being back home, back in school; he told me about the band's latest happenings. We each avoided the subjects of Chris and Teri—a conscious effort on both our parts. As we talked, it became easier and easier to relax, the comfort level increasing with every minute that went by. He was still Steve Potts: rock star, rock idol, and normal guy. And I was still Jean Heck: former lover, rape victim. But we didn't belong to each other anymore.

I don't know how long we remained in that hallway, chit-chatting. It could have been minutes; it could have been an hour. We always were good at losing track of time, getting lost in each other. It seemed that had not changed. Somewhere along the way we had sat down on the floor, backs against the wall, literally and figuratively; when his knee touched mine and he didn't move it away from me, my heart palpitated. A few times he poked me with his finger in the leg to emphasize a point and it set my nerves on fire as I hungered for that touch again.

There were a few times there in the hall, when he looked at me and I could see the traces of—what? Love? Passion? Sadness? A mixture of all three? And what was he reading in my face? I couldn't bluff my way out of a lie if I had to. I was sure he could read my emotions easily as we locked eyes several times, holding each other in gazes of yearning, past memories, past love.

The tension between us was abruptly stifling. We both shifted uncomfortably on the floor several times as our conversation waned. I didn't want to leave him—I couldn't stay—but I didn't want to go.

We stood from the cold cement floor and made our way slowly—ever so slowly—down the hallway, swinging our arms at our sides, our hands occasionally bumping into each other until he finally took my hand into his; we wrapped our fingers silently around each others' in a familiar gesture.

Surprising? You bet.

He and I finally ended up in the band lounge, separating our hands from each other's prior to walking through the door. One last look; one last blink; one last sigh.

And, again, life went on. I didn't hear from Steve again. Didn't expect to. As celebrity entertainment news gained increased popularity, TV shows and magazines began carrying new stories about him and the band. Plus he was the focus of many articles in the teen magazines like *16* and *Tiger Beat*, which had been my favorites when my crushes were on David Cassidy and Bobby Sherman. I kept up with the gossip. So many of the stories, though, particularly those in the teen realms, were filled with inaccuracies. And it was mostly gossip. So many stories were also blatantly skewed to produce and sustain a crush in a teenager.

I didn't go to another concert—his solo tour, his band, or any other band. I couldn't bring myself to go to any—could barely bring my self to listen to music in general. All except Chris' singing—him I could listen to.

I graduated with a journalism degree in August of 1981. Didn't attend the actual graduation ceremony—didn't feel like dealing with all that pomp and circumstance—literally. I wasn't aware of it at the time but James, Steve's brother, got married that month. Wish I had known—I would have sent him a card. I always had liked James—he didn't judge, didn't lecture.

I landed a job working as a features writer for the local paper. One advantage of working for a paper was that I had access to all the news—fit to print or not—and that meant I could get all the news on the band and Steve—able to keep tabs on them—couldn't help it. Chris was enjoying his duties on the fire department; he had only gotten burned on the hand once when it was his turn to cook the dinner at the station and he accidentally touched the hot stove. Guess I could handle that kind of injury.

1983—the year that Cabbage Patch dolls were introduced and caused riots in toy stores; Sally Ride became the first American woman in space, expanding the dreams of little girls everywhere; CDs were introduced; and Karen Carpenter died of anorexia too young. The final episode of *M*A*S*H* aired, giving way to a bad spin-off; *Dallas* stayed in the top ten along with other dramas that helped push sit-coms out of the tope five TV spots. Phil Collins had multiple hit singles, from *You Can't Hurry Love* to *It Don't Matter To Me*; Billy Joel wrote a song about a model from uptown; and Culture Club sang about a chameleon that had great karma. It was a good, full year all around.

My relationship with Chris grew into a romance as I healed and settled into a comfortable routine with him. I moved in with him on March 6, 1983 and we were married five months later, in August, to the day. We didn't make love on our wedding night, not that we hadn't in the past, but it just wasn't to be on that night—I don't know if it was pain, a lost love still attaching itself to my brain, or what. I just couldn't do it. Chris was remarkably patient with me, working around the echoes of my pain and fear and loss.

Unfortunately, all I did was compare him to Steve in my mind, part of which would become a problem throughout our marriage.

During August and September of 1983, the band produced their 8th album together, *Dependence,* and Steve put out his second solo effort, *Winds of Change.* Music videos were becoming all the rage—to be successful, it was not only necessary to get the radio play, but also video play on MTV and the fledgling VH1. Steve had two videos, released from his second solo album, both of which featured Rose in fairly large parts. What a camera hog! She wanted to be a star, a model, or anything famous.

Hmphf. Well, she couldn't act—*that* was obvious by her performance in his videos. Her movements were stiff and unnatural. The only time she looked genuine was when she walked—her stride was a floating athletic movement, much like that of a panther stalking its prey in the jungle. She looked more at the camera than she did at him, the man she was supposed to love. It was obvious to me that she didn't really love him—why couldn't he see that?

Wow! *That* was the rambling of a jealous female—a jealous female who had no business being jealous or overly critical.

Chris and I had a cozy marriage. He understood when I was moody, was patient when I was depressed. He never pushed me to do things I didn't want to do and never denied me anything I wanted. We didn't have the romance, the fiery emotion that Steve and I had had, though. My biggest flaw was never letting Steve out of my heart completely; had I done that, perhaps I could have let Chris in more. I tried not to show it to Chris but, deep down, I am sure he knew.

June, 1985, was a critical turning point in the triangle that was to foreshadow my life. Ronald Reagan was President of the

United States; Tina Turner asked a nation *What's Love Got To Do With It?*; and TV dramas dominated the AC Nielsen ratings— *Cagney and Lacey, St. Elsewhere* and *Hill Street Blues.* It had been 10 years since Steve and I met, nearly to the day. So much had changed—so much that had gone right had suddenly gone so wrong and ripped us apart, physically and mentally, and drove us into the arms of others.

As hard as I tried, I could not totally turn my back on him— on Steve. He had hurt me deeply and, in the midst of a trauma, had done a lot of damage. I was already suffering with depression; his desertion made that all the more painful. But I understood; now, after all these years, I could understand it.

I had to understand my marriage too—something that was a more difficult task. I loved Chris—I truly did—but it was a different type of love than with Steve; a friend-type love. I kept telling myself that I would grow to love him romantically—just give me more time. Was that fair to him? Definitely not. But, it was all I could do, all I could give.

My brother appeared on our doorstep one evening—late one June evening—after 10 PM. John never came by that late—I figured he'd had a fight with Mom and Dad and had come by to sleep on our couch—he had done that on several occasions. When I answered the door, though, I could see there was something else going on—something more serious. I knew right away something was wrong and fought to keep the panic under control, as well as that strange feeling in the bottom of my stomach.

James had called my parents', at the request of his parents; it was the only number they had for me. Steve was in a Los Angeles hospital, critical condition after a suicide attempt— heroin overdose. John told me the message—call James at Steve's house—here's the number—what? He thought I didn't have the number to his house?

My heart sank. The tears immediately flooded my eyes and it was difficult to see through them. Panic set in with ease. John dialed the number for me and, when James answered, he handed the phone to me. When James heard my voice, the story started.

Rose had left him months earlier (thank heavens); packed up and left with no note, no phone call, no nothing. All she and Steve had done was fight. She left him for a record executive who could take her on a higher path. Whatever. He realized she had never loved him, that he had been a stepping-stone to fame and riches.

Steve's suicide note had stated regret over leaving me, his unhappiness with life in general. He had shot a large amount of heroin and had been found on the bathroom floor by his housekeeper who had performed CPR on him before the rescue squad arrived.

Paramedics had continued CPR as Steve had no discernable respirations, and had an erratic, faint heartbeat, no pulse in his extremities. They had defibrillated him with electric shocks several times in their rig, on the way to the hospital, after a tube had been inserted through his mouth for artificial respirations to be administered with increased effectiveness. He had had multiple IV lines started by the medics and a medication had been given—one that reverses narcotic action in the body— given several times without success. Steve remained unresponsive. The drug, usually effective in arousing overdose victims from their drug-induced stupor, was not effective. Steve was beyond that and remained comatose.

Can you come? When? Tonight—now—hurry, Jean; we'll get you plane tickets—pick them up at American Airlines. Just say you'll come. Hurry.

The urgency in his voice was all I needed to hear. Chris was at the fire station in the middle of a three-day on-shift stretch—I called him and explained what had happened. He knew I had to go and why. Never an argument. Never a harsh word. He said I was to keep him informed and come back soon.

Six hours later I was landing in Los Angeles—LAX—a nervous wreck, full of anxiety and a horrible feeling of doom. James and his father were at the gate; I thought for sure Steve was dead—that is why they were both there to greet me. I didn't want to leave the jet-way—if I didn't cross the threshold into the airport, I wouldn't know.

But, he was still hanging on. Silently they drove me to the hospital and lead me to his bedside, next to his mother. Steve looked so small, so helpless in the large bed. His skin was pale, almost grey under the harsh lighting. He was on a ventilator that was rhythmically breathing for him. There were smears of blood on his neck where a central IV line had been surgically inserted; four bags of different fluids hung above him on the IV pole, being pumped in at different rates. A tube was taped to his face that snaked into his nose and was attached to wall suction; a catheter hung on the side of the bed. Electrodes were attached to his chest, connecting him to a heart monitor, audibly and visually displaying his heartbeat—a slow but steady rhythm. A blood pressure cuff inflated and deflated on set intervals, and he had some contraption on his finger. He had so many tubes and wires—those are the times when you find out just how much more you can take.

Was he going to die? No one could really say. He had apparently injected a huge dose of heroin, determined to die, according to his note. I got a quick lesson in heroin overdose, which affects the central nervous system. Steve, we were told, had approximately 1700 mg of heroin in his system—a potentially lethal dose, depending upon his tolerance level, depending upon current usage. When his housekeeper found him, the needle had fallen from his arm, the tourniquet still in place and so he had been in a puddle of blood. His fingernails and lips had been blue. There was partly dried frothy white fluid, speckled with blood, coming from his mouth and nose, a clear indication that his lungs had flooded with fluid, pulmonary edema, an indication of overdose.

His note had been brief—he still had terrible handwriting (he could have been a doctor with such terrible, near illegible handwriting), and was not good at putting his sentiments into words—unlike the beautiful songs he could write.

Dear Mom, Pop, James:
So many times—so many nights—I am alone. I don't want to be alone. Can't be.

Tell Jean I have regrets—huge regrets—treated her wrong—love her still. Tell her I miss her—come back. She'll know.

I love you all—Mom, Pop, James, Jean—the band, Ned, Richard, Joss and Phil.

I just can't go on with the empty sadness.

Tell Jean I am sorry—she will always be my love. Tell her I will always love her through time and space.

Steve Potts

My God.

His family and I waited nearly five days for him—to what? Live? Die?

He woke up slowly. First by showing leg movements, then hand. His eyes opened; beautiful brown eyes that were now cloudy and lifeless; and he tracked movement after a day, but it didn't appear at that time that he was registering what he was seeing.

I kept in touch with Chris as the days passed and it almost angered me that he was so understanding. He kept in touch with my boss at the newspaper so that I wouldn't lose my job. Did I want him to come to Los Angeles to be with me? No—*that* I couldn't handle on top of all of this.

Five days—Steve was receiving physical therapy, still on the ventilator, still with multiple lines and wires and IVs. His eyes began to focus and take on more life and light. Finally, on day eight, he seemed more alert, nodding and shaking his head in response to simple questions. I kept out of his line of sight—I didn't want to disturb his brain any further than the doctors said it was already.

Day twelve dawned on a man who was fully awake and appropriately responsive. His family and I were ushered out the door into the waiting room so the ventilator could be pulled; he was, thankfully, able to breathe on his own. Unfortunately, we were all in the dark about his continued ability to speak, or even sing due to length of time the ventilator tube had been in his throat, in between his vocal cords. No one mentioned that lovely fact to him yet.

I still remained out of his sight. With the vent in place, he had not been able to turn his head much so he had yet to realize that I was there. I was actually dreading him seeing me, not really knowing what he would do, and how he would react. When he had started coming around and saw his mom leaning over him, he cried. But with me, who knows? When we had last seen each other, four years ago, we had parted on fairly good terms, and his note had said that he loved me still, so why be afraid? It made no sense to me but I was.

Would he want me there? Would he be angry with his family for bringing me out? For even calling me? A thousand questions raced through my head in panicked bursts, to which I was about to receive an answer.

His mom leaned over him and faced him closely. She simply said, "There's someone here who wants to see you." He raised his eyebrows in expectation as his mom straightened and James nudged me forward from his place behind me.

I gradually came into his line of sight, moving deliberately forward, watching his face for signs of changing emotions.

What I saw, as he saw me, was happiness, pure and simple. He blinked several times, not hard, just as though he was trying to clear his sight, grinning widely at me. He opened his mouth as if to speak, remembered he was advised not to do so just yet, and snapped it shut. But his eyes spoke volumes: the tears were there and flowing down his temples into his hairline; his eyebrows up, causing the wrinkles on his forehead; staring at me, boring into me.

He weakly raised his hand and I took it; he held it tightly, wrapping his fingers around mine. I cried—sobbed and bent over him, wrapping my arms around him in the bed as he did the same to me. We were back. Nothing would tear us apart again. I loved him, more than ever.

What were we doing to each other?

ortunately, the news of Steve's suicidal overdose never hit the papers—he had been admitted to a hospital that was very discreet with their celebrity patients. He remained in the ICU a few more days, the medical unit for a week, and then we took him home. Physically he was okay—no therapy needed; he was weak but, we were told, everything would come back. A speech therapist worked with him but his voice, apparently, was not harmed—thank goodness. However, she also told us that intubation complications sometimes appear later, particularly stenosis of the vocal cords, a stiffening of the tissues. But, for now, there had been no trauma to his mouth, teeth or vocal cords—no paralysis, no ulceration. We were all relieved to hear that good news.

I called Chris on day 16, the day Steve moved from ICU to the medical floor, and told him I would be awhile longer, and that I was taking a leave of absence from my job to stay in California until I was assured that Steve was on the mend. Chris was none too happy; neither was my boss at the newspaper—life went on—I was staying here and that was all there was to it.

After our eyes had met in the hospital, we were back together again. I didn't plan it and Lord knows he didn't either. All thoughts of suicide vanished; even the staff psychiatrist was impressed with how upbeat he was in their sessions. For someone who had apparently been extremely serious about taking his own life just weeks ago, this man was now extremely serious about staying alive and getting on with life.

I didn't leave his bedside for his entire hospitalization, except to go out and get changed, just as he had never left me after my rape. We held hands—his grasp, at times, was almost desperate.

His family left us alone after he was transferred to the medical unit; they were satisfied that he was on the mend. It was our turn to have some time together. I couldn't sit on the bed with him, something about hospital rules, so I pulled a chair up to the bedside and lowered the siderail for better access to him. His arm lifted as I laid my head on his hip, his arm settling back down, around my back. How I had missed that sensation—his arm around me, his hand touching me. It still sent those little shivers down my spine and caused great warmth to spread through me. Precious memories.

His hand brushed the tears from my cheek then he brought his fingertips to his lips—those pouty lips—I wanted to taste them—did I dare? Not yet.

In a voice that was hoarse and raspy, he spoke, playing with my hair.

How long have you been here? Since the first night. The first night?! I had to come to you—James called my parents. Why?—why are you here?—how can you care for me?

He slammed his head down on the pillow and looked at the ceiling, tears flowing down his temples into unwashed hair. He didn't understand how I still cried for him in the dead of night, how I wished it was his ring that I was wearing on my left hand.

"Steve—how can I not care for you? You are still the beat that drives my heart—you are all that I am."

He raised his head from the pillows and I raised mine from his hip. Our eyes were connecting our souls again. There was no denying it at this point: I loved him, with all my heart and soul.

"Kiss me?" He said it more as a question than a statement or request.

I stood up and moved to the head of the bed. His arm came around my waist, up my back and he pulled me into him. Our lips met in a soothing, short burst of kisses, which slowly became more inflamed with passion as his tongue met mine. No familiar taste—his mouth tasted of plastic medical equipment, similar to how the room smelled, and two weeks of only glycerin swabs for oral care. But it was okay—because it was him—it was all him.

I was in heaven—knocked off my feet—my knees feeble, wanting to buckle. My arm wrapped over him in the bed, my hand found his and I grasped onto it. His other arm on my back, swept up and down my spine, sending tingles through me—no better way to describe it. His mouth and mine were still a perfect fit, a perfect match, and he continued exploring mine as I did his.

My free hand touched his face, caressed his nose with my thumb; the oxygen tubing was still there, as was another tube, but it didn't matter.

He had several day's growth of beard—shaving patients in ICU was not a priority. His chin and jawline were scratchy with chestnut brown hairs growing in. I touched his hair that was tangled and a mess—washing hair was apparently not a priority either. That was okay—it still felt wonderful to run all that hair through my fingers, dirty or not.

We came out of our kiss but remained in our makeshift embrace, forehead-to-forehead, nose-to-nose. Our special silence filled the room. My tears flowed and dropped onto his face, mixing with his own. I loved him *so* at that point, grateful to whatever god or goddess had saved his life for his family, his fans and me.

I had to say it, shout it, and proclaim it. "I love you."

Three little words with so much meaning.

"I love you too. I was such a damn fool."

It felt so good, so right to hear that out of his mouth after so long. We fell into another kiss; I languished in his arms, in his love. The door opened, but we never noticed until James said, "Well, it's about damn time." I rose to a standing position so fast, our lips came apart with a pop, and we both giggled.

His mom smiled—she looked so much more relaxed than she had. We had had some time to talk, she and I, while waiting for Steve to come out of his coma; she told me how sorry she had been for everything; that she had been devastated when her son and I had gone our separate ways. She even revealed to me that he, too, had shut himself away from life for a while; that he *never* believed that I had cheated on him.

She had met Rose several times, although, Steve had never brought her to their home, which I found interesting—she had felt that they were an odd match from the beginning. She knew Rose had only been there for the money and the fame; she had seen it in the woman's eyes. But she could never reveal that to her son.

Mrs. Potts and I also spoke of my marriage, of the anger Steve had felt when he found out that Chris and I had married. What I wanted to know was how did *he* know about it? We had had a small circle of friends and family to the ceremony and reception—no one in Steve's circle of friends and celebrity. He was receiving a daily copy of my newspaper by mail—that way he could read my stories, my writing. My God! He was keeping tabs on me, just as I was on him!

Then she told me that when he had seen the wedding announcement and had been devastated. I twisted my wedding rings as she spoke to me, nervously wondering if she was wondering what the hell I was doing there, being married to another man. But she never asked.

So, now that Steve and I had proclaimed our enduring love to each other, and his family was aware, we had to get him home, get him healed, both physically and mentally. It was time for his release, 23 days after he had been rushed into the emergency room.

Back at his home, his staff had arranged a small celebration for his homecoming—balloons, a cake, and a cookout of his favorite foods. It was only his family and I, but it was very nice of them, and Steve was very appreciative and thankful.

The night of his homecoming, after the house was quiet, I found him standing in the bathroom where he had tried to kill himself, hands shoved into the pockets of his jeans. There were no traces of the heroin or of the blood that had been spilled; no evidence that five paramedics had been in the master bathroom with their life-saving equipment; nothing appeared out of place. The only thing I could see that might have been different was that the bathroom rugs appeared to be brand new—no trace of wear. Perhaps the old ones had been stained with his blood. I didn't know.

Steve's eyes seemed far away; he was, no doubt, going over whatever he could remember from that day. I watched him for several moments; he never moved. The room was, potentially, the last room he may have ever seen; it must have seemed strange for him to be there now.

He opened the large medicine cabinet behind the mirror, slowly regarding everything in it—Tylenol, aspirin, deodorant, razors, oral care items, one bottle of Valium—for sleep—one bottle of Darvon—for pain; nothing unusual there. No syringes, no heroin. I wondered if that was what he was looking for. There was a bottle of Methadone on the counter—given to him in the hospital to help him overcome his heroin addiction—whether he chose to acknowledge that he was addicted, he needed to get off of it. I hoped and prayed that he would, once and for all.

I stepped to him at long last and wrapped my arms around his waist from behind, burying my face in his long hair. He had showered when we arrived home; clean-shaven with hair that was back to being luxurious. He held my hands in his and squeezed. It was late—nearly midnight. His parents were in one guest room and James was in another; his staff had gone home for the night.

My bag was in a third guest room—James had nearly put it into Steve's room when he carried it up for me earlier, but I insisted he place it in the guest room—the blue guest room.

Steve and I hadn't been together intimately since 1979—six years ago. It didn't seem like it had been all that long but then again, it did. Sometimes it felt like forever. We hadn't made love since before I was raped.

In my arms, Steve turned to look at me, his face solemn, his eyes afire. He led me from the bathroom into his bedroom where we stood near the large dresser. I noticed the décor had changed a bit since my last visit—was that Rose's doing? If so, I didn't like it.

There was still a collection of pictures on his dresser—his family, James' wedding picture, a group shot of him and the band from several years ago. I was there too—after all this time: my old band picture, one of he and I at a concert back stage and that sad little picture from San Francisco, when we first met. Did he put them out recently? Probably, as, I am sure, Rose would not have approved.

It made me feel so warm inside to see that I had become part of his life again. I had pulled out his pictures also—they were in my wallet—two of him in concert, and one of him—publicity still from his solo album—on my desk at work.

His room was clean—the advantage of having a housekeeper; but I missed seeing the clothes draped all over everything and the tennis shoes kicked into corners. Even the clothes he had taken off earlier when he came home had already been swept away.

It was nice being in his room again—I had wanted to be here but truly never considered I would ever see these four walls again. The room was still cozy, as if I belonged there. Steve came up to me and slid himself in front of me, brushing the hair from my face with both hands, allowing his fingertips to trail along my skin. He cupped my chin in a loving, caressing manner; he was tender in his touch and in his stare.

I am so glad you came. I had to—there is no doubt that I had to. How long can you stay? Maybe another week, not much more. I'll take it!

He lifted my face, lowering his, our lips meeting in the middle. At last—a real kiss—not one in a hospital bed. His mouth was still a friendly place to be, familiar in its taste. His tongue probed my mouth in a full open-mouth kiss that was both passionate and calm all at the same time. Our arms wrapped around each other; his were comforting in their strength and touch.

This was a well-known position for us—we had been good kissers together; apparently still were. My problems at this point, though, were several, including Chris—waiting patiently for me to get home; the considerate husband who had seen me through my break-up with this man. My second problem—our break-up itself—it had been very hard on me, as Steve had not truly given me the reasons for leaving me, as if he simply wanted to be rid of me. While Steve acknowledged in his suicide note that he had made a mistake, there was still the memory of that horrible TV interview and the multiple print interviews during which he accused me of sleeping with Chris while I was still with him. His words had stung me like a slap in the face and had been some of the hardest things I have ever had to endure.

That whole issue had been discussed at the hospital between us—he explained that he had used infidelity as an excuse because he couldn't deal with the pain we were both experiencing—his lie was a psychological defense. He felt that, if he walked away, I would heal sooner without the pressure of his life to deal with on top of my trauma. I didn't quite understand it all, and it didn't make much sense, but I accepted his story. He apologized many times to me while in the hospital bed—I finally did accept, but I kept him guessing for a time.

There was also another problem with any kind of reunion between he and I—a more serious problem than the others; one that might not be able to be resolved. That was my psyche—my psychiatric condition. The flashbacks and nightmares had all but disappeared; the pain was minimal; the fear subsided, not quite gone. Chris and I had been together but not steadily, and had had many long dry spells due to my reluctance to even try.

Steve and I sat on the edge of his bed—I needed to talk to him about some of these issues; I had to make him understand how much I had changed, not just physically (I was heavy-set now—clinging to extra weight as a protective force against further attacks), but mentally as well. I explained my problems—my uncertainty—I was married—unfaithfulness had never been a part of my vocabulary. I remained hurt over the way he and I had broken up. And my mental condition hinged on it all—I was bipolar—fearful of many things I hadn't been before—and somewhat scared of him. I never expected to have to have this conversation with him; I never really expected to have any conversation with him ever again.

He was most interested in the psychiatric issues, as his own psychiatric issues were the reasoning behind our break-up. I explained the bipolar diagnosis—a disease of severe mood swings—from very high highs, almost euphoria, to very severe depressions. All fairly controllable with medication which had been prescribed and I had been taking religiously. The mania, the highs, weren't that bad but at their worst, would cause severe recklessness. It was the depressive episodes that were bad—I too had had suicidal thoughts, refusal to leave home, leave my room. As long as I took my medication, I was okay.

He understood the depression, obviously, having just gone through a severe episode. He understood fear—he admitted to having been extremely fearful about my rape, fearful that I wouldn't fully recover; fearful that he would hurt me; fearful of my pain, my misery. These were the reasons, in part, that he had left me behind—his fears, my pain, our sorrow.

In his breathy, hoarse voice, he spoke, his eyes boring into mine. "Jean, I made such a huge mistake and we both paid for it, but you have paid for it more. I have missed you—missed us. I want you back: body, heart and soul; if it has to be part-time, so be it. My life had been swirling out of control since I screwed it all up—I need to fix that."

He was so close to me, I could smell his warmth; I was drowning in the scent coming from his body. My own body was beginning to respond, coming alive in a way I hadn't experienced in a long while. I had to let go of the guilt over betraying Chris, the sadness over what Steve had said to me many years ago, and the fear. Time to let it all go or hold on to it all and turn away from him.

Time to let it all go. I once told Randi to listen to her heart regarding her relationship with Dean, 25 years her senior—they were now married. Could I take my own advice? Could I listen to my own heart? Did I dare?

I loved this man—this rock star. The mere sight of him, sitting with me on the bed, sent thrill tremors to all my nerves, nearly breaking me into goose flesh. He obviously still wanted me in his life, having said so earlier. Could I trust my heart? My heart wanted to leap and take the plunge and make love to him.

Look into his eyes, Jean, what do you see?

I heeded the directions my heart was giving me. I looked into his eyes: his deep, dark brown eyes as he stared back at me. My heart told me nearly immediately that I had to find out if we were still soul mates, meant to be together; I had to find out if we were still meant to be.

Be slow with me, please take it slowly.

He smiled, his overbite relaxed, eyes sparkling.

You're sure? I'm sure—I want you—in every way; just take it slowly—it's been awhile.

He stood from our position, helped me up and led me up to the head of the bed, pulled back the sheets, then began to undress. First the t-shirt—some small amount of hair had appeared over his sternum but it was pretty much hit-or-miss. The bandage was still intact to his right collarbone where the central IV line had been; and there were faint circles on his chest from the EKG electrodes: reminders of a near tragedy that nearly took him away from me forever.

In his typical style, he tossed the t-shirt over his back, toward the dresser and missed.

Next came the tennis shoes—blue ones—he pulled each one off with the other foot without untying them and kicked them across the room—*that* was nice to see—I smiled widely at him and got the same in return as he said, "Some things will never change." Thank God.

He kissed me softly, at a slow pace, unbuttoning my blouse. When he finished with the buttons, he opened it widely, draping it slowly down my shoulders, deliberately assisting the fabric off of my arms. I shivered as the blouse tickled my skin, my body responding with more force to his actions.

Steve leaned into me, kissing my face, working his lips onto my jawline, and to my neck. As he kissed my neck, my body answered with full-blown goose flesh now, stirring in ways it hadn't since I was last with him.

I turned my back to him to give him access to my bra—as long as he could see the hooks he wouldn't have any problem with them. Once it was unhooked, Steve sensuously slid his hands under the fabric from behind, drawing his hands forward to the sides of my breasts. I turned to face him, slowly, and he removed the bra as I moved.

We hugged each other again, chests bared to each other, flesh to flesh. The sensation of him against me—nothing in between— was blissful. How I had longed for this for years. Did I feel like that because he had been my first, or because I truly was in love with him? Had to be love.

"Okay?" he whispered into my ear, his breath hot against my skin.

"Definitely."

"Lights on or off?" There was a small bedside light on and a nightlight. I didn't want any lights on—I didn't want him looking at me because of my out-of-control weight. But did I want the lights on so that I could see this gorgeous man?

"Leave them on."

He grinned. His pants came off next, along with his white briefs. Exposed in front of me, he looked fabulous. Nothing had changed as my eyes took him all in. It was evident that he was excited, hard to his full 6-inches—nothing had changed there either, even after having a catheter for 12 days while in the hospital. What an odd little thought.

He then pulled my own pants and underwear off, steadying me as I stepped out them. He stood up in front of me, about a foot away from my body; I could feel his warmth radiating from him in the stillness of his bedroom. How would he react to the extra weight? Very self-conscious about having his eyes on me, I started to turn away from him, but, mid-turn, he stopped me and pulled me around to face him again. There was no disdain on his face, no shock, no disappointment. His face simply registered love, lust. Did it really not matter to him how much I had changed?

I was naked in front of him, for the first time in a long time, and it felt right, natural. After all this time, he still felt so right to be with. But I was also terrified. How would my body react when he entered me? How would my *mind* react?

He stepped to me, taking me into his arms, wrapping them around my back, hands flat against my skin, his manhood finding the wetness between my legs. I placed my arms around his waist, drawing him to closer me.

We had brought to each other our deepest shadows in our own time, our own way, and time was drifting by, leaving me helpless in his wake. I had attempted to live my life without him; we had taken a midnight train in opposite directions into the lonely darkness on separate tracks; to hell and back, and we were now climbing out of that chaos, making our way home to each other. It was time to admit I couldn't live without him. His light was still shining within me and mine within him; we had been unable to do anything to change that.

As we held each other, quietly, peacefully, we listened to the other's breathing and, unconsciously drew in our breaths together, letting them out, spreading warm air over the other. His heart was beating quickly — I could feel it in his chest against mine. He laid his head onto my shoulder and rested there, his face turned slightly toward my neck, his long hair gently brushed against my chest and back as the strands draped across my skin. An amazing feeling that set all my senses leaping with delight.

Steve was still a perfect lover, never trying to go too fast, even if he wanted to, proceeding with tenderness, consideration and kindness. He was mindful in the way he left the next move at that point up to me, knowing that this would be my move, my play — that I had to set the tone, the pace, in order to get through it without flashing back. We had talked about this moment a little during the day, a few hours earlier; I reminded him that he and I had not been together sexually since before I was raped and that I was now a different person; so was he. We'll never change what was, what had been. He had been with someone else, pretty seriously, and so had I, equally as seriously if not more, even though Chris could never replace Steve in my heart and soul.

Steve said he wasn't serious about Rose, but, then again, he had been serious, to some degree. He did admit that she was a dalliance; she was also his rebound girl, as Chris was my rebound guy. Oh, the tangled web we were weaving as we tried to rationalize all of this mess in our heads. Had I been able to look into the future and see what was in store for us, how complicated our lives were about to become, I may not have gone forward with any of this. But, the future is something I couldn't see; so jumping headlong into it was all I could do.

Steve lifted his face off of my shoulder and kissed me, almost hard, on the mouth, our teeth knocking together in ecstasy as we ground our lips together, our tongues finding the other. His teeth were still uneven on the bottom; his upper teeth had some slightly sharp edges—we had noticed that they were very slightly chipped at the edges, probably a consequence of having a tube inserted down the throat while in the throes of an emergency; no one had noticed until now.

We kissed, causing my fluids to flow freely in an uncontrollable flood of sexual energy. His mouth still tasted like the man I knew long ago. He felt harder and larger against my legs, if that was possible. We came out of the kiss and moved slowly to the bed behind us. I sat down on the bed in front of him, his belly at my face. I leaned forward, holding him around the waist, pulling him to me as his hands played with my short hair. He moved down, caressing my shoulders. Holding him at the side of the bed was good enough for me; I could have held onto him like that forever.

He knelt on the ground in front of me, wrapped his arms around my waist, his head in my stomach now, his body between my legs. I felt so sheltered in his arms, in his care, in his house; like I would be able to endure anything, get through it with ease, so long as he held me and kept me safe.

He looked up at me and blinked his eyes, slowly, luxuriously, long eyelashes brushing his cheeks. He looked nervous; like there was something he wanted to say but wasn't totally secure in what it was or how to say it. He reminded me of a young man I once met in San Francisco who had also been somewhat unsure of himself at times.

He took my left hand from his shoulder and held it with both of his hands, resting back on his legs in front of me.

I love you. That was all he said. Softly, in his hoarse voice with the slight Southern drawl, more prominent now that he was on edge about something. He suddenly slid something onto my left ring finger, above my wedding bands. When I looked down, I saw that beautiful ¾ carat diamond—my engagement ring that Chris had sent back to him.

"Take it back—it belongs to you—it always has."

I didn't know what to say, how to react. He realized I was still married, but there on my finger was that beautiful ring, a promise to be his for all time. Could I take it again?

"Steve, I love you so, I just don't know."

He sighed heavily, resting his forehead on my knees. Not looking up, he said, "Then just wear it while we are together; we can pretend, can't we?"

I melted in his words, bringing his head up to mine, kissing him again, letting him know that it was time for us to lie back into the bed, become each other's again, become lovers again, be in love again. We were definitely feeling the same way about each other; there was no denying it. We touched each other's lives and were not going to look back again.

Still kissing me, he stood up and turned me around in the bed so that I lay lengthwise, and crawled on top of me. The sheets held his scent—strong and male. I breathed deeply, taking in the odors from both the bed and his body with memories flooding my brain, tied to those scents.

He took great care to be slow and deliberate with me. His caresses were soft and warm, spreading all over me as he re-explored my body with his fingertips, while I did the same to him.

He kissed my face, the emotion becoming stronger with every touch of his lips on my skin. We could smell each other's arousal; feel it as well. I finally relaxed and spread my legs, allowing him in. He took the cue, becoming a part of me easily, without pain, without fear, without flashback. It was a marvelous feeling to be relaxed again, in love again, in ecstasy with this man. Joyous abandon; not thinking about the past.

He began a slow rhythmic thrusting that felt unlike anything had before. I joined his rhythm, as we were one in our passion. Several times, he lifted his body up and off of mine, looking down the length of us, watching what he was doing, then brought his face back to mine and kissed it.

Something about him doing that, watching our love-making, something about being with him after being without him, something about him being in me, being a part of me, touching my soul, was overwhelming in the best of ways.

His body was speaking to mine, as mine was to his. There was not going to be any turning back from here. We were a couple again and my life was about to change more than I had ever imagined.

Our lovemaking continued until he climaxed and collapsed on top of me, sweating profusely, smiling as he did so. He had brought my body to heaven several times during our passion, and I was just content to be in his arms, in his shadow, helpless in his arms.

We lay quietly in his bed for a time, wrapped in each other, silent. He traced my body with his hand, occasionally finding an erogenous zone that set me aglow. I was in awe of the man. He was a star—a huge star now, known the world over as a rock idol; on the cover of hundreds of magazines and in the pages of hundreds more. He had gold records all over his walls, and other awards he and the band had won over the years; he received thousands of letters through the record company weekly; he was loved by thousands, maybe millions, and couldn't leave his house without a disguise due to fanatics who wanted a piece of him, literally.

And who was he sleeping with tonight? The girl from Ohio that he had left behind but with whom he had now reconnected.

I had him again. Over everyone else—over anyone else. He could have his pick of any woman, and he picked me—again. Why me? Time to find out. I shattered the blissful silence with a question I had always wanted to ask but had tried to avoid.

"Steve, why me?"

He looked up at me from where his head was resting on my shoulder and arm. There were circles under his eyes and he did that thing with his mouth that said, this is making me nuts but I'd better deal with it.

"Why not?"

Not exactly the answer I was looking for, but it was a typical Steve answer. Short, sweet, to the point. Uh-huh—he wasn't going to get away with that tonight.

"No, seriously, why me? When you could be with anyone— why are you with me?"

"Because we fell in love—because when I saw you, I knew there was no one else for me. Because I love you; that is the long and short of it. You are the music I write, the words I sing. I love you. Please believe me. I love you."

There was nothing else he could have said that would have made me feel any better about being back in his arms. He laid his head back down on my arm and sighed—don't know if it was a sigh because we were finished talking, or if he was just exasperated with me, with my constant doubts.

I fingered the hair that was hanging over my arm—I missed that hair; that proud mane of hair which he continued to wear long, but which was now very layered, almost wild and big, as "the big-hair of the 80s" was. Everyone has a favorite part of the one they love. Steve knew my favorite part of him was his hair; second would have to be his beautiful nose. Did he have a favorite part of me? He once told me it was my eyes, followed by my chest (typical man), followed closely by the Elton John t-shirt I had worn when he saw me from stage in San Francisco; I told him that the t-shirt wasn't a part of me and he told me yes, it was, in his mind—when he sees me in his dreams, I am in that t-shirt because it represented my innocence, my naïve nature, my teenage soul.

The house was quiet. His family was asleep down the hall. His cat was prowling somewhere in the house, every so often we would hear him running through the downstairs. The air conditioner came on and off at intervals, keeping us all comfortable as the summer had come on like gangbusters with high temperatures and high humidity. I was at peace with myself, even though I probably shouldn't have been. And Steve was content in our new arrangement.

He should have been asleep, as he had been released from the hospital that day, but I think both of us were too keyed up to sleep at that point. We were a couple again; we had declared our love for each other again; we had made love again.

We threw on some clothes—he put on a pair of shorts and I put on a nightshirt from my suitcase and went downstairs for something to eat. It was 2 AM; we were not the only ones hungry—James was in the kitchen fixing himself a sandwich from the food in the refrigerator, all the while talking on the phone, propped into the crook of his neck, to his wife.

Steve threw me a soda from the refrigerator and took James' sandwich off the counter, cut it in half, gave half to me and then bit into his half; James had his back to us and didn't realize we were there yet. These two brothers were like big kids when they were together, even in the middle of a tragedy, as they had just gone through.

James told his wife good-night, that he loved her, then made a few kissing sounds into the phone, causing Steve to snort laughter through his nose, as James hung up and whirled around to face us, startled that we were there, even more startled that his sandwich had been pilfered, as he lifted the empty plate off the counter, displaying its emptiness to Steve.

"I find this funny—not," James said as he made a face at Steve, and smiled at me.

Steve nearly doubled over with laughter—that was very nice to hear. I began to apologize when James picked up a slice of ham and winged his brother with it. There it was—the beginning of a food fight that would leave more than a few sandwich fixings on the floor. I could see these two being holy-terrors as children; they still were.

Steve and I stayed in bed most of the next day, despite the fact that he had just gotten out of a hospital bed, having laid there in bed for nearly three weeks. But this was different. He sent his mom and dad out to visit Los Angeles in his limo; they were going to go home the next day and wanted to get a look at the big city. James stayed home—he was going back to Atlanta that afternoon—his wife, Betty, was missing him.

I stayed on another ten days, pushing my luck with Chris and my job, no doubt, but I couldn't help myself. I wanted to stay as long as I possibly could, as long as I could get away with it. Steve was doing very well—taking the methadone and not experiencing much in the way of side effects, participating in psychotherapy for the suicide attempt. We both went to a few sessions together as he had done for me. He was off the heroin; no signs that he was thinking of killing himself any longer. We were back together in every way possible. His life was less complicated at that point as the band was taking a break from each other and from touring.

But, I had to go home. Suddenly, as his life was smooth and uncluttered, mine was becoming complicated and very cluttered. He took me to the airport this time, unlike the last time I left his house; floppy hat perched on his head, his hair tucked up under it. We made quite a scene at the gate: kissing, tears, saying good-bye. If anyone recognized him, they left him alone, left us alone.

My brother picked me up and drove me home; Chris was on-shift at the fire station. John had taken one look at me and knew that Steve and I had been together. Was it really that obvious? He said I had better tone it all down; erase the goofy grin, before seeing Chris. Great. More complications.

Things between Chris and I were, obviously, strained, but he never asked what had gone on in Los Angeles, in fact, he never asked about anything. He didn't really want to know and I didn't really want to say.

Steve and I spoke on the phone the nights when Chris was at the fire station, sometimes for hours at a time. Phone sex was tame, but we had it nonetheless; it felt very strange, erotic and risqué all at the same time. He wrote to me every couple of days, sending the letters to a post office box I had rented so Chris would not get to them before I could. His letters were sexy, but disjointed, as they always had been, but I loved them.

I sent him Chris' work schedule and, about once every couple of months, Steve flew into Cleveland, drove to my hometown, so we could be together for a day or two, holding each other, acting out what we had spoken of on the phone.

He bought himself a motorcycle, a small one for getting around short distances in Los Angeles, for Christmas 1985; it was something he had always wanted. He bought me a computer, something I had always wanted; we could e-mail each other much more effectively than using snail mail, as the USPS was affectionately being called. A friend of his set up my computer e-mail accounts with a password in order to get into the mail, and a program that would automatically delete Steve's mail in 24-hours so prying eyes, hopefully, could not see it should the password be discovered. This affair was becoming very high-tech.

A year later, after Steve and I had seen each other multiple times in 1986, the band was ready to do it all over again—they had all rested, were all refreshed and raring to go. Steve was the lone holdout, not so sure he wanted to go through all of the hassle again. He was financially secure at that point, having been smart with his millions, but, the record company was anxious—they wanted their biggest-selling band back out on the road, back onto the charts. They offered an exorbitant amount of money; a share of the profits for a new album and subsequent tour; and Steve finally agreed.

Steve was beginning to put pen to paper with the other band members to develop new songs and a new sound for the album—their ninth, *Apprehension*, a word that described their feelings about it and the tour to follow; it was a word that described how I felt about my affair with the lead singer.

1987 would be a year for couples—the scandal between presidential hopeful, Gary Hart, and Donna Rice would be exposed; Bruce Willis would marry Demi Moore in November, a marriage doomed to divorce in the future; and Prince Charles and Princess Di would begin to live separately. On TV we would watch an Alien Life Form move in with a normal family and request a cat for dinner; children trying to make it through *The*

Wonder Years; LA Law would show us that big city law on the West Coast is very serious and full of sex; and *Night Court* would show us that big city law on the East Coast was very funny. The Bangles would try to convince America to *Walk Like An Egyptian;* George Michael sang about wanting our sex; U2 still hadn't found what they were looking for; and Whitesnake went again, with their lead singer's girlfriend, Tawny Kitaen, writhing on the hoods of Jaguars in the video.

The year would also uproot me from my hometown—my home state—Ohio. Chris, I think, wanted a fresh start—he figured if we were living somewhere else, our lives would be better. So, we moved—he found a firefighter/paramedic lieutenant position in a northwest suburb of Chicago. I was not happy to leave family and friends but I had to go where my husband went. Had I thought about it, this would have been the perfect opportunity to leave Chris—allow him to move on, and I would stay behind. That could lead to a divorce—then I could be with Steve. But my mind didn't work quite that way. So, in the Spring of 1987, I became a Chicagoland suburbanite. Sigh.

I was miserable. No job—one small newspaper in my county wasn't hiring and had a waiting list for jobs. Fast food? No way. Retail? Forget it. I stayed home, adopted a black cat at the local shelter, and e-mailed Steve. Their tour was getting ready to kick off in Milwaukee in May. I was going; not just to Wisconsin but on the whole summer leg of the tour. Nuts to staying home, doing nothing, being miserable.

Chris said he would let me go as long as I came back. Between the decision to go on the summer *Apprehension* tour, and telling Chris, I had enrolled in nursing school—a totally different direction for me but it was something I had always wanted to be, ever since playing with the plastic medical bags kids get for Christmas with plastic thermometers and band-aids and candy pills. At one point, all of my stuffed animals were covered with gauze and bandages when I was a child.

Chris was actually happy about my schooling—he knew I

would be back to go to school. He never asked why I wanted to go on the tour—he figured, I think, that I just needed to recapture some of my youth (I was all of 27), and, if I was going to get closure of any kind, I was going to have to do this. I am pretty sure he knew the real reasoning: I was with Steve again and wanted to be with him through the summer, alone and on the road. There aren't many husbands who would turn a blind eye, allowing their wives to run off on tour with an old flame who happened to be the lead singer, and be with him for nearly four months. Bless his heart, he never asked me any questions. Chris was a uniquely compassionate and sympathetic person who knew, as my parents had known 13 years ago, I would go to Steve with or without permission. This time was no exception.

I had to go; run to Steve and cry on him about the move; about my new house, which I hated; the lack of a job; the change in career paths.

He and I met in a Milwaukee hotel six days prior to the start of the tour. He was all mine, completely, for six days. We drank each other in and were all that really mattered. We rarely left the room for the full six days. By then I had his scent all over me and enjoyed how it made me feel to smell him embedded in my skin.

We arrived at the concert hall, after six days of ecstasy, in a limo several hours prior to the show. Fans were already gathering in the parking lot, partying, sharing stories of past concerts. The tour buses and semi tractor-trailers were around the side of the huge building. We pulled up to an entrance next to the main door where the driver escorted us out of the limo. It felt so much like old times; so many memories came flooding back. A few screaming fans noticed us, noticed him, and headed toward us but were stopped by security guards at the barricades. Steve graciously waved to them from the hall doors as we went inside and raised my own hand in his to do the same; like the fans wanted *me* to wave at them.

I had told him earlier that I wanted to see his band mates prior to the concert, particularly Richard, who had always been a silent friend to me. It had been years since I saw all of them; it was time to say hello again. Steve was okay with my request—he took me to the band lounge, looked at me momentarily as if to be sure this is what I wanted to do; I smiled; he let me in.

They were all there—and they looked fabulous. Ned looked a little older, his hair a little shorter, curlier; he seemed less serious in his mannerisms, not off in some corner with his guitar, but sharing an animated conversation with Joss, arm slung around a blonde's shoulders. Taking a closer look, I realized that blonde was his formerly-brunette wife.

Richard was—amazingly—alone, at least for the moment. He came over to Steve and I, sweeping me into his arms, a bear hug from the six-foot musician—he had always been my favorite. He asked how I was—how I *really* was. I got the jist of his question: how had I been since the rape and since Steve's and my break-up? I told him I was fine, still in his arms, looking up into his unshaven face. He looked at Steve. Puzzled. He didn't know—none of them knew we were back together—as back together as we could be at that time. I noticed the distinct absence of a wedding ring; I didn't ask.

Steve stepped to the middle of the room and cleared his throat, garnering the attention of everyone there. It was all family—band and crew—at that point. No groupies yet; no radio station contest winners; just the people who mattered to him. He announced that I would be joining them for the summer leg of the tour and we would be together. If anyone had a problem with that, with my marital status, they were to keep it to themselves. I wished he hadn't said that.

Then he added, almost as an after thought, that he loved me, I loved him; and no one was to talk about us to the press, per my request(!).

Richard tightened his hug around me, still wrapped in his arms. He seemed genuinely happy for us both. I could always count on Richard to be honestly supportive.

Joss came over and shook Steve's hand, then gave me a quick hug. He was as tall as Richard and I had to stand on tip-toe to get my arms up around his shoulders as he bent over to me. He seemed happy for us; and himself—he had a girlfriend whom he would soon marry. Phil also came over, and said a quick congratulations to us both; I got the distinct impression he did not approve. Oh, well.

Ned was last, strolling over with Nancy, his wife. I half-expected him to be blunt, curt, and quickly walk away from us, but he was actually human. The years had melted away some of his outer layers of ice. He patted Steve on the back; no, he clapped Steve on the back enthusiastically, much in the way a true friend would do. He then turned his attention to me and said he had been sorry to hear about the rape; his words sounded heartfelt and honest—and he was glad to see me. With that he leaned in and kissed me on the cheek. What a shock!

I could see Richard's face over Ned's shoulder; an exaggerated jaw drop. He was as shocked as I was—Steve too.

The band had grown up; they had changed over the years: mellowed, greyed, cut their hair (all but Steve). I was pleasantly surprised, but somewhat disappointed too as I hoped they were still the same band on stage.

Steve and I stayed in the lounge a little while longer. He went over a few things with Joss and Ned; they even laughed a few times. They had had a rehearsal three weeks ago: long-distance rehearsals through phone lines via computer hook-up: not exactly the ideal way to rehearse but Ned and his own band were in Europe; this was the only way; it had to be good enough. They would be playing their old standards for the most part, and a few new songs from *Apprehension*. The line-up was taped in front of everyone on the stage or on their instruments so they would know their way through the show, something that was done only for Steve in the past; this tour really was quickly thrown together.

An hour prior to the concert start, Steve and I made our exit to his dressing room; the lounge had begun to fill with other people: groupies, fan club people, radio people; a little too overwhelming for us both. His private dressing room was something he still insisted on having—it was his wish—he was the lead singer, after all. He was the one most people came to see, much to the other band member's dismay. They all had their own groupies too with letters of proposal of everything from marriage to affairs, to straight out sex, but Steve got so many more.

He was invigorated that night, his excitement about the beginning of a new tour increasing as every minute ticked past. His dressing room was full of flowers—some from radio stations, some from fans, some from record execs and sponsors. There was a stack of telegrams on the dressing table that he never even looked at.

A tub of ice with beer, water and soda in it sat on a table along one wall; he never requested anything else. His concert clothes—a t-shirt, jeans that were torn in strategic places to make females swoon and think they may have seen something they shouldn't have, and his black tennis shoes—hung on a rack in a suit carrier. For all the clothes were, they could have been folded and carried around in a grocery bag.

45 minutes: the opening band, a local group of four girls, was starting to play; we could hear them faintly through the ceiling. Steve was looking at me from his place on the couch—I was reading some of the telegrams: fans who wanted to meet him, radio stations wishing him good luck, the mayor welcoming them to the city. I looked over the top of a telegram I was holding and saw his eyes staring at me, through me, smoldering in liquid chocolate.

I knew that look—he was thinking about sex. So was I.

I went to him on the couch and straddled his lap, wrapping my arms around his neck and pulled off his t-shirt, causing his hair to fall in a cascade of brown strands around his shoulders. I gathered up his hair in my hands and threw it down his back.

His arms came around my waist, caressing my back, unfastening my bra through the shirt; suddenly he was an expert at getting it undone. I allowed him to pull the shirt over my head and the bra came with it.

He took one of my breasts into his warm hands and lifted it to his even warmer mouth, exciting me further. We exhaled at the same time, as I arched my back into him and felt his hot breath on my skin, causing a rush of warmth between my legs.

I sat up straighter in his lap and unsnapped, unzipped my pants, allowing room for his hand to slide underneath my panties to the wetness beneath. His long fingers were manipulative in all the right places as he skillfully put his middle finger inside of me, all the while rubbing me with his thumb. He was an expert in his ability to bring me to a climax in minutes, as I bucked slightly against his fingers, my breaths panting forcefully as I fell forward against his face, kissing him with all the love and passion I had within me.

I could feel him hard against me in his lap as I climbed off and undressed the rest of the way, exposing my curves and the slickness of my thighs to him. This was a very brazen thing for me to do, as I normally did not undress in front of him in such a way.

I bent over him, knelt on the floor and began to undress him where he sat, slowly, deliberately. He was fully rigid as he lifted his bottom off the couch, allowing me to remove his pants and briefs.

I reached out and took his erection in my hands, lovingly stroking it with long, even strides, producing whimpers of euphoria as I rubbed him to fullness like he had never been. He laid his head back on the couch, placing his hands on the tops of his thighs. I finally decided to give in, abandon all decorum— my tongue found the tip and my mouth followed, enveloping him in the moist heat within. Steve drew in a sharp involuntary inhalation of air as I drank him in, using my tongue as a weapon of love and sex, causing him to drown in breath taking shudders of pleasure.

When he was beginning to thrust with increased force against my mouth, respirations increasing, moans louder, he grabbed my head and lifted it until I became detached from his body. He told me to "Come back to my lap." He didn't have to tell me twice.

I straddled his legs again as he slid into me with ease. I leaned forward into him, bringing my lips to his, kissing him with a sexual force I didn't recognize. It didn't take long until he came deep within me, his body quivering with uncontrollable spasms.

My body ached to stay connected to his—this is where I wanted to be for the rest of my life—this is where I wanted to die—in the arms of this man. This is who I wanted to be with— a man who loved me for me, who didn't love me because of my looks of lack thereof, my intelligence, my anything—he loved me for me—who I was, who I had been, who I was to become.

He kissed me—not with the fervor that he had as we had made love, but with all the intimacy two people could share. I had missed these lovemaking sessions before concerts the most—these were the times when we truly connected— figuratively and literally. It didn't make his stage performance any different; it just made *him* different.

Ten minutes to stage—we uncoupled, reluctantly, but quickly, and dressed. Richard knocked on the door five minutes to stage, and slowly opened it as if he knew what we had been up to. Without putting his head all the way into the doorway, he called out to Steve, who told him to go ahead and come in. Richard poked his head in to see us dressed and sitting back on the couch. We could dress in a hurry when we needed to.

Hand in hand we made our way to the stage with Richard on our heels. Stage left; always stage left. If nothing else this band was consistent. The opening band had finished five minutes earlier; the road crew had readied the stage; Steve's band was anxiously awaiting their cue. Ned's wife, Nancy, and I were the only other people back stage at that time. Ned had his arm around Nancy; I was standing behind Steve, my arms wrapped around his waist, my face buried in his back and strands of hair, inhaling the scent of him, of us.

Their intro began, an eerie mixture of lights and almost a new-age-type sound that Phil had written and recorded on a synthesizer; Richard left to go to his drum kit ahead of the others. In 30 seconds he began playing the cymbal, in time with the growing volume of the sounds emanating from the speakers. The music Phil had designed was meant to evoke a sense of apprehension — pretty cool how it accomplished that. The crowd was on their feet with screams of building anticipation, adoration. Steve pulled me around to face him and kissed me hard but gently at the same time. Breathily he told me he loved me and was then off to the show.

The fans were older now — I took several peeks at the audience from stage left and saw they were a mixed bag of people — all shapes and sizes and ages — from teenagers to middle-aged to, well, older. This band's music seemed to speak to everyone, young and old; to everyone except the critics and reviewers.

Their latest album had been a critical disaster — reviewers had never much cared for Steve's voice or even his looks, the band's sound, anyone's ability to play an instrument. I always figured it had to be jealousy at their tremendous success. The fans didn't pay any mind to the reviews — they made up their own minds — and we loved these guys. We didn't care what kind of names they were called — "bubble-gum pop rock trying to be adult contemporary," "corporate rock," and the all-time favorite: "sickeningly sweet, honey dew, dripping with sentimental songs of sap." Nice. Very nice. Nastiness like that is why I refused to take the journalism courses to teach me how to write reviews; I didn't want any part of that.

Today the fans, the most loyal ones, the die-hards, still spend time on-line in chat rooms and e-mail groups, discussing the band and their latest solo activities and the concerts of old. If someone dares say a bad word about any of the band members, they attack each other verbally, kind of like a lioness protecting her young, provoking long discussions over what we all really liked—the music of this band or the persona of a lead singer or another band member. Did it really matter why the music was loved?

Despite the lack of in-person rehearsal, despite poor album reviews, despite time away from each other, this concert went off without a hitch—it flowed smoothly—the guys *all* looked like they were having a good time. Even Ned and Steve appeared to be getting along out there and I don't think it was all for show. It was nice to see—they were more like the two young men I had met in San Francisco, having fun with their music.

Steve came off the stage about halfway through the show, as he had always done, to rest his voice, giving his band mates a prime opportunity to show off their instrumental talents. He grabbed me around the waist, practically spinning me around—he was thrilled with the way things were going, not something he had been able to say very often. He held me tight as the music played, our arms around each other's waists, caressing our backs; loving, touching each other, in love. When it came time for him to got back on stage, he grasped my hand tightly and squeezed, then, with our arms outstretched, our hands slowly came apart as he walked away. As he backed away from me, his arm still stretched toward me, it had to be very obvious to the audience that he had been back stage with someone that he was apparently very fond of, his face showing emotions of love and fire. He picked up the cordless microphone from Phil's keyboard and was lost in another song.

I was in heaven being backstage again, being on tour again. As we traveled from city to city, night to night, I felt like a teenager again, only I was no longer that teen hanger-on that everyone had raised eyebrows to when Steve and I kissed or held hands. I had always been the recipient of the snide remark or stern look—no one on the road believed that he and I had waited until I turned 18. Like his mother had told us so long ago, even when we were simply talking to each other or looking at each other, it appeared like we were making love.

But now we were both full-grown adults—were we really as much in love as we felt? As we appeared? It sure seemed that way. We were together in every way possible and it wasn't all sex. We were so much more.

No more obnoxious glances, no more concerned stares. We were just us—Steve and Jean—together again—on the road and staring down another highway. Together we had found the power, the strength, to love each other.

Summer Tour 1987 took us into Chicago in July, to play an arena just on the outskirts of the city to the northwest. That was about 40 miles form my house…Chris was coming to the concert—he knew about it from the itinerary I had given him. Was I stupid to do that? He could have gotten the schedule from any source—it might as well have come from me. I couldn't exactly tell him not to come.

Steve and I arrived in Chicago at 2 AM the night before the concert—it seemed stupid to stay in a hotel when my house was so close. Chris was working the 6 PM to 6 AM shift at the fire station so when I opened my front door, we were greeted with a deafening silence. This was my house and yet it felt so foreign.

I gave Steve the grand tour of the downstairs. My cat came out to greet us and took a shine to Steve right away—he was the only one of my friends that cat had actually ever liked. Smart kitty. I called Chris at the station—it was just after three, he had a few more hours to go on his shift. He sounded odd when I told him Steve was here. He should have expected it though.

As we talked, mostly about what he had been doing with himself, Steve sat in a chair reading a magazine—I think it was *Woman's Day*—wish I had a picture of that. He kept looking up at me and smiling. As Chris and I talked, the fire tones suddenly went off on the scanner next to where Steve was sitting and in the fire house—startled, Steve jumped out of the chair, not sure what to think. I laughed, let Chris go rescue an elderly female experiencing radiating chest pain, and listened to the busy signal on the phone for a few seconds after he hung up. I was suddenly sad.

Steve stood at my fireplace mantel, looking at the pictures, his nerves calming. There was my mom and dad, John; Chris' brother; Country Blue in a performance at Rabbit Hole; my kitty, my Charlie; my wedding picture; and a picture of Steve in concert many years ago. He was surprised that Chris had allowed it to stay out—I told him that was my call; I wanted it there, so there it stayed.

We finally went upstairs; I showed him the three bedrooms. The third was a craft room, the second a guest room with twin beds, much like my parents guest room had been. The large master bedroom was fairly clean; clothes not on the floor but draped over a chair. Chris must have been to some fires because I could smell the faint scent of smoke hanging in the room from his dirty clothes.

Steve went to the guest room and threw his bag onto one of the beds. I followed close behind, watching him, enjoying the sight of him from the rear, in his shorts. He turned on a small light with the light switch, which put out not much more light than a candle would have, casting a subtle glow over each of us.

Steve looked so innocent, so good standing in my house for the first time. Chris would be home in three hours—I wanted this man—badly—but did we dare? What if we fell asleep and Chris came home? And found us? What would it do to him? What would he do to us?

But, I wanted to make love to Steve in my house, in my sheets, under my roof. I went to the window, which faced the front of the house, and could see the white limo we had been in since Detroit, parked like a silent sentinel in the street at the end of the driveway, awaiting our return. I closed the curtain and turned toward him. He was already pulling his t-shirt over his head, shaking out his hair once it was off.

My wish came true—I made love to him in my home, exhilaration like no other. He was slow, gentle, ever mindful of my past. I loved every hair, every freckle, every mark on him. I knew every inch of him. Our few hours in each other's arms were blissful.

Chris came home just after 6:30 AM and I greeted him at the door, fresh from showering; the last thing I needed was him to be able to smell Steve all over me. Chris and I had coffee together at the table, talked about the tour, and his fire calls over the summer. He finally asked where Steve was—upstairs asleep— he said he figured as much as there was a "big limo outside."

I didn't understand Chris at all; I wouldn't have understood any man in his position. We talked that morning about us—he and I, Steve and I—the threesome I had created. He told me how hard it was to know that I really did care for Steve; that I could care for him after what he had done to me. I asked him if he wanted me to answer any questions for him; he declined, saying his imagination took care of him realizing how serious my affair was. He had to put up with the façade of a normal life and pretend that everything was fine between he and I, never let anyone past the masquerade. He had made up his mind to live up to what his dream should be and not what it had become.

I asked him then if he was going to leave me and he was silent for a time, eyes closed, carefully going over his answer in his mind. He finally looked at me with his blue eyes, which seemed a little more pale, a little more tired that morning. His answer was a good one—he couldn't give up the memories we had together from the *real* times. He had no doubt that our real times were ours alone, without interference from outside sources, meaning Steve.

Then he said it—he knew I was in love with Steve; that I always had been. He wasn't ignoring that fact—he was quite cognizant of it. He told me he had no plans to leave me—that to do so would, in his mind, be admitting defeat. He loved me, even if I didn't love him in "that way." He was willing to share me rather than lose me.

This was the most uncomfortable I had ever felt in my own home with Chris. He knew—I had always known that he knew; now it had been confirmed.

It was Chris I always came home to, but he was beginning to suspect that I had been doing that simply out of some skewed sense of duty. At least we had managed to get some of this out of his system and into the open, even if it made both of us more miserable. I was just relieved that Steve's and my relationship was not known in Illinois. Chris explained my summer absence to his friends as I was home with family, avoiding scandalous rumors that would have been fodder for the gossip mill at the fire station—yes, men do gossip—just as much as women.

I was beginning to understand.

Steve abruptly appeared in the kitchen, dressed in his shorts and, obviously, nothing else; he hadn't even thought about it. Probably not the smartest thing to do. He shook Chris' hand, who was gracious in his defeat, if that was what it was to be called. Chris then yawned in dramatic fashion and announced he was going to bed—it was 10 AM and he had picked up that night's shift.

You're not coming to the concert? Huh?—oh, no—sorry—duty calls.

In some ways I was disappointed, watching him leave the room. It was all very sad, very unsettling, very complicated.

I teared-up at the door saying good-bye to Chris later that day, he was quietly allowing me to go again. I should have left him, allowing him to find someone who would love him in the way he deserved to be loved, someone who would give him their whole heart and not just a piece of it. But I couldn't let him go, any more than he could let me go.

Thankfully, Steve was already in the limo during our good-bye scene. Chris held me—loosely—in the doorway and kissed me, but it was a forlorn feeling I sensed from him. He didn't say much more to me than to take care of myself, take my bipolar medicine and come home soon. He let me go back to rock-and-roll and the life with a star; he let me go because he knew he had to.

I waved to him as I got into the limo but he had already turned and gone back into the house. I looked around my neighborhood, the small cul-de-sac we lived in—a lot of the neighbors were out and about on this late Summer afternoon—trying to get a look at who was in the limo, trying to look casual about doing so.

We arrived back at the Chicago arena around 6 PM; I leaned my head on Steve's chest the whole way, intermittently crying softly and sniveling, whining. We met the rest of the band inside, and they rehearsed for about an hour as the crew completed final set-up. This was an open stage in the middle of the arena so the show could be seen from all angles. Made it logistically difficult to set up the light scaffolding so that views were not obstructed. Steve hated these concert set-ups—he felt the audience behind him was always looking at his butt—he was right.

Smart audience!

The tour continued on, the cities a blur after awhile. Time was going fast, seemingly quicker every day as the end of August loomed in the immediate future. Steve and I were inseparable, together every waking moment, lost in each other's world. My place during the shows was stage left and it was becoming increasingly obvious to the audiences that he was singing certain songs to someone back there. During the nights I was in his bed, in his arms, safe and secure in his love and his endurance; during the days I was at his side, a mate, a consort to a star.

Mid-August was blazing everywhere we went; the heat didn't even subside at night. Arenas set up multiple fans to keep the band cool and had ice and water on stage for them. They finally started taking a 15-minute intermission due to the heat while in the South. Even at 9 PM temperatures remained in the 90s.

We pulled into his family's Atlanta home on a Thursday, after midnight, after two shows at the Omni. The air outside was close, hot, hanging sticky as we walked through it. Summer heat pressed down on us; even at the stroke of the Witching Hour, it was nearly suffocating to walk even short distances.

His dad met us at the door—his mom was in the family room, waiting for us. I hadn't been to this house in years but nothing had changed—the furniture was all the same—even our couch: still that flowered material covering overstuffed cushions which were now just a little less overstuffed, tamped down with age. The house even smelled the same—cherry tobacco and smells of home cooking hung in the air. And thank heavens for central air!

His mom didn't look well. She seemed pale, weaker, smaller somehow. Steve had told me to be prepared—that she was having increased problems with her kidneys due to the diabetes and would probably have to start dialysis soon. So, her appearance was understandable. But she looked so much worse than she had in California just a short while ago.

Steve shooed his parents off to bed shortly after we arrived— he scolded them for staying up to begin with; he had told them we would see them in the morning, they were not to wait up. But they had wanted to see their oldest boy get home safely.

Slowly his mother rose from her chair, using a walker for balance and strength; she kissed Steve, then me, which did my heart some good, and she and her husband went upstairs, leaving Steve and I alone on our couch. The couch—we had spent so many hours, so many nights together, wrapped in each other's arms—it had been the first place we had slept together in 1976, without sex. We sat on it that night, fresh from the Atlanta concert that had been an overwhelming success, at least according to Steve's point of view.

Now that we were in his parent's house and he had seen his

mom, he mellowed a little, coming down from the concert high. He was clearly worried but had a lot of trouble admitting that—don't know if that was ego or a macho-type thing rearing its ugly head, or just a son's fear.

We talked about his mom a bit, as if he needed the debriefing. He seemed to have a lot to let out so I sat quietly and listened as he described his feelings. After about 30 minutes he had said all he was going to and turned to face me on the couch.

"Are you okay?" I asked him the question after several minutes of uncomfortable silence.

He nodded and smiled. This man, this rock idol with the golden voice, was so family-oriented and so different from his counterparts in other bands, or even the guys in his own band. He wasn't a user of people and he wasn't a hard-hearted jerk who didn't care about anyone other than himself. After so many years with his band and other bands playing the same festivals Steve's band did, I had seen many musicians who had forgotten their roots, their families, them selves.

But Steve forgot no one—he was kind to everyone in his circle of family and friends. He had turned his back on no one.

I leaned to him and kissed him softly on the mouth, holding his face in my hands. I was gentle in my kiss and didn't attempt to press him into anything he wasn't prepared to jump into. But he responded to my kiss with his own.

I wanted him to make love to me there on the couch—for the first time, there on the couch, the one piece of furniture that held so many memories for us. We might not ever get this chance again, not knowing what the future had in store for the two of us. But, I didn't want to push. I didn't have to. We had made love across the country all summer. Why not Atlanta? Why not here? Now?

Our kisses built, and yet I kept one ear on the alert for any sign that his parents were coming downstairs—definitely not cool to have a parent catch you in the act. Fortunately, his parents stayed upstairs the entire night.

As our excitement built, our clothes were tossed onto the floor around the room in reckless abandon, and I realized once more why I loved this man, why I had fallen so hard in San Francisco—he was a gentle, loving man who loved me back, just the way I was, whether I had extra weight on me, wore glasses, wasn't all that attractive. He loved me despite multiple flaws. Yes, we had both made mistakes, some we couldn't ever rectify. But we always ended up back together somehow.

So, here we were, in his hometown, in his parent's house again. I was comfortable in his arms, ecstatic with his touch, enamored by his smile.

When he flashed that smile at me, my heart melted; when he stared at me with those chocolate brown eyes, my breath caught in my throat which would then tighten up; when his mouth met mine, there was an explosion that sent shudders rippling through me.

There was no denying the love we shared. And that is what we did in Atlanta that night, on the flowered couch in his parent's house—we savored each other in the dead of night. I never wanted to leave him and yet I would be doing just that in a very short time, to return to Chicagoland to start a new life in nursing.

As Steve and I lay in each other's body heat on the couch, he asked me to stay with him, not go back to Chris. The thought of staying with him made my heart swell and I actually took a few moments to consider the whole idea. I so wanted to be a full-time piece of his life and not this part-time thing we had going on. I was a part-time lover and didn't want it to be that way forever, but I just could not leave Chris. I just wasn't strong enough.

He seemed disappointed but not surprised.

The two-day stay in Atlanta was uneventful from that night on. Steve had hired a housekeeper for his ailing parents, allowing his mom to save precious energy for more important tasks—she didn't like being a lady of leisure but knew that her health depended upon it. I sat with his mom all afternoon the day after we arrived, and helped her glue a backlog of pictures and articles about her son into albums. She was almost up to 100 albums about him. She was still such a proud Mama.

Steve spent the same afternoon in the basement with his father, puttering around on some project. I wondered what the two of them talked about when they were down there—neither one of them were big talkers so I am sure there was a whole lot of peacefulness going on, unlike his mom and I. I had to tell her why I was going to go to nursing school; what I was doing at home, how my family was. If I felt he had recovered in the last two years and, more importantly, did I think he was off the heroin?

Steve and she had such an open relationship, I wondered why she just didn't ask him, but she had asked me and I felt an obligation to speak to her. Yes, he is fully recovered with no signs of suicidal ideations. Did I think he was off the heroin? I had no answer for that because I didn't know. Addicts of any substance are very good at covering things up and I supposed that Steve was no different. I just didn't know and he had never said.

We spent one more day in Atlanta then flew on to Cleveland for a concert at the Coliseum—sold-out for three nights. I had misgivings about going home to see my parents while we were in Ohio—my parents were not as forgiving as Steve's were regarding our relationship. I called ahead and they did want to see us, so they said. Yes, both of us.

Steve and I arrived at my house mid-morning after the second night's concert—Steve had actually rented a car and drove the hour to my house. That was nice—no one looking in the rear-view mirror at us.

My parents were gracious hosts once again. They hadn't seen Steve since he broke up with me in January of 1980—it had been a long time—I hadn't realized how long. Steve still looked the same but his hair was much longer now.

As far as my parents were concerned, he and I were friends now and I was simply reliving my youth, prior to venturing into the world of nursing. They had no idea we were sleeping together once again. That was something they didn't need to know—but, if my mom was as perceptive as his mom was, she could read it in our faces.

We had a nice lunch together; my brother was living in Florida now so there was no one there to gape at Steve or to spread it around the neighborhood that he would be in our house. My bedroom upstairs was no longer my bedroom—it had been turned into an office for my dad; John's room was about to change also—into a dressing room for my mother and her shoes.

Our next tour stop was obnoxiously all the way across the country—Long Beach Arena in Los Angeles. Steve and I flew along with the other band members and some of the assorted managers in charge. Fun flight. Everyone was relaxed for a change. Steve and I didn't know what kind of storm we were flying into.

Two nights at the arena went very well. California is a relaxed state of mind and that attitude permeates everything. However, the third and last night of the concert series was very nearly the end of my perfect world.

As the final preparations were made on stage for the band's opening act, Steve and I were in his dressing room, sitting on a small well-worn couch, my legs draped over his, his hand lazily resting on my chest, the other gripping the sheet music tighter and tighter. I was half sitting up and had a handful of his hair in my hand, fondling its full 18 inches lovingly.

He was gong over the words to a certain song from *Apprehension* that he continually flipped around, no matter how many times he tried to memorize it. He was fun to watch while he was doing all that fussing over something that no one noticed anyway. So he mixed up a few words—maybe he should have written them that way to begin with.

A knock came on the door, and, right away, I checked my watch reflexively—not time to go on up to the stage yet. Steve called out and a roadie stuck his head in sheepishly and announced that Steve had a visitor; was that okay? We looked at each other—had we given out passes to anyone for this show? No. Well, let them in anyway. We would find out who it was in a second. That was a mistake: in strolled Rose, wearing literally nothing but a white cotton dress that billowed out around her as she strode into the room.

Neither one of us moved, riveted to the couch by shock and a sense of severe uneasiness. Rose still moved with the skill and litheness of a sleek big cat; you could almost hear her purring as she glided and jiggled past us to a chair across from the couch. Steve watched her over the sheet music, his expression neutral. His hand was still resting on my chest, my hand tangled in his hair; he made no move to withdraw his hand so mine stayed put also.

In an instant this woman had managed to make me feel inadequate and unworthy all at once. Looking at her slim frame, her full lips, full breasts, I suddenly couldn't understand Steve's choice in women again: that he was with me. But, my brain reminded me that Steve and I were together and he had left her behind.

Finally, after a pause of silence and, as she looked directly at me, her eyes trailing the length of my body, from my head to my legs over Steve's and back again, I shifted and made a move as if to remove my legs from Steve's but he stopped me with the hand holding the music. I was stuck.

At long last she spoke, introducing herself to me. I did the same and she told me she knew who I was—she had seen the pictures. Her voice was nearly a sneer, her mouth screwed into a scowl—but not quite. Steve cleared his throat slightly and finally asked her what she wanted—did I hear an air of annoyance in his tone? His words were curt and with some force as he practically spat out the question to her.

"Just here to see you, love." Her voice was as lithe as her walk, cat-like in its lilt. He bristled when she finished her sentence with the word "love."

"You've seen me." Steve's voice could not hide how bothered he was that she was invading our space; his space.

I kept my eyes lowered, not looking at either of them. She hadn't come to see me—or had she?

"Can we talk in private?" She directed the question to Steve but was looking directly at me. It wasn't me she wanted to see in private. There was nothing she could have to say to me that she couldn't say in front of him but I was sure there was plenty she could say to him that she didn't want me to hear. I raised my eyes and looked at Steve who was already shaking his head.

"No—she stays. Whatever you have to say, say it and go." His grip tightened on the sheet music, twisting it slightly.

She uncrossed her legs then crossed them the other way. She smiled like a cheetah about to take off across the Serengeti to catch its prey. She was good at playing a bitch; but was she playing?

"Okay, Steven, I want you back. There, I've said it."

I shifted; he shifted. The air in the room was suddenly thick, making it difficult to suck air into my lungs. My head felt fuzzy and dizzy as things began to spin, almost as if I was in rewind mode to replay the statement she had just made. And she called him Steven?! How formal.

It was Steve's turn. What would he say? My heart assured me he'd stay with me; my brain was telling me something completely different.

"No way, Rose, no way."

Relief washed over me like a sudden rainstorm.

"You left me—I never really loved you. You need to go. Now."

Rose's face never changed—she held that same expression—sickeningly innocent—I wanted to slap her.

"You're sure? You want to stay with her?"

"Yeah, Rose, I do—I have always loved her and always will."

Again—great relief. Rose's face was beginning to register some emotion—what was it? Sadness? Dashed hopes? A wasted plea?

"And don't stay for the show."

With that, she stood and stomped to the door, no longer the long, sweeping strides of a hopeful lover. She turned at the door, opening it behind her and looked at him.

"You're sure?"

"Definitely."

She turned and left, however, seconds later, Steve untangled our hands and legs and went after her. That really worried me, and the panic set in. I sat quietly on the couch, wondering if he was coming back.

A few minutes later he was back and closed the door. It had felt like he had been gone an hour. I scrutinized his face for any trace of the fire-engine-red lipstick she had been wearing; I didn't see any. And I smelled him—trying to detect her perfume; I wasn't able to.

As Steve got called to go on stage, I told him I would be up in a bit. He kissed me on the mouth, a full kiss of his love, and was gone, leaving me to think. Think about our future—did we even have one? Could we ever have one?

I heard the band's intro and envisioned them going out onto the stage. I would soon be leaving the *Apprehension* tour—my time with them would soon be coming to an end. I would be starting a new chapter in my life. Suddenly I was in tears thinking that I needed to concentrate on my life, free from distraction. I loved Steve with all of my being but nursing school was going to be hard enough without the complications of a serious affair.

My bipolar depression must have been kicking in at that point as I thought more and more about Chris, school, Steve and life. I could hear the songs being played—the songs of love, courage, triumph, hope; songs of denial, and a strange song about a band member's friend.

I loved that band, loved its lead singer. They had all become an important part of my life, a very large part of my life. Steve and I were getting along well; Chris and I were too, when I was there, but that was all going to change when I got home in a few weeks.

I didn't want to deal with that now. Too many variables were playing into whatever decision I was trying to make. I shrugged it off for now and went upstairs to stage left. Their performance was in its second hour; it was nearly time for the instrumentals. Steve would be coming off the stage.

I waited for him, pensive but in a heightened sense of awareness of everything around me. Two roadies—a guy and his girl, new crew this summer, were about four feet away from me, holding hands, gazing into each other's eyes. Must have been what Steve and I looked like to the people around us. They looked no older than 12 but had to be at least 18 to get on the crew. Why they were at stage left, I didn't know; generally, no one from the crew is back there, other than a senior-staffer. These kids probably hadn't been told about all of the unspoken rules yet.

The stage lights went off, flooding everything with darkness; Steve was coming off the stage to rest his voice, guided by a laser pointer from a roadie over on stage right; those new devices were quite the help in getting him safely off stage. He had 20 seconds before the lights came back on—he made it in 15.

When the lights came back, he found me there, holding a towel and a bottle of water. The girl must have been really new to all this—she audibly squealed upon seeing Steve in the light—and so close. He shot her an irritated expression, brows furrowed, lips pursed, then turned back to me, face relaxed, smiling.

We had about ten minutes while the band did their instrumental thing. He downed some of the water and threw his arms around me in a hug that set my heart ablaze. How could I even consider leaving this man? He touched my lips with two fingers; his sensuous mouth close to mine, so close I could feel his breath. He removed his fingers from my mouth after I kissed them, replacing them with his lips. His tongue searched my mouth, probing, thrusting, exploring, and spreading his taste throughout me.

His hands dove beneath the bands of my jeans and underwear, and fondled my cheeks as he nuzzled the space on my neck, just below my ear; that place that stimulated every nerve, turning my will to gelatin with his irresistible power of excitement and sexual energy.

His teeth scraped across my skin, resulting in an erratic heartbeat in my throat, which felt as though it were closing quickly in an involuntary gasp. When he brought one of his hands forward in my pants, and slid a finger into the wetness between my legs, my own hand went to his hardness and massaged it through his jeans.

I didn't know what the hell we were doing—we had rarely done anything like this before; rarely considered doing anything sexual back stage, especially in front of people.

But, whatever we were doing, it was unbelievably arousing. His nimble fingers brought me to a quick climax as he continued to nuzzle against the erogenous zone of my neck. He came quickly also, thrusting his hips into my hand, still outside his jeans. A growing wetness appeared on his jeans as we uncoupled a few minutes later, after kissing like there would be no tomorrow. I was worried about him going out on stage like that, offered to go get him a new pair of jeans, but there was no time. He had solved the problem anyway—as he walked back out onto the stage, to thunderous applause and grateful hoots and hollers, he pretended to trip over a stage wire, spilling the water in his bottle down his front. Smart guy. Good save.

I watched the rest of the show, biting my cuticles, totally embarrassed by the couple that had witnessed our antics. They didn't say a word to me but did glance at me several times—amusement I saw on their faces? Probably. Okay, so now they had seen the famous lead singer make out and nearly have sex with his girlfriend right back stage—how many other roadies could say that?

The concert and the subsequent encores were over sooner than I thought they would be. We were driving to San Francisco that night; I couldn't wait to get back to our past, our beginning, our roots. I hadn't seen San Francisco since that family vacation of 1975. Back then I had begged my parents to leave me home; I was 15—what teenager wants to be seen with her parents, even if it is a different state? What 15-year old wants to do anything, anywhere, anytime?

I had not been in search of a life with a rock star but that is what I inadvertently discovered on a July evening in San Francisco. When Steve and I returned to the city, we went to the Golden Gate Bridge—it loomed majestic in front of us, the symbol of the city—our city. I had been able to see it 12 years ago from my hotel room that I had been forced to share with my brother.

The driver of our limousine had prior instructions—pull below the bridge to allow us the chance to get out and gaze longingly at it. No San Francisco fog today—the day was sunny and gorgeous; the bridge shone bright reddish-orange in the sunlight that warmed my heart, flooding my brain with memories.

Steve and I leaned against the limo, his arms encircling me as we took in the bridge—San Francisco had saved him so many years ago when he had been a lost soul on the streets; the city took him in, sheltered him until he landed the gig with the band that sent him on his way. San Francisco had also rescued me from the horrid family vacation, and had propelled me into the magical world of love, happiness and rock-and-roll.

When we pulled into the hotel parking lot, feelings of deja-vu suddenly flooded my head—we were going to stay in the same hotel where we had met; he even reserved the same room on the sixth floor where we had gone after the pool.

Twelve years—the color of the walls and upholstery was the same, and room layout was the same; I think the paintings nailed to the wall were the same. To make it truly seem like his room from the past, he kicked his tennis shoes and sent them flying across the room, to land in a helpless pile near one of the beds, smiling all the while, a glint in his eyes.

This was our room—from a time gone by—the room in which we had sparked a romance that continued on, despite life's many twists and turns, ups and downs, ebbs and flows. We had endured and continued to love each other. I loved the man who was standing at the window, gazing at the Golden Gate, hands leaning on the sill. As I stared at his back, my body wanted him, ached for him, as it did twelve years ago when we were unable to consummate our feelings.

Steve turned to face me; in his jeans and a white button-down shirt, he looked relaxed, happy, anticipatory. His shirt was undone to the fourth button, not tucked in, hanging loosely below his hips. His long hair showered over his shoulders, laid neatly on his chest and down his back. His jeans were torn and fraying at the knees and the bottom edge, well-worn but bought in a store in that condition. His feet were covered with plain white socks—one had a tiny hole in it. He was so normal it was scary.

He could have been draped in gold with designer clothes, socks without holes, shoes that reflected his dazzling face, but he preferred simple things; the simple life, as simple as he could make it. He could stay in the very best hotels and be waited on hand and foot but he liked staying in simpler places, dealing with room service and that is all. Fame had not captured this man's integrity.

He turned and looked out the window again, and as he continued looking out the window, I took the opportunity, grabbing silk out of my suitcase, dashing into the bathroom. I cleaned up from the long ride and changed into something I wished I had had twelve years ago—a light lavender (his favorite color was purple) negligee: very revealing, very silky, very lacey in all the right places. This was something I rarely did—show up in something slinky—we just figured it would end up on the floor anyway, but this time was special.

He was still staring out the window as I emerged from the bathroom and cleared my throat. He turned slowly to face me, his expression changing from neutral to longing—I could see the hunger in his eyes, feel the magic between us cross the room. As he stared silently, he lit fires in my soul that would burn for days, keeping me warm deep inside with his love. His stare took me all in as if he were memorizing everything he saw for future reference. He mouthed the word WOW, and walked to me, arms open wide.

We met in the middle of the room, the silky material of the nightgown sweeping lazily along the floor as I stepped into his arms. The mere touch of the fabric against certain areas of my body acted like some sort of drug. As his hands roamed my back and then trailed lower, his touch set me aglow with passion. I rested my head on him, in his hair, and held him tight against me, enjoying the feel of the silk between us, the lace against my nipples as they became aroused and strained against the roughness of the lace.

Steve stepped back and again drank me into his eyes. I felt almost liquefied as my knees threatened to give way and my arms felt heavy and useless.

"You are so gorgeous."

His words were almost a whisper and I reacted to them a quiver—he thought I was gorgeous. Our lips met and we kissed each other, exploding into a craving, an eroticism that grew with every touch, every sigh, every movement. His kiss was pure excitement, pure love, pure him. When our tongues met, we both let out a sound—mine was similar to a cat's purr, his was more like a whimper.

He dipped his face to my ear, humming a new set of music I hadn't heard prior to then. It was slow and easy, probably one of his new ballads. Then he sang part of it to me, a breathy rendition of a new song—one that he would never finish.

Always on my mind, during day and night
She rests in my thoughts and desires
Her scent lingers on me when she has left me
With an exhilaration of my spirit
She's never afraid, never shy, never worried
When she's with me—she is magic and allure

We hang onto each other, making dreams come true
We don't have to pretend—we just are
Two of a kind, brought to one by a twist of fate
She is my love, my light, my love
Friends forever, lovers in body, mind and soul
In spirit—our loves goes on

Lost in her eyes, lost in her love
She takes me all the way to heaven and back
Picks me up and never lets me down
She loves me as I love her

Our unfinished song.

His hands continued to caress my curves, my hips, easily gliding over the material, finally finding my breasts with his hands, which he tickled, sending me into a feverish pitch of sexual response. He backed me to the bed, nearly gliding us over the carpet. I unbuttoned his shirt and let it fall to his feet, spreading kisses down his neck, onto his chest, circling his nipples with my tongue, causing them to harden as he had mine.

I trailed my tongue down around his navel, to just above the waistband of his jeans, which I undid and pulled down along with his underwear, freeing his erection. I rose up to take his mouth onto mine, wanting to feel him between me and the silk; wanting him to enjoy the experience of the silk as much as I was.

We swayed together next to the bed—his lead—a rhythm in his head only known to him. My fluids were beginning to flow with increased intensity. As we swayed, his arms around my shoulders, I dropped mine and lifted the silk above my hips, allowing him access to the wetness spreading between my legs. My arms went back around his waist and I pulled him closer into me.

He pulled the nightgown over my head, slowly allowing the material to flow over our bodies in the luxurious fluidity of the silk, leaving me weak in its wake and longing for his continued touch. He and I lay back on the bed where he hovered over me as I drew up my knees, giving his easy entrance, which he took full advantage of.

As always, the experience was a combination of ecstasy and excitement. He was slow, building in pace and thrust as his own excitement grew.

We turned over to face each other on our sides, my top leg over his, still coupled, locked in an endless kiss. His fingers found the sensitive spot between my legs, and slowly used two fingers to caress me into a frenzied sexual explosion that began at my toes, causing them to curl. He knew what to do to a woman and when and how to do it; there was no doubt.

The feel of him inside of me, the touch of his skin against mine, the smell of his excitement, the taste of his mouth, the look on his face—it all added up into a sensation of pure elation as he thrust one last time, climaxing deep inside of me.

We lay together on the bed, kissing, caressing, lost in the love and look and feel of each other. I loved the feel of him still within me, the kisses with the slightly swollen lips from the fervor of our lovemaking, his fingers as he played with my hair and my face. It was made all the more sensual as this was the room in which we had first started to explore each other—our first passion—our first discovery of each other. And we had just rediscovered each other.

We found the lounge later in the afternoon—he had donned that awful hat, pulled his long brown hair back into a ponytail and wore the mirrored sunglasses to complete the look. The lobby of the hotel had been remodeled—there was no longer a computer there that a 15-year old could dump her little brother in front of while she went off in search of some new experience.

The lounge was completely different—it had definitely been updated and I wasn't so sure that was a good thing. It was no longer a dark space with tables and chairs with a small stage. It was now a tropical paradise with torches and tiki masks, palm trees that were neon in bright pinks and blues, and waitresses in grass skirts and coconut bras (which did not look comfortable at all), bartenders in Hawaiian print tops and shorts.

We went to the stage and sat at a table where ours had been so long ago. A far away look came over his face—he was remembering the hard times and the times at this lounge as he climbed out of poverty to find fame and fortune, almost overnight. I was remembering the wall I had leaned against, watching his every move, memorizing his face, his eyes.

What a flood of memories were pouring over both of us— watching him and the band make their way through new songs that they didn't quite know yet, on their way to open for another band, on their way to stardom.

I had been so young back then—15 and totally innocent— never been kissed, certainly had never had anything even close to sex. Why had he picked me out of the crowd that fateful night? Neither of us could answer that. Never could. Was it love at first sight? Must have been. It still boggles my mind when I think of that first night.

I looked into his sunglasses, seeing my own reflection in the lenses. My head resting on my hands, elbows on the table, much the same way I had gazed at him back then. A candle on the table, casting odd little shadows whenever one of us sighed, illuminated our faces. He finally removed the sunglasses and laid them on the table, and continued to stare at me; at least now I could see the fire in his eyes.

A waitress came over; neither of us looked at her, we just kept staring at each other; Steve finally simply said, "Two Buds," and she was off to the bar. When she came back, her demeanor was clearly different—she had recognized him and was nervous, giddy, shaking, as if she had downed the two beers herself on the way back to our table. She stood at the edge of the table as Steve paid her without his eyes leaving mine, and still she stood for a few moments, finally sighed and walked away.

We were lost in love.

"Do you know how much I love you?" He asked the question in a low, hushed tone to his voice.

"Tell me."

"Do you really not know?"

"I know; I just want to hear it."

He smiled again at me—his beautiful smile, no teeth showing, cheeks rounded and flushed.

"I love you more than anything. There is nothing I wouldn't do for you. I would die for you and not think twice about it. I ache when you're not with me. I see you in everything I do, everything I am."

My heart was beating wildly in my chest, threatening to beat out of my chest—he rarely said such eloquent things to me. Had he thought about his words prior to this moment, or were they impromptu?

Then he said it: "Marry me."

Time stopped, and the words hung like a billboard on the air. He hadn't said that when he had given me the ring back after his suicide attempt. Why was he saying it now? I still had the ring on my right ring finger.

"Steve—I—I love you. I love you more than anything."

Did my love border on obsession, I wondered? Almost seemed like it with all the things we were saying to each other.

I had always wondered if I was obsessed with him or in love or a mixture of both. I decided that night it was all love, nothing else. I loved him and I wanted more than a part-time relationship—I wanted to stay with him and never leave his side. If that meant giving up everything I knew, everyone I knew, I was willing to do it. All I needed was him—all we needed was each other.

We continued to look at each other. He took my right hand into his and removed the ring, placing it on my left hand, above Chris' rings. It was still a perfect fit, as we were. This all felt so right and yet, I was already married, already spoken for, already taken. Yet, I was willing to give that all up.

We truly were two lost souls, lost in our own hell that we had created, coming together for a summer band tour, to love, to become one with each other again, destined to part at summer's end—one more time.

Did I want to marry him? No doubt. At that point, had I been single, we would be running off to Vegas. I could tolerate the life of a star, couldn't I? Could I be a recluse right along with him between tours? Could I be a wife, watching him with the fans, watching the fans with him?

Could I tolerate all of that as a wife? I was doing okay as a groupie, a girlfriend, whatever I was, but could I as a wife? It's different being married—you look at things differently; you see things differently. I wasn't sure I had it in me to live the reclusive lifestyle he was accustomed to.

I just wasn't sure of anything.

We were silent in the little lounge; he drank his beer and then mine as we watched each other with wonder and love, unaware that we were being watched ourselves by a small crowd that had gathered, fans that had recognized him in the semi-darkness, gawking, talking excitedly among themselves, but keeping a distance.

When we finally realized that they were there, there was nothing we could do about it—nowhere we could go. I told him that we needed to make like a couple, kiss, be into each other and just walk on by—maybe they would leave us alone if we seemed like we wanted to be left alone, which, of course, we did. He shrugged; put his sunglasses on. We stood and hugged, bringing our lips together for a long, fiery kiss, our hands fondling each other's backs. An audible sigh rose from the crowd behind us and smiled against each other's mouths.

Arms around each other, we walked close by the girls, heads held high. They watched us intently and Steve finally lifted his sunglasses at them and smiled with a glint in his eyes. He paused, and said, "Thanks for leaving us alone." And we left. Twenty pairs of eyes followed us down the hallway.

We traced our steps around the pool, drawing interested looks and suspicious glances as people weren't quite sure if who they were seeing was really who they were seeing. Then we rode to Haight Ashbury. It wasn't quite the same corner it had been in 1975 but there were still obvious traces of the hippies. We got out of the limo a few blocks south and made our way to the famous corner, passing lots of people along the way. Steve even felt comfortable enough to take off the sunglasses but not the hat— he said he fit right in with the hat. And he was right.

He ran into a few people he had known, most of which were still considered to be a part of the counter culture. They congratulated him on his success, on his ability to "make a go of things," and on me (!). This was a life I could have easily been a part of—no real responsibility, take things as they come, no worries. Steve probably would have welcomed this lifestyle too—it would have made his life a whole lot less hectic. He could blend in with the crowd and no one would be the wiser. Something to definitely consider.

If he had asked me to join him in living there at that point, I would have surrendered in a heartbeat and left everything behind. We could have hidden in San Francisco and never been seen again. But it was not to be, not yet. He had too much to do yet. He had not done all he could in the music business and I would not be the one to hold him back.

The San Francisco concerts were an overwhelming success—the guys were all thrilled to be back in the city that had launched their careers. They were electrified, sending that energy into the crowd where it bounced off of everyone and made its way back onto the stage to invigorate the band.

Three nights they played to sold-out, standing-room-only crowds. Three nights the band was the best they had ever been on stage. Three nights Steve and I made wild, exciting love in his dressing room before the shows, then again back at the hotel. We were like lovers should be—together in heart and soul.

The Summer *Apprehension* Tour was over in August, 1987, with a bang in San Francisco. The guys all scattered when it was done—Joss to Chicago; Richard to Philadelphia; Ned to New York City; Phil to Los Angeles. Actually, Phil rode with us in the limo to LA after the last concert. We heard all about what he was going to do with his children to try to cram an entire summer down their throats in two weeks while he was with them. I had a few weeks to go before nursing school—Chris would be looking for me to come home soon.

We slept for a time in the limo, fitful sleep, each on their own seat; Steve's and my heads together at a corner, my feet at Phil's feet at another corner. We dropped Phil at his apartment on Wilshire Boulevard and went to the Laurel Canyon house. Home. It could have been *my* home; *our* home. Something else to consider.

Coming home after a concert series is like needing to go to sleep for the next several days. Steve and I retreated to his bedroom and didn't come out for three days. His housekeeper left food at the door for us when we didn't answer—brought it in when we did. We mostly slept, caught up on TV and news, and slept. And we read the fan mail that his secretary sent over.

His fan mail was generally answered by a few secretaries at his manager's office, but some made it into his hands—some were from teenagers and younger who wrote him passionate letters of love and hope and "I will simply die if I can't meet you!" Those were the ones he never saw. Some were touching—asking for an autograph for a sick friend or family member. Some were long and sentimental as people described what his music meant to them over the years—sometimes his music had been able to bring the writer out of a dark depression, on the brink of suicide.

He personally answered those that touched him the most, particularly those from sick children and people who had been considering suicide. I helped quite a bit with the mail, as it got overwhelming at times.

Time was drawing near for me to leave him again. My heart wanted to stay, to be his wife, to love him for all eternity and be a piece of his world. There was a place for us and it was there in that house—it could have been my house, it could have been my town.

But, I had to go back to reality—my reality, not his. Four more days and my plane would take me home the day after Labor Day.

Labor Day would turn out to be very laborious mentally and physically.

*W*e were home, his home, for a few days—Labor Day, three more days away from my own home; time to go would be here soon enough and I would be going to my own home. Back to the mundane life of a soon-to-be nurse, married to a firefighter, the secret consort to a star. What could be more out of the ordinary? I always wanted to be different. Guess I truly was now. I was one exception to the rule and I had no business being that exception.

I wanted to stay with Steve. I was fighting the urge to remain in Los Angeles and leave everything else I had behind me in a trail of stardust. The temptation was great—greater than anything I had faced in the past. My life loomed long and boring ahead of me—there was nothing left for me in Illinois at this point. I had a husband who was tolerant of my lifestyle but it was hardly fair to him what I was doing. My cat was in Illinois, and I loved him dearly, but, uprooting him from the home he loved and plunking him down in a new home with a strange cat would be unfair; he was better off with Chris. My new direction in life—nursing—was waiting for me there too, but I could go to school in California without difficulty, and get a nursing job when I was finished, but I didn't really think I would have to work if I didn't want to.

On the downside, there was still that lifestyle I would have to deal with—Steve was a bonafide rock star—there was no getting around that. I would have to deal with a whole lot of other girls' love and desire for him, and their attempts to get at him at any cost. He was always going to be leaving on a tour, or a personal appearance, or an interview, or…the list goes on and on. The man was in great demand and he was committed, at least, for now. Could I handle that demand?

There were pros and cons on both sides of the issue and I had to take the time to look at each side, make my decision rationally, with a lot of thought—yeah, right.

For now, Steve and I spent most of our free time alone and in seclusion in his bedroom or somewhere in his house, but mostly in his bedroom. There were few times when we were separated—either when he was on the phone discussing music or management issues, or when he got an idea for a song and was off pounding out the music. Even then I usually tagged along and watched, fascinated by his abilities.

I had to reconcile the fact that I was going to stay with him— by the time I only had one day left to decide, the decision had been made. I wasn't going home; I was staying, destined to become a California girl. Everyone in Illinois called California the land of fruits and nuts—I guess I was going to fit right in.

I decided to tell Steve that night at dinner. I knew he would be pleased, thrilled probably. He and I had been waiting for this moment for a long time. It was time that I wore his ring on my left ring finger for real and have it mean that we truly belonged to each other, not just for the moment but for the lifetime.

Dinner was moments away; his housekeeper silently nodded her head toward the table. Steve was on the phone with the band's manager, telling him no, absolutely not will he agree to another tour this soon; the band needs a break and some time away from each other; the families need a break. The fans will wait and they will have to understand. I went upstairs to change my shirt for dinner—I had been a little too chilly in the one I had on—the air conditioner was cranked in the late summer heat, the way Steve liked it, but I was actually cold. Must have been the nervousness over telling him my decision to stay.

In the master bathroom, I stood in front of the mirror and looked at myself, critically, as always. I had lost some weight being with him—didn't eat much when we were together—he ate more than I. That was okay—I cold have stood to lose about 40 more pounds, but that would come.

I still didn't see what he saw when he looked at me—he saw confidence and beauty and loved me for it. I saw self-doubt and no self-esteem, a woman who didn't think much of herself and of whom she had become, and still couldn't understand why she was with such a handsome, famous person.

I was still an extremely curious person—some things never change—and, as I stared in the mirror, I noticed a panel that was ajar, a cabinet I didn't know existed; I knew there was a medicine cabinet on the left side of the mirror but had no idea there was one on the right. Curiosity killed the cat, right? I didn't care. I went back and forth about opening the cabinet, not sure what was right—I was living in this house—his house—I had made the decision to stay on and be his wife. Did I dare open what could potentially be a Pandora's box and find out what was in the cabinet?

There are some things that should be left alone—left hidden—because they are so destructive and so deadly that nothing good can come of them. I should have learned that lesson long ago in Salt Lake City, but some things I never learn or never remember.

It took me about five seconds to look into the cabinet, opening it slowly and cautiously—he would be the one to put a bunch of loose marbles or something else in there ready to fall out at the first opening of a latch, just to catch me snooping. But, nothing fell out as I swung the door further.

Nothing, except for my heart.

What I saw caused panic and despair to wash over me as my blood ran cold, turning me even cooler standing near the air conditioning vent.

In the medicine chest was his stash—syringes, a vial of a brown liquid and several vials of a brown liquid. How I wished that they had all been there for a very long time, but, seeing as how the door was ajar, there was what looked to be a drop of fresh blood on the needle of a syringe, I knew he had been using again—recently—very recently.

My head spun. He had told me, assured me, promised me that he had quit using. That his suicide had been enough of a scare and a wake-up call that he needed help and that he needed to stay clean from the drugs. I should have known better—I should have paid attention to the signs I was seeing, but I thought he was simply happy with the way things were going on the tour; I thought he was happy being with me. I was so stupid. I blamed myself for not noticing, for not being aware enough of what was going on in front of my eyes.

My head reeled and I felt as if I might spin out of control there in the bathroom, but I stayed standing, lost in a whirlwind of thoughts, feelings and the irresistible urge to run. That is the urge I acted upon—I ran.

I removed the engagement ring from my left hand and placed it on his pillow on the bed, along with a few syringes that were in the cabinet and the vial of liquid. He would get the message. It was a very clear message. Then I left.

I went downstairs and could hear Steve still on the phone, insisting that there was nothing the record company could do to get them back on tour in the fall. His cat was at my feet and I bent down and scratched him one last time before silently going out the front door and into the evening. Into an evening that had suddenly turned foreign and frightening.

I don't know which direction I actually went in or where I thought I was headed; I just walked; it seemed endless. I was not aware of things around me, except that I had managed, somehow, to grab my purse off the couch as I left his house. Not that it mattered anyway because I didn't know what I was doing. I had no plan; nowhere to run.

"I have to leave this town" was all my mind kept telling me — "leave this town before it's too late." It almost was too late. What if I hadn't found out? Would he have ever shared it with me? Would he have let me know before we decided to take the plunge and get married? Would it have mattered so much if he had told me and been honest with me?

I was so disappointed in him, in me, in us. Why the drug and why now and why heroin? Why didn't he tell me? Why didn't I know?

I walked the streets of LA, lost in tears and anger and sadness, a deep sadness like I had never known in the past. A sadness that we were over now; I could not be with him. I just didn't know how to handle the drug thing, pretty much the way he didn't know how to handle the rape thing.

I sat on a park bench in a small inner-city park on a corner the next morning; it was morning? How did it get to be morning already? My feet hurt and my knees were aching; I must have been walking all night but I didn't remember a thing. I still had my purse slung over one shoulder; that was a good thing. But, as for the time, I had no clue where that had gone.

I sat, not really knowing what to do next, where to turn. My first inclination was to call Chris—he was always the one I thought to call first. But I put that thought aside—what was he going to do? Tell me he told me so and hang up on me probably. It would serve me right.

I thought briefly about calling Steve, but immediately put that thought to rest as well. What would be the point? He would come and get me, tell me some cock-and-bull story about the heroin not being his or not being something he was actively participating in at that point in time, and I would go back to him without a doubt. I was so stupid!

So, as my thoughts rambled on, around in my head, I wandered on, around the streets of LA. I was unsure of destination, not familiar with the city, and didn't really care anyway. I didn't see anything, didn't know anything, didn't care about anything.

A second night I spent on the street: wandering, stopping to sit, dozing-off at times. I didn't know where I was, if it was even safe to be out and about, sleeping on a bench or sidewalk. I wasn't alone in that respect—I had a lot of company, but none looked too friendly; no one spoke to me and I spoke to no one. That I can remember.

The third day, after two days of almost stifling big-city heat, a cold front must have been settling in—I remember waking up in that little park again, feeling cold and chilled. I figured it was my depression kicking in as I always got cold when I was depressed, but, looking around at other people, I could see they were wearing sweaters and layered clothing.

And there was fog: it seemed to be rolling into the city in waves like the sea at the beach. The clouds were in my hands; I was able to touch them as they advanced through the city, wrapping everything in a covering of white and grey mists. The cold front had come seemingly out of nowhere and had wreaked havoc on all kinds of traffic and people's lives, mine included.

When the fog rolled in, it was as if the California world of sun and fun, of models and beautiful people, was plunged into my world of gloominess. It covered everything in a haze of humid air that glazed my exposed skin with a damp layer of heavy dew as I sat on my bench. I felt like a statue must feel covered in the foggy darkness—as though the fog would swallow me and there were times that I wished it would. I didn't want to be a part of this world any longer, or any world, for that matter.

My flight home was due to depart that night and I wondered if I could get out of this town. I wandered the rest of the day, thinking and crying. People on the street avoided me—I probably looked a little crazy, unwashed, unkempt, crying and sobbing like an idiot. No direction, nowhere to turn to, no one to go to.

I took a cab from somewhere in the city to the airport. The fog had thickened, and LAX was at a stand still—no flights coming or going and, apparently, that was the way it was up and down the coastline. I hadn't told Steve when my departure was so there was no way he would be trying to find me at the airport that night. I hadn't thought I would be leaving so there had been no reason to tell him.

There was a scramble at the airport for other means of getting the hell out of town—I was finally able to make it to a phone after standing in line for hours it seemed. Amtrack was it and I didn't care what the woman at the other end of the phone did—I just wanted to be on something to get out of Los Angeles, out of California. I didn't hear where I was going, but I was on a midnight train—#304, track #7. I would be there.

Another cab ride took me to the train station where I numbly awaited my train. Midnight—I boarded at 11:45 PM, found my seat and sat. Packed with other passengers, the train rumbled out of the station at midnight exactly—going somewhere; going anywhere. It was like the song *Midnight Train to Georgia*—LA turned out to be too much for me and I had to get out of there. I didn't care to where, as long as it took me away from this city.

As the train pulled away from the crowded station, into the night, I could see up ahead as we went around a corner that it was still horrendously foggy—the headlight from the train's engine cut through it like a saber, carving in it a path for this silver machine. I hung my head against the window and cried. Cried like I had been doing for days—I was amazed that I still had tears to cry.

I took the opportunity to think about what had happened over the past several days and found I could remember very little from being on the streets of Los Angeles. I am sure I ran into people, had contact with someone, but I couldn't remember a soul; and I am sure that no one remembered my anonymous face in the crowd either.

I missed Steve, almost desperately so. I felt so alone; I didn't know what to do. There were so many times that day that I had wanted to call him and have him come get me—I didn't care about the heroin or the deception—what kind of nurse was I going to be if I couldn't have compassion for an addict that I loved?

I did still love him; for all his faults, for all my faults, for his addiction and his fame, I loved him. What could be so bad about the heroin use? Maybe I should get off at the first stop and go back; maybe this was all so stupid and I should just grow up and deal with it and help him deal with an addiction that obviously had a great pull on him as he hadn't been able to give it up. Maybe I was still that stupid little girl from Ohio that didn't know anything and should just buck up and deal with it. Maybe.

I didn't know what to do and as the train pulled farther away from Los Angeles, my doubts became louder and stronger in my head. Doubts about going home and attempting to have any semblance of a normal life with my husband, doubts about turning around and having any semblance of a normal life with my lover.

I was in a tailspin of emotions that were threatening to take me over.

A lack of sleep and food were obviously working against me as my thoughts rambled in my head as much as the train was rambling down the track. The clatter of the train was repeating, "Going away—going away—going away" in a sing-song rhythm as it became faster and faster and drowned out my thoughts.

The gentleman sitting next to me was reading; he didn't notice the tears that flowed from my eyes and down my face; no one noticed the poor heavy-set woman who had no luggage, no purpose, who had wandered the streets of Los Angeles in search of something—no idea what—and who was now destined for where?

286

No plan, no destiny, nowhere to go.

The more distance put between the train and Los Angeles, the more I physically throbbed all over, the more I mentally agonized over the whole situation. No position was comfortable; I continually shifted in the seat, probably driving the guy next to me bananas.

I still had no idea where we were headed—I was so directionally-challenged it wasn't even funny; I literally didn't know East from North. If I had the presence of mind to look at my ticket, I would have seen that we were on the way to Indianapolis, but I didn't actually care.

Looking back on the Summer *Apprehension* tour, I can obviously see what I had chosen to ignore: the euphoric highs and the crashes during which he slept for hours on end. The sex we had in out of the ordinary places, in surprising and unexpected ways. Had that all been as the result of the heroin use and not really about us being together again? In the back of my mind, I guess I really should have known, but just didn't want to see.

It just couldn't have all been only the drug, could it?

I was beginning to regret just leaving the heroin on his pillow along with my ring, but he was smart—he would get the message. I also regretted leaving my belongings behind—everything I had taken with me on tour was still at his house, including my pictures, tour jacket, clothes, everything. All that stuff was at his house and would have come in handy now—I am sure I was a little filthy from a lack of hygiene and clean clothes. Poor guy sitting next to me; he didn't seem to notice or, he was polite enough that he didn't show it.

My relationship with Steve was forever over; that was the realization I came to halfway through the day; it was by my choice this time, which made it all the more bizarre. I loved him—I loved him to the core of my being. My heart was breaking leaving him and Los Angeles and California. I already missed him desperately and had to fight every moment not to get off at some stop and race back to him. But, I couldn't; I knew that in my brain, but my heart was still fighting.

He was using again; the heroin was winning and the rest of us, including me, were losing. It had been heroin that had nearly taken his life in a suicide attempt; obviously rehab and methadone had not been effective. I just didn't understand the draw of the drug. The few times I had shot heroin with him were unlike anything I had ever done before—intense sensations, heightened awareness, euphoria. All exhilarating but the side effects were hell—nausea, sleepiness. Didn't like those much. I guess I just don't have an addictive personality—drinking only makes me sleepy as do the drugs; I smoked for several years, but Steve put an end to that and I was able to quit with ease. The only thing I would consider myself being addicted to was him.

He was going to be very hard to give up.

Time rolled on. So did the train. I must have cried myself to sleep at some point because I lost time: few hours. The sun was shining brightly through the windows of the train and there was no more fog—obviously we were far enough away from Los Angeles that it had dissipated. That thought started my tears again. I finally found the bathroom and cleaned up as best I could with what I had in my purse and a hand dryer.

The train rolled into Indianapolis three days later, after rambling through the mountains and the plains. I had been gone from Steve's home for five days…I wondered what Steve and Chris were thinking, if either of them was thinking about me. I sat in the Indianapolis train station for a long time; it was early afternoon and I wasn't really sure what to do. I didn't have the money to get home from this far—I had spent most of what I had left on the train ticket. I finally got my courage together, found a pay phone and called home.

Chris showed up five hours later, running through the double doors of the station and scanning the small crowd for my face. He appeared relieved and exasperated, still in his fire uniform—he had been at work when I called him. He came to me on the large wooden bench and sat next to me and grilled me endlessly about where I had been and what I had been doing; I only wished I could have answered most of his questions. He told me he was booked on a flight that night to go to California to try to find me—Steve had finally called him two days after I left his house and told him I was, basically, missing.

I walked into the front door of my house four and a half hours later. My heart recognized it all but I was so tired that everything looked strange and unfamiliar. Chris drew a bath for me—guess that was a hint that I was filthy—and then went into the bedroom. While I sat in the warmth of the bubbles and water, I heard him talking; it took a few minutes but I finally realized he was talking to Steve. I wondered how much they had been in contact the last several days.

I went to bed and slept like the dead for nearly 24 hours. I was home, in the comfort of my violet wallpaper, my husband and my cat. Numb, I went about some routine that was fairly normal, sleep-walking through much of my days. But, as before, Chris was there for me. He never judged; he never said a word about California, and more importantly, he never asked me anything. He didn't care about what I had been doing; he was just happy that I was home.

Nursing school was next on my agenda and I had to physically and mentally prepare for it by picking myself up and out of the funk I was in. The courses I had to take in preparation for the core classes began the second week of September, and I was ready. I had always enjoyed being a student so I knew I would enjoy this.

Time passed all too slowly; days and hours dragged on; things seemed to be happening in slow motion. Steve called and I wouldn't answer the phone, wouldn't allow Chris to answer it either—thank goodness for caller ID. He wrote letters too but I sent them back, unopened. I half expected him to show up on my doorstep but he never did.

Around Christmas, as I was finishing up my first semester of classes, I received a box from Steve; I recognized the return address and the horrible handwriting. I almost sent it back without opening it but I was too curious…all that was there was my stuff—my suitcase and all the other things I had left at his house. There was also a note—brief, but well stated—the sentiment was that he knew how badly he had screwed up, he was sorry, and that he loved me and knew that he messed up a good thing and was sorry for that too.

I pretty much kept to myself at school, not really making any friends. I went to class, drifted through English, organic chemistry, microbiology, anatomy and physiology; all A's once again. Sickening, isn't it? I don't even remember those prerequisite classes—the only one I recall even a little is microbiology, because I enjoyed it so much.

The nursing classes were much more interesting and held my attention. I had never had anything like these classes, had never even worked in anything medical, unlike the majority of my classmates. Nursing school was much more structured than journalism school. There were a lot of grey areas in journalism, but, in the medical field, there are no greys—it's life or death. And the grade scale was much more strict—anything below an 85 was failing.

Clinical time was something else all together. I had never walked into a patient's room and now we were all expected to not only walk into our assigned patient's room, but also do a quick assessment and a bed bath. Sounds easy, right? I thought so too until I saw the door I was to go through to meet my very first patient; that doorway loomed imposingly in front of me like a great yawning giant; I wasn't sure I was going to be able to go in there and make nice to a patient and try to give her a bath.

The anxiety level was huge that first day as I wrestled with myself, reminding my brain that this is all part of nursing, and if I was going to be a good nurse, I could at the very least, give a bath. Then I saw my classmates lined up in the hall, much in the same way I was, leaning against the wall, agonizing over the same predicament. We all looked pretty comical, pale and very nervous. It was nice to know I wasn't the only one who felt the same panic.

Finally heaving a deep breath, I went on in to meet my very first patient; she turned out to be a very nice lol ("little old lady" in medical-eze), who was there with pneumonia. She had just finished receiving a breathing treatment and the therapist was encouraging her to cough. He handed me a basin to give her something to spit in and he left; as she spit into the pink basin, I threw up in the waste-basket. I never could handle anything remotely respiratory. Still can't. Yuck. All nurses have one bodily function or fluid that they cannot handle. I found out what mine was that day.

At least the day could only go up from that point, and so did the rest of nursing school.

Nursing was challenging and gratifying; stressful and grueling. Decisions had to be made in an instant—people's lives depended on my ability to think and make those snap decisions. No one could teach anyone to care, though—that had to come from the heart. I had always seen nursing as more of an art than a science; an art that takes courage, patience, compassion and an open mind.

Two years of school in the actual nursing program—two long years that I am happy I had the chance to enjoy and experience. My decision to become a nurse was the right thing to do, at the right time. No distractions now that Steve and I were through. I missed him but school kept me plenty busy. Plus I forged a whole new relationship with Chris as he helped me with my studies with his paramedic background. After a few months, I didn't even check the online web site to see what the band was up to. It didn't matter anymore, at least, not to my brain; it did to my heart.

I graduated in May of 1992; again I didn't attend any of the ceremonies; not the graduation and not the pinning. All I wanted to do was get on with my nursing career. Most everyone from my class was going into hospital nursing; I chose long-term care—the elderly.

And time continued to pass. I got my license without any difficulty and was a practicing registered nurse, extremely proud of those two initials after my name: Jean Tanner, RN. Nice. Yet there were still times that I wanted to write Jean Potts, RN. I worked night shift for a while; six months later I moved to day shift with a title and more responsibility.

1993 would turn out to be a very unusual year, all around. We were watching crime dramas on TV—*Law and Order* and *Homicide*; laughing at a show about nothing; wondering what was going on behind the *Picket Fences*; and watching the normal, blue-collared life of a domestic goddess. *Philadelphia* showed audiences the human face of AIDS; *What's Eating Gilbert Grape* introduced Leonardo DiCaprio to fame; and *Sleepless in Seattle* made even the cynics believe in love again. Meat Loaf sang about doing anything for love, except for that, whatever that was; Alladin and Jasmine sang of whole new worlds; and Aerosmith was *Livin' on the Edge*, as were we all.

The Midwest suffered severe flooding to the tune of $10 billion; 72 people were killed in a government raid of a dangerous cult in Waco, Texas; and two police officers would be convicted in the Rodney King beating in a case that would change the lives of police officers and video camera owners everywhere; and China would break the nuclear test moratorium, placing nerves on edge.

I had managed to keep a part of my past a deep secret at my job at the nursing home—nearly six years since I last saw Steve. I never spoke of anything at work other than my husband and his duties at the fire department, and my cats. We now had two—a black one and a white one—Pepper and Salt. My first baby had passed away, leaving me broken hearted. I didn't have children to talk about or any family in the area. I had a secret past but I knew no one with whom I could share it. Steve had to stay buried like a dream that, if allowed to rise, could cause a cascade of grief and sorrow.

Unfortunately, my worlds were about to collide and there would be nothing I could do to stop it.

We Couldn't Hold On
By Steve Potts

So many memories of a time long past
There was never enough time to say what I wanted
Days turned into months into years—all so fast
We turn around, we've grown, we're gone

Too many promises, too many doubts, too many
When it's over, there's no music, no song
Through all the silence and through all the noise
We had it all, we had it good, we had each other, it was so wrong

You walked away and I let you go
I should have listened to the angels on my shoulder
There were so many dreams we had
So much hope and so much love
We couldn't hold on, or did we hold on too tight?
A short good-bye whispered on the wind
A tear down my cheek, down my cheek
And it was over

Inside all of the promises, all of the dreams
We should have seen the truth, the light in each other
I stand alone, walk isolated, listening to my screams
Bewildered, floundering, I search for your face

Can we try again? Could you come back to my world?
Or, can I fit into your world, would you allow it?
It felt as thought there is not turning back, no look back
What have we done? We're breaking our spirits bit by bit

We couldn't hold on—to each other, to ourselves
We couldn't hold on—through the darkness, through the light
We couldn't hold on—to the love, to our lives
Could we try again? Can't we try again?

I had heard his mother wasn't well. Concerts that were cancelled so he could be at her bedside were news on all the entertainment programs. I considered calling him but decided it was no longer my place; not anymore. I also considered calling James, but decided that was out of the question also.

The story of the cancelled concerts continued for two weeks, then the announcement came: Steve's mother had died at home, in the arms of her sons; funeral to be private for family and close friends. I wanted to go but I wasn't even a friend at this point; we hadn't seen each other since 1987, six years ago; was I justified in going? His mom had been like a mother to me for many years; I had to swallow whatever pride I had left and go to Atlanta, to acknowledge her death, her life.

Chris, my faithful, ever understanding husband, was not too sure he wanted to let me go; to fly off to Atlanta to see the man who had meant so much to me. But, he finally seemed to get it— that I had to go—as we stood in Chicago's O'Hare Airport, saying good-bye. I cried the entire flight; don't know if I was crying about leaving Chris behind, about seeing Steve, about Steve's mother. I just cried; for all of us, I guess.

The taxi took me directly to the family house—it still looked the same—same geraniums on the porch, same well-manicure lawn, new coat of paint. I hesitated to get out—Steve and James were both on the front porch, coffee mugs in hand. James looked good—hair a little longer, but still nicely trimmed, as always. He was facing the street; his older brother sideways from the street.

Steve—my heart fluttered at the sight of him. His hair was feathered to his shoulders, maybe a little below them, so much shorter than it had been. He looked older—so much older, even from the side. He had gained some weight—it was evident in the way his pants fit around his waist, and in his face. His eyes looked tired, even from that distance.

I didn't want to get out of the taxi—I suddenly wanted to go back home and not have my life in any more upheaval. Why was I here? What was I thinking? This was no longer my place. I had a life in Illinois—a good life, a good job, a good husband. My mind was panicking as thoughts raced with many reasons to run away and only one to stay—Steve.

Too late. James was coming down the steps, a smile on his face, Steve close behind him, hands shoved in his pants pockets, head down, face hidden by his hair. James pulled me out of the taxi as the driver handed my bags to Steve, who paid him and sent him on his way. My escape route was gone. James held me tightly and told me he was glad I had come. I told him how sorry I was—there really was nothing else left to say.

Steve was suddenly there, face to face with me as James stepped away. His face seemed a thousand years old as we looked at each other. The grooves near his mouth and between his eyebrows were well worn with the years of glory and loss. His eyes spoke volumes as he stared at me with those dark brooding eyes, looking me up and down as if he were contemplating an extravagant, price-too-high-to-pay purchase.

Was he glad to see me? Did he want me to leave? His eyes glistened with unshed tears as he opened his arms and took me into them, encircling my waist. He visibly and physically relaxed in my arms, burying his face in my neck as I melted at his touch. He cried softly against me as I allowed my own tears to flow. We stayed in each other's arms for what seemed like forever. I opened my eyes and saw James carrying my bags into the house.

Still holding me, he spoke, we spoke; nearly at the same time.

You're here—I can't believe you're here! I'm here. I've missed you—more than you'll know. I've missed you too; I didn't come for this—I came because of your mom—I am so sorry. She loved you. I loved her too. I love you—still. Me too.

What had we just said to each other?!

He kissed my neck lightly, still holding me close. His lips on my neck had the power to make me think and say anything—always had been that way, and he knew it. I wanted to abandon everything, after all this time, to be with him again. Did anything from the past mean anything anymore? Were we firing things up again?

Walk with me.

He took my hand and led me down the road. The sun was just setting on the horizon as we headed toward it, talking, going over the last several years. The last tour I had joined him for was the Summer of 1987, celebrating the ninth album, *Apprehension*, which had been a not-so critical success, but fans didn't care what critics had to say. Fans were loyal and only cared if their band was speaking to their hearts. After the tour of '87 and into '88, the band went their separate ways, not officially breaking up, just taking a long break. They had decided to take time for themselves, to get to know their families, to discover who they were.

So, how was I doing in Chicagoland? Me? I had just graduated nursing school as an RN, something I had always wanted to be. Chris had pushed me to go for it. Married life was fine, I guess. Comfortable, that was the perfect word for me too. Chris was wonderful, patient, understanding. No—no children. Cats.

We walked to his old high school and sat on the outdoor bleachers at the stadium. A slight breeze was blowing, making it was a little chilly on that June evening. He took his suit coat off, placed it gallantly around my shoulders, leaving his arm around me, pulling me into him.

Still the silence. We were always good at silence; we had never been good at talking. So we sat, watching the shadows grow long into the evening. No one bothered us; I kept looking for someone following us, but no one had; people were keeping their distance due to his loss, allowing him time to grieve.

Steve and I looked into each other's eyes, both of us searching for the light, the spark that had once been there; it still was. We had both spent sleepless nights, searching for a reason that we were over, that we had changed our minds. That I had run away and never looked back. Someone had to say it—someone had to admit that we had made an awful mistake that had sent us in separate directions for so many years. We hadn't said good-bye after the tour of '87, as I walked away, convinced that we were too different, too intense, too stubborn.

And yet, here we were, still the same people who had been in so much love, in the midst of so much passion. We made promises to each other so many times—they couldn't all have been in vain, could they?

I searched his eyes, his face, as he searched mine. There was still something there, despite everything. Nothing that strong just fades away like a shadow in the mist. We had both changed over the years: we were both a little heavier, both a little more cynical. But, did that make it all truly over, or simply just put aside? Does true love ever really desert your heart or does it remain there, hidden, until it is brought out again in the right moment, the right place?

San Francisco seemed a hundred years away, yet I could still see his face in that hotel bar, young, swept away in me. He never really changed—just aged—and today—in this place—in this hour—I didn't want to say good-bye ever again.

Then we talked. About what happened in Los Angeles in 1987.

"You never said what happened when you left me. Chris kind of told me some of it, but I need you to tell me."

I hung my head and said, "I couldn't stay. The drugs, Steve. I couldn't handle the drugs, and now being a nurse, I have learned a lot—I think I can understand it all now. Much better than I could back then."

"Are you sure?"

"I'm sure—I just need you to be honest with me, about it all. How much are you using?" I didn't want to hear the answer but I needed to hear it and understand it.

"Once or twice a week—no more. I swear. I don't know why. Stress, I guess." His voice had become weaker. His face was full of pain and anguish. It was very hard for him to talk about this and yet, this was exactly what we needed to talk about.

"That's all?" I was pushing but he needed to be pushed.

"That's all—I swear."

He showed me his arms—two areas were red and swollen slightly but not near what I expected. For the first time he offered to show me his feet as some addicts inject between their toes, but I declined. He had admitted his drug use to me—I finally was able to believe all that he said to me.

"Do you still love me?" he asked with a face still in doubt and fear and pain.

I nodded, unable to speak for a change.

"I love you," he said. "There has been no one else since you left me."

That hit me like a brick.

I felt the pull between us getting stronger, willing us to give in to the love that was spilling from our hearts, out into the evening. His arm on my shoulder grew warm with a heat between us, a heat that had never really cooled. When he pulled me into him, I didn't resist, couldn't resist.

His lips crashed into mine with a hunger that had not been

satisfied for years. He tasted the same, except for the coffee he had been drinking. The smell of sweat had been replaced with a scent of yearning I had not experienced in years. It was all too familiar, too exciting, too heady.

We broke away from the passion for the span of three heartbeats, long enough to say three little words I have not said and truly meant in years; three little words I have only truly meant for him.

And we said them together, this time, in perfect unison, feeling every nuance, every thought, every word, every heartbeat.

"I love you."

Through space and time it hit us—we still needed each other—we were still each other's soul mate; that could never change. We had met as strangers, and became what we were that minute, that second, that instant—a couple, tied by fate, lost in a world working against us. We had turned to other people in our grief and had, in that one instant, turned our backs on anyone else.

I held Steve; held him tight against me, willing my soul to go back to his and touch him, hold him, keep him. I can't explain what happened on those bleachers, but we connected again— never to be lost again. It all came flooding back—all the love, the passion, the pain. It was all there. What the hell were we going to do with it?

He kissed me again and I let him in—his tongue explored me as I did him; we exploded in the heat of the moment, hands roaming over body parts that had been forbidden for so long from each other's caress. His suit coat was tossed off my shoulders as he undid my blouse; his hands found me through the lace of the bra.

I didn't want our reunion to be here, in stadium bleachers that teenagers used as their own romantic settings, but we certainly couldn't go back to the house—it didn't seem right to be in his mother's house, under the watchful eye of his father whose own heart was breaking. At least not tonight. I also didn't want to be reminded of his mom that night—too much sadness.

He looked at me for a moment.

You have a hotel? Sure—for tonight. We could go there.

He was like a kid again—the grief replaced by apparent happiness and anticipation. He was giggling, almost giddy. He kissed me quickly on the mouth and called James on the cell phone he carried everywhere these days. The conversation was brief.

"Come to the football field to pick us up—don't bring your wife."

James, always the good sport, did as he was told, smiling suspiciously in the rearview mirror. We didn't know it at the time but it was obvious to James what we were up to—in putting my blouse back on, I missed a button. Sigh.

I checked into the hotel with Steve close on my heels, every so often, kissing my neck or cheek as I tried to sign my name on the register. The desk clerk gave us a stern look which I ignored, as I had to re-sign my name—I had written "Mrs. Steve Potts." Wishful thinking?

Our walk to the door, down a long hallway several flights up, took on shades of past hallway walks, going all the way back to San Francisco.

I handed him the electronic key—I could never make work—and he let us into the room. Typical hotel—two chairs, a desk, TV, bed—bed—soon to be our bed. And I was nervous. So was he. This man had introduced me to sex and everything that came with it; we had been together for years. And we were nervous.

Steve sat my suitcase on the floor and came up behind me as I had been contemplating the bed. His arms went around my shoulders; I leaned my head back against his chest and chin. His closeness could still cause my heart to beat in that funny way that made me feel it would stop at any second.

I took his hands into mine—his fingers were long, a little chubbier, the nails rough at the ends, cuticles red from biting them—a new nervous habit. He fingered my wedding band and engagement ring—the rings of another man—then quickly stopped. My nails were short as well, rough from years of biting them to the quick; the skin of my hand dry and cracked form all the hand-washing we nurses do on a daily basis. He ran a finger over several small skin tears on my hands—cat scratches from roughhousing with my babies.

He rubbed his cheek against mine and held it there for a time. How I had missed that cheek, the feel of that hair against my face.

I turned, his arms still around my shoulders, and gazed into his eyes, which were now sparking, the opening to his spirit. His eyelashes were still longer that most; his eyebrows naturally poised at a degree that made him appear sad most of the time. That nose—still long, thin, chiseled at the end with small nostrils that flared only as he slept. Small thin lips covering straight teeth on top, uneven teeth on the bottom. I remembered every scar, every mole, every pore. He had a few more grey hairs framing his face and in his eyebrows; so did I.

He spoke first.

"So, where did we go wrong?"

"We got stupid. I got stupid."

"How do we fix that?"

"I'm not sure we can now."

He sighed heavily and pulled me into him, holding me tightly, as though his life depended on it, as though we would never let me go. We stayed locked in our embrace until he let go.

The room was dark so he went into the bathroom, turned on the light, came out and left the door open a crack so that light would shine through. He sat down on the end of the bed, bounced on it a few time, declared it "fit" and stood up in front of me.

"I want you—I think you know that." His voice was breaking up a little as he spread his arms for me to come to him.

My heart was torn—for several seconds. Yes, I was still married to Chris and was poised, once again, to break the vows we had taken. But ours had truly become a marriage of convenience—it was a marriage between two friends. I loved Chris—for everything he was to me, for everything he had been to me. I had betrayed him before by being with Steve; I was about to do so again. There was no turning away from this man—I couldn't stop destiny, couldn't stop love.

Steve pulled his t-shirt over his head, shaking his hair out during the process. His chest was still, basically, hairless. His belly was more rounded, a sign he hadn't been on stage for a bit, working off extra calories—he admitted a lot of his mom's friends had been cooking for the family, and they were pretty good cooks. He undid his suit pants and let them fall, kicking off his tennis shoes as he kicked away the pants. Still the white brief underwear—nothing fancy—nothing obnoxious. I had forgotten—almost—how fabulous he looked in his underwear and sweat socks.

As he stepped to me, I could smell his arousal, mingled with the familiar scent of his sweat starting to bead on his skin. His lips found mine as his hands, once again, began to unbutton my blouse. There was more of me at this point since I had continued my numb eating after the rape in an effort to make myself unattractive to any man. And nursing school contributed to extra weight with stress eating. Always an excuse; never a solution.

He removed my blouse then the bra. After all these years he still had slight difficulty with the clasp—that always made me smile. His hands came up and cupped the fullness of both breasts, found the nipples with his fingers, kindling my desire further.

My hands found his stiffness and freed it from his briefs, caressing him between our bodies. He pressed his mouth against mine harder, his tongue prodding every corner of my mouth. He still tasted of the coffee he had been drinking on his front porch. His moans began, at first light and breathy, continuing to crescendo in tone.

I pulled away from his mouth and looked at him—I wanted to take all of him in—I wanted him emblazoned in my memory.

He finished undressing me, taking off his underwear at the same time, and then took me into his arms once more, holding us together, skin-to-skin, body heat to body heat. Together we fell onto the bed where we made love—unhurried, full of each other, delightful—love. When we were both spent, laying in each other's arms, aglow with the passion and the sparks that had passed between us, glistening with sweat, I spoke.

"I want you to know, I don't do this with just anyone."

"Neither do I," he admitted.

"I don't want to lose you again; I don't want to let go of you again; I can't let you go again, but I can't ask you to wait for me, to put your life on hold." I was fighting back the tears as I spoke to him.

"I'll wait—no matter what—how long—I'll wait."

We spent the night relearning each other, rediscovering each other. We talked a lot; seemed like we said more on that night than we ever had. He was like the young man I had met in San Francisco: full of life, hope and future. There was no anger in his head about the band or any past difficulties.

We cried for his mom—he loved her so much—she had meant everything to him because she had always believed in him, supported any decision he made. As we talked about her, I think I was most concerned that this reunion between us was more based in grief than anything else; that his mother's death had caused a shift in his rationale; was that what was driving this? Would he wake up and realize that time marches on, that things don't necessarily change overnight, and we would be through again.

I asked him if that was what had happened—if his thoughts and actions were being driven by his loss, and I had simply gotten swept up in it. He put my fears to rest—he had wanted to see me, he said, since the day we parted six years ago; since the day we said what we thought would be a final good-bye. He's thought of no one else—he has been with no one else.

His mom's death made it all final in his mind: we were meant to be together, even if only part-time again. He would let me be with Chris for now, because he knew I still didn't have it in me to leave my husband. In my own way, I loved him too; Chris was my sanity, the rock that kept me steady; he was my support, my solace. He had been there during the rape, its aftermath; during my depression and struggle with bipolar disorder; during Steve's and my break-ups, consoling and strengthening me always. Standing by me despite my many flaws, my infidelity.

But then there was Steve: my danger zone. I could be myself with him, always had been; I had never had to pretend and, to some degree, I had always felt I had to do so with Chris. I loved Steve with a fervor that had no comparison. He and I could have an entire conversation without saying a word. Steve was my first true love, my soul mate, my star.

Did I think I could handle this? Did I think he could handle this? What the hell were we thinking?

The next morning we took a taxi to his house where his father greeted us, smoking a pipe on the front porch, rocking in a glider. He hadn't seen me yesterday but James must have told him I was in town because he didn't look surprised. He peered over his glasses at his oldest son, then at me, then back at Steve, and smiled. A man of few words, like his son.

He dad reached out his hand to me, which I took. He pulled me to him and I gave him a hug, told him how sorry I was, holding him tighter. A tear fell down his cheek as he simply nodded. He told me he was glad I was there, releasing his hug.

Steve took me inside the house, through the kitchen where a housekeeper was cleaning up from yesterday's wake that I had missed. She acknowledged me with a professional nod, and went about her business.

The house still looked the same, smelled the same. It was as if his mom would come peeking around the corner at any second. She never did but her spirit hung heavy in every corner of the house.

Our couch was still in the family room; new throw pillows on it but the same flowery upholstery. There was a sheet and blanket folded in the recliner in a corner—Steve said his dad had been sleeping there—couldn't sleep in the empty bed upstairs. I more than understood.

Nip, the old cat, was asleep in a puddle of sunlight on the carpet, content in the warm bath.

Steve then led me up the quiet stairs to his bedroom; I was near as nervous this time as the first. He was still obviously a slob—some things never change, thank goodness. It was these qualities that endeared him to me from the beginning. Clothing was strewn about the room, some on the furniture, but most on the floor. Piles of music everywhere. Tennis shoes everywhere. A very pleasant reminder of the past.

My eyes fell on his bulletin board; I was still there: the Homecoming Dance, a picture from the '87 tour, my dog Charlie and I from '75.

We spent a week in Atlanta, rarely leaving the house. I called Chris who was refined in his patience, and work—I was a long-term care nurse in a nursing home—new job—at least they understood in letting me take a few extra days. I had kept this part of my life very secret, in some ways—my jacket had the band's logo on it; I had several tour jackets; but I professed only to being a groupie. Nothing more. Didn't want people thinking once again I was lost in a fantasy world, locked in a make-believe romance with a rock star.

James brought his wife over for dinner—she actually wanted to get a look at me—a person she had heard a lot about from both brothers over the years. Betty and James married in August, 1981—she was a nurse too. James told me since he couldn't be a nurse, he'd marry one. Steve chimed in, said he was going to marry one too—in the future. His family gave him a look of cautious surprise then let it drop.

The week was up, too fast; time flies when you are allowed to dance in the clouds. Steve and I were together again, his father and brother happy about it, my husband in the dark about it or, at least, he was pretending to be. I had to leave Steve at week's end. I had to go back to my life and try to make a go of it, try to fit back in. He had given me his all; had it been enough? More than enough. I just wasn't sure if I could give anymore.

We had plans—to meet in certain cities when I could—to reunite and be who we once were—two lost souls on the road to adventure and love and who knows what else at this point. It was good enough for him at that point; it had to be. It was good enough for me—for right then.

I went back to my life. Chris realized right off the airplane that something was different, but I tried not to be obvious about it all. I went back to nursing, he continued to be a firefighter. Life truly does go on, for better or worse. Life finds a way—so does love.

I only wished I knew where it was we were to go from there.

*T*he story was that he bought another motorcycle for himself, tiring of the lack of energy the first one had. It didn't take him long until he decided to buy a Ninja—a competition-oriented bike—painted blue—they didn't come in purple. Unfortunately, no one told him that he should have taken time to become acquainted with the bike, its subtle nuances and the throttle response, prior to getting on it, but he probably would have thought he knew better anyway. He figured he knew motorcycles—he had one, after all, and this one was just a little faster, exactly what he wanted.

The man always was stubborn when it came to things he felt he knew about.

So, he left his car at the dealership and took the bike right out onto the road—the winding curves of the Hollywood Hills—not a real smart thing to do. At least he was wearing a helmet—the man did have some sense. Apparently he had a ball too—cranking the throttle, seeing what the bike could do, taking it around the sweeping curves, nearly doing the "slide for life" several times as he powered up the bike faster and faster. He managed to control it for a time. He had probably felt lucky there were no cops around at that time; later, I think he wished that there had been, to put a stop to him.

Pulling up to a stoplight he considered blowing it off and continuing on his speed ride, but decided to stop and regroup for a moment; to decide which way to go next, which road to chose—the really curvy one or the not so curvy? The bike had great power and control, he felt. He felt he could handle anything he would give it. He felt invincible.

There wasn't any cross traffic as he waited impatiently for the light to turn, thinking that he should have gone ahead and rode through it. He revved the engine and the power between his legs, combined with the heroin high, was nearly sexual in its driving force. When the light turned green, the adrenaline pumped and he gave the bike the juice, into second gear, causing an explosion of power that sent the front end of the bike skyward with too much instantaneous power off the line, flipping him backwards off the bike, which came back with him. Still with some advancing motion, his head hit the pavement hard, causing the helmet to crack as he saw white stars for a moment.

Steve lay on the pavement, battered, bruised; not totally conscious, not totally unconscious—in a state we nurses call twilight. He says now he doesn't remember a lot: the stars, the dizziness, the pain. The fog in his head had been intense and he says he remembers being scared, almost terrified of any injury, but was mostly embarrassed, actually hoping that no one would come along.

Unfortunately for his state of mind, another driver did happen by, recognized the seriousness of the accident and called it to the 911-system. The police were the first on-scene—then the paramedics and fire department. Steve, still in the twilight state, was taken to the nearest hospital where his blood was tested—obviously he was positive for heroin; alcohol too.

His injuries were fairly serious—a severe concussion—he does remember being told, if he had not had the helmet on, he, most likely, would not have survived the accident. He also had a fractured right forearm and wrist, requiring casting. And had a pretty healthy road rash to the back of his legs and his bottom.

The worst part he remembered is being placed under arrest for DUI—heroin; thank heavens he didn't have any on him or he may have been charged with possession too.

"Rock star arrested in possession of heroin—film at eleven." I could hear the TV news stories now.

But he was back in the same hospital he had been in when he attempted suicide—he had still been helmeted when the other driver saw him and she hadn't recognized him. There would be no press on this incident either.

Again I received a call in the night; James was on the other end, from Atlanta; he was preparing to dash out the door to catch a flight to Los Angeles. I could hear his babies in the background fussing. He started the conversation with "Steve's hurt," and ended with "Will you come?"

How could I not go?

Chris was understandably upset, fearful that I would not come back, fearful that he'd lose me to Steve once and for all. He did not want me to go and he made that clear. He didn't know I was seeing Steve and had been for nearly a year. But he was hurt—badly—and I had to go, despite my trepidation over the heroin use continuing. I had to resolve in my head that he wasn't going to stop using—not anytime soon, anyway. Nothing I had done was enough to satisfy his addiction, a very hard thing to wake up to.

I had known, though—in my heart of hearts, I had known he was still using. I just didn't allow my mind to acknowledge it. I had taken many nursing courses for continuing education credit on recognizing addiction; I was slowly becoming an expert, not for my patients, but for the man I loved.

I had to go to him; I couldn't stay in Illinois and worry, not seeing for myself if he was okay. James was going; I was too. James arrived that night; he couldn't get me a ticket until the next morning. A limo driver met me in baggage claim, holding a sign with "Potts" written on it that I assumed was for me. We headed out into the Los Angeles traffic crunch of the early morning—and I thought Chicago traffic was a nightmare.

I expected Steve to be either in a neuro unit, due to his closed head injury, or on the medical unit but he was on neither—he was on the psychiatric unit. Not really a surprise, I guess—the medical staff was probably attempting drug detox and rehab. It was a secure unit, which surprised me but I guess they didn't want anyone slipping out to go get high. I signed in at the desk and was told by a snooty nurse that they would notify Mr. Potts' brother that I was there.

I waited awhile, scanning the magazines left on a table, and the morning newspaper. The hallway was dark and it was hard to read in that light. I watched the nurse at the door as she went about her routine. Every nurse has a different way of doing things.

Finally the large steel door to my left opened and James walked out, shuffling his feet slightly, hands in his Dockers' pockets, head hung. When he looked up and saw me, I was stunned to see how much he looked like Steve at that moment. I don't think I ever noticed that much resemblance before.

James also looked tired, eyes heavy and red; clothes slightly disheveled, which was out of character for him. He took my shoulders in his hands and kissed me on the cheek, then sat with me on the couch in the lounge.

"He doesn't want to see you, Jean."

Stunned, I searched his face for some sign that he might have been joking, but he was deadly serious. He told me the story of the accident and the charges pending against him. He told me about the heroin use; that Steve had never really been able to quit, even after the *Apprehension* tour when I left him because of the usage. His use hadn't been heavy but it was enough. And it was a direct cause of the accident.

And here he was, in the psych unit, under arrest for DUI. His injuries were fairly serious—particularly the head injury—the others would heal with time—but the addiction needed to be seriously addressed and conquered. It would be a condition of him staying out of jail. The doctors had put him into rehab and detox. But, he would have been in psych anyway due to his past history of the suicide attempt; was the motorcycle accident another attempt on his life?

But, why won't he see me?

He's embarrassed. The accident was just that—an accident that could have easily been prevented. He's under arrest, Jean.

He's embarrassed and disappointed in himself, afraid you'll just leave him, afraid that he screwed up too big this time. He's angry and pushing everyone away before they push him away.

My head started to spin; lack of sleep, lack of food, lack of thought about what Steve was thinking.

James and I talked further; he described his brother's injuries which, he said, were not all that bad. His arm broken in three places, road rash and a concussion that was the worst of it all. It had erased all recollection of the accident. He had been damned lucky operating a motorcycle with heroin and alcohol in his system. He had no business being on it and no business even driving his car to the dealership. What was that man thinking?!

But, why wouldn't he see me?? That question was badgering me with all it was worth. James didn't really know one way or the other what was wrong with Steve. He could only tell me to give him time and maybe he would come around. But, time was a luxury I didn't have—I had a job and a husband to get back to; so did James but it was different for him—Steve was his brother; he was only my—my what? Lover seemed so cold and impersonal to call him; boyfriend is so high school; affair is correct but sounds stilted and taudry.

I stayed in Steve's house when I left the hospital later that day; James offered to give me his keys but I had my own. I slept in Steve's bed that night—it was somewhat uncomfortable because he wasn't there with me. I had never slept in that bed alone. But it was also disconcerting that he had shut me out. I couldn't understand why.

I sat in a chair in his bedroom for a while and watched TV, then noticed he had some videos in a cabinet—some labeled, some not. Turns out they were performances of the band on a variety of television shows over the years, including a video taped from an 8mm film someone had taken of them in that lounge in the hotel in San Francisco. That was so cool to see right now. The very beginning of his musical shot to the stars.

There were several from the show *Midnight Special*, hosted by Wolfman Jack. Looking at the tapes brought back so many things I had buried or forgotten along the way. How I miss those days, the simple days of love and purity and no complications.

It was very odd seeing myself on those tapes, sitting in the front row of the shows—I was a kid but the love was evident, and it was more than the puppy-love of a teen-age crush on a rock star. You could also see the adoration in his eyes and passion. We were both so young and innocent then, so many years ago. Where had all that gone? What had happened to those two young people?

I watched the old concert tapes into the night, enjoying how he had sequenced them all together in ascending order; the band grew up on those tapes. The songs were varied—the old standards. Concert venues ranged from Japan to Europe to all over the United States.

And I was there on way too many. I hadn't realized half the time that someone had been taping us, whether we were behind the scenes or on stage. I looked lost half the time, star-struck part of the time, in love all the time.

Finally tired after watching hours of videos, I changed into a nightshirt and regarded his bed. As I crawled under the sheets, I was pleasantly surprised to find that they had not been washed yet—a rush of a familiar scent stirred on the breeze I created with the sheets. The smell was all him in the bed. I drifted off to sleep with Steve on my mind.

The next morning was no different at the hospital; Steve was still refusing to see me. James and I talked by telephone — figured there was no point in me going all the way there just to be turned away. Days turned into a week with him refusing me a visit. I didn't understand — did he think I was going to berate him for the drugs, for the crash? I wasn't going to and I wasn't going to leave him either. Yes, I had left him once before for the drug use and that had turned out to be one of the dumbest things I had ever done in my life. It wouldn't happen again. James told him all that and still I was left out in the cold.

I even wrote him a note for James to give him. It said that I had suspected he was still using and I hadn't left him, had I? I wasn't going to leave him; I couldn't leave him.

Ten days and he was finally released; I remained in his house, awaiting his arrival, placing my marriage and my job in serious jeopardy. A condition of his release, to keep him out of jail, he would have to do outpatient rehab, which included frequent and unannounced drug testing.

When he arrived home, I stayed as much in the background as I could, so as to not upset him. He looked terrible — there was absolutely no life in his eyes, his face was pale and puffy. He walked with a pronounced limp and his short shorts revealed the road rash he had suffered, the worst of it still bandaged and hidden. His right arm was in a cast, his fingers were purple and swollen where they emerged at the end of the plaster. He held his head at an odd angle as if straightening it made him dizzy or ill.

His face was emotionless, his head hung, as he made his way through the entry hall, into his family room. James was directly behind him with his bag and a handful of discharge papers and court papers. When Steve had his back to me I got a better look at his leg wounds; always the nurse assessing things. Even the wounds that weren't bandaged were very inflamed, still draining.

Steve finally lifted his head and appeared to be trying to decide if he wanted to sit on the couch or go upstairs, intermittently looking at both. That's when he saw me, standing in the doorway between the family room and the kitchen, watching his every move. He looked at me with the same expressionless face with which he regarded the furniture. Not a word, not a nod, nothing. This was all very sad.

He slowly climbed his stairs, taking them one leg at a time, steadying himself with every step, every movement. When he reached the top, he looked over the railing at me, then silently turned and went into his bedroom, closing the door behind him, shutting me out. James said nothing to me as he collapsed in a chair. I bit my bottom lip as I remembered that all of my things were in Steve's room; I half expected to see them all come flying through the door at any moment.

Later that day, I decided I had had enough of the silent treatment—he was going to see me whether he wanted to or not.

I didn't care how he felt about it. This was ridiculous. He ignored my knocks on the door, and my eventual pounding. I carefully tried the doorknob but it was locked. Locked! So I entered the master bathroom and found the door from there into the bedroom ajar; he had forgotten that door. I peeked into the bedroom and knocked softly as I did so. He was sitting on the small couch, the drapes were pulled, clouding the room in semi-darkness. My belongings were all where I had left them—he hadn't touched anything that I could see.

He had a pillow under each thigh to cushion his wounds and had removed the shorts; they were lying on the floor presumably where he had dropped them. He was still hanging his head, as he was when he walked into the house and was holding it at an odd angle. Eyes closed. His hearing was okay—he had heard me come in and grunted at me as I asked if I could come in.

I shrugged off the grunt and entered the bedroom fully, slowly walking to him, and sat next to him. He lifted his head slightly and looked at me skeptically; there was an air of disdain in his eyes and face. Then he hung his head again. I wanted to reach out to him, touch him, wave a magic wand and make him all better again, but only he possessed the power at this point to be all better.

We sat in silence, the room continually darkening as the daytime sun set. I could hear him breathing: slow, even breaths. That was all I heard. It was so hard to see him like that, drowning in sorrow, loss, shame and pain. I would never tell him "I told you so," or chastise him about the DUI, or be one of those people who lecture about how he could have put others at risk with his behavior. I just wanted him back to normal, but wasn't sure how to get there.

My stomach growled and shattered the silence, causing me to giggle a bit. Steve didn't make a sound but did raise his head and look at me again. His emotionless mask had turned darker, almost angry, and it was directed at me.

What's going on with you, Steve? I had finally gathered up the courage to ask, exasperated with the entire situation.

His eyes flashed something but I wasn't sure exactly what I had seen. I almost thought he was going to remain silent but, at long last, he spoke.

"Why are you here? This isn't your place anymore."

What did he mean by that? The blow of those words dumbfounded me—I stared at him, feeling my eyes involuntarily widen. The venom in his words coursed through me in a poisonous race against time to my brain. I had nothing to say to him, no way to respond.

He continued to stare at me, his eyes dark and blank.

In that instant, I made a decision—it was time for me to go home. For some reason, this man whom I had loved and had given myself to for nearly 20 years, was seeing me as the enemy. I could tell by his actions, his face, the words that he spit at me. I was no longer welcome in his life. The accident had affected him more that I had imagined.

But, had I thought about the anger, the pain, I would have seen it as what it was—heroin withdrawal. Uncontrollable anger; withdrawal from friends, family and life. That consideration never entered my mind. Some nurse I am!

I gathered up my belongings and left him alone in his pain. James drove me to LAX and put me onto a plane going home. He held me and wished me good luck. He was going to stay awhile and try to get Steve through everything. I told him I loved him and his brother and that I would always be there for them both if they needed anything. Then I was gone.

oing home this time was hard — not because I was leaving him but because I was leaving him in his mentally unstable state. He was a broken man — in spirit, in love, in physical condition.

I had to walk away, though. I couldn't handle staying there; couldn't stand the use of the drug, the lies, the deception. I was again hurt that he hadn't told me he was still using; I could have dealt with it if he had told me. But he chose not to — again. Instead of saying anything, he said nothing.

I would have stayed, helped him get through the withdrawal, helped him get back to life, but he didn't want me there — for a variety of reasons he turned his back on me. At least he was okay with James being there. The next several weeks were going to be hell as Steve's body continued to crave the drug and he, hopefully, refused to give in. The worst was over at this point in time — the worst withdrawal side effects had been suffered at the hospital, but he still had a rough road ahead of him. Now he had to work through the emotions — I should have been there at his side, but he didn't want me there.

Chris was pleasantly surprised to see me come home so quickly. I settled back into nursing, working then in a hospital; I decided that nursing homes weren't for me: too much sadness.

So, I became a pediatric nurse: talk about sadness. Fortunately, the hospital was a small one and the pediatric floor was also the medical floor so my patients ran the gamut in ages, from newborn to 100.

My husband, now 60 and a deputy chief with the fire department, had always thought his dream was to be in music, but he had found his true love to be firefighting. That is where he had been able to shine so brightly. He was an excellent firefighter, an even better paramedic, and was an inspiration to every rookie he trained.

Our lives went on—we were basically living together as friends. I loved him—he loved me. But it was definitely a different love than most married couples experience. We went through the motions with friends, at business events, but, behind closed doors, a dark curtain hanging between us separated us.

I didn't hear anything at all from Steve, but I did occasionally hear from James. He had remained in Los Angeles for several months after the accident, helping Steve through everything. He called several times during those months to fill me in, letting me know how things were progressing. Steve had been passing his urine tests with flying colors, and was able to keep his driver's license. He was still harboring a lot of anger at himself, which he internalized, and was not able to get through it with any amount of ease. Rehab and counseling were going to take awhile to work him through everything he needed to get through.

James had told me that, while he and I had talked on the phone, many times Steve had been on the extension, listening, curious about what was going on in my life, and to my reactions as to how he was doing in rehab. I wished I had known he was there, hovering in the background. I wished I were still in California.

May, 1995 he was back in the media—releasing another solo album: his third, *Final Countdown*. Of course I had to run right out and buy it when it hit the stores. It was musically different than anything he had done before, alone or with the band. The music bordered on melancholic new age with lyrics of loss, separation, depression. The title would prove to be prophetic.

I spoke with James after buying the album and caught up on his life and Steve's. It was important to me to keep up with them both as I always hoped Steve and I would find a way to be together again; that he would get over his anger and his depression and his drug use. James assured me he was well: no further drugs in his system. He did test positive for alcohol once, much less than the legal limit—he had had a beer the afternoon before the hospital called him in on a random test run. But, alcohol he was allowed to have; it was the narcotics that were forbidden.

He was attending a counseling session twice a week and a Narcotics Anonymous meeting at least four times a week, something he would probably have to do the rest of his life, sometimes more often, sometimes less, in order to stay clean.

James also let me know that Steve had not been out of the house except to go to the recording studio, the hospital for counseling, rehab meetings and testing. There was no one in his life. And he was getting ready to go out on tour with the new album.

He had a tour scheduled July through December, 1995, criss-crossing the country with a rag-tag bunch of studio musicians who were only too thrilled to be backing up the famous Steve Potts, and a road crew, thrown together at the last possible moment as Steve waited to get the okay to tour from his doctors in rehab. So long as he found an NA group in the concert cities, and attended regularly, contacted his doctor every few days, he would be okay. He also made it clear to everyone hired for the tour that there would be no drug use tolerated; a condition of hire was a drug test. Unusual in rock-and-roll, but very necessary in this case.

His tour was, to put it mildly, a no-frills affair, with none of the trappings of his band's concerts that had light shows and pyrotechnics. They were playing small venues—the smaller the better—nothing over 4000—that was the way he liked things; always had.

His tour dates were on the record label's web site: there was nothing in Chicago, nothing even close to me at all; I couldn't help but wonder if that was deliberate. I wondered if he was avoiding me on purpose because the closest show was Columbus, Ohio. Did I want to go there? Not really. Too many memories from my college days.

But, I did decide to go to the New York City show in October: a Halloween show, my favorite holiday, my favorite singer. The tickets even stated, "wear a costume." My friend, Pat (not the Patty I had gone to high school with, but a whole new friend in Illinois with the same name), went with me; the cover story to our husbands was that we were going on a shopping trip for the weekend. Why either of them bought that lame story was beyond me, since neither of us could be considered shopaholics.

The concert was at a very small theatre, capacity 3500—sold out, of course—all of his concerts had been quickly sold out as this may have very possibly have been the last time to see the man on stage. As we waited in line with the rest of the fans, my excitement grew to a nearly uncontrollable edge. I had on my tour jacket from several years back with ten or twelve backstage passes clipped to it; a t-shirt with the band's logo on it in sequins; buttons; pins; a lot of memorabilia. When asked what I was supposed to be for Halloween, I simply said I was a fan of the band. Pat was a witch—a real Wiccan witch. We were both Wiccan and proud of it. Another reason to love Halloween and to make that night special.

We had seats in the middle section, fourth row; having a family member of the performer obtain tickets for you comes in handy for good seats. James had offered to get us front row but I had declined, not wanting to be all that close. I swore James to complete secrecy. This would be odd, actually spending the entire concert in a seat in the audience. Not something I did often.

Steve's show was refined; only him and several lit jack-o-lanterns flickering; and a few musicians who were young and psyched up to be on stage with a true star. His voice sounded tired; heavy and very raspy, hoarse at times, but his energy was up there on the high end. Not bad for a 46 year-old rocker.

He was heavier than he had ever been on stage—probably since he was no longer using the heroin, he was eating and gaining weight finally. His hair was long again—hanging partway down his back, freely swaying around his gorgeous, but tired, face. He wore a simple t-shirt and jeans, and, as always, the famous tennis shoes. It was all him and it was all fabulous.

About halfway through the show, he instructed the lighting crew to bring up the house lights so that he could take a look at the costumes. I felt like scrunching down in the seat, but figured he would never see me with everyone on his or her feet in the three rows in front of us.

How wrong I was.

He saw me.

On his fifth scan across the audience, laughing at the costumes and the crowd as his eyes roamed over everyone, he found me; it was obvious by the look on his face. It was as if the gears in his head had suddenly ground to a screeching halt. He stared hard at me, no real expression on his face at first. His laughter stalled and the smile disappeared.

Some of the audience members in the three rows ahead of Pat and I turned to see what or who had captured his attention. Pat nudged me. I raised a hand with a short, noncommittal wave; he did the same. Very disconcerting.

He finished the performance, pointing to stage left as he vanished behind the curtain at the end. His eyes had met mine and we clicked again; just as we had in San Francisco, our eyes had held onto each other and spoke volumes. I stayed in my seat, thinking. Did I want to go through all this again? I didn't know. But, wasn't that truly why I was there—to find out how much more I could handle? I sat with Pat, an anxious friend holding my hand. She tried to convince me to go see him; she knew I wanted to go see him, but that I was nervous and just not all that sure about anything.

At least say hello—you have to find out what will happen. She was right. What could it hurt to go say hello?

A roadie was at the stage door and allowed us to pass. He told us to go straight—second door on the right. We went straight, past stage left (stage left brought back the best memories of tours and love and passion and strength), past about 40 girls in the hallway, waiting: for what? Probably to get with one of the road musicians, to get into the band lounge. To get their turn.

The second door to the right was brown and heavily painted, many areas of paint chipped off, revealing all of the other colors it had been previously. I knocked softly on the door, getting the attention of most of the girls standing around who looked at me with the same note of surprise I always got in the old tour days.

The door opened to a small, dimly lit room; Steve was standing to the side, doorknob in his hand. Being only a few feet from him, my heart jumped. Pat and I walked into his dressing room and he quickly closed the door behind us, and I made the introduction. Pat was gracious and not giddy; we were both too old for that. She shook his hand as my own hands broke out into a sweat. She pulled me aside and told me to talk to him—that she could see something in his eyes, she wanted us to have our time; to see if what could have been may still be. Then she was gone. She was right; Steve and I needed to be alone. We were left staring at each other.

He looked great, like he had aged all of five minutes. He had track marks visible on his arms but they were well healed and had not been used in awhile. That was a relief. Only I would have noticed that.

I am sure he noticed the changes in me—I was heavier, looking ridiculous, I am sure, in all my tour paraphernalia. Had the aviator-style glasses frames again (the "man frames") with the lenses tinted a light blue gradient.

Steve was looking at me with a smile, not a wide smile, but a smile. It was as if he was seeing me as the same person I was 20 years ago. That same look of amusement sparkled in his eyes as he took me in. I worried for an instant that his love for me might have been influenced only by his drug use. Did he love me now?

I leaned against a wall and crossed my arms in front of me and grimaced at him, wrinkling my nose at him, which he did right back at me and came closer, slowly striding across the room, slightly dragging his heels. He looked suddenly like such a little boy.

When he was directly in front of me, he stopped. Our eyes locked and held each other in an electric gaze. What was I doing? What was I thinking?

Steve must have read my thoughts earlier, as he turned his forearms outward for me to inspect.

Could it really be true that he was off the drug? Could it be possible after all these years? Did I dare believe him and James? This was the first time he had brought up the heroin issue himself since he first told me about it in 1976. Had he really changed?

I hoped so. I prayed it was so.

The tension between us was rising as he moved a few inches closer. There was nowhere for me to go—my back was literally against the wall. My head was full of his scent—sweat and aftershave—and the vision of him. I wanted to say it—shout it—scream it for the entire world to hear.

"I love you." Did those words actually come out?

They did—they came out so easily that they surprised us both—I hadn't meant to say them out loud.

"I love you too."

There—he had said it too. His words seemed just as easily spoken.

We had done it again—declared our love for each other—where did we dare go from there?

He leaned into me, one hand on either side of me on the wall at each side of my head. He kissed my nose, then my forehead, then each cheek and he finally found my mouth. His kiss was amazing as it always had been. His taste was sweet and minty, as though he had recently crunched a breath mint, something he hadn't done in the past. His bottom teeth were still uneven and rough, as were the top ones, an everlasting painful memory from the intubation after the suicide attempt.

Did we dare take this further? Could we even stop now? I didn't know if I could. Didn't think I could. The feelings were all still there—they had never gone away; no matter how angry, how disappointed, how disillusioned I had been at different times over the last 19 years, I never stopped loving this man. I never could. Love just doesn't go away, no matter what happens. If it is true love, it remains, for a long time, forever. Sometimes it's buried and dormant, but it is still there.

Steve's kiss was as exciting as it had ever been, bringing my love for him to the surface and back into my being. His touch on my shoulders, as he grabbed me, sent tingles below my waist that I hadn't felt since the last time we were together. I wanted him—as much as I hated to admit it, I wanted him to take me to his bed again, make love to me and never let me go.

We parted from our kiss and stared at each other. His eyes again took me in, gazing at me, head to toe. His face seemed to be awestruck as his breathing increased in depth and rhythm. His cheeks flushed and his pupils dilated—only a nurse would notice that.

I watched as the emotion changed in his face from happiness to love to need. The same smoldering reaction must have been evident on my face as well—he was doing nothing to try and hide how he felt and neither was I.

"Take me back to your hotel." My words were hushed, but clear. He smiled, the smile of a man who knew he was about to get what he was aching for.

His hotel was two blocks away from the theatre. He donned his hat—that worn, tired hat, tattered with years of wear and of being tossed into a suitcase, the ribbon band had come loose at one end, secured with a an old button with the band's logo on it. I still hated that hat but now it was developing a bit of an endearing quality.

He still insisted on wearing his basic disguise from the prying eyes of fans; I had to admit, it had been effective after all these years; it had kept him safe. Who would imagine that a rock star would be caught dead wearing such an ugly hat?

We walked, holding hands, to the hotel, talking all the way. He was clean: as we walked, he showed me a copy of the drug test he had been ordered to take over at Bellevue yesterday—all clear.

The hotel was not a Hilton, not the Waldorf, but it was a nice one. He could have afforded any hotel in the city but he went with simple elegance. The room was nothing fancy, but it had him all over it—clothes were strewn about, piles of music and newspapers were on the dresser and nightstands. Typical Steve Potts—a mess. He made a small effort to clean things up but stopped as I laughed at him. He dropped the armload of clothes and came to me, arms wide.

The hug was like two old friends who had had a long absence, which is exactly what we were. He held onto me, almost as if his life depended on it. Then, quickly, he pulled away, went to a briefcase on the dresser and dug through some papers until he found what he was looking for—a file folder with many lab slips in it—all negative for narcotics as he made his way across the country.

He really was clean. It made my heart soar for several reasons: he was following the court's ruling; he was healthier; he still wanted me—drugs or no drugs.

My happiness made me grab him where he had sat down on the bed; we fell together onto the squeaky mattress and faced each other.

"I am so proud of you."

"Yeah, well, it's been rough; toughest thing I ever did beside leaving you, walking away from you, letting you go. But you did it—how many days? 326 days without it and counting; I can do it; thinking of you has gotten me through."

Thinking of me; he thought as much of me as I did of him. He made everything so good, so right. We had been together since 1975—20 years off and on. I still had Chris but couldn't remember the last time he and I had had sex. Steve sated there had been no one else; concentrating on sobriety and getting me back were all that kept him going. He has been with no one except me since Rose. The man was truly a stand-out in the world of rock-and-roll in more ways than one. I never would have imagined that he wouldn't have been with someone else, when so many wanted him, when he must have had basic male urges. But he denied anyone.

We talked for a time on the bed, in between kissing and the slow, occasional removal of pieces of clothing. We chattered for hours, going over the past year; his solo tour and album, the band's tenth album: *In the Line of Fire*. Both albums were doing well on the charts but he apologized to me for the way both his solo and the band album sounded—they had both been recorded near the same time and he had had the flu, not to mention had still been heavily into heroin withdrawal, so his voice was not "great." I thought they sounded wonderful, but I always liked his voice. I told him about nursing—he had many questions, as he usually did about anything I was involved in.

Hours later we were under the bed sheets, down to underwear, fondling and caressing each other, increasing the heat in the room by several degrees. I don't remember removing my clothes or his, or climbing under the sheets; it didn't matter. He was suddenly nuzzling my neck in that familiar way he had, where his teeth came into contact with the skin and caused the involuntary release of goose flesh all over me, and the hardening of my nipples against his chest.

His hair draped over my neck and chest like delicate brown wedding dress lace. Where it touched my skin, it was oh-so slightly scratchy and erotic; I ran my fingers through it, enjoying the feel of it once again, and after all this time, remembering its split ends, its wonderful scent.

His mouth moved to my breasts and his tongue expertly stimulated then with his tongue, swirling and stirring those feelings between my legs until I could feel my juices flowing. We both squirmed out of our underwear and he entered me quickly, thrusting gently and swiftly, his fingers playing over my skin on every part of my body. Even his toes against mine caused me to shiver.

We made love twice that night, the second time with more touching and feeling of each other. He hadn't changed his lovemaking technique and for that I was grateful. He had always been an expert lover. We became reacquainted that night and rediscovered our love, our hearts and our need for each other.

As we lay in bed seeing the sun beginning to come up over the New York City skyline, I rolled onto my side and looked at Steve, my Steve. He turned his head and returned the gaze. I just wanted to look at him and touch him and make sure he was really there; that we were really together; that we had made it back to each other; our love had found a way at last.

He kissed me with all the love he had in him and my mouth replied with all the love I had. We didn't care that we were older now and that we were a little heavier, a little more tired. We didn't care that we had a logistical problem, a marriage that was still halfway intact. We didn't care about anything at that moment.

I turned and picked up the phone off the nightstand and called James with Steve watching me, puzzled, not knowing what I was doing. I think he figured I was calling Pat.

"Hey—it's me. I'm with him. We're together. I love him. Here he is."

And I handed the phone to Steve who looked at me with a strange expression. When he figured out it was James on the other end, he was surprised. And pleased that his brother had gotten the tickets for me.

We slept for a few hours, still pretty excited about being back together, so our sleep was fitful and short. I called Pat at the hotel she and I were supposed to share, told her to meet us for dinner at a restaurant he liked nearby, and then he took me shopping. First for some clothes since mine were at the hotel, then to a jewelry store. When he would have bought me diamonds, or anything else I wanted, I was looking at ID bracelets, still a child of the 70s when they were big. An ID bracelet was something I had always wanted but had never received. He shrugged, picked out one, and told the clerk what to engrave on it. Fifteen minutes later he was fastening a silver ID on my left wrist—it read: *In the Line of Fire*—the band's latest album. It pretty much summed up everything about us in the last 20 years.

From that point on, Steve and I were back together.

After we had dinner, a very nice dinner, Steve took Pat and I to the theatre—the line was already down the block to get in. The limo pulled up to the front of the theatre and it was like old times—the crowd went crazy to see him up so close, and security had to hold them back. Then he assisted Pat and I to get out and the crowd looked at us like who the hell were we?! Yep, just like old times.

I asked Pat if she wouldn't mind going to the band lounge while I went with Steve—she didn't mind. She was such a good friend.

Once Steve and I were in his dressing room, it truly was like old times, only less so as the show was much smaller, much simpler. There was so much less anxiety and so much less anticipation. We sat on the couch and were like kids again, sharing each other, loving each other.

He and I made love before the show and it was sweet, as though nothing had changed, as though we had never been apart.

When the show was over, we went back to his hotel and spent the night together. He was supposed to have pulled out with his band to go to Philadelphia but stayed to be with me and sent his band on by themselves. He'd meet them there the next night.

That night in bed, he and I talked about where we go from this point. We wanted to be together as much as possible, which meant a lot of traveling for him, some for me. Missing work too. I was willing to do whatever it would take to see him; so would he.

Then he told me that he didn't think that he and the old band were ever going to get together again. They had been apart since the tenth album was recorded, and they were not likely to get together again. He seemed sad about this but there was a tone of relief in his voice also. When he spoke about the problems at the last recording sessions, he didn't get as angry as I expected. He got whispy, and the sadness was evident on his face. This would be his last solo effort too.

There was a sadness within me as I realized there would be no more tours, no more passes, no more back stage or dressing room fooling around.

Steve and I were together until mid-morning then he had to catch a flight, so did Pat and I. His limo took me to my hotel and we said good-bye—for then. This good-bye was easy because I knew I would be seeing him again—maybe not sometime soon, but it would happen. We were still the couple we had once been; we had made it this far.

Less than six months later, the band announced, in a statement given by their record company, that they were through, severing all ties to each other. The proclamation would send a ripple through the music and entertainment world and shock waves through the fans. I was with Steve when the announcement was first seen on a television entertainment show. He had flown into Chicago to be with me during that very sad time; he did not want to be in Los Angeles when it all came out. We watched it from a private room in the airline lounge.

It was a very sad thing to watch; we both had tears in our eyes as pictures of him and the band flashed on the screen from the past 20 years. I had thought I would be able to stay strong and not sob since I knew this was coming, this was why Steve was in Chicago, but we both sobbed when the story was over. This was the end. The end. His solo tour was finished; his band touring was finished. He was a private citizen again. The title of the last album *had* been prophetic—he was now in the line of fire as people began to make up stories about the break-up and who was at fault, as if anyone needed to be at fault. No one was, but rumor had it that Steve was since he was the one with the solo career; no one mentioned that other band members were in other bands and had other musical responsibilities. It was simply no one's fault—they had grown apart and were tired, ready to move on to other projects.

The title also pointed to personalities that could no longer pretend that everything was fine; management that insisted on more and more touring, more and more records, more and more everything—more than any of them could give; security issues; family issues. The list could go on and on.

What it meant for Steve was that his privacy would be restored. He would still be an icon who sang his way through two decades of varied musical styles, but, with time, fame would ebb and he might be able to recapture some of his life, at some point. He was thrilled—he had wanted to walk away for years—the music could go on forever—but he wanted it to stop; so did Joss and Richard. It was time.

The band was over; in one fell swoop, the music fell silent. Steve was now a nobody—well, hardly—but he loved every moment of not having any responsibility. I wore my ID bracelet with pride because it bore the name of the last album—their last hurrah. Oh, there would be greatest hits albums, but nothing new. Ever again. Most of them parted on fairly good terms, happy if only for their own reasons.

Four years went by, to 1999. Steve and I saw each other a lot—

several times each month when he flew into Chicago. Sometimes he stayed in a hotel near the airport for a day or so, sometimes he was only in town for a few hours and we met in the airline lounge. We were passionate and loving as he became more and more relaxed in his ability to be out in the world, at least the world of Chicago—he still did not go out much in Los Angeles.

His father passed away in July, 1999. Now he and James were alone in the world. Chris saw me off to go to Atlanta; he didn't know that Steve and I had been seeing each other all along, so, he felt that my going to Atlanta would be no big deal. As far as he was concerned, Steve and I had not seen each other since October, 1995, at the Halloween concert.

James and Steve decided not to sell the family house—at least not right away. They figured it would have sold quickly the minute it came out that it was his childhood home, but neither could part with it just yet. They took some of the belongings out of the house to go to their own houses; Steve took his bed, because that is where we spent our first night together, he said, and the couch from the family room. They each took special items; Steve took all the scrapbooks his mother had kept about him and found that his father had continued to glue things into books after his mother had passed away.

The night before the movers were coming to take the things away, James and Betty, and Steve and I spent one last night in the house—the house that still smelled of pipe tobacco and his mother's cooking, even though she hadn't been there in years. We spent the evening talking with his brother and Betty, catching up with each other, telling family stories, laughing and crying off and on.

We all went upstairs together, Steve and I to his old room, James and Betty to James' old room down the hall. The house was quiet and still, as if waiting for someone to breathe some life into it. When he closed the door to his bedroom behind us, I knew something had stirred in him that would not be denied.

His eyes shone with the light of his soul and reached into my soul and danced with it.

He took me into his arms and held me tight for a time. His dark hair hung in my face and I could smell the shampoo from his morning shower, his scent was clean and musky. It made me blossom in places he knew well. And still we just held each other, breathing in unison.

I don't know how long we stayed like that, or what time it was. I was comfortable in his arms and never wanted to leave. The room was darkened with only the desk light casting long shadows on the walls. He reached to turn the light off, but I touched his arm and stopped him. I trembled as he looked at me again with those eyes that were now smoldering.

There was something different in this night—was it because this was potentially our last night together in this very special place? He stood in front of me and wrapped his arms around my waist, burying his head in my shoulder. I held his head tight against me and closed my eyes, going over the many times we had spent together in this bedroom, remembering the first time we made love in this room. He had been so patient and gentle on my 18th birthday, and had taken me so easily.

He backed away from my shoulder and looked again into my eyes, a question there that I answered with a slight nod of my head. Once again we had had a whole conversation without saying a word—we always were good at silence. He took my hands in his and moved the diamond ring I wore on my right hand over to my left hand, saying that, someday, that ring would be sitting atop his wedding band on my finger.

He reached up and unbuttoned the blouse I was wearing, tentative at first, almost as if this was out first time, forcing himself to take it slowly, wanting it to last. When the blouse had fallen from my shoulders and onto the bed, he backed away and removed his suit jacket and then his tie, tossing them carelessly aside to join the other clothing in a corner. I always enjoyed watching him undress in that way he did—he was such a young man still and yet he was 50 years old now. He unbuttoned his shirt and tossed it aside also. It's funny how the smallest things can set your heart on fire—undressing and the way he threw his clothes would always be a trigger point for me.

I reached out and cupped his face with my hands, feeling the scratchy growth of a day's beard on my palms. My thumb wiped away a silent tear that was making its way down his cheek. I kissed him and his kiss was passionate and full of fervor. His tongue probed my mouth with urgency as it met mine and mingled with it. His hands on my back found my bra and removed it, still experiencing a problem with the three rows of hooks—I didn't know if he really had difficulty with them anymore or if it had simply become a tradition.

I loved this man so much as we stood chest to chest, his hair draped over my shoulders. I would do anything for him if he asked; I would die for him. I had felt that way for over 20 years and didn't see it changing anytime soon.

He pulled out of our hug and moved back slightly to look at me standing in front of him. I sat on the bed and pulled off my shoes as he kicked his away and removed his pants and underwear, standing before me in his socks only. He was still gorgeous, in every way.

I stood and removed my own pants and sat back on the bed with him beside me. Our mouths came together and ground together as we lay back onto the pillows. His touch was soft on my skin and felt as though there would be visible blue electricity wherever his fingers were.

We were still locked in our kiss when he touched me through the panties I had left on, feeling the wetness that was growing there. My breath was coming harder and faster as he slowly rubbed me and set me afire. He took my hand and moved it down his side to between his legs and guided me in movements that did the same to him as he was to me.

He maneuvered my underwear off and slowly crawled on top of me, holding me with his mouth over mine. I felt him enter me and it was heaven as it always had been. He was slow and easy, using his hips and his fingers to bring me to the edge several times. When he and I climaxed together there was no denying our love for each other.

As we lay together in the bed, under the sheets, occasionally running our fingers over each other's bodies, causing shivers of excitement through the other, he laid his head on my shoulder and purposely draped his beautiful hair over my chest.

We said nothing; there was nothing that needed to be said at that point.

He fell asleep on my shoulder, sleeping very peacefully, with very little movement or sound. He sighed a few times and did grind his teeth once or twice. I never did fall to sleep that night. I watched him sleep and wondered where he went in his dreams, what he was thinking to make him grind his teeth. His mouth was closed and his nostrils flared.

And he was mine.

September, 2001, saw a mass terrorist attack on our American soil—the World Trade Center was attacked with jet airliners, killing many, including firefighters and police officers. People in America finally raised their awareness of the dangerous jobs that firefighters and police do everyday, giving everyone a sense of pride. The whole episode caused a flurry of changes at airports everywhere and caused it to be somewhat more difficult for me to meet Steve at the gate—non-passengers were supposed to wait outside of security for the passengers to come to them now. Chris and I joined a federal disaster team and were now considered part of Homeland Security, which made it easier for me to get to airport gates if I flashed my ID. Our lives had all changed dramatically on that day in September, never to be the same again.

The war in Iraq began in 2003—we invaded, searching for elusive weapons of mass destruction; what we did find in the desert was Saddam Hussein cowering in a hole. Soldiers were also stepped up a notch in respectability, as they deserved to be.

The Viet Nam protest chant held strong in this war too—"We're not against the soldiers, we're against the war." Yellow and red, white and blue ribbons were everywhere as patriotism took on a whole new meaning, from 2001 on.

Toward the end of 2004, Steve got word that he and the band were being given an award in San Francisco—a lifetime achievement award for a band formed in the city that went worldwide. He did not want to go; did not want to be in front of any crowds. He valued his privacy deeply; he was and always will be a very private person. Part of his love of privacy was what drove him into self-induced solitude. It was a type of agoraphobia—not truly afraid to leave the house, but not truly comfortable with the outside world that had shut him away.

There were times when the pain on his heart was obvious on stage. There would simply be something missing in his smile or in his energy. I always knew when something was weighing heavily on him. My role in his life was the one he ran to: to talk to, to confide in. I held the man's deepest thoughts, feelings and secrets, many of which ended up in his songs, some of which only I could understand.

I was his love and he was mine, had been for twenty-nine years now. Twenty-nine years. My God. No one ever thought someone like me would be with someone like him. I remember the cold and puzzling stares I would get from the skinny, beautiful girls and women at concerts when I was on his arm or would disappear into his dressing room. I was an unlikely girl to be on the arm of a superstar, crossing the forbidden line to the lives of the band.

Being in the backstage arena, hanging out in the room behind the stage or under it, was a dream come true for anyone—for me, for awhile, it became old hat—the place I should be—the place I was expected to be. And he was always there waiting for me. Even when he didn't know I was coming, he was waiting. The other band members had girls in every city that wanted to be with them and most of the time, they were.

But I meant something to Steve and he never did fool around. He loved me; I loved him. We were special. My heart kept his and his kept mine.

But, we couldn't go on the way we were, with him traveling across the country nearly every week, just to come see me. He had the money; he wasn't worried about it, but I was. I worried about everything; just a part to my personality that usually got in the way.

The next year would be hard on both of us for many reasons, but we would make it through, stronger than we had ever been, tighter than we had ever been, and closer then we had ever been.

2004—The war in Iraq celebrated its first anniversary in search of weapons of mass destruction; President Bush was re-elected easily to a second term; Los Angeles saw massive mud slides as they went from drought status to flood status overnight; and a tsunami would devastate island nations in the Pacific.

Bubble gum rock made a bit of a comeback with Britney Spears as she tried to grow and expand her repertoire from school girl to woman; Nick and Jessica on TV not sure if chicken of the sea was tuna or chicken (is anyone really that much of a ding-bat, or was she simply as crazy as a fox?); U2 was a force to be reckoned with on the top 40, as was Matchbox 20 and Rod Stewart, who was now singing the old classics of the 50's and 40's after a scare with his vocal cords. And it could all be heard on an I-pod, the best portable musical device since the transistor radio. We watched Joey continually repeating, "How you doin?"; the end of Angel in a vampiric last stand against evil doings, following Buffy into the deep gorge of reruns; *Sex and the City* on non-premium cable in episodes cut too that the girls were tame in comparison to *Nip Tuck*; and the Soprano family continued to knock each other off.

Movies helped us stay young and find Neverland; rediscover

the aviator in Howard Hughes; cheer for an incredible family of super-heroes; and root for a female boxer, a million dollar baby.

2004 would also see massive changes in my life as the year came to a close. And, there would be nothing I could do to make any changes to see the year through to a happy ending. It was all out of my hands.

Steve flew into O'Hare International Airport on a wintry November day, anxious to discuss an award thing he had been fussing about for weeks; to get my opinion and convince me that he shouldn't go. I had until March to convince him why he should go.

I met him at the gate, federal ID in hand.

He saw me and was obviously glad to be there. His arms opened wide and we fell into each other; the passion still there, and the love. He pulled back and looked at me, as we stared into each other's eyes: both pairs of eyes are a little more tired than they were on our last meeting, about a month ago. But he is still the same breathless talker with the low, throaty voice that can set my heart on fire and my body aching for his touch.

We moved through the crowd at the airport; he no longer had to wear that goofy floppy hat. I have the hat now; I still maintain that we will have to have a ritual burn for it someday; it was such a huge part of his life, though, and kept him safe so long; maybe just a ritual burial would do. Very few people recognized him without his signature long hair these days; he cut it a few months ago and sent me the ponytail—22 inches of brown hair had now been reduced to barely a few inches, brushing the collar of his suit. I am still not so sure I like the new look but he loves it, saying it is so much easier to take care of. He had asked me before he cut it if it was all right as he knew his hair is my favorite part of him; I told him he could do what he wanted; I would love him regardless.

We walked arm in arm, slowly and deliberately, through the terminal, my head sometimes coming into loving contact with his upper arm, into the lounge of his frequent flyer airline. He removed his suit jacket and threw it over the seat in a booth and followed it in, scooting over for me to join him.

We talked for a long time; he is still writing songs but there is nothing really big brewing right now. His songs show up on other artists' albums, and he does, at times, do back-up vocals for friends. More often, though, it is his songs that are on albums and not his voice. He is pretty much living the life of a true recluse—not really afraid to leave his house—just preferring not to do so unless necessary.

This man sitting with me is intense in his conversation and colorful in his speech about his life. As the years have passed, he has become less and less fond of being with, and around, people. Just being in the lounge was making him slightly uncomfortable even when there was no one around us. He wants to be out in the world but he cannot; for reasons he will not entirely explain. He still keeps many of his feelings bottled up inside and away from the public view; even away from me until I can get him to talk about it. And yet, I keep my secrets from him too.

But we were there, and the love was there: an electrical current still flowed between us. Just being with him is enough to set my soul on fire and my heart aching for his touch.

We went out into the terminal and concourse after a time; there were very few people still in the airport and those that were couldn't have cared less about us. We window shopped at the many shops O'Hare had to increase customer satisfaction during their famous flight delays. Still nearly a month until Christmas but the decorations are gorgeous; the place actuall had a festive air.

He missed his flight back to Los Angeles; this was supposed to be a brief meeting, a quick look at each other and then it would be over. Chris was only working until midnight; it was past that now. I had blown it. What was I going to tell him? I'd figure it out when I got home. Steve arranged to be on the 7 AM flight back so we had almost six hours together; that was more like it. I never liked it when he flew in for less than three or four

341

hours at a time, but I guess it was better than not seeing him at all.

We went back to the lounge and the private room he had arranged for. He liked to be comfortable when spending time in the airport with me; sitting in a lounge booth is not his idea of comfort. The bed was not made for comfort but it would do.

Steve had a present for me for Christmas—he pulled a small velvet box out of his suit pocket and handed it to me: a beautiful ring, platinum setting with three stones in it. Gorgeous. Did I want to know the significance of the stones? One was my birthstone; one was his; and one was the birthstone of the month in which we met. He had it custom-made for me with an antique-looking scroll around the stones. He remembered; he always remembered the little things. In all of the chaos of his life, he remembered.

So we talked about his dilemma—the reason he had come to me that night. The band was being given award in San Francisco that they were to accept it in March, 2005. They didn't have to make any speeches; they didn't have to perform. All they were being asked to do is show up and accept. Why wasn't he thrilled to see his old band mates? So many memories were tied to those five men whose songs had become the anthems for a generation and whose ballads were the make-out songs during which there were probably a lot of children conceived. His songs, their songs, had meant so much to so many, he just had to go and accept this award.

His presence was being requested—strongly. He was expected there. He was the lead singer when they were still together—he was what made them who they were, what they had become and what they still were. Their songs continue to get airplay daily on radio stations throughout the United States, and they show up on commercials, TV shows and in movies. Their music was important to a generation who grew up with it and, even today, their songs are recognized with gusto and remembrance. And he was a part of that—he *was* that.

But he was bogged down in multiple problems—he had a habit of remembering all of the bad stuff and none of the good—and there was good. There were good times with them all together, impromptu jam sessions back stage prior to shows; recording sessions that resulted in no useable tape due to multiple screw-ups and laughter; practical jokes played on each other and the roadies; the Vaseline put on Richard's drum seat so that he slipped off it when he sat down at the beginning of shows; the change in the line-up written on Steve's paper taped to the stage so that he would be singing one song while the band was playing something totally different; the synthesizer turned on instead of the keyboard when Phil came out on stage; vodka substituted for water in the bottles on stage. They did have good times, but as the years dragged on, the good times became fewer and farther between. Pity.

He remembered the bad things: Richard taping his wrists with ice packs due to severe swelling and pain; Ned's bloody fingers from too much touring; the fights and jabs taken at each other; the way his own voice became so raspy that he could hardly speak between shows. Didn't I remember the months we were separated from each other? Didn't I remember that, as they grew in popularity, all the problems grew in proportion? Tempers, angers, prima donnas.

Sure, I remembered, but I remembered the good things more strongly. Those are the memories that were precious to me: those were the memories I chose to hold close to my heart.

So, aside from bad memories, what the heck else was going on in his mind?

He finally admitted it was what he was reading on the Internet, the fan boards and the chats. He went onto them quite a bit, simply a quiet observer, curious about what fans were saying about him after all this time. People were not expecting him to be at the ceremony and were having a field day on the chats, placing odds about the chances of him coming. There were remarks about the band break-up and how he was at fault;

about the final album not being up to snuff with the others; how Steve would never do anything great again because his voice is shot.

Fans can be a wonderful thing to have, supportive in their devotion, faithful in their love; when the times are good, so are the fans. But, when the music is silent and the band has gone home, fans can become nasty, expecting the rock-and-roll to continue on, even when band members are exhausted and ready to collapse, either mentally or physically. The fanatics tend to believe they are the only ones that matter and that the show must go on—despite whatever ill effects it may have on those doing the performing.

It becomes very tiresome listening, or rather, reading the fans' posts about poor singing, poor song writing and other things about which they have no idea.

People criticizing his performance were probably the worst for him. He had always known that the critics hated his voice, but he believed that the fans loved it—loved him. But, not these fans—they had hateful things to say about the last album and he was giving his all—in the haze of the flu—and people were still blasting his sound. Personally, I liked the way his voice had sounded. Yes, his voice was lower than on earlier recordings, but it was also mature and sexy. A deep, throaty kind of sexy underscored with the raspy quality he now speaks with. The songs themselves were grown up, less bubble gum (he hates when I use that term for any kind of music), with meaning; some even took some thought to figure out what they meant. But I understood them.

I have never understood the make up of the fans that hound bands and band members into obscurity, taking away their very lives at the end. The fans can be so full of devotion at one moment, spewing hatred and lies the next. Many fans of Steve's band felt deeply betrayed when he walked away—when they all walked away; like the band had done something to them on purpose, to hurt them directly, without much thought or reason.

Like he owed them an apology, an explanation. Good luck waiting on that—an explanation and an apology were two things no one would ever get from him, or the other band members, for that matter. It was his life and he was through with that part of it. For good.

So, without much more than a simple good-bye, he retreated to his house in California, rarely to emerge again. And the other band members spread out through the country, doing their own thing. Some retired from music and some were out with new bands.

He had heard all of the exaggerated rumors and stories about why he turned his back on the music industry. He told me, his family and very close friends the truth and that was all he cared about. He didn't want to hold a press conference to tell his story—he was trying desperately to escape the harsh lights and attention. Unfortunately, he and all of us soon found out that when the only ones who are talking are the ones with the rumors and innuendo, those are the things that people listen to and believe because they have no one else who's letting them know otherwise.

But Steve never saw fit to come forward and deny the drug rumors or the stories that said he was the ogre who controlled the band and the others had had enough and kicked him out. There was some truth to each story that circulated—he had done drugs, he had been depressed, he didn't want to do the music thing any longer. But he wasn't the one who quit—the whole band did. He said good-bye and felt that was all he had to do.

He had gained so much during his years on the top of the charts, but had lost a lot too. It was the losses that he no longer wanted to deal with.

The statements on the Internet were getting tiresome to him but still he wanted to lay low and ignore them. The statements hurt him more than he would admit—words do hurt people, sometimes as much as physical weapons, and he was hurting now. Fans can be very cruel, even after many years of his solitude he couldn't escape the noise.

He finally admitted the real reason he is not, no way, ain't gonna go to the award ceremony: he is afraid of being heckled and even booed. To me that is unimaginable, but he truly believed it would happen. How do you convince someone, a star, that he is still beloved by fans worldwide and that it's only small factions who are so petty?

I told him to stay off the Internet when home, and not pay any attention to what anyone was saying about him. And if he did go online, he was not to pay any attention to the fanatics—half the time they were only trying to get a rise out of the other fans. His self-esteem was very poor that night; his confidence waning—that was usually my problem. Here he was, leaning on me for a change.

We had two more hours until his flight. A lot of talking, something he had needed to do that night, had taken place; he got a lot of things off his chest and I helped him through that. But, once again, our time was running short. I would have to get home as soon as his plane took off; I was going to be late for work. Bummer. This was worth it. Did I want to try to get some sleep? Hardly. I wasn't ready to let him go. I needed him—needed his arms around me—forever. We had wasted enough of this visit with the talking. This was a difficult web we had woven for ourselves.

My new ring shone brightly on my right hand. The stones caught the light and bent it into thousands of facets of lustrous radiance. We were on the bed and he suddenly took me into his arms—he clung to me as if his world was crumbling; he held me with all his insecurity in an attempt to borrow some of my security. I had never seen him so unsure of himself, of so many things.

His hug, his touch, kindled all the feelings. That was the reason for the private room—always was—so we could be together. He began to kiss my neck because he knew that was the way to sparking my fire inside. We hadn't been together in a month, only by phone and that wasn't enough. I needed him and he needed me at that point. So I told him.

I whispered in his ear that I wanted to run my tongue all over him until he quivered with delight, and hold him so tight that he would go right through me; that I wanted him to make love to me and never stop.

As he nuzzled my neck and listened to my slow, deliberate words spoken into his ear in a breathy voice, my warm breath sweeping over his ear caused excitement in him like none other.

I stood up from the bed and slowly did a striptease for him as he laid back and watched, head propped up on one arm, sighing heavily as he would bite his lower lip and draw blood several times. When I was naked in the dim light of the room, I climbed onto the bed and began to undress him as his hands began to roam their way around my body, rediscovering all the places he had been so familiar with for so long. His suit came off easily in my hands and when he was naked too, we made love, several times, almost in a manic frenzy, as if he didn't know if this would be the last time, the last dance. He had to dash to the plane, and almost missed that one too.

I watched him go through the gate to the airplane, as he walked backward down the gangway to the plane, waving, a tear running down his cheek. Just as he began to disappear from view, as the ramp crew was getting ready to close the door, he stopped, blew me a kiss and yelled, "We'll be together again — I promise — for always. I love you." I blew him a kiss back and nodded, wiping my own tears from my face. I drew interested stares from the gate crew there as I turned to the window to watch the plane pull away; they all knew who he was — they wanted to get a look at the woman who had been with the star.

I wanted him to stay. I wanted him to go. I wanted to go with him. I wanted to remember every inch of him (as if I could ever forget).

We were a couple in secret and no one else needed to know. Well, that wasn't exactly true. When I went back to the nursing home, after realizing that is where I needed to be, I got a desk job; I got a desk. I like pictures on a desk—I think it makes the boss seem more personable, like we actually have a life beyond the four walls of the office. So, I put up my pictures—of my cats, of my husband, and of Steve and the band. It took a week or so until the rumors flew and finally some people got up the nerve to ask.

Yes, I know him; have been a groupie for years—nearly thirty years. Do you still see him? Sometimes; not as often as I would like; but we do get together. Do you—you know—do it?

No answer; good enough for the rumors to fly.

I let Steve know that night that the stories were flying at work and that there was everything from outright belief to outright disbelief. It was very hard for most people to look at me and think that I was the consort to a rock star. People like me are housewives and nurses and normal. Not sleeping with rock gods.

Steve always thought it was funny when people would find out about us; whether it was his friends, or mine. He would never deny us to anyone unless I asked him to, and I never did, but I still did not want to jeopardize his reputation in the business. So, when we were in California I kept a very low profile, and when he was in Illinois, I kept him sequestered away. There were people at work who would have loved to meet him but, being the private person he always was, I would not subject him to that, per his request. Yet another reason that no one really believed me.

All we had to prove our relationship were a few random pictures, a few gifts given to each other, the occasional flowers sent to each other, cards and letters, and love. The love that only two people can give to each other who care more about each other than anything else.

We didn't have to prove our relationship to anyone—we

knew what we had and that was all we cared about. Never ones to hog the media, we stayed behind the limelight and he stepped in front of it only when he had to.

So, the people at my work were beginning to figure out that something was going on and it was actually a relief to confirm it at times. But, then I wondered what kind of a boss I would be if people thought I was fooling around on my husband. There were too many problems with all of this.

Steve and I e-mailed and talked on the phone daily, sometimes late into the night. We continually grew closer as I drifted ever farther from Chris, emotionally and physically. Chris was getting ready to retire from the fire department—he had been a member for seventeen years, now 70 years old, becoming slower and more exhausted with every fire call.

Thankfully he wasn't involved in any actual firefighting any longer, generally assigned to incident command to direct the crews. He was active in the paramedic runs, though—those he loved the best. It was always strange having him come to my nursing home if we called 911, but it was awesome watching him work; he knew his stuff.

Everything changed, though, on December 23, 2004 causing my world to disintegrate; I would never be the same.

Chris was home that evening, off shift, watching TV; I was in my chair, he was on the daybed, wrapped in a blanket. We had surfed the channels many times, and, unable to find anything to watch, had finally put in a DVD of the Lucille Ball, Henry Fonda movie *Yours, Mine and Ours*. Always good for a hearty laugh.

Our serenity was shattered, however, when his fire pager went off—structure fire in a nearby town; requesting mutual assistance from neighboring towns as the fire was quickly becoming out of control. Chris kissed me, told me he was going, that he loved me and was out the door, pulling his coat around his shoulders as he went.

I heard him on the radio a few moments later announcing that he was en route to the fire station; shortly I heard him again announcing that he and another firefighter were on their way to the fire in the engine. I took advantage of his absence and called Steve. He was home—as always—watching the news—he always had the 24-hour news channel on; how anyone can stand that much news, I just didn't know. He had adopted a kitten that had appeared on his doorstep a few days ago. Kitty spent all of her time with Steve, rarely leaving his side.

Steve and I talked for a while, hours actually. Sometimes we just breathed at each other, sometimes we thought of things to say. We both wanted to know what the other had done all day— it was boring—work and that was about it. Christmas was a busy time at the nursing home—we were the family to most of the residents. I was also doing a lot of training for the federal disaster team online and in person over in Iowa. He wanted to know all about that all the time, very concerned that I would end up having to go to another disaster scene like that of 9-11 in new York City or worse (what could be worse?!). His day had been routine—he didn't go anywhere. Rambled around the house with Kitty, trying to decide what to do. I tried to convince him to go out and at least see the city lights of Christmas but he wouldn't.

As we talked, I could hear a lot of excited voices on the fire band of the scanner as something was apparently intensifying. I didn't pay a whole lot of attention as the anxiety level is always high at a fire and voices get raised, usually in both octave and volume.

Our phone conversation went on. It is amazing how much we could find to say to each other night after night. He told me he was coming back to Chicago in a few weeks; this time he had a hotel reservation for the night—we would have more time together. He had Chris' schedule and knew he would be working that night. What were we going to do when Chris retired? We would cross that bridge when it came up.

Just prior to us hanging up, the doorbell rang; at that point I realized that the fire band had gone silent. Fire must be out. I heard the rescue helicopter on another channel transporting someone to the hospital from the scene; sounded pretty bad. It was 1:02 AM. My panic level began to rise—I told Steve to stay on the line with me as I went to the door. Through my front window, my driveway looked like a parking lot at the fire station: the squad was there, the small truck and a rescue squad. I told Steve what was happening, that I would hold onto the phone, but something was wrong, very wrong. My voice was a whisper on the phone.

I opened the front door to find the Chief, the Chaplain and two paramedics on my porch, all looking somber, heads slightly bowed. My heart dropped—this is the moment that every fire fighter's family dreads—the moment when the red car pulls up in the driveway to deliver the bad news. It is never good news. Never.

I knew all these guys; I knew the procedure. This was not a good thing.

I let them all in and noticed their grim faces immediately. I still had the phone in my hand but had dropped it to my side. One of the paramedics took it from my hand and went into the other room to explain what was happening to whomever I was talking to. The Chief directed me to my couch and sat with me as the Chaplain sat across from us.

The chief began his story:

There had been a partial roof collapse; Chris had been up on the roof, helping to ventilate when he and two other firefighters suddenly fell through the roof, crashing through two floors. The three men had been trapped for nearly an hour as the fire raged around them and the others couldn't find them. Incident command had had to make changes to their attack plan after Chris had reported that the roof appeared unsafe, but the plan hadn't been changed in time. What Chris was doing on that roof, no one knew. He should have been at Incident Command—someone had probably asked for his help, which he was always ready to give. They had to use hydraulic jacks and airbags to free the men once they were discovered, which took even more time. Chris was the only one who had made it out of the building alive.

He had been airlifted by med-evac hospital, which I had been listening to on the scanner, unaware it was my husband they were talking about. He was very unstable, critical with burns over 60% of his body, mostly above the waist, and massive head trauma. He was not conscious and hadn't been, apparently, since the fall. That was a blessing.

I had stopped understanding anything after the Chief said that Chris had fallen and was critical. I do remember being handed the phone.

Steve's voice was full of anxiety as he told me he was coming: "Don't argue with me—I'm on the next plane out."

I was going into shock and it was settling in fast. I never thought anything like this would happen; Chris was going to retire; he was going to be done with this life. I started to stand, swooned and quickly sat back down, dazed and confused. The paramedics stepped in and gave me oxygen, bundled me in a blanket and kept me safe. When they thought I was ready, they led me out the door to the squad and drove me to Chris.

When I saw my husband lying in that burn unit bed, he appeared dead. I could only see him through the glass initially but his face was swollen with fluid and there were tubes everywhere. A nurse was removing the dead, burned skin from his face and head. Thank God he was unconscious. There were about twenty of his colleagues in the hallway, who all came up to me when I came down the hall.

I was allowed into the room to see him after he had been cleaned up and the skin was removed that could be up to that point. I had to wear special protective equipment to protect him from me. Chris had been ventilated as his lungs and trachea were burned. His wounds were severe—his burns massive. The smell of burned flesh was overwhelming; the smell of death hung heavy—I knew that smell from the nursing home, as morbid as that sounds. I knew he had a very slim chance of surviving—I was a nurse—I wasn't stupid. I was going to lose him.

Steve was there a few hours later—Christmas Eve—how he found a seat on a flight is beyond me. Was it inappropriate for him to be there? I didn't think so. I needed someone there; my parents were in Florida visiting my brother; they would come the day after Christmas, the only time they could get a flight out. My other friends had their own families to be with during the holidays. No one wanted this kind of tragedy overshadowing Christmas.

My parents did come up from Florida, my brother in tow; even James came up from Atlanta. My friends drifted in and out, stopping by to check on me, to check on Chris. The firefighters all stopped by and kept a vigil day and night with Steve and I. They were devastated and couldn't help but let it show. And Steve stayed at my side.

As we passed into 2005, Chris began to take a turn for the worse. His lungs were filling with fluid and chest tubes had to be inserted; his brain was swelling daily, little by little as a result of the head trauma—a monitoring device was inserted into his head to monitor the pressure. As the days wore on, his organs slowly began to shut down as the burning of his body continued from the inside out.

Two weeks from the day he fell through that roof, I made the decision to turn off his ventilator and not put him through anything more. That was the hardest decision I had ever had to make. I was just glad I had family around me when I did it. I kissed his face through the bandages as the doctor in charge disconnected the ventilator, and I told him I truly did love him, and I cried. He had been my husband for 21 years; he had stood by me when no one else could or would. He had been my rock, my safety net, my friend, my best friend.

My mom and dad were in the room with me as Chris drifted peacefully away and never took a breath on his own. The alarms were all shut off so there was no shrill ringing when his heart stopped. My family gave me time to be with Chris alone for a few minutes, to cry, to be a widow, and then I stepped out of the room, allowing his firefighting brothers to say their good-byes.

He was buried three days later, a full firefighting funeral that everyone attended, from my friends at the nursing home, to all the county firefighters that were available, to my family, to Steve. My tears did not want to stop flowing—sorrow, guilt and depression set into my silence.

I rattled around my house alone after everyone left from the funeral. Steve went out with my family and James to give me some time alone in my house. My cats were looking for Chris, expecting him to come through the door any minute. But he never did. He never would again.

I felt him in every room of the house. His spirit was there and I think even the cats felt it as they would pause every so often and stare at something I couldn't see. The house smelled of him—his scent and the scent of his fire clothes. The department had given me his helmet, the one he was wearing when he fell. I didn't want it but I took it. It was on the mantel; I couldn't even look at it—it was scorched and all black, very small areas of the yellow showing through. The label on the side that read Deputy Chief was burned and peeling off.

Now what? My parents wanted me to come back to Ohio, unaware that Steve and I had been seeing each other. Steve wanted me to come to California, when I was ready. James suggested Steve and I go to Atlanta. There was a huge decision to be made—my life had been in Illinois for 17 years—my job, my husband's grave, my house, my friends.

One by one my family left me—James back to Atlanta; John to Florida; Mom and Dad to Ohio. Steve was with me, but even he left, at my request. I needed to think, to make decisions about the rest of my life and where I was going. I was full of emotions— guilt, sadness, grief, anger. I had to work it all through.

I tried to go back to work but couldn't make it through a

whole day without breaking into uncontrollable tears. I finally quit in mid-February, turning my management position over to a very capable nurse who had been on the floor. I just didn't want to be a nurse any longer, still struggling with the loss of my husband and having to be the one to turn off his life support.

I rambled through my house for two weeks after that, stumbling through some semblance of a life in a depression that seemed to grow on a daily basis. Chris' firefighting co-workers' visits grew farther and farther apart until they stopped all together. My cats still looked for Chris and never found him.

Steve called daily, sometimes two and three times a day. I needed those calls—they were my lifelines at that point. He never pushed me into any decision; he just let me know he was there for me if I needed him and that he would come back the minute I said so, but he understood I needed my space.

Mid-March came and I was still in a fog. Steve's concern grew as he questioned me daily about my medications and how I was feeling. I saw him on *Entertainment Tonight* as he and his former band mates accepted their achievement award in San Francisco; he had told me to watch. Steve looked calm, poised in front of all the fans and cameras. He even made a full speech at the podium.

I was surprised to see him there and very pleased. It woke me up: if someone like him, a self-imposed recluse could get up in front of several hundred people and speak, I could climb out of my mourning and get on with life.

He called from the San Francisco hotel that same night. He was excited that he had been able to do what he did, and proud of himself for the way he had gotten along with his band mates after so many years. Including Ned. They had all talked after the ceremony and had all made amends. Closure. Something we all desperately needed.

Two days later, he showed up on my doorstep. It was snowing like crazy and he said he thought his plane had been the last to land at the airport before the powers that be closed it. The black limo was covered with white ice and snow when I opened my front door and found my rock star there, 56 years-old, short hair, tired smile.

We talked the night away; we had changed so much since 1975; we were both kids then and grew up in front of each other. Circumstances drew us together and, at times, kept us apart. He was a rock star at night, a normal person during the day. He taught me about rock-and-roll, life and stardom; I taught him about love, staying normal and being himself.

Our relationship had survived and was going into its third decade. We had gone from heaven to hell multiple times in our journey through the years, but always managed to find each other, even in our darkest moments.

As the light was peeking through the curtains of my family room, it found Steve and I still talking, weighing all of our options, laying on the daybed, my head on his chest, his arm around me. A snowplow could be heard running up and down the road outside, scraping loudly against the pavement, scaring my cats.

I looked into Steve's eyes and said what was in my heart: "Let's go to Atlanta."

He blinked twice and appeared surprised but pleasantly so.

"You're sure?" He sounded incredulous.

"I'm sure. Let's go home. Your home."

Atlanta had been his home but it also felt like my second home. California was never home to either of us and it had become the realm in which he felt the most uncomfortable. Ohio was my home but had never been his. Illinois was home to neither of us. Atlanta was the logical choice.

We're going home.

Life goes on; life blooms again in the Spring; life takes a chance and goes forward.

Love endures; love takes us home together; love had found a way with Steve and me.

Printed in the United States
39396LVS00004B/1-51